FADED LINES OF GRAY

AN HISTORICAL NOVEL

BY

STEVEN D. HARRIS

www.bookstandpublishing.com

Published by
Bookstand Publishing
Morgan Hill, CA 95037
3725_3

Although this book is a work of historical fiction, many of the
characters did exist and many of the events described in this book are
documented. However, the author did utilize artistic license to create
certain events and characters as well as much of the dialog for the sake
of telling the story.

Cover map of Lake Erie Islands courtesy of Michael Gora, Middle Bass
Island, Ohio

ISBN 978-1-61863-356-9

First Printing 2012
Second Printing 2013

Printed in the United States of America

ACKNOWLEDGEMENTS

In the course of gathering background information to shape the story and to reflect the personalities of the characters and the times as much as possible, I soaked up insights from every available printed media I could find, including historical documents, artifacts, newspaper articles, and books about John Yates Beall, the Johnson's Island Prison, the U.S.S. *Michigan* and Confederate operations in Canada.

The initial research for this book was done in the pre-internet era, and so thanks are in order to those institutions that provided assistance to develop the story into one that is not only fascinating and inspiring, but also as accurate as any novel can be, especially when dealing with information now nearly 150 years old.

I am indebted to these organizations and their staffs for all of their assistance:

Library of Congress, Washington, DC

National Archives, Washington, DC

Follett House Museum, Sandusky Public Library, Sandusky, Ohio

Charles Town Library, Charles Town, West Virginia

Thanks also to friends and relatives who provided encouragement as this project progressed from concept to outline to manuscript to finished book.

Special thanks go to my wife, Ann, for her support, not only in typing the manuscript and proofing it, but for the moral support to keep me focused on getting this project done.

Thanks also to my cousin, Carol Wagner, an accomplished author in her own right, whose guidance with respect to story line and plot development were invaluable. Finally, thanks to Kelle Urban for her excellent editorial assistance.

INTRODUCTION

Throughout the ages, there have always been heroes and villains. These tags have often placed with the benefit of hindsight and are influenced by which side ultimately prevailed in a conflict.

So it is with the American Civil War. With the passage of more than 150 years since that conflict began, principles that are alien to modern society were matters for which people would be willing to die. This is the story of two men – one virtuous and the other not – who were charged by Confederate operatives with carrying out one of the most daring exploits of the war. While this novel does present an interesting historical perspective on the war and its intrigue, it is also a character study in how two men responded differently to the challenging events of their time.

One of the men, John Yates Beall, was a man of principle, valor and courage. He was well educated and came from a prominent Virginia family. He willingly undertook dangerous missions, even after being severely wounded early in the war, all in support of the Confederate cause to which he was dedicated.

But not all men then (or now) had the same strength of character and devotion to principle as John Yates Beall. One of them, Charles Cole, was a shadowy figure about which little can be confirmed. There is no doubt, however, that he was a man who could not be trusted.

In 1864, it was apparent that the Confederate cause would not prevail on the battlefield. A master plan was developed to bring the war behind the Union lines and cause havoc that would influence the upcoming Presidential election. The Confederate hopes were pinned on a war-weary North rejecting Abraham Lincoln's bid for a second term and replacing him with a man who would reach a negotiated peace with the South. Confederate Commissioners operating out of Canada, at that time a British colony, would direct components of the plan.

Through fate, Beall and Cole find themselves tasked together in the summer of 1864 by Confederate operatives to liberate the nearly 3,000 Confederate officers held captive by the North on Johnson's Island, located just offshore from Sandusky, Ohio and tantalizingly close to neutral Canada. Simultaneously, Confederates commandos would take over the U.S.S. *Michigan*, the only U.S. warship on the Great Lakes, which lay at anchor just off the prison camp. Once the *Michigan* was in rebel hands, it would sail up and down the Great

Lakes shelling and generally wreaking havoc on Northern cities just before the fall presidential election.

Both Beall and Cole wear the rebel gray colors, although Cole's rebel *bona fides* are suspect. The fading hopes of the Confederacy rest squarely on their ability to successfully carry out the mission.

Although this book ostensibly is a work of historical fiction, many of the characters in the story really existed. To the extent events and statements attributed to them were documented, I have attempted to incorporate them into the novel. People often told conflicting stories for their own reasons or as memories of events dimmed with the passage of time. And no matter how well-documented some of the events are, holes and conflicts in the facts necessitated use of some creative license to tell this story.

PART I: THE CRUCIBLE

"Reputation is what men and women think of us. Character is what God and the angels know of us."

– Thomas Paine

1

OCTOBER 1861
JEFFERSON COUNTY, VIRGINIA

John Yates Beall knew it wasn't thunder rumbling through the verdant contours of the Blue Ridge Mountains and down along the rock-strewn Shenandoah River. No, the rumbling was white-hot cannon fire, and men of all sorts were dying as a nation was being torn asunder in a bloody conflagration. More men would die today, too.

The spark for the battle came from the actions of a single bearded zealot. Some called him a prophet. Others called him Satan personified. There was no doubt, however, that the abolitionist John Brown had awakened the fears of stalwart Virginians two years previous with his raid on the federal arsenal at Harpers Ferry, just down the road. John Yates Beall had been there at the zealot's hanging, when his neck had been snapped like a dead twig.

Even though he had been executed and the rebellion put down, Brown's futile attempt to incite southern slaves to rise up in rebellion against their white masters caused a predictable reaction among the men who had called the Shenandoah Valley their home since before the Revolutionary War. Local volunteer militia companies quickly formed as protection against any future surreptitious attempts to strip Virginians of what they perceived to be their property and, more important, of their fundamental freedoms. One of these militia units was organized by Caption Lawson Botts of Jefferson County and was known as Botts Grays. John Yates Beall, despite his wealth and family pedigree, had enlisted as a private in Botts Grays, now known as Company G, Second Virginia Infantry.

At Walnut Grove, the Beall family estate located three miles northeast of Charles Town, John sat on a comfortable walnut settee in the English garden just behind the mansion house. But John was not in the least bit comfortable, and he alternately twitched his right leg or got up and paced nervously. Since early morning, the echoes of cannon fire had rumbled intermittently across the lush hills of the Shenandoah, now mottled in autumn hues of golden maize, crimson and bronze.

The tranquil beauty of the garden, originally planted by his grandmother with seeds and plants sent from her native England, offered John no solace this afternoon. The Yankees threatened his beloved Virginia, cradle of American democracy. He felt the invading army posed not only a menace to his own personal freedom, but an immediate threat to the very safety of his family. Since the death of his father six years previous, John had assumed complete, personal responsibility for his mother, four sisters and little brother, Willie.

John stared intently across the orderly rows of apple trees to the Blue Ridge Mountains rising in the distance. The speckled skins of thousands of Grimes Golden alternated with the deep ruby coloration of the Black Amish apples for which the Beall farm was justly famous. But beyond the orchard, he could tell from the way the clouds of gray-blue smoke wafted down the Shenandoah Valley that the fighting was around Harpers Ferry, four miles east of Walnut Grove. John had heard nightmarish tales about the depredations of Union soldiers in nearby Fairfax and Prince William Counties during the Manassas campaign. He was determined to be a part this time in driving the northern invaders from his home, from his family's sacred soil.

Although John had heard these stories of Yankee depravity, he had not experienced them personally. In early July he had obtained a pass from Captain Botts for him and his younger brother, Willie, to return to Walnut Grove to bring in the first cutting of hay; Willie had joined Company G in June, also as a private. Captain Botts understood that, with most of the men of Jefferson County serving in the militias, John's mother and four sisters would be unable to supervise the cutting by themselves.

Because of the special consideration extended by Captain Botts, John had missed that glorious victory at Manassas, where the Second Virginia fought valiantly at the Henry House in support of General Jackson. And here he was at home again, with another battle underway.

This time, Captain Botts had detailed John to convey Willie, suffering from dysentery, back home. Captain Botts knew Willie would have a chance to fully and quickly recover under the gentle, constant, loving care of his mother, away from the rough conditions in the field. Although John felt compelled to stay with his unit out of honor and duty to his comrades, he also knew he had a duty to his family to get Willie home where he would have a chance to return speedily to full health. And so, he had brought Willie home.

As he now pondered the significance of the fighting just a few miles away, John knew instinctively what he must do. He would not shirk his duty to God and Virginia. He would serve the cause in which he so fervently believed by joining the battle already brewing at Harpers Ferry.

4

John set his empty glass of apple cider down and rose from the settee. Upon entering the house, he walked though the main hall, passing by dark oils of stern-looking ancestors as he headed up the stairs to the sick room. His mother would be tending his brother there, as she had been for seemingly countless days.

Willie had come late in life to Janet Yates Beall, and as with most mothers, her youngest child occupied a special place. Ever since John had carried him through the front door of Walnut Grove two weeks ago, his mother had stayed with Willie, doing everything she knew possible to reduce Willie's discomfort and to hasten his recovery.

John knocked twice, gently, on the sick room door. He could hear the rocker creaking as his mother moved it away from the bedside. Several footsteps later, the door was opened a crack. His mother stepped into the hall and closed the door gently behind her so as not to disturb Willie, who was now asleep.

"Have you heard the cannons, mother?" John whispered.

"I wasn't sure if those booming noises were cannons or a little fall thunderstorm," she replied.

"I'm sure they're cannons." John related to his mother how he had seen the telltale smoke floating through the valley.

"I expect it's those infernal Yankees again, causing trouble at Harpers Ferry," Janet sighed.

"Yes, I'm sure it is," John stated matter-of-factly. Pensively, he stroked the whiskers that came to a little point on his chin. "Mother, you know it is my duty to join my Virginia brothers who are fighting there, and perhaps even dying there, this very moment."

Her son's proclamation had an immediate impact on Janet Beall. She wished that there were some way to dissuade John from pursuing this thought any further. But she knew her son only too well, and once John made up his mind to do something, there was no way to get him to change course.

Janet supported the Confederate cause, although not nearly as fervently as did John. In that respect, John was more like his father, George, who had been a States Rights Democrat until the day he died. Still, it was with a great deal of typical mother's reluctance that she had concurred in John's decision to join Botts Grays. In fact, there was not much she could have done to stop her 26-year-old son from doing what he believed to be right, anyway.

Janet looked up into John's light blue eyes. She knew she should not make a scene now, and fought to control the fear for her son's life welling up inside her. "If you feel you must go, then do so," she stated with as much courage as she could muster. "Just promise me that you will try to stay out of harm's way."

"Mother, you know I cannot promise to give less than my all to anything I endeavor," John said firmly. Then a gentle, pleasant smile lit up John's face, as he realized he should attempt to calm the fears of his 60-year-old mother.

"But don't worry. My guardian angel will be there with me. And who knows, by the time I get to the Ferry, we may have driven the Yanks back anyway," John said.

An awkward silence filled the air, as each of them knew there was no use in discussing this topic any more. The ticking of the grandfather clock at the end of the second floor hall was the only sound to be heard.

It was Janet who finally spoke. "It's getting late in the day," she observed. "It will be dark soon, and you haven't even had any supper yet. Why don't you wait until morning to go to the Ferry?"

John knew his mother was right. Even if he could make it to the Ferry before dark, the fighting would be over for the day by the time he got there and found where he might be needed. John also knew his mother believed that, as long as he was out of the battle zone, he couldn't be injured, or worse.

"All right, mother," John replied. "I'll wait until morning. That will give me more time to get prepared. I'll be cleaning my musket, and then I'm going to be in the library reading my Bible. Call me when supper's ready."

John gave his mother a long, warm embrace. He gently patted her on the small of her back. She returned dutifully to the sickroom, as giant tears filled her eyes. John turned to go downstairs, his mind at ease. He was strangely at peace, now that he knew he too was about to contribute something to the struggle.

* * * * * * *

Although he had told her he would wait till daybreak, John tossed and turned in bed fretfully, pondering what might have happened at the fighting yesterday. And he wanted to make sure he was there by dawn to avoid missing any of the action. So he left Walnut Grove in the pre-dawn darkness, which had the incidental benefit of avoiding any more entreaties from his mother not to join the battle. She would understand in any event, he felt.

He walked in timeless solitude through the cold, crisp mid-October night. The only sounds came from nocturnal animals that dwelled in the woods on both sides of the road. John liked the still quiet. It was at times like this that he felt closest to God.

The trance-like state came to an abrupt end. "Halt, who goes there?" A picket's sharp challenge rang through the pre-dawn darkness.

"A friend!" John shouted back.

"Identify yourself!" the still unseen picket barked.

John did not answer immediately. Had he encountered a Union picket, he wondered? Had the Union driven the Virginia boys back all this way? He trusted his instincts, which told him that the Yankees wouldn't be this far west of the Ferry, even if things had really gone poorly for the Confederates the day before.

"I am Private John Yates Beall. Company G, Second Virginia," John shouted back. He paused, but the picket made no further reply. John took a step forward. He left his musket slung over his left shoulder. "I've come to join in the defense of Harpers Ferry."

The picket finally spoke again. "Advance and be recognized," he commanded, but in a tone now slightly more friendly. John sighed deeply, now that it appeared to him that the picket was not from the North. In fact, there was something familiar about that voice.

John stepped briskly up the steep path through the woods for about ten paces when he was challenged again. "That's far enough," the picket ordered. "Now lay your musket down on the ground in front of you."

Now doubts arose in John's mind again. The picket hadn't identified himself. Maybe he was a Yankee after all. John realized his musket was not primed and ready to fire, and therefore was of no real self-defense value. But surrendering control over his weapon gave him considerable cause for concern. Still, what choice did he have? John obeyed the picket's command and laid his weapon down.

"Good," the picket replied sternly. "Now take off your breeches there, man. We want to see if you're hiding a weapon."

"What?" Anger boiled up inside John. But before he had a chance to say or do anything more, loud raucous guffaws exploded from the woods. Three soldiers stepped from behind the trees, their gray uniforms revealed by a lantern, laughing uncontrollably and holding their sides.

And then John realized that he knew these men. They were Jefferson County boys like him. The man laughing the hardest was George Belcher, a Charles Town friend and neighbor.

"What the hell are you doing here, John?" George asked between guffaws.

"I thought I was coming here to help drive the Yankees back across the Potomac," John replied, his voice frosted with anger. "I certainly didn't come here to strip in the woods for you."

The laughter reduced to occasional titters.

"Come on, John. Be a sport," George pleaded, with at least a slight amount of sincerity. "We've been out here in the cold all night. It's a damned boring job, too, waiting and watching for nothing to happen," he continued. George spoke with the authority of someone who had been sitting all night on the cold, wet leaves. "You say you've come here to fight. Well, you'll see after you've been in a scrap or two how important it is to not only keep your wits about you, but your sense of humor, too."

The laughter had now stopped completely. John stooped over to pick up his musket. He wiped the damp gunstock across his breeches. "Maybe so, maybe so," John said. "But this is a serious business. If we don't drive the Yankees back, they'll be on our doorsteps tomorrow. They'll burn our houses, steal our cattle, rape our mothers, wives and sisters. I don't know about you," he continued, "but I can't be distracted by silly, childish games when there's so much at stake."

George and the other two men now looked sheepishly at the ground in response to John's lecture. George nervously shifted his weight from foot to foot. He had known John all his life, and it was not until his father died several years ago that John had become so intense about everything. Before that, John was always pulling pranks, just like other boys his age. With broad shoulders and a muscular chest, John could get away with anything, because nobody wanted to challenge a fellow the size of John Yates Beall. George didn't want to take on John now, either, but for obviously different reasons.

"George?" John's tone of voice was now subdued.

"Yes, John," George answered.

"I'm sorry. I didn't mean to lecture you." John's voice resonated a sincerity that was unmistakable. It was this sincerity that was one of John Yates Beall's greatest virtues.

"It's all right, John. I don't disagree with what you said. It's just that I – that we – have damned few chances to do anything that's the least bit fun anymore. We shouldn't have used you for our entertainment, though."

"I understand," John said. "Now, who's in charge here? If it's entertainment you want, I'm in favor of watching the Yankees wade back across the Potomac with minie balls nipping at their heels and whizzing over their heads."

A sly smile crossed John's thin, compressed lips. The tension that had previously existed dissipated like the misty vapors of the night air, as John and George slapped and hugged each other like the old chums they were.

Walking together toward the camp, George explained the events of the last several days. Lieutenant Colonel Turner Ashby had been given the responsibility of keeping the Union Army bottled up in the Ferry. If Ashby's men could keep the Union Army from advancing through the Harpers Ferry Gap, the rest of Jefferson County and the Shenandoah Valley beyond would be safe from Yankee depredation, at least for now. It was an awesome responsibility.

George related that several days ago the Federals had moved west out of the Ferry, which lay deep in the valley, and had taken Bolivar Heights, overlooking it. Ashby's job was to drive the Federals from their positions on the Heights, now fortified with breastworks, and then turn his attention to the Federal positions in the Ferry below.

To accomplish all this, John learned, Ashby had under his command only 300 Virginia militia armed with ancient flintlock muskets, about 200 cavalry and two cannons. The larger of the cannons, a 24-pounder, had not been used since the end of the Mexican War, except during Fourth of July celebrations, and then with only a modicum of success.

"I'm really glad I came," John said to George as they neared Ashby's tent. "There could be no more compelling reason to risk your life than to protect your family and your home. The Yankees may outnumber us, and they may have better equipment, but there's no question we have right on our side."

"I should get back to my post now," George said as they arrived in front of Ashby's tent. "It's been good seeing you, John. I expect we'll meet again soon."

"I'm sure we will, although after this thing is over, I'm obliged to rejoin my regiment," John replied. "And George."

"Yes, John."

John's deep, soothing voice now quivered with emotion. "God bless you and watch over you."

"Thanks, John. You, too."

Their exchange of greetings complete, the two men shook hands, patted each other on the back, and waived goodbye as each headed toward his own destiny.

* * * * * * *

The golden rays of the sun were just starting to peek over the Potomac when John arrived in front of Ashby's tent. An enlisted man stood in front, holding the reins to the Colonel's steed, a magnificent snow white charger. John saw that the flap of Ashby's command tent was open. Although he had never met him before, John knew immediately that the self-assured man rising from the field desk inside the tent was none other than Lieutenant Colonel Turner Ashby himself. Although there were other officers around him, it was instantaneously clear who the leader was.

Ashby was already a living legend in Virginia. Just 33 years old, he stood tall and erect, with a flowing black beard, long coal-black hair, thick, bushy black eyebrows and intense, steely-gray eyes. He was a larger than life figure to all who met him. But while Ashby's persona made people take notice, it was not until he escorted John Brown to the gallows two years ago that his fame in the Valley had grown. The daring exploits of Ashby and his cavalry in the Virginia countryside during the first months of the war were totally consistent with the perception the public already had of the man. In a word: fearless.

The Colonel's brow was furrowed, and he walked with an agitated quick step toward the soldier holding his horse. Before Ashby could mount the horse, John snapped to attention and offered a crisp salute. John's militia uniform consisted simply of baggy breeches and a pale gray shirt, open at the collar. Members of Botts Grays were, for the most part, ordinary farmers and working men. Their uniforms had been designed by Captain Botts to not only be comfortable, but also to fit within their means.

Ashby caught a glimpse of John out of the corner of his eye as he mounted his horse. John spoke first, though, before Ashby could say anything.

"Private John Yates Beall, Second Virginia Infantry, sir. I hear there's been some fighting, and I'd like to help out," he said, his eyes riveted straight ahead.

Ashby liked the bearing of this ramrod-stiff young man. "At ease, private," he said. "Yep, there's been a little fightin' the last couple of days. I expect today we'll see some real action. What outfit did you say you're with?" Ashby dismounted from his steed to get a closer look at the eager, intense soldier in front of him.

"Second Virginia, sir," John replied. "My company is from Charles Town."

"Who's your captain, son?" Ashby's use of the word "son" did not strike John as unusual, even though he and Ashby were roughly the same age. John expected all officers to take a fatherly interest in the soldiers under them.

"Captain Botts, sir," John answered crisply.

"I know Captain Botts very well," Ashby nodded. 'He's a fine gentleman and a true patriot. Why aren't you with your outfit, private?"

"I've been on furlough, sir. A member of our company got a touch of dysentery, and Captain Botts detailed me to take him home to Charles Town," John replied in a strong voice.

"Well, that's fine. But why did you come here," Ashby asked pointedly, "when you could have just stayed home and out of danger?"

"Well, colonel, I just couldn't stay put, knowing that, just a few miles from the portico to our house, other Virginians were risking life and limb to defend my family as well as theirs. I have a duty, just like the other men here, to contribute something to the defense of all of our homes." John paused and chose his next words carefully. "Even at the cost of my own life, if need be."

Ashby knew full well that he could use every man he could get. His infantry militia consisted for the most part of raw, untested men, many of whom were barely old enough to shave. And while somewhat more mature than the infantry, his cavalry had little battlefield experience. He could use every man he could get. And Ashby's instincts told him that John was not only fearless, but that others would follow him too, if need be.

"Private," Ashby said, "if you'll follow me on up the hill a ways, I believe you'll get that chance to contribute something to the defense of Virginia."

With that, Lieutenant Colonel Turner Ashby put his left foot in the stirrup, lifted himself up and swung his right foot effortlessly over his magnificent white horse, all in one fluid motion. The steed snorted with anxious anticipation. As he pulled gently on the reins to steer the animal to the right and up the hill, Ashby, ever tall and erect in the saddle, did not notice John's crisp salute as he galloped away.

* * * * * * *

John and the other men who formed Ashby's ragtag army gathered around the colonel at the first little crest of the hill. Farther up the hill, Ashby could glimpse frantic activity. Federal soldiers scurried to build their breastworks just a little bit higher, in anticipation of the impending onslaught. The frenetic cadence of Union drummers echoed down the hill. While it may have electrified the Yankees on their side of the breastworks, Ashby noticed the mounting anxiety among his soldiers, especially the infantry. It would take divine intervention, he thought, for his plan to succeed.

"Men of Virginia!"

Ashby's authoritative voice brought an immediate hush to the whispered conversations among the men gathered around him. The only sound now was an occasional whinny from the several hundred horses being held by the dismounted cavalry. Ashby himself remained mounted, almost regal on his powerful white charger. Ashby had remained mounted when the rest of his cavalry had dismounted, ostensibly so that the men could all see and hear him better. But Ashby also knew that his commanding presence would be tangibly evident astride his steed. Immediately next to him were the company commanders for the regiments that had been hurriedly assembled for the battle.

"Do you see those Yankees running around up the hill there?" Ashby asked no one in particular, not expecting an answer. A smattering of grunts was his only response.

"Do you know what those fellers are doing up there?" Again, no noticeable response from his motley regiment.

"Why, they're hurryin' to get their rucksacks all packed, so that they can leave for home!" Ashby joked. A nervous twitter now rolled through the assemblage.

"Boys, I don't think we should let them leave, without showing them a little Virginia hospitality, do you?" Ashby asked. Now the men were all broadly smiling. They didn't know what their colonel would say next, but they knew they would like it.

"What say we go introduce ourselves?" The men roared their approval, while waiving their muskets over their heads.

John himself got caught up in the excitement. Adrenaline coursed through his veins as the roar around him rose to deafening levels. So this is what it's like, he thought. It's hard to imagine that the thought of willfully taking the life of a fellow human being could be so thrilling. Now he understood a little better what motivated men like his friend George, sitting on the picket line.

The company commanders had learned their plan of attack in the early morning meeting in Ashby's tent. Each of three infantry captains now gathered their companies around them to communicate the plan and to form ranks for the attack. John drifted into the same group as the rest of the irregulars.

Behind John, the artillery crews wheeled into position the only two available cannon, a rickety old 24-pound smooth bore, veteran of the Mexican War, and a more modern rifled 4-pound cannon.

Although generally better equipped, the Union forces did not have any cannon at all, and even these two minor pieces of Ashby's had been effective in the skirmishing of the past few days, if only for psychological value.

In front of him, John could see the cavalry massing in ranks. When finally organized, the horsemen stood, with their animals at their sides, in ranks ten deep. Ashby, as John had expected, was in the front rank, waving his hat wildly over his head while nudging his white stallion up and down the line.

The morning sun was now well over the horizon. Puffy white clouds filled a turquoise sky, and a light breeze from the northwest kept the temperature comfortable. The beauty of the scene reminded John of the view from the veranda at Walnut Grove.

He was glad he had enough foresight to have eaten that loaf of bread and three boiled eggs he had brought with him when he left Walnut Grove. There had been no time to eat after arriving at the camp. Now it appeared things were moving so quickly that he would not have had an opportunity to have breakfast at all. He would miss his two cups of Earl Gray tea, sweetened with just a bit of honey and lightened with fresh, sweet cream. John had become accustomed to drinking tea this way when he was in England ten years ago with his grandfather and namesake, John Yates. Still, he reminded himself, there were men here who probably had not had a cup of hot coffee or tea for days, if not weeks.

"Cavalry, mount up!" Ashby ordered. It was apparent to all who was in control of this battle.

All 200 cavalry instantly mounted their horses.

John could see Ashby staring up the hill at the Union position. Because the sun would have been in their faces if they had attacked from the west Ashby maneuvered his forces to the south, so that the sun would not be in their eyes during the attack.

"Artillery! Fire at will!" Within seconds of Ashby's order, two huge explosions rocked the ground where John was awaiting the order to attack, along with the rest of the infantry. A sulfurous blue-gray fog of acrid smoke settled over the men, filling their heads with some of the sights, sounds and smells of war. John could not see where the cannon shells came to earth, but several seconds after the cannons were fired, he heard huge explosions up the hill, presumably the direct consequence of the Confederate cannon barrage.

With the sound of the shells landing, John and all the other men each let out excited whoops, even though they did not know if the cannonade had found its mark.

"All right, cavalry. On my command, prepare to charge!" Ashby barked. He paused momentarily. Looking up and down the ranks of now-mounted cavalry, he saw that all was ready.

"Charge!"

In pre-arranged sequence, the first rank of cavalry left, with Ashby in their midst, spurring their horses up the hill to the Union position. After the first rank had gone but fifty yards, the second took off, whooping and hollering like the first. Similar waves of frenzied mounted soldiers followed until all 200 mounted men had started their charge up the hill. A second rebel cannonade groaned over the heads of the advancing cavalry units.

"Infantry! Prepare to charge! "Double time!" Major Finter, the impetuous commander of one of Ashby's militia companies, now barked out commands to the troops.

Even before the first wave of cavalry had come within range of the Union positions, John found himself running up the hill, as though in a dream.

He had lost sight of the cavalry in front of him, but John could hear the discharge of muskets and pistols in the direction of the Union fortifications. The first wave must have made it, he thought. And then, in what seemed only a few seconds more, the firing stopped.

John continued his run up the hill. His head throbbed, his lungs ached and his mouth was dry from the sheer magnitude of the physical effort. His rubbery legs nearly buckled near the crest of the ridge as a single tiny stone slipped under his shoe.

As he drew closer to the top, John saw that many of the cavalry had dismounted, and were standing next to and inside the Union breastworks, holding their well-lathered horses. The men around him, exhausted by their run up the hill and their adrenaline stores expended, slowed to a walk. So John did, too.

"Where's all the Yankees?" John, breathless, asked one of the dismounted cavalrymen. Before he could answer, John realized the reason the fighting had stopped so quickly. A few Union soldiers lay on the fringes of the breastworks, groaning and bloodied. A few lay forever still, with gaping, scarlet holes in vital places, faces frozen and contorted in their death agony. A few others had been herded to a corner of the flimsy breastworks, now Confederate prisoners. But most of the Federals had retreated down the opposite side of the hill before Ashby's cavalry charge had even commenced.

I suppose mother will be happy, John thought, now that I've come through the battle unscathed. Little did he know that, even as the

Confederates were milling around the Union fortifications, the battle was far from over for him that day.

* * * * * * *

An hour had passed since the charge up the crest at Bolivar Heights. It was mid-day and some of the men had pulled cold biscuits from their backpacks and were devouring them voraciously. They were all well rested and raring for the action they hoped was coming.

"Gentlemen, we've got the Yankees on the run," Ashby told his ragtag army as he walked through the fortifications which had been just hours earlier crawling with Yankees. The men cheered lustily.

"But our wives and families won't be safe until we've chased every last one of them back across the Potomac," Ashby continued after the cheers subsided. Ashby sensed the men understood what he was about to ask of them.

"I believe the Yankees went just far enough down toward the Ferry to regroup. I'd like volunteers to scout out the Union positions," he continued, "while the rest of us hold the Heights in the event of a counterattack. Those of you who would like to volunteer, raise your hand so that I can get a count."

Almost immediately, nearly every hand shot up in the air, without thought or hesitation. Turner Ashby inspired a deep sense of loyalty and devotion among his soldiers, even those who had not fought under him before. The man emanated trust and invincibility. It made his men feel like they could do anything, even charge St. George's dragon with nothing more than bare knuckles, if need be. The full retreat of the Federal forces before Ashby's brazen charge only served to further this innate sense the men all felt.

John Yates Beall also volunteered. He was driven not only by the emotions generated by Turner Ashby, but also by a feeling deep in his gut that he had somehow shirked his duty by not being with his unit during the Battle at Manassas. He needed to prove to himself, and, on a larger scale, to his God and his country, that he was a man of honor, a man who knew his duty and met it head-on.

Ashby could see that another tact would be required to form his reconnaissance group.

"Mister Finter." Finter had accompanied the Colonel on his walkabout through the hilltop.

"Yes, sir."

"Major, take your company down the hill in the direction of the Ferry," Ashby ordered, loud enough for all the men to hear. "Be on the lookout for where the Yankees may have set up picket lines. If you spot anything that might signal they're regrouping for a counterattack, I want you to skedaddle back here and let me know."

"Right away, sir."

John had stayed close to Ashby soon after the legendary colonel had arrived atop Bolivar Heights to inspect his troops and new defensive position. After an initial, fleeting feeling of deep relief at having been spared from any serious risk of harm, John was soon bothered by the same sense of duty, honor and yes, even guilt, that had motivated him to seek out Ashby in the first place. He had been waiting for the opportunity to satisfy that inner drive in some way. Now is the time, he thought.

"Colonel, I believe the Major may need my help, too," John said boldly.

John was standing just a few feet to Ashby's left. The Colonel turned in John's direction, his black, bushy right eyebrow raised inquisitively.

"How is that, Private?"

"With all due respect, sir. Major Finter's troops are fine fighting men, but none of them know the area as well as I do. They're from Page County. I've lived in this area all my life. I know where everything is in these hills."

"Major, do you have any objection?" Ashby asked.

"No, sir, I think the Private can help us out a great deal."

"Very well, then," Ashby concluded, nodding his head to reinforce the verbal command he was about to give. "I'm detailing Private – what's your name again, son?"

"Beall, sir."

"I'm detailing Private Beall to your company. Are your men ready to move out now, Major?"

"Yes, indeed," Major Finter responded.

"Then you may proceed immediately," Ashby ordered. "And Private Beall?"

John was surprised to hear Ashby mention his name again. "Yes, Colonel?"

"Just make sure these men don't get lost in your Jefferson County hills."

Ashby's eye twinkled and, beneath his heavy black beard, John could detect his mouth crinkling up in a wry smile. John returned the smile, saluted sharply, and followed Major Finter toward the edge of the path where the troops were gathering for their expedition toward the Ferry.

* * * * * * *

John walked beside Major Finter, as he led the Page County militia down Bolivar Heights. Chatting amiably, the men traded stories about the time each had spent at the University in Charlottesville as they ambled along the leaf-strewn path through the woods towards Harpers Ferry. John recounted how he had finished his pre-law studies, when the death of his father six years ago had forced him to change his career plans. Now, he said, he was happy being a gentleman farmer. Not as much anxiety, he said.

The patrol had been uneventful until the sudden crack of musket fire filled the air. Instinctively, John dove behind the nearest tree. Finter lunged toward the adjacent tree. There was no need for Finter to order the troops to take cover. The sound of Union minie balls whizzing through the trees all around them had done that.

Based on the frequency of the volleys, Finter estimated there might be as many as 50 Union rifles pointed their way. With a strength of over 100 men, he knew he had numerical superiority. He and his men were pinned down, though, and he still hadn't determined exactly where the shots were coming from.

Where do you think they are, John?" Finter was glad the earnest young man next to him had volunteered to guide him and his troops through the woods.

"It's likely the Yankees are holed up in an old farm house just through the clearing," he said. "If that was their pickets that shot at us, the rest of them will soon know about us, too."

When he was a boy, John had often hunted in these woods with his father. Just about 100 yards farther the two-story brick house of the Widow Wager stood in a clearing. John fondly remembered the times he and his father had stopped there on a crisp autumn day like today, just to chat with her. The kindly old woman with the cheery, cherry-colored cheeks and ready smile always had the sweetest cider, too, he recalled.

The thud of a minie ball into the limb just over his head brought John's mind back to the serious business at hand.

"Major, why don't I go on ahead and scout around?" John said. "I'll get behind the house and see what the situation is."

Finter nodded his assent.

John loaded his musket, pouring the black powder carefully down the barrel. He firmly tamped the shiny lead minie ball in place. Assured that he now was prepared to deal with whatever he might encounter, John scampered through the woods, ducking behind trees at every opportunity until he was safely out of the Union line of fire.

As he came around the top of the ridge that bordered the Widow Wager's farm, John spotted one group of three or four blue-coated soldiers, then another, leaving the old brick house below. It was obvious to John that the Yankees were up to the same thing they had done at Bolivar Heights. Their job, he surmised, was simply to slow down the advance of Virginia troops towards the Ferry.

Must be the Yankees are expecting some reinforcements at the Ferry, he thought. Well, I can play their game, too.

John slowly lifted his musket to his right shoulder. He pulled the hammer back with his right thumb, until he heard a familiar click. Closing his left eye, he sighted down the barrel until the blue blouse of a Union private, who was in a group of four running down the hill toward the Ferry, was in his sights.

He paused momentarily, as he contemplated the morality of ending this young soldier's life so brutally, so abruptly, so prematurely. But then he thought of his mother and sisters back at Walnut Grove, and he hesitated no longer.

With a gentle squeeze of the trigger, the ball exploded out of the barrel of John's musket. Quickly, he reloaded his weapon, oblivious to the shouts of the Union soldiers or the cries of agony of the man he had hit. An almost surreal calmness enveloped John. At last, he now was able to do something.

John could see that a group of Union soldiers was gathering at the southwest corner of the farmhouse, moving cautiously up the ridge in his general direction dashing from tree to tree. There's time to get off one more good shot, he thought, before I hightail it out of here.

John had not changed his position since firing his first successful shot. He now took careful aim once more, this time picking out the man closest to him. The Yankee troops had moved cautiously, and getting a bead on the target was no easy task. John squeezed off his second shot, just missing a Yankee solider as he ducked behind a tree.

Now it's time to get out of here, John thought. He knew he had precious little time to make good his escape. Glancing quickly down the ridge, John observed that his second shot had the Yankee soldiers scurrying for cover. Good! he mused. I'll make my run for it, and I'll be long gone before they know what's going on. A wry smile crossed his lips as he thought of how he, just one man, had slowed up the retreat of a whole company of Union infantry.

John jumped quickly to his feet. He had taken only a few quick steps when he heard the sound of a single distant musket.

Almost instantaneously, his body was thrown backwards as what felt like a huge hammer slammed into this chest.

His body lay sprawled on the moist blanket of fallen leaves. Not realizing that a Yankee sharpshooter had skillfully planted a minie ball in his chest, John attempted to get back to his feet and continue his escape.

It was then that John felt the unspeakable agony of three broken ribs and a punctured right lung, damages caused by the internal ricochet of the Union missile. His vision quickly faded to hundreds of shooting stars in a field of gray, and then mercifully went to black.

2

Charles Cole barely noticed the roaring, crackling crispy flames in the massive stone fireplace in front of him. Within the last hour of creeping winter afternoon darkness, he had quickly consumed four consecutive double shots of extra smooth Kentucky bourbon. The alcohol surged through his veins, and brought with it that dull, tingling sensation that now had become an everyday occurrence for him.

The door to the parlor creaked open as Charles' father entered the room. Dr. James H. Cole was a tall, stately man with a thick mane of magnificent hair the color of pewter. Countless craggy lines crisscrossed his clean-shaven face. Constant exposure to the elements as he drove his buggy on house calls across the rolling farmland roads in all seasons and temperatures had weathered him. Dr. Cole was an institution in Springfield. Everybody knew him; everybody liked him. And everybody trusted Dr. Cole. He was the quintessential small town physician.

His younger son, Charles, was another matter, though. Physically, he did not resemble his father in the least. Charles was short and rotund, with a ruddy complexion with straggly black hair and beard. His eyes were the color of coal, normally black, but which flashed fiery red when his temper was up or he had had too much to drink. For Charles, both occasions happened all too frequently. To most people, it was obvious that Charles' physical appearance was attributable to his affinity for alcohol and his aversion to physical labor of any sort.

At 24 years of age, Charles had yet to assume any real responsibility for himself. And he had been unquestionably spoiled by his doting mother, who did not agree with her husband that what Charles really needed was discipline, and lots of it.

The creaking door drew Charles' attention. Dr. Cole stood just inside the room, waiting for his son to invite him in. Unfortunately, getting Charles' attention was something that had become increasingly difficult. One of the few times when his father had any real influence on Charles was several months earlier, when he was able to persuade his son to answer President Lincoln's call for volunteers. After considerable prodding and thinly veiled threats by the good doctor to force him from the nest, Charles had reluctantly volunteered. But, ever mindful of the dangers of combat after reports of the horrors of Bull Run, Charles was able to talk his way into the regimental band, where he had joined 20 other musicians.

Charles' eyes caught those of his father. Embarrassed and saddened at the sight of his inebriated son, Dr. Cole swiftly averted his glance toward the oil painting of his grandfather which hung over the fireplace mantel. He stood stiffly inside the door, waiting.

Charles sighed deeply. Then slowly, haltingly, he attempted to raise himself from the sofa. As he struggled to sit upright, he lifted his right hand and waived at Dr. Cole. "Come on in, doc," he slurred. "What can I do for ya?"

Dr. Cole bristled at being beckoned like some common servant. After all, it was *his* house. He was a pillar of the community. He has no right to talk to me like that, he thought. I am his father; he should at least show me some respect. But the good doctor kept his tongue, at least for now. He knew what he had to discuss with Charles would be difficult enough.

Dr. Cole steeled himself up for the anticipated verbal battle with Charles. He had carefully rehearsed over and over in his mind what he would say to his son.

"Well, Charles, I think we ought to talk about your future," he began hesitantly. Having gotten the first words of the intended speech out of his mouth took some of the tension out of the doctor, and his body now noticeably relaxed. He entered the parlor, and closed the door gently behind him. He stood there, waiting for some response from his son.

Dr. Cole's tentative offering was met with a fierce verbal assault from his son, the sot. "What do you mean, *my* future? I'm not interested in any more of your preaching on what I ought to do with my life. I'm 24 years old, and *I'll* decide what I'm going to do and when I'm going to do it!" Charles smiled smugly at the way he was able to keep his father off-guard. But through the thick alcoholic fog that swirled through his consciousness, Charles still could sense that his father meant to talk with him about something considerably more intense than even the snowstorm, which howled with growing intensity outside around his parents' stately brick home.

The doctor avoided the inclination to lecture Charles. His ne'er-do-well son was probably right. There was very little he could do to persuade Charles to do anything, unless of course his mother agreed. "Your mother and I have been talking."

"Yes," Charles responded cautiously. If his father and mother agreed on something, which now appeared likely, Charles knew he probably was not going to like to hear about it.

Dr. Cole cleared his throat. Unknowingly, he folded his lanky arms across his chest, a subconscious effort to symbolize his authority.

"I'm sure you know how proud you made your mother and me when you enlisted last November. We know you weren't particularly excited about the prospect of spending the winter in a tent in Virginia, so far from home."

Right about that, doc, Charles thought. It was colder than shit there. Lousy food and not a goddamned thing to do except drill, drill, drill. It didn't take Charles long to figure out he had to get the hell out of that place.

"We know how hard it was on you. And when you came home at Christmas, I could see that you were not adjusting well. That's why I wrote that letter, as your doctor, to your commander saying you were just too sick to return to your unit."

Charles chafed at the lecture from this oh-so-pious, oh-so-respectable man. He knew that his father's letter had saved him from desertion charges. Still, he couldn't just sit here like a child and not say anything.

"Look, doc. It wasn't my idea to sign up in the first place. You forced me into it. I know this is a big deal with you, but I don't really give a good goddamn about whether the Union whips the South or not. In fact, I'm inclined more every day to the view that Jamie's probably got the right idea."

The mention of the name "Jamie" had a noticeable impact on Dr. Cole. He had forbidden all members of his household from speaking the name of his eldest son, James C. Cole. On a similar cold winter's day ten years ago, he and Jamie had nearly come to blows on Jamie's insistent refusal to go on to college and, ultimately, medical school. Jamie stormed out of the house, without so much as even a good-bye, and headed south.

Dr. Cole's wife, Victoria, still received letters sporadically from their son. Dr. Cole had heard from her, in occasional intimate moments when he let his guard down, that Jamie had opened a pharmacy in Memphis. He knew Jamie was married, but didn't know his daughter-in-law's name. He knew Jamie had produced him some grandchildren, too. She pleaded with him to go to Memphis, to make amends. But Dr. Cole had refused. He was a stubborn man. And what's more, he could not leave his patients for the weeks it would require to make the trip she insisted upon. And of course, now with a war on, travel was even more problematic, even if he had wanted to go, which he did not.

"I don't see what Jamie has to do with this," Dr. Cole responded icily to Charles.

"Well, let me tell you," Charles replied. He knew he had touched a nerve when he mentioned Jamie's name. He wryly concluded that he had successfully deflected the discussion away from his own inadequacies. Lord knows, he had many.

"Jamie knew that he had to get the hell out of here. If he stayed here, you would have tried to control every single aspect of his life, just like you are trying to control mine. That's why he went as far away from here, from you, as he could."

Dr. Cole stood in stony silence, his arms still crossed. Only the nervous tapping of his fingers on his elbows betrayed an increasing depth of disgust with this pathetic excuse for a son.

"Charles, I can't believe you mean what you are saying," he responded coolly. "You know I only want what is best for you."

"Well, doc, it's like this. The thing is, you don't really give a damn for what I want to do with my life." Now flushed with the influence of alcohol and anger, Charles' voice climbed both in volume and in pitch. "All you care about is your god-damned reputation and your pissy little patients, suffering from incontinence, hemorrhoids, or some other such afflictions. Frankly, I wish you'd leave me the hell alone, and I'll do the same with you. You pay attention to what you want to, and I'll do likewise!"

Dr. Cole's superficial coolness now disintegrated into a smoldering rage. He clenched his fists so tightly his knuckles turned white. The tracks on his weathered face looked like narrow white trails across a sandy fiery red desert.

Charles sensed that, for one of the few moments in his life, he now held sway over his father. He pushed himself to his feet and stumbled off the sofa. He proceeded toward his father, still standing stiffly at the parlor door. Now is the time to really tell him what I think, he thought. As he negotiated his way across the pine-planked floor, Charles swayed slightly from the influence of the four double shots of whiskey.

Only the persistent rapping at the parlor door behind Dr. Cole kept the scene from disintegrating into total bedlam. He raised his hand, both in an effort to keep Charles at bay and to signal that there was someone at the door.

Gently, Dr. Cole pressed on the latch. He pulled the door open. It was Victoria, his wife and Charles' mother.

"James, I know you and Charles are having a discussion." A classic understatement, he thought. "But Mr. Maloney is waiting in the hall. He wants to speak with you."

"What is it about?" Dr. Cole inquired, under control again.

"He wouldn't say," she responded, "but he seems mighty upset."

"Tell him I'll be right with him," he directed. Closing the door behind him again, Dr. Cole turned to face Charles.

"Mr. Maloney is here to see me. I know you've been friendly with his daughter Tess," Dr. Cole stated. "Do you have any idea what has caused him to come out in the middle of a blizzard like this to see me?"

Charles knew full well why Maloney was here. Charles had been swilling down more booze today than usual in an effort to drown out his concern about a visit from Tess's father.

Tess Maloney was an admittedly flirtatious, raven-haired 18-year-old Irish beauty. Charles had had an on-again, off-again relationship with her for the last few months. A cheerful lass with a twinkle in her eye, she was the kind of girl who liked a little fun, but never wanted trouble.

Yesterday Charles had called on her while her parents were attending the wedding of a distant niece in Philadelphia. He had a little too much to drink and, as they sat on the love seat in front of the fire in her parents' living room, Charles brazenly and without any invitation whatsoever put his hand up her dress, his stubby fingers pushing roughly through her dainties in search of the flower of her femininity. Tess firmly resisted Charles' advances. Angered at the rejection, Charles threw her onto the floor. There he forcibly and swiftly torn off her dress and undergarments and raped her. He had left her on the floor, crying and whimpering, with a warning to tell no one of what had occurred. Obviously, Charles thought, she had ignored his warning. No matter, it was his word against hers.

"I haven't seen Tess in weeks," Charles lied. "I have no idea what her father wants to speak with you about." In addition to his ability to consume large quantities of alcohol, Charles had developed a real knack for telling lies so convincingly that people would believe them.

He was a little too cool and composed to fool his father. "Well, I'd like you to stick around just the same," his father said. Charles shrugged his shoulders, and headed toward the Queen Anne table next to the sofa, where the whiskey decanter sat. He retrieved his well-used glass from the table, and poured himself another double shot.

Dr. Cole nodded his head back and forth sadly. "Show Mr. Maloney in please, Victoria," he said to his wife. "And Victoria."

"Yes, James," she answered dutifully.

"I think it would be better if you do something else while Charles and I talk with Mr. Maloney."

Mrs. Cole nodded her head in assent, turned and retreated down the hall to retrieve Mr. Maloney.

* * * * * * *

Dr. Cole stood just inside the open parlor door, waiting to receive Michael Maloney. Charles must have been up to something again, he thought. Victoria had probably surmised as much, too, when she first sized up Maloney's somber, no-nonsense visage at the front stoop. No visitor would come calling in a whiteout, refuse to state his business unless he had serious matters to discuss. And Charles' speedy move to the liquor decanter at the announcement of Mr. Maloney's visit was a pretty good clue as well.

This was not the first unannounced visit from the father of a Springfield girl that Dr. Cole had endured. Charles could be a real charmer, he knew. But after even just a few shots of liquor, Charles' personality changed, and he became domineering and aggressive to the point of brutal.

"Mr. Maloney, how good to see you again. How's the hardware business?" Dr. Cole's attempt at friendly banter had no impact on Maloney, who stood grim-faced just outside the door.

"Please come in," Dr. Cole said, now very formal. Maloney nodded curtly and brushed past Dr. Cole.

Charles was sitting in a rocker in a shadow-filled corner of the room. An afghan covered his knees as he rocked gently back and forth. He made no effort to acknowledge Tess's father, who had noticed him, but who likewise had made no effort to recognize Charles' presence.

"This won't take long," Maloney said. "There is a matter of utmost seriousness that I would like to discuss with you. It concerns your Charles and my Tess."

Dr. Cole remained standing, his hands clasped tightly behind his back. He rocked gently back and forth on his heels. "Go on, Mr. Maloney. I invited Charles to join us so that he may provide his insight on whatever it is that is troubling you."

Charles continued rocking silently in the corner. He had finished his most recent double shot, and the empty glass lay across his lap.

"You're damned right I'm troubled!" Maloney had now found his voice. His face flushed crimson with rage. "Your god-damned son raped my Tess yesterday!" Maloney's voice boomed off the rafters; his hands quivered with anger.

"Now wait just a minute, Maloney," Dr. Cole interjected. "How do you know all this happened? And why do you think Charles is responsible?" Even though just minutes earlier they had nearly come to blows, Dr. Cole now instinctively defended Charles. He also was concerned that this matter not be conceded too quickly, lest it affect his own reputation in the community.

"How do I know it happened?" Maloney stared incredulously at Dr. Cole. "How do I know this happened?" he repeated. "Very simple. When the Missus and I arrived home last evening, Tess lay crying on our living room floor, her dress and undergarments in tatters. Her face was covered with huge welts where someone had beaten her. And . . ." Maloney paused, not knowing whether he could continue. He sighed deeply, which seemed to give him the stamina to go on. "And all around her privates her mother tells me, she was scratched and bleeding," he stammered. "You're a god-damned physician! You want to examine her?" Maloney's voice trailed off. He could go no further. He buried his head in his hands, sobbing inconsolably.

"This is just dreadful," Dr. Cole said. "I'm so sorry."

Maloney heard not a word of what the good doctor had said. He was lost in his own world of grief and continued to sob inconsolably.

"What about this, Charles?" Dr. Cole turned to his son. "Do you know anything about what Mr. Maloney has said?"

Charles raised his head and looked directly into his father's eyes. Even in the twilight darkness the sugary smile on Charles' face was unmistakable.

"Look, doc," he said sweetly. "I'll admit to seeing Tess a few times the last month or so, but I haven't been anywhere close to her within the last week." The lie was easy to tell, Charles thought. He always tried to build one of his fabrications around a kernel of truth, so as to make it all the more believable. Who would know?

"That's a god-damned lie!" Maloney bellowed. He charged across the room toward Charles. Dr. Cole jumped in his path, and wrapped both arms tightly around the struggling Michael Maloney to restrain him.

"Charles, get out of here!" Dr. Cole screamed. "Get out of here now!"

Charles sensed the imminent danger. He leapt to his feet, the shot glass tumbling from his lap to the floor, where it shattered into hundreds of tiny pointed crystalline shards. He nearly tripped over the afghan, but managed to stumble toward the door.

"You son-of-a-bitch! You son-of-a-bitch!" Maloney bellowed incessantly as the figure of Charles Cole slipped through the door and out into the white void of the raging winter night's storm.

* * * * * *

The blizzard had stopped by the time Charles returned to his parents' home several hours later. He had little enough time to escape with his life from Tess's father, and so had left the house without boots, coat, cap or even so much as a muffler. Still, Charles hadn't really needed much protection from the elements, since he had headed only a block down the street to the corner tavern. There he had warmed himself by the fire, with glass after glass of mulled wine to help calm his nerves. He left for home only because the bartender told him he would not serve him any more, that he had had enough.

The massive cherry grandfather clock had just chimed out eight times as Charles opened the massive front door. The smell of roast beef filled his nostrils. He could hear glasses and china clinking in the kitchen. Mother must be doing the dishes, he thought.

Dr. Cole sat in the dining room, listening attentively for Charles' return. Maloney's visit had dramatically interrupted his conversation that afternoon with Charles. But Dr. Cole was now more firmly convinced than before that he needed to lay down the law, once and for all. Drinking to excess and shirking military duty were bad enough. But forcing oneself upon a woman. There was no way that could or should be tolerated, he thought.

"Charles," he called out. No response.

"Charles!" he shouted, more firmly.

Charles Cole sauntered into the dining room, pulled a chair out from the opposite end of the table from where his father sat, and plopped into it.

Dr. Cole grimaced. This will be hard, he thought, but it's got to be done.

"Charles, I had a lengthy conversation with Mr. Maloney after you left," he said authoritatively. "I believe I have been able to convince him to not report this little incident to the police." He paused. Charles stared at the flickering candelabra, seemingly ignoring even his father's presence.

"If it happens that Tess becomes pregnant as a result of this, your mother and I have agreed to make appropriate compensation to her and her family," he continued. Charles grimaced, but still said nothing. "But Mr. Maloney has insisted that you must leave Springfield immediately."

"And I suppose you and mother have discussed this, too?" Charles inquired sarcastically.

"Actually, yes, we have," Dr. Cole said. He rose from his chair, walked slowly to the fireplace, and then turned to face his son.

"We believe it would be best for everybody if you volunteered to rejoin your old regiment again."

"Look here, doc," Charles declared bitterly. "I ain't <u>never</u> going to do that again! A fellow could get killed out there."

"Charles, I don't think you understand," Dr. Cole declared firmly. "You must either volunteer for another three years in the Union army or . . . ." His voice trailed off as he groped for the right words to speak now.

"Or what?"

Dr. Cole sat back down at the table and generated the most intent, serious expression he could muster. He knew he needed to make absolutely sure that Charles firmly grasped what was at stake here. "You will find yourself in jail on rape charges filed by Mr. Maloney," he replied. "Your mother and I will do nothing to deter him from pressing charges, as he is already inclined to do."

"This is ridiculous!" Charles' tone had now changed from sarcastic to bellicose. "I didn't do a god-damned thing to that whore," he lied. "Now you are telling me I'm gonna have to re-up in the army? I could get killed. Is that what you want?"

"Of course not," Dr. Cole responded. Increasingly angry, Dr. Cole's response was less than completely convincing.

"Then why are you telling me I'm going to have to volunteer for another three years? Don't you believe me?"

"Actually, Charles, no. I do not."

A leaden silence hung over the tension-filled room as father and son glared across the table at each other. The only sound that could be heard was the seemingly interminable tick-tock of the grandfather clock in the hall.

"Well, father dear. Let me tell you something," Charles said icily. "There's no way in hell that I'll ever go back to the Union army again. And you know what else?"

His anger seething over, Charles continued, barely taking enough time for a breath, let alone time for his father to respond.

"I think I'll go visit Jamie in Memphis. Maybe he can use some help in his store."

The mention of Jamie's name twice in one day was more than Dr. Cole could bear. "Do not speak that name in this house!" he commanded. "It belongs to a man who deserted his family and has betrayed his country."

Charles knew that Jamie's rebel tendencies irritated the hell out of his father. And while that in and of itself may be sufficient reason to bring his brother's name up again with his father, Charles also began to realize that his brother and he shared a common bond – hatred for their domineering, demanding, overbearing father.

"Look, doc. Why should you care where I go? As long as I'm away from here, you're off the hook with Tess Maloney's father, and I'll be out of your hair."

Charles nodded his head in smug agreement with his own brilliant analysis. Yes, his father really had no choice. He could not force him to enlist in the Union army. And his father could hardly allow his precious reputation, that most priceless of his possessions, to be sullied by allowing him to be thrown in jail on rape charges.

Dr. Cole also realized that, frankly, getting Charles out of town to anyplace would be a solution to his immediate problem. And while he would prefer to act as though Jamie did not exist, assisting Charles in this endeavor was a better alternative than having to explain why he was in prison. Still, he knew he should proceed cautiously.

"All right, Charles," Dr. Cole said calmly. "If you believe that your brother can assist you, I'll agree to help get you there. I surely wish that it didn't require you to go into rebel territory, though."

Charles knew that he had won. He had finally showed his father that, at least on this one matter, Charles H. Cole was a man to be reckoned with.

"Can you be out of here tomorrow?" Dr. Cole asked. "I mean, so that Mr. Maloney is convinced that you have satisfied our end of the bargain?"

"Gladly, doc. And maybe even sooner!"

Dr. Cole rose from his chair, sliding it back carefully so as not to scratch the varnish that had been painstakingly applied to the yellow pine flooring in what appeared to be endless coats. He walked around the table and blew out the candles one by one, in an obvious sign that the conversation was over, the deal concluded.

"Oh, doc." Charles said casually.

"Yes, Charles?"

"It's a long way to Memphis, you know. Especially with the war on and all. I'll need $100 in gold for expenses on the way. Do you think you can loan it to me?" Charles knew perfectly well that his father not only had the money, but that he would gladly part with it if it meant this thorny, uncomfortable problem were behind him.

Dr. Cole was determined to maintain at least the appearance that he was in control. "We'll talk about it in the morning," he answered, in a noncommittal voice. He walked out of the dining room, and turned up the stairs to go to bed, leaving Charles to stand alone in the dark.

3

FEBRUARY–MARCH 1862
PASCAGOULA, MISSISSIPPI

"John, wake up. We're almost there."

The sweet, lilting soprano voice of Abigail Williams drew John Yates Beall from the respite of sleep. His eye fluttered open. As consciousness returned, so did the reality of his condition. Every excruciating, shallow breath now reminded John of that day four months ago on Bolivar Heights when a Yankee sharpshooter found his mark.

John felt the urge to cough and fought to suppress it. Every time he had not resisted, seemingly endless, intense coughing spasms erupted. The inevitable consequence of these episodes was that the wound to his right lung was reinflamed. Once he started coughing, John would disgorge huge quantities of blood before momentarily losing consciousness from the toll of the exertion and reduced oxygen. Then, for the next few days, the pain would be incessant and intense.

Since leaving Tallahassee five days previous, John had been reclining on one side of the Williams carriage, attempting to sleep as much as possible. Sleep, he knew, was slowly restoring him to strength. But it was also an escape, however brief, from his constant companion, pain.

Abigail and her husband Robert occupied the other side of the carriage. John had met the Williamses several weeks ago aboard the train from Richmond. John was en route to Tallahassee, the southernmost rail terminus. As soon as he was able to travel, his Virginia doctor ordered him to go as far south as he could, where the warmer climate might aid in his recovery. The sharp turns in winter weather in Virginia were not conducive to a speedy recovery and could in fact cost him his life.

Robert and Abigail Williams had both grown to admire and to like John, whom they believed to be a gallant young patriot, over the course of the trip to Tallahassee. They invited him to stay with them at Runnymede, their plantation near Pascagoula. There the gentle Gulf climate would aid his recovery. He had accepted, not only because he thought the locale would be therapeutic, but because of his reciprocal fondness for the couple.

"Runnymede?" John whispered.

Abigail nodded, silently affirming that the painful jolting and bouncing over rutted roads through the swampland was nearly at an end.

A wan smile crossed John's face as he felt the tender touch of this angel of mercy on his forearm. She reminded him so much of his own mother. She was a good, solid Christian woman who cared for his every need. John hated having to rely on someone else. But he realized that it was the constant, unwavering attention of people that cared about him that was responsible more than anything for his survival and gradual recovery from the near-fatal encounter at Bolivar Heights.

The carriage slowed, then turned from the main road and entered Runnymede. The path to the mansion house was covered with crushed oyster shells that crunched underneath the carriage's wheels and horses' hoofs.

Robert Williams' father had carved Runnymede out of the swamp some forty years ago. Actually, it was not Williams, but hundreds of powerful black backs and biceps that had cleared and drained the land. Several hundred slaves, many of them the children and grandchildren of those who forty years previous had carved thousands of acres of productive land from primeval swamp, now tended luxuriant fields of indigo and rice.

Late afternoon sunlight flickered through Spanish moss hanging from massive live oak trees. The warmth of the sun crept into the carriage as it progressed up the drive to the mansion house. Powerful perfume from countless gardenia blooms wafted through the open windows on cool, gentle breezes. So far, John had only experienced Runnymede from a nearly prone position, but already he had begun to sense the enchantment and tranquility that the Williams' associated with this ethereal place.

The carriage slowed to a halt and John struggled to rise from his seat.

"Lay still," Robert admonished, gently touching John's shoulder. "We'll have you carried into the house. You need to save your energy. It's been a long trip."

John understood that his host's counsel was based on concern for the effects of the lengthy ride from Charles Town, Virginia to the gates of Runnymede. Still, it was important to John to make the effort himself.

"Thank you, General," John said softly. "But I believe I can make it. Just give me a little support as I step out of the carriage in case I faint."

During the ride from Tallahassee across the pocked roads of the Gulf shore, the two men had plenty of empty time on their hands. When John was awake and felt up to it, they each discussed their involvement in the war. Williams had explained to John that, because of his advancing age and lack of any military experience whatsoever, he had been unable to obtain a military commission. However, his personal wealth, persuasive talents honed from years of courtroom experience as an attorney, and connections with similarly-situated wealthy, well-educated gentlemen across the South were assets that the Confederacy could use. Williams had journeyed to Richmond, at the request of President Jefferson Davis, to discuss just how he might be able to assist in the war effort. Following a recitation by Williams that rivaled any jury summation he had ever given, Davis had asked Williams to serve as an Aide-de-Camp, or ADC, to General Beauregard, with principal responsibility for troop recruitment.

Williams had told John that, although he had not been given a military commission, an ADC is entitled to all of the benefits and privileges that befit a General. Jeff Davis himself had told him that, he said. John sensed the pride welling within Williams at the thought of being so honored by the President, and began calling him "general" thereafter. The name stuck.

"All right, John," the General responded. He stepped sprightly from the carriage as his servant opened the door. Stepping onto the drive, little crunching sounds from crushed oyster shells in the drive emanated from beneath his feet. Turning back to face the carriage, Williams offered his hand as support to John in his struggle to disembark from the confines that had been his home on wheels for a good bit of the last week.

Abigail remained inside, assisting John in getting up from a prone position on the bench. John grimaced in pain as he put pressure on his right side, which still had not entirely mended. Abigail acted as a brace upon which John could lean, although her own age and petite size prevented her from doing much more. Like her husband, she too was well into her sixties, and gnarled fingers revealed her battle with arthritis.

Through steely determination, John overcame the searing pain shooting through his body. Tears welled up in his eyes, but his lips remained tightly pursed. His thinning brown hair was disheveled, his clothes rumpled. The once massive muscles covering his upper body had wasted away some, but not so much that he couldn't carry his own weight. He still could, if only just barely. A stubby growth of beard covered his face. John Yates Beall looked like he had been through hell. But the fire of determination in his eyes spoke volumes about the internal strength with which he would overcome this impediment, too.

He took one tentative step down from the carriage, then another. The worst was over. John now began walking in slow, measured steps to the main entrance door to the mansion house, some fifty feet away, concentrating intently on each step. Robert and Abigail Williams grasped both of his arms, gently but firmly, steadying him as he shuffled slowly along. Household slaves started to unload luggage from the top of the carriage.

"Uncle Robert! Aunt Abbie!"

Two young women came running through the portico door and down the walk, their arms open in greetings. John and the Williamses stopped and looked up.

"Oh, I'm sorry," one of the two young lasses chirped. "I didn't realize you were bringing home another houseguest," she said, her green eyes twinkling mischievously.

"Well, Martha, we didn't know you and your sister were going to be with us either," the General said. His efficient exterior quickly melted as he observed the two sisters' forlorn look. "But don't worry. We've always got room for the two loveliest belles in the South." The corners of his mouth crinkled up in a sly smile, and the two young ladies quickly regained their exuberance.

"Oh, I'm so sorry," Abigail said to John. "I've completely forgotten my manners. Let me introduce you to our two nieces."

"I understand perfectly," John replied. "No apology is necessary."

"Helen, Martha, would you come here, please? There's someone I'd like you to meet."

The two sisters, sensing a pending formality, composed themselves. Arm in arm, they gracefully strolled down to meet the stranger with their aunt and uncle.

John had paid little attention to the two young women immediately upon arrival at Runnymede. As they drew closer to him, however, he noticed how lovely they both were. In particular, he felt an attraction to the younger of the two sisters. There was something about her spirit that sparked his interest.

"John, I'd like to introduce my two nieces to you," Abigail said. "Helen and Martha O'Bryan, my sister's daughters."

"John Beall," John said as he introduced himself, "I'm delighted to make your acquaintance." He bowed slightly. The two young ladies curtsied in acknowledgment.

"Mr. Beall, you certainly do look a mess," the younger sister stated matter-of-factly. "Where have you been?"

"Martha! Mr. Beall has been through a horrible ordeal." Abigail Williams could not believe how forward her niece was. Of course, she had always been that way. Even as a little girl, she remembered, Martha was never afraid to go up to any adult, known or unknown, and ask for candy, speak her mind or otherwise embarrass her elders. "You must apologize."

"No, that's not necessary," John said. He rather admired the young woman's boldness. "I…." His voice trailed off.

Tiny white sparkling stars began to spin in John's head, and his knees went limp. Since he had spent most of the last four months on his back, he had lost much of his considerable strength. He had only been able to endure the weeks aboard the carriages and trains, and then overland through the countryside to Runnymede, by drawing on that reservoir of energy deep within his very soul.

Abigail Williams caught John by the arm, and steadied him. The General came to his side/, too, to keep John from falling.

"I believe Mr. Beall needs some rest now," Abigail stated firmly. With that, she and the general half-carried John through the Runnymede front door. Helen followed behind, while Martha pondered alone on the drive this very curious stranger who had entered her life.

* * * * * * *

John's strength grew daily after his arrival at Runnymede. His doctor could not have prescribed a better regimen to aid his recovery. Abigail Williams made sure that he ate three substantial meals a day, that he got plenty of rest, including a nap every afternoon, and that he began exercising so that the weight returning to his frame consisted of muscle, not fat.

The laudanum prescribed for him by the General's doctor had also facilitated his recovery. John had at first resisted use of the drug. "I'm not interested in any opium or morphine," he said. It was only after the doctor had assured him that laudanum contained only one percent morphine that he relented. And now he was glad he had. The drug worked miracles. It reduced the chronic pain in his lung and suppressed the desire to cough. Although he had been told he would likely continue to have some pain and difficulty in breathing for the rest of his life, John's wounds had now started to heal, and he felt noticeably better. The doctor had also told him that the laudanum would help him sleep. And he had been sleeping better, as advised.

Abigail and the General's doctor had both suggested to John that he exercise by taking walks every day. Martha had cheerfully volunteered to join John on his walks. "What else have I got to do around here?" she said when John reminded her that he could walk just fine on his own.

Initially, John was thankful that Martha was joining him because he enjoyed the company. As they traversed the countryside in increasingly longer strolls, though, his original curiosity about his vivacious companion grew into something more. Now John's entire focus was on Martha. He spent every waking moment with her. When not on their walks, he would accompany her as she tended her aunt's flower gardens, or as she went into town to shop. He could not imagine an existence without her, although he was too shy to verbalize this to her.

In fact, Martha felt the same way about John. Since she had first met him as he struggled out of her uncle's carriage, haggard and sickly, she had been drawn irresistibly to him, like a moth to a flame. His brilliant blue eyes had first caught her attention. Then, as they began taking their walks, she learned about, and was drawn to, his compassion, intelligence and determination.

It was a picture perfect morning as John and Martha embarked on their current morning stroll. Fluffy white clouds coasted lazily overhead against an azure sky. Robins chirped merrily in the springtime air. Deep blue hyacinths, white and yellow daffodils, and tulips of every shade filled in the spaces between the moss-draped live oak trees lining the path from the main road to the Runnymede front door. Despite his occasional pain, and although he was still weak from his wound, John had never felt more alive. Especially with Martha at his side.

Martha could hardly contain herself with exuberance over the beauty of the day. "Is it as lovely as this in Virginia in the springtime?" she asked as they ambled along the path toward the main road.

John had spoken with Martha about many things on their walks, but usually matters of deeper substance than the weather. The twenty-year old Martha had not been to the University, as John had. But her parents both believed that a woman of means should also be well educated. And so they sent her and her older sister Helen to an exclusive finishing school in Nashville, where they had studied classic Greek poetry, French political thought and similar ethereal subjects.

"Every bit as lovely," John responded softly. He had not thought about home in weeks, ever since Martha had begun to occupy the principal spot in his mind. A lump formed in his throat as his thoughts returned to his widowed mother and four sisters, alone at Walnut Grove. And what had become of Willie? When he journeyed south after Christmas, John's baby brother, not yet 18, had rejoined his unit, the Second Virginia. The Stonewall Brigade would be moving through the Shenandoah Valley by this time, he mused.

Martha could sense that John's thoughts had turned introspective. "You miss your home, don't you?" she queried. "I mean, we all find something special in that place where our roots are, don't we?"

"Is it that obvious?"

"Yes, John," she answered softly. Silently they walked down the path, just breathing in the beauty of the day. Reaching the main road, they turned east into the sun.

As his thoughts turned toward home, John realized that he was troubled. He didn't really know Martha that well, but felt that he could share his thoughts and his feelings with her.

"Martha?"

"Yes?"

"I really feel like I have shirked my responsibilities to my family and my country." The words gushed out of John's mouth. How will she respond? Will she agree? he wondered. My God, it would kill me if she did!

"That's ridiculous," Martha said firmly. She had heard all about John's exploits from Aunt Abbie. Stopping in the road she took him by the arm. "Why do you feel that way anyway? Because you were unlucky enough to take a Yankee bullet?"

Before John could answer, she continued. "What you did was the act of a brave man who loves his country. No one forced you to be there. Nobody forced you to lead that reconnaissance patrol. You weren't coerced into scouting out the old farmhouse. You *volunteered* to do all of this. Why? Because you were crazy?"

The corners of her mouth turned up and her eyes twinkled mischievously. John could not help but chuckle himself.

"No," she stated emphatically. She maintained control of John's arm. Unwittingly, her hand clasped it tighter, as if doing so would better make her point. "Look at me, John Yates Beall," she commanded. John knew it was pointless to argue with Martha now, and so he peered intently, longingly into those lovely green eyes. "If every man in the South were as brave as you, this war would be over by now."

Suddenly realizing that she had John's arm firmly in her grip, she let go. John's arm dropped to his side.

The young warrior's face flushed red. He wasn't sure if that tingling sensation he felt now was pride or embarrassment or something else. But he knew intuitively that the passion with which this petite young flower of the South had spoken her mind directly reflected the feelings that she had for him.

"But I will never be able to fight again," he protested. "Even after I have completed my recuperation, only one lung will be fully functional. I will likely develop and have to live with tuberculosis. It will be impossible for me to do anything productive any more, not only in the defense of the South against the Yankees, but even back home at Walnut Grove. Can't you see? I'll never be fully a man again."

"Listen to me, John," Martha said. She stepped one step closer to the man she had come to know so well, and took both of his hands in hers. She gripped his firmly, yet gently, a reflection of her own feelings for him. "I don't want to get into an argument with you about this. And not only because I learned at Miss Babcock's Finishing School that young ladies do not argue with young gentlemen."

She paused, searching John's eyes for some response to her latest witticism. She noticed only tiny tears forming in the corners of both of his eyes, which were tightly closed. Dear God, she prayed, let this man see how much he means to me.

Impulsively, or perhaps in response to her prayer, Martha tossed aside convention once more. Standing on tip toes, she planted a peck on John's cheek. "I love you, John Yates Beall," she whispered in his ear. "You mean more to me than life itself."

John could not believe his ears. For weeks, he had dreamed of little else but Martha. Her image filled his mind during those rare moments when they were not together. He could see her shiny hair – parted down the middle with a cute little braid at the back – her turned up button nose, her penetrating green eyes and the way the corners of her mouth crinkled when she smiled. But John had always been taught that things must be done properly. And it was not proper for Martha to pursue him like this. Still, he felt the same way about her.

Opening his eyes, John was greeted with Martha's sweet smile, the one that had captivated his heart. He could resist no longer.

"And I love you, too, Martha," he said, his voice cracking. Martha flung herself into his arms. He wanted to smother her with kisses and never let her go. He still couldn't believe that this sassy young beauty cared so for him.

Tenderly, John lifted Martha's chin from his shoulder. Her arms still tightly around his waist, he took her head in his hands. He could feel her feminine softness pressing against his body. Sparks shot though his entire being as he pressed his lips against hers. Gently at first, and then more firmly, he caressed every inch of the face of the woman of his dreams. Afraid of his own deepening desires, he pulled himself gently away from her.

"Oh, John," Martha cooed breathlessly.

"Yes, my darling."

"Do you think Miss Babcock would approve?" She giggled at the cuteness of his reference to the prim and proper dowager who ran the young ladies' finishing school in Nashville.

John wagged an index finger back and forth in front of Martha's face, in his best imitation of an elderly spinster who thought she knows everything about the world, but has never experienced it. "Just make sure your young gentleman knows how to waltz. It is important to have an escort who can dance," he mocked. They both guffawed at their juvenile silliness.

Still laughing and joking, hand in hand they strolled back down the lane toward the mansion house. John filed away in a back corner of his mind that he had not yet completed the prescribed morning exercise. Oblivious to the springtime beauty on all sides, they both were caught in the rapture of their own blossoming love.

* * * * * * *

The therapeutic powers of new love had a profound impact on John's recovery. He expanded his regimen to include daily pushups, situps and other exercises designed to strengthen and tone up his entire body, now that he had regained his endurance courtesy of the long walks with Martha. His coughing fits were mostly controlled by steady doses of laudanum, and only an occasional wheeze indicated outwardly that John's lung capacity was still significantly impaired.

Of course, he had an additional motivation in restoring his physical prowess. Martha was there to firmly but gently provide the catalyst every day that he could become again the specimen of a man he once was, before Bolivar Heights. She had him convinced that he could become, as John had put it, a "full man" again, capable of contributing something to the betterment of mankind and the care of his family.

In the course of only a few short weeks from their mutual affirmations of love, John and Martha learned nearly everything there was to know about each other. Not only did they continue their discussions of history, philosophy and religion, they poured out even their deepest personal secrets to each other.

And although they both felt the flames of passion licking at their resolve, thus far they had managed to keep their physical relationship perfectly respectable. For John, it was a matter of principle. God abhorred fornication, and the Bible clearly forbade carnal relationships between unmarried individuals, he told Martha when the topic inevitably turned to this. Martha professed to share John's religious beliefs, and she did. But she had also resisted the temptations of the flesh because she feared the unbridled power it would give her over John, which she was neither willing nor prepared to exercise. She knew that, at this vulnerable time, her man needed to feel once again that he was in control of his life, not someone else, no matter how dear.

John's interest also returned inevitably to the progress of the war. He read every line of every newspaper he could get, searching for new dispatches from the front lines. He mapped out the locations of enemy and friendly forces and the sites of engagements on a huge map, provided to him by the General. His insatiable appetite for news from the front strengthened his resolve to return to duty as soon as possible.

Martha cried inwardly at the thought that John would ever dream of putting his life in danger again. She tried unsuccessfully to wipe from her mind the thought of losing the man she now loved so much. But Martha also knew that his was not an issue to be trifled with. For John, his own sense of manhood, the essence of his very being, hinged on his ability to meet the obligation he felt he had to the country he loved so much. So she kept her peace when John asked if she could understand why it may be necessary that he go back into battle some day. She said nothing, feeling that it was a topic to be discussed at another time, when he was stronger.

That day came at last. Jacob Thompson, another ADC to General Beauregard, arrived one evening in late March for a prearranged meeting at Runnymede with the General. Over the last month, Williams had been in more or less perpetual motion, applying his considerable powers of persuasion to encouraging and, if need be, cajoling, enough men to meet General Beauregard's demands to raise 10,000 Confederate troops from the Gulf counties.

Like Williams, Jacob Thompson was a man of considerable power and influence throughout the South. Before the war, Thompson had served long and well as a distinguished member of Congress from the sovereign state of Mississippi. President Buchanan had even tapped him to join his cabinet as Secretary of the Interior. However, Thompson's implacable, intransigent and unswerving support of what he perceived to be the South's inviolate and irrefutable right to secede, even while sitting on Buchanan's cabinet, had earned him the enmity of many men now in power in Washington.

Throughout the day, as Williams and Thompson conferred, John had been preoccupied for the most part, as usual, with Martha. But as he moved through the main hall on several occasions during the day, there they were in the General's library, two men huddled over numerous maps and papers spread across the General's rolltop desk and onto the floor. John knew intuitively, by the intensity and length of the men's conference in the library, that planning was underway for a major campaign.

Abigail told John all about the powerful and influential visitor holed up with her husband in the library, soon after his arrival that morning at Runnymede. John had hoped all day for an occasion to meet Thompson. An opportunity finally presented itself that evening.

After dinner, Abigail and her two nieces excused themselves to attend to their evening devotions. The General and Thompson arose from the table. "Would you care to join us on the veranda?" the General asked.

"I would be honored," John said, and followed the two men from the dining room through the sitting room to the hall, which led to the portico. Once outside, they situated themselves on oversized rattan furniture, painted white to match the four massive columns that held up the roof over the porch. The sun had not yet set, and the open sky in front of them was a virtual kaleidoscope of color. The men sat in awed silence, drinking in the beauty of the sunset.

"Mr. Williams tells me you're quite a hero," Thompson said to John, finally breaking the silence.

"I've done no more or less than any other man would have done," John said humbly.

"Horsefeathers!" Williams retorted. "You singlehandedly attacked a fortified Yankee position. If it hadn't been for a lucky shot by a sharpshooter, you would've driven a whole company back across the Potomac!" The General was as proud of John's heroics as though he were his own son. He also tended to stretch the truth a bit, too.

John simply blushed. How could he tactfully contradict a man of such prominence, and in the presence of another person of considerable influence?

Thompson leaned back in his chair and turned to face John directly. "The Confederacy could use a lot more men with your courage. We've got a helluva long, hard fight ahead of us, I'm afraid, before this war is over."

"I fully intend to return to my unit as soon as I am able," John said politely. He resented the fact that everyone assumed his fighting days were done, just because he only had one fully functional lung. But he knew that this man could be of assistance to him, so he went out of his way to avoid ruffling his feathers.

"What unit is that, son?" Thompson inquired.

"Second Virginia Infantry."

"Isn't that part of the Stonewall Brigade?" Thompson asked.

"Yes, sir, it is."

"Fine man, that Jackson." Thompson and the General both nodded their heads in affirmation at the mention of General Jackson's name. Thompson's questions continued. "And what is your rank?"

These questions were likely more than just polite conversation, John thought.

"Private, sir."

"Private? But Mr. Williams tells me you've studied law. The combination of brains and guts is tough to find in many soldiers. You should be leading other men."

"Thank you, sir," John said. He was flattered at the compliment. But it also appeared obvious to John that the General had already spoken with Thompson about him.

Thompson leaned forward in his chair. He uncrossed his legs, and then placed his elbows on the arms of the chair. "Look, son, you come very highly recommended by Mr. Williams. He has asked me to use some of my influence in Richmond to find a spot where your talents can be put to good use. And where your physical infirmity won't be a hindrance. Would you like me to do that?"

John could hardly believe his ears. Just hours earlier, he had only hoped to meet Thompson to get his insights on the progress of the war. And now, Thompson was offering to open doors for him that seemed only a dream before.

"Thank you, sir! Thank you! I would be most appreciative of your help!" John tried hard not to appear too exuberant. But it was difficult not to gush at the thought of being able to return to the service of his country in some meaningful position. In his heart, John felt Thompson was right. He should be leading other men.

"Well, then," Thompson said. He rose from his chair. John and the General stood up, too. "I will write a letter of introduction for you to the Secretary of War before I leave for Corinth tomorrow morning." Taking the General by the arm, he motioned toward the door that would lead them back to the library. "But right now, Mr. Williams and I have to discuss how we can stop those damned Yankees from coming any farther down the Mississippi than they already have."

"Certainly, I understand," John replied. "Good night, then."

Thompson and the General nodded their salutations, and proceeded back to the library. John followed behind, turning to go up the stairs to his bedroom, as the two older men continued down the hall.

John knew that the time had come to discuss his future with Martha. He could put it off no longer. Best to think and pray on it tonight; I'll discuss it with her in the morning, he thought. Having resolved that he would wait until the morning to share his news with Martha, John climbed up the stairs, one step at a time, pausing briefly midway to avoid irritating his still-tender lungs.

* * * * * * *

He awoke early the next morning after only a few fitful hours of sleep. Thank God for the laudanum, John thought to himself as he threw his legs over the bed to the cold hardwood floor below. If not for the calming effects of the laudanum, he would not have even got the few hours of sleep that he did.

Despite the numbing feeling that comes when a body is not properly rested, John Yates Beall felt like a redeemed man. Certainly not in a religious sense; he already had that peace that passes all understanding, which all believers in the Christian faith experience. No, John had been given another chance to fight for the Confederacy, even though his wound continued to sap him of his full strength.

As he had tossed and turned in his bed, John swiftly concluded that there was nothing that he should hide from Martha. She knew how he felt about doing something, anything to aid the cause. What pained him most was the fact that he would have to leave her soon, perhaps never to see her again. And that thought was completely unacceptable to him.

John loved Martha, more than he could ever hope to express to her. He loved everything about her; she was all a man could ever want in a woman. She was cultured, attractive and witty. She cheered him up when he was down, and encouraged him to dare to dream. That had been quite a job as John embarked on the difficult road to recovery over the last few months at Runnymede. But even more important – she loved him. Knowing that made John feel as though anything were possible. And it made John's decision all the easier about his future relationship with Martha.

The first hints of daylight were just peeking over the horizon as John came down the stairs to the kitchen for breakfast. Every day for weeks now John had arisen at the crack of dawn, so that he could go out on his endurance-building walks with Martha through the countryside as the sun rose over the well-cultivated fields of Runnymede. This morning, he had dressed in his usual attire – a loose fitting cotton shirt and black breeches, held up by brown leather suspenders. His thinning brown hair was neatly combed, and he had already shaved, except for the area around his chin and upper lip where wispy hairs formed his only facial hair. Ever since that day when he was introduced to Martha all smelly, dirty and disheveled, John had made a noble effort to dispel the first terrible image he thought he had created.

It was important to John that the discussion with Martha about his future, about their future, happen at just the right time. So, as they sat down to their usual early breakfast together, he avoided talk about anything except the most banal of subjects. He sat across the kitchen table from her, which is how they normally took their breakfast.

Martha sensed something was different about John this morning. Although hardly a chatty person to begin with, he was even more reserved than usual. But she felt she knew him well enough to believe that he would talk about whatever was on his mind when he was ready. And no amount of coaxing and prodding on her part would speed up the process.

"Martha," John finally said as he swallowed his last gulp of steaming black coffee, "you know your uncle had a very important visitor yesterday."

"Yes, Aunt Abbie told me about Mr. Thompson. She said he was here to plan mobilization of the new troops Uncle Robert had recruited." Martha was not quite sure what direction this conversation was headed. They both apparently knew that something important was happening right here at Runnymede. But what did that have to do with John?

"Your uncle has been quite successful in mustering in lots of men very quickly," John said. "He has done more than any single man could do to bring victory to the South, except perhaps General Jackson. It's because he has been so successful that Mr. Thompson was here to seek his counsel." Martha beamed at the accolade given her favorite uncle by the man she loved. And for John to compare anybody with Stonewall Jackson, whom he had once said was his role model, was high praise indeed. Her feelings of apprehension dissipated into the cool morning vapors blowing off the Gulf.

"After you left to do your devotions last night, I was fortunate enough to be invited to join Mr. Thompson and the General for a few moments," John continued. "They are both truly remarkable men."

Martha nodded her assent, but otherwise said nothing. She had learned that when John wanted to discuss something, it was best not to interrupt his presentation. Otherwise, he would become irritated that he had not been allowed to finish his thought and would either .repeat what had already previously been said or get moody and unresponsive. She loved John deeply and with no reservation, but this one personality trait was a little annoying.

John pushed back his chair and walked around the table to where Martha was sitting. He pulled a chair from the corner of the room and put it next to hers. Martha turned in her chair to face him as he sat down.

Taking Martha's hands, John caressed them gently between his own. He reached up with his right hand and gently stroked her milky-white face. Oh, how I love this woman! he thought. How can I bear to leave her? But John had already made up his mind for what needed to be said. He swallowed hard, and then proceeded.

"Martha," John said, "Mr. Thompson is writing a letter of introduction for me to present to the Secretary of War." Martha sat impassively, looking deeply into John's crystal blue eyes. "He believes I can play an important role in the war effort."

"I do too, John. There is nobody more loyal or dedicated to the cause of liberty than you. And nobody cuter either."

Blushing slightly, John smiled at Martha's remark. This may be an agonizing moment for her, too, but she had still not lost her sassiness. "But you know what this means, don't you?" John continued. "This means that, as much as I would like to spend the rest of my life here in paradise with you, I must be leaving soon. And I don't know when I'll see you again."

The significance of this was not lost on Martha. She knew that war is a dirty business, and that John would be exposing himself to all sorts of danger. But she had been preparing herself for just this moment, for she too knew that John must do this. If he did not, the man who was left behind would not be the same person she had grown to love so deeply. He would be just the mere shell of a man.

Even though Martha had anticipated this moment would arrive some day, the reality of the situation was difficult to accept. But she too had an important role to play. John needed to know that she supported his decision, and understood why he must leave. Biting her lip to maintain control, she told John the words she knew he needed to hear.

"John, I love you more than life itself. I cannot bear the thought of living even one second without you," Martha said. John frowned; he had hoped that she would not make this difficult for him. She continued, "but I also love liberty. And I can accept the fact that I may have to sacrifice part of you for the greater good of others." John sighed, almost imperceptibly. What a woman!

They fell into each other's arms, the chairs clattering to the floor. They kissed, deeply one time, and then stood there, hugging and embracing silently. As Martha embraced John, her hands moving gently, lovingly, up and down his back, he reached deeper for what he now must say.

"You are the very reason for my existence, my love," he breathed in her ear. "I want you to be mine, always."

Martha could hardly believe what she had just heard. She had always dreamed of this moment. "Is that a proposal, John Yates Beall? Because if it is, I want you to do it properly," she teased.

Pushing Martha back gently, John fell onto one knee. The cold, hard floor did not cause him any discomfort. He was floating on air. Holding her right hand in his, he looked up at her and said tenderly, "Martha O'Bryan, would you do me the honor of taking me as your husband?"

Martha smiled sweetly. John could see tears welling up in her eyes.

"Yes, John," she said softly. "I will marry you."

John tried to rise, but lost his balance as his right leg slipped out from under him. He had gripped Martha's hand tightly in his, and as he fell, she fell with him. Laughing and crying on the kitchen floor, they hugged and kissed each other as rays of sunlight beamed in through the kitchen window onto the happy couple intertwined below.

4

APRIL 1863
MEMPHIS, TENNESSEE

Private Robert Williamson paced methodically back and forth in front of the long row of jail cells. Not too many months earlier, guarding of civilian prisoners had been performed by local authorities. Soon after Memphis fell into Federal hands, however, the occupying Union Army carried out many police responsibilities. Despite the strong Confederate sympathies of the city's residents, the jail was not overflowing with spies, saboteurs and others inclined to action against what was commonly considered to be an army of occupation. Persons who were that hostile to the Union had already enlisted in the Confederate Army, where they could express their views more directly, with sabers, rifles and cannon.

Prisoners for the most part continued to be run-of-the-mill drunks, horse thieves and petty criminals that generally constituted more of a nuisance than a threat to Federal authority. Still, the provost marshal had decided that discretion was called for, and so assigned around the clock guard duty to make sure no embarrassing incidents, such as an escape, could occur while he was responsible.

"Hey, Bob. Anything exciting happening today?" came a familiar voice as Williamson approached the steel bars and locked door at the end of the hall. He had lulled himself into a sort of trance-like state as he marched for hours up and down the dank and dirty jail, and failed to notice that Private David Proctor, his replacement for the 8 a.m. shift, had arrived. Proctor had a big wad of chaw in his mouth, and expertly spit a stream of saliva the color of water in a creek swollen by spring rains toward the smoothly worn wooden floor.

Williamson stopped and leaned casually against the bars that separated the cellblock from the outside world. Proctor pulled up a rickety chair, on the other side, plopped himself in it, and stretched his feet out in front of him. Both men had keys, but neither was in any particular hurry to change places.

At the sight of Proctor's expectorate, Williamson felt like having a smoke. Unbuttoning the flap of his breast pocket, he pulled out a well-worn corncob pipe. Gently tapping the bowl, he struck a match on the steel bars, held it expertly above the half-burned tobacco in the bowl, and drew on the pipe. As he exhaled, hazy blue smoke circled in a lazy little cloud around the oil lamp that burned above him. "Not too much going on, other than the usual trouble from our friend, Mr. Cole."

"He's something else, isn't he?" Proctor explained in mock wonderment. "I wonder when the man has time to sleep, what with all the banging and screaming he makes. That constant clamoring about how his brother is going to come here and kill us all is getting real old, too."

"I don't know why he keeps talking about his brother so much," Williamson said.

"Oh, haven't you heard?" Proctor grinned widely, revealing a mouth full of yellow and half-rotten teeth. Slimy tobacco juice dribbled out of the right corner of his mouth and disappeared into Proctor's matted, graying beard. He was always grinning like that, and Williamson turned his head ever so slightly to avoid staring. "Cole has told me, more times than I care to remember. It seems his brother is a big-time local businessman, druggist I think."

"So why would a druggist want to kill us?" Williamson interrupted.

"Because he is also a colonel in the rebel army." Proctor leaned the chair back against the wall and clasped his hands behind his head. There weren't too many occasions when Proctor knew more than anybody else, and he was reveling in the glory.

"But why would his brother want to risk breaking him out, even if that was possible? The whole thing doesn't make any sense at all to me," Williamson asked.

Proctor hadn't thought about that before. He shrugged his shoulders impassively. "I dunno," he finally replied.

"I don't know either," Williamson said, "especially since the marshal is going to let Cole go today anyway."

"He is? Gosh, that's news to me." Proctor spat again, this time just missing a hard-shelled, shiny black beetle scampering across the floor. "When is he being released?"

"Just about an hour or so. As soon as the marshal can sign the papers."

"Does Cole know this?"

Before Williamson could answer, a noise like the bellowing of a wounded bull came from the opposite end of the cellblock, a good twenty paces away.

"Hey, god-damn it! Where the hell is my breakfast? The sun's already well up on the horizon, and you sons-a-bitches are too goddamned busy jawin' away down there to get me somethin' to eat? You damn well better get a move on and get me my grub, or there'll be hell to pay!"

Williamson and Proctor looked at each other knowingly. It was Cole. Of course.

Proctor pulled a watch out of his pocket and held it up to the light coming in from the window behind him. "Not eight o'clock yet, old buddy." He smiled that nearly toothless smile again. "You're still on duty, so he's still your problem," he said as he clicked the watch cover closed and returned it to his pocket.

Muttering something incomprehensible under his breath, Williamson turned and headed back down the hall to try and quiet Cole down. It's amazing, he thought, how one man can become such a big problem in only three days. Thank God he's being released.

Cole had taken his tin water cup and was now raking it back and forth across the bars of his cell, just to make sure that he wasn't ignored. The other prisoners, many of whom had been asleep on their straw tick mattresses when Cole started his ranting, started to yell, too. Not for breakfast, but to Cole, telling him to shut up. Cole ignored the shouts directed at him by the other prisoners, and continued his tirade.

"OK, that's enough!" Williamson shouted as he reached Cole's cell, barely loud enough to be heard above the din. Cole continued banging his cup and spewing obscenities until Williamson drew his government-issued Colt revolver and leveled it at a spot midway between Cole's two deep-set black eyes. Cole threw his cup on the floor, and retreated to sit on his bunk, still glowering at the Union private on the opposite side of his cell door.

The other prisoners let out hoots, hollers and whistles of contempt at Cole, now that he had been silenced, at least temporarily.

"What's your problem, Cole?"

Cole was clearly agitated. He stood up and walked in quickstep toward the cell door, his arms flailing wildly. Even though he knew the door was securely locked, Williamson backed away a step, just in case.

"My problem, Private, is that I am hungry!" Cole responded, his voice seething with thinly disguised anger. He grasped a cold steel cell door bar in each hand, his knuckles turning white because he gripped the bars so tightly. "For the last three days, you've brought me my breakfast promptly at dawn. Well, we're long past dawn, and . . ." Cole paused, visibly trying to keep his temper suppressed. He continued, "And I haven't seen any god-damned thing that even remotely resembles food."

Williamson did not like this insolence one bit. How dare this arrogant son of a bitch order him around like some common servant. Who in the hell does he think he is? "Listen, Cole, you're damned lucky someone hasn't beat the shit out of you yet. All you've done since you got here was to insult me and the other guards, create a lot of noise, and generally make a nuisance of yourself. Seems to me you ought to consider yourself lucky that somebody hasn't killed you by now."

"Yeah, but what about my breakfast?" Cole shook the bars of his cell door for emphasis, just to make sure that he got his point across.

"You're not getting one today."

Williamson meant to tell Cole that the reason he wasn't getting fed was because he was being released within the hour. But Cole exploded before he could. "Why you no good, rotten bastard!" he screamed. He shook the cell door violently with both hands, as if somehow he would be able to shake the door free from the floor.

"I'll kill you, ya hear? I know who you are! As soon as I get out of here, you're a dead man!"

In the short three days since Cole had arrived at the jail, Williamson had been exposed to Cole's temper before. But he had never seen the man this violent. He was downright concerned about Cole's threat to kill him, too. The short, squat Cole did not physically menace Williamson, who had well-developed biceps and shoulders from chopping wood and shoveling manure for years back on his father's farm in southwestern Ohio. But Cole was mean enough and certainly smart enough to get a gun and find Williamson out on the street some day. Right now, though, what he needed to do was to calm Cole down.

"Hold on, Cole. I'll see what I can do."

Williamson still had not told Cole that the marshal planned to release him soon. And for good reason. The man obviously could not be turned loose onto the streets. Based on this last temper tantrum, Williamson decided he'd better talk with the marshal and tell him about Cole's behavior. And in particular, Cole's threat to kill him. He was going to recommend that Cole be kept in jail for another three days, or at least until he had hopefully cooled down enough to not be a threat anymore.

As Williamson turned to go back down the hall toward the main cell door, where Proctor was waiting to relieve him, he was oblivious to Cole's rain of epithets and threats, and to the noisy jangling cell door as Cole shook it. This man was not getting out now, no siree, not if he had anything to say about it.

* * * * * * *

A cold, bone-soaking rain had been falling all day on Memphis. It was that damp kind of early spring weather that everybody knew was necessary for crops to grow properly and for cisterns to be replenished with fresh water. But it was also the kind of day where folks felt those twinges in their bones and joints caused by arthritis, rheumatism, gout and various other ailments that are most pronounced in the damp and the cold. And despite the foul weather, it was the kind of a day that Amanda Cole looked forward to. It was on days like this that business boomed at the J. C. Cole Pharmacy.

Even though it had been a very profitable day, Amanda was exhausted and glad when she finally pulled the shade on the store at 6:00 that Saturday evening, revealing the big "CLOSED" sign. Every day was hard for her, ever since her husband Jamie left last July, right after Memphis fell. Jamie joined the Fifth Confederate Infantry, better know locally as the "Irish Regiment," since it was composed primarily of sons of Eire. He was well liked and respected, and had been given the rank of Lieutenant Colonel.

With Jamie off to war, Amanda had to assume primary responsibility for running the store. This was a role to which she was unaccustomed. Before the war forced a change in circumstances, Jamie had insisted that she was to stay home and take care of the children. That was her job. Now that Jamie was gone, she had no choice but to run the business. Jamie's brother, Charles, was supposed to help her out. He had not been any help at all for quite some time, and in fact, had caused Amanda untold headaches ever since Jamie's steadying influence was no longer available.

When Charles arrived unannounced a little over a year ago, Jamie had viewed it as a godsend at first. It was hard to find men to work in the store, he reminded Amanda, since most able-bodied hard working ones had already joined up to fight. Jamie had taken Charles under his wing and taught him the basics of the business. Charles at first seemed to Amanda to be a willing, hardworking kind of soul, even though she found some of his personal peccadilloes disgusting, and perhaps even despicable. Her brother-in-law seemed to have much too much interest in women and alcohol, she felt. Still, she had tried to ignore those faults. He was her husband's brother, after all.

Since Jamie had gone off to fight, Amanda's widowed mother had moved in with her, making it possible for Amanda to run the business during the day, while Grandma took care of her two little ones. The children had been fed and bathed and were in their nightshirts, ready for bed, when Amanda arrived home every evening.

Grandma usually waited on Amanda to come home so that the two of them could have dinner together. It was a time that Amanda looked forward to, since she had so little time to chat with someone other than a customer. But tonight, Grandma had already eaten and gone to bed with the children, accompanied by a hacking cough and a fever.

Amanda worried about her mother. Grandma, as even Amanda called her, had lost a lot of her spunk in the last year or so. Amanda wasn't sure if it was because of the Yankee occupation, which Grandma described as "contemptible" and "loathsome," or because of the increased rigors of advancing age. After all, Grandma had just celebrated her 65th birthday.

Still, Amanda was frankly glad to have this one night to herself. It was in these rare quiet times that she read Jamie's letters, over and over until the pages were now tattered and torn, and until she was brought to tears at the thought of what he had to suffer through. She never got this impression from Jamie's letters, of course; they were cheerful and chipper, and contained newsy reports on just about everything. But she knew what was really going on out there, where men were bleeding and dying, often over agonizingly long periods of time.

No, Jamie's letters never mentioned any discomfort to himself, nor did he even briefly allude to the dangers, although Amanda knew they were legion. She had seen all of the limbless men straggling home after Shiloh. And she knew many of her mostly female customers at the pharmacy had at one time or another worn black mourning clothes, grieving over the loss of yet another loved one. She prayed daily that God would shelter and protect Jamie from harm, and if that was not His will, to at least take him swiftly.

Amanda sat before the crackling fire in their spacious drawing room, eating a small bowl of chicken and dumplings, which Grandma had prepared earlier in the day when she felt the onset of fever. The stack of Jamie's letters, including one delivered just today to her at the pharmacy by special courier, sat on the floor next to her. Amanda had lit every lamp in the house, even though a faded sliver of gray light still crept in through the dusky twilight sky outside. The brightness, although vanishing into night, in some way dispelled the gloom which otherwise might come as Amanda sat there alone, with the only reminder of her best friend, lover and husband being a stack of tattered letters.

Tap, tap, tap. At first, Amanda did not hear the gentle rapping on one of the drawing room windows. Her eyes were closed in contemplation and meditation, which had become her usual practice before she took out Jamie's letters to read and reread again. In her mind's eye she again relived that day nearly eight months ago when Jamie held her in his arms, telling her over and over that he loved her, giving her a kiss to remember, hopping gallantly on his horse and riding south towards Mississippi to fight for the Confederacy. She could see his soft brown eyes, with little tears forming in each corner. She could touch his shiny, flowing jet-black hair. She could feel the caress of his beard against her ear as he blew mischievously into it one last time before he left. She smiled, the memory as real as that glorious day when it last happened.

TAP, TAP. TAP, TAP. The sound at the window was now harder, firmer. Amanda opened her eyes with a start and turned her head in the direction of the noise. She could hardly believe her eyes. Was this a dream? No! It was Jamie!

She flung the door open. "Jamie, Jamie!" Amanda called out her husband's name in little squeals of disbelief mingled with delight. Flinging herself into his arms, she gently stroked the nape of his neck, kissing him full and hard on his lips, which were still wet and cool like the weather outside. Jamie was covered with a thick brown ooze, and his clothes were completely soaked. His normally beautiful hair was wet and matted down with mud. But Amanda didn't care or notice, not in the least. Her man was home. And that was all that mattered. She could mop up the mud from the floor and wash her indigo-colored wood shawl and calico dress later.

"I've missed you so much, my love! You can't imagine how lonely it can get surrounded by hundreds of dirty, smelly men!" gushed Jamie between frenzied kisses.

"We can talk about that later," said the ever-cautious, ever-practical Amanda, pulling herself away from him just to take in once again that he was there, standing right in front of her. "First, let's get you out of those clothes and into a hot bath. I don't want you getting sick on me now." Amanda went toward the closet where she kept her spare bath towels. They were there primarily to clean up after her young boys, but certainly would suffice for this purpose.

Jamie had come around the back of the house to tap on the window. Not just because he did not want to be observed by curious eyes; after all, the Union army was occupying the town. But also because he knew that Amanda would be sitting in the drawing room after supper, just like she had written him describing her ritual of reading his letters over and over. Amanda had let him in through the kitchen door, right next to the drawing room, where Jamie now stood dripping onto the throw rug designed to keep splinters from the wooden floor from penetrating unprotected feet.

"Don't you think it would be better if we turned down some of the lamps?" Jamie asked as he started to peel the soggy mass of chestnut-brown clothing from his body.

Amanda blushed, and then smiled. Jamie has removed his breeches, which brought back memories for Amanda of what a man's body, her husband's body, really looked like. "Of course, my dear. No need to have to share you with the neighbors." She handed Jamie the two carefully folded, fluffy white cotton towels she had retrieved from the pantry and stood there, happy just to be looking once more at the man she loved, regardless of how rough his appearance had become. Then she remembered that she had not yet turned down the lights, and quickly darted around the room, extinguishing all but one of the lamps, which now burned dimly over the sink.

Amanda slid gently past her Jamie to the kitchen stove. She pulled the big copper kettle to the side of the old wood-burner, carefully putting it under the pump. Pushing down hard on the handle, she primed the pump, and eventually filled the pot with water to heat up for Jamie's bath. As the kettle was filled, she struggled noticeably to try and slide it back onto the stove.

"Here, let me help you with that." Jamie, now stripped down to nothing more than his dingy long johns, left the rug, walked over to the sink, and gently but firmly lifted the kettle back onto the stove. Amanda's soft smile glowed in the dim light, the shadows from the flickering flame bouncing off her cheeks. She was taller than most women, a fact that proved to be helpful in reaching for bottles of elixirs from the top shelf at the pharmacy.

Amanda added two hefty pieces of well-seasoned oak to the glowing embers in the stove. Quickly a bright yellow flame popped from the tinder, the flames licking up the sides of the old kettle.

Jamie moved to the kitchen table, pulled one of the well-worn Windsor chairs around and sat down on it. A huge sigh escaped as he took the weight off his feet for the first time in hours. He had been walking through the mud and the rain since 5:00 in the morning. He had left his horse in camp, where he deemed it was safer than trying to get it across Union lines into Memphis. It had not been an easy trip, as he dodged the Union checkposts on the way into the city, often wading through icy creeks or hoofing it through the thorny blackberry and wild rose brambles over the mountains.

"You look bushed, honey. Can I get you anything while the bath water's heating up?" Amanda smiled that sweet, caring smile that had first attracted Jamie's attention years ago.

"A cup of coffee would be nice. I'm really not too hungry," he said.

Amanda went to the sideboard and poured out some of the still steaming java that she had cooked for her own supper. She added the two teaspoons of sugar that Jamie always took with his coffee and set it on the kitchen table next to him.

"I sure have missed you, Jamie. The kids have, too. It's just not the same without you," said Amanda as she took Jamie's hand in hers, brought it to her lips, and gently kissed it.

"I know it's been hard on you, my love. Every night before I would lay my head down on whatever rock or bush happened to be my pillow for the night . . ."

"Like Jacob?"

"Exactly," Jamie said. He knew Amanda liked to find parallels for everything in life to events that had happened in the Bible. And she knew her Bible stories well, like the one about Jacob using a rock as his pillow and dreaming of the ladder to heaven. "Every night," he continued, "I would say my prayers and ask the good Lord to keep you safe. And to give you the strength to make it through another day. It gave me a lot of comfort to know that you were praying for me, too," said Jamie, referring to the promise Amanda made when he left eight months ago that she would say a prayer for him every day.

He took the cup to his lips, the steam swirling from the rounded top and took a long sip. Cradling the cup between his hands, he asked, "And how is Charles doing? Is everything working out alright?"

Amanda, who had been staring deeply and longingly into Jamie's eyes, now directed her gaze to the floor below. Jamie had suspected there was some kind of trouble, for in all of her letters to him she had never once mentioned Charles. Everything else, just not Charles. And now he knew his suspicions had been correct. There was indeed a problem, and he bet it was a major one at that, too.

"Come on now, honey. I can tell something's wrong. You know I can help with my brother if you're having any trouble with him at all. I'm one of the few people who ever treated him like a human being, and he'll listen to me." Amanda remained silent, biting her lower lip harder than she thought, until the salty taste of blood rose in her mouth.

She lifted her gaze from the floor, and looked back into Jamie's eyes. With only one lamp burning low over in the corner, it was hard to see on this moonless, starless night. But there was no mistaking Jamie's love and concern. Yes, maybe she should tell him. She wasn't very good at keeping secrets anyhow.

"Jamie," she said, her voice quivering like that of a little girl about to admit she had broken her mother's good china, "I have had so many problems with Charles, I just don't know where to begin."

"Any place is fine, dear," said Jamie. He squeezed her hand, hard, as if he could somehow pass on the strength in his grip to get her through this.

"Everything was fine with Charles for the first few days after you left. You know you were a very positive influence on him. He was wonderful with the customers, so charming and courteous, just like when you were still around. He did anything I asked him to, without one complaint." She paused, as if unsure about how to proceed. She believed that Jamie should know. And she believed that Jamie could actually help Charles. But Amanda was afraid Jamie might be angry with her for somehow causing Charles to go astray.

"Go on," Jamie coaxed.

Amanda took a deep breath, letting the expended air escape slowly. "Well, I don't know what happened, but one day he didn't show up for work when I opened the shop. I waited for about an hour or so. When he still hadn't arrived, I got concerned. Lord knows, I was worried."

Jamie stood up, slid his half-naked body off the kitchen chair, and went to the kitchen cupboard where he always kept his tobacco. Yep, it was still there. He took the humidor out of the cupboard, and rolled a smoke with hands that had performed this task countless times previously. Licking the paper to make a tight seal, he put the cigarette in his mouth, walked over and stuck it into the middle of the flame of the one glowing lamp, and took a deep draw. He knew this additional time would give Amanda an opportunity to regain her composure.

"Was everything OK with Charles then?" Jamie asked, exhaling the smoke through his nose.

"Actually, no," Amanda responded, as Jamie sat back down in his kitchen chair with the damp seat. "I closed up the shop and went over to his hotel to look for him. Just as I was inquiring about him at the front desk, in he stumbles. To make a long story short, I learned that he had been at a bordello all night. And here he was, coming home at 10:00 in the morning, drunk as a skunk."

"Now Amanda, you know men have needs," chided Jamie. "Don't begrudge Charles a chance to enjoy himself. Every man is entitled to that now and again."

Amanda stared intently into Jamie's eyes. They had never talked before about these things. She hoped her Jamie had been faithful to her.

"I understand, Jamie, that lonely, single men sometimes have no choice as to where to find some female companionship," Amanda said, stressing the word "single." She thought that would make it clear that she disapproved of marital infidelity, especially if it was her spouse that was involved.

She continued, "Anyway, it only got worse. You could see every day that Charles was losing any sort of self control. On the days when he did show up, he was usually drunk. He would take liberties with the young ladies who came in, and was vulgar and abusive with everybody else."

"And . . ." She paused here, for she knew that Jamie would not believe that the outgoing hardworking brother he had left eight months ago would have changed so much. "And he was stealing pharmaceuticals from the store."

Jamie flicked an ash from his cigarette, so that the glowing red ember at the end was plainly visible. He sat his coffee cup down, and motioned for Amanda to sit next to him. Compliantly, she sat down, stiff-backed, in the chair closest to Jamie.

Jamie could see that his wife was upset. There must be something to this, he thought. "Why do you think that, sweetie?"

"At first, I thought that we were selling an awful lot of laudanum. But then, one afternoon while Charles was in the front of the store, I went to the backroom to do some paperwork. I had forgotten my receipts book, and came back out front to get it. And there he was, swilling down a bottle, his head thrown back to receive every drop."

Jamie knew now that Charles had a problem, a major problem. He had been in the pharmacy business for ten years, and had come to know a bit about medicines even before that when he was on better terms with his father back in Pennsylvania.

"It sounds to me like I should maybe have a little talk with Charles. Can you go over to his hotel and get him, and bring him here?" Jamie knew that, as a Confederate officer, it would be unwise for him to walk the streets. His wife would have to be his legs.

Amanda swallowed hard. Now she would have to pass on even more bad news concerning Charles. "Actually, no," she replied.

Jamie said nothing, but raised his eyebrows quizzically, encouraging Amanda to continue.

"He won't be released from jail until tomorrow morning."

The room was filled with a deafening silence. Jamie got up from the chair, walked over to the sink, and doused the stub of a cigarette in the sink. Amanda had not yet told him why his brother was in jail but Jamie suspected it had something to do with Charles' out-of-control behavior. Probably got in a barroom fight, and beat the stuffing out of somebody. Jamie knew from first hand experience that his brother may be short and stout, but he was also scrappy. He was angry with Charles for making Amanda's life so difficult. But he also felt that Charles could be salvaged. After all, hadn't he done that once already?

"Well then, we'll deal with this tomorrow. Let's just put this out of our minds, since we can't do anything about it tonight, anyway. I've got something else on my mind," he said mischievously, "and, if you don't already, you will soon, too."

Jamie waked around behind Amanda, still sitting stiffly in her chair, staring straight ahead. He put his arms around the nape of her neck, softly massaging the tension out of her. He bent over, his wet, bushy beard brushing against her ear, and blew into it, just like when he had left eight months ago. Amanda stood up, took Jamie by the hand and led him down the hall to their bedroom where a glorious homecoming and renewal of their marriage bond would soon erupt in matrimonial bliss.

* * * * * * *

"So, tell me Charles, what in the hell has happened to you since I last saw you?"

Jamie knew the answer already. He asked the question because he wanted to hear how Charles responded. Jamie had sized up his brother immediately when he entered the house that morning after Amanda had fetched him from the jail. At first glance, Charles looked OK; after all, he had been in jail for a while, with no liquor, no drugs and no ladies to distract him. But he still had that hollow, hungry look in his eyes. Jamie had seen that look many times before as a druggist, and as a field officer with responsibility for hundreds of men.

"I really don't know how to answer you, brother," Charles said sheepishly. "I'm not going to stand here and tell you I haven't had some trouble. We both know I have." Charles knew full well that

Amanda had told Jamie everything about her views of his problems. So there was no use to try and lie to him.

When she drove the surrey from the jail downtown back to their house, she said nothing more to Charles than that Jamie was home. Charles knew he was lucky that Amanda had pled so successfully for him to be released because she needed him at the store. And his jailers had been relieved, even happy, to get rid of him.

Charles knew that Amanda was still upset. So he had honored her unspoken request and likewise said nothing as she negotiated their way around the countless ruts filled with muddy water the color of burned sulfur.

"Yes," Jamie said thoughtfully, his head nodding in silent assent to what Charles had said, "that is wise. It's always better to face your problems head-on than to try to run from them."

Right, Charles thought. That's why you and I had all of our disagreeable disputes with Father. *He* was the problem, and we tried to face him head-on. But Father was insistent on total obedience and respect for *his* authority.

The house was empty, except for Jamie and Charles. At Jamie's request that morning, Grandma had taken the children to their cousins' house to play. Amanda had gone to open up the pharmacy after retrieving Charles from the jail.

Jamie walked over to the kitchen table where Charles was sitting, a mug of coffee in front of him. "It seems to me," continued Jamie, "that you might do better if you and I were together." Jamie pulled out a chair and sat down, and began rolling another cigarette.

A chill came over Charles, and he frowned noticeably. His one exposure to military life had left a bitter taste in his mouth. If Jamie is talking about me joining the Confederate Army, I'm in a peck of trouble. I can't go home to Pennsylvania, he thought. And I sure have no interest in exposing myself again to military life in anybody's army.

"Look, Charles, I know you hated the time you spent in the Union Army. But it will be better this time. I promise."

Charles took a swig of the murky bitter swill in the mug, and spat it back out. He looked up and realized that Jamie had interpreted his action as a response to his suggestion. Jamie is my only friend, the only person I can trust, he thought. He felt he should let Jamie know he had not rejected the idea.

"Jamie, you know how much I respect you. And we both know how much I need you around to keep me on the straight and narrow. But I really did hate all of the marching around, sleeping in the mud, and getting shot at while I was in the Pennsylvania volunteers." He hadn't mentioned that he had been in the regimental band at the rear, not on the front ranks of the battles.

Charles paused, and observed Jamie's demeanor. Jamie's face had lost that hard edge it had when Charles spat out the coffee. "You said it would be different if I joined you. How so?"

Jamie took a quick puff on the cigarette he had just lit, then laid it down on the coffee table, the glowing end dangling precipitously over the side. He could tell that Charles was receptive, but just needed a little more convincing. Not only would this be good for Charles, he thought, but also for Amanda as well as for his business. I can't afford to have him stealing so much out of the store, when it's so hard to replace. And I sure don't want him driving customers away, like Amanda said he was doing. It would be better, though, if I didn't have to sell him too hard.

"Well, to begin with," said Jamie, "this time you would come in as an officer. And you would be attached to the field staff. You would be working for me, just like you did when you first got here and started at the pharmacy. I can't promise you won't see any action, but I can promise you this. I will never, ever put you in harm's way without putting myself there first. And we will be there together, as brothers."

Charles pushed the half-empty mug to the center of the table. He stood up, walked over to the kitchen sink, and looked out the window as he contemplated his choices. The rank and prestige of being an officer appealed to Charles. So did the prospect of being with Jamie all the time. But the thought of serving more time in the military and getting shot at was definitely most unappealing. Why was it that the only decisions he had to make were always the difficult ones?

"All right Jamie, I'll do it," Charles said.

A broad smile crossed Jamie's face. He walked over to his brother, slapped him on the back, and shook his hand, pumping it up and down four or five times. "You've made the right decision, Charles, really you have. I'll take care of you. You'll see."

"So when do we leave?" Charles asked. Now that the deal was done, he wanted to get on with it. The thought of hanging around here waiting for something bad to happen did not appeal to him.

"We'll pull out first thing tomorrow. My leave is up anyway; it was only for a few days," said Jamie, still glowing from Charles' decision to join him.

"Sounds great," Charles said halfheartedly. He went to the stove and poured himself another cup of coffee. He knew where he was going tonight, though. One last stop at Madame Witherspoon's.

Hope she's got three or four nice girls for me. Charles grinned as he thought about the last orgy he had there, as he drank from the new, hot mug of coffee.

5

FALL 1863
COASTAL VIRGINIA

John Yates Beall was worried. If his men could have seen his face here in the inky void of night, they would have observed his brows furrowed so deeply that it seemed like his eyebrows were joined together at that point where the wrinkles met, just above the bridge of his nose.

"Captain Beall!"

John did not hear the voice of his brother Willie above the din of the storm. He was preoccupied with trying to keep the *Swan* and the eight Confederate sailors in the little boat from being swamped by one of the massive, towering waves being swept ahead of the gale force noreaster blowing in from the Atlantic over the Wachapreague Inlet, or from smashing into the towering hulk of the Union schooner bobbing wildly like a punch-drunk fighter just a few feet away. And he was also worried about the survival of the adjacent *Raven*, the *Swan*'s sister boat, and its crew.

John's original plan had been for Lieutenant Ed McGuire and the crew of the *Raven* to board the Yankee supply ship from the starboard side. John and the *Swan* crew would simultaneously board the ship from the port side. Together, the Confederate sailors would subdue any resistance, forcibly if necessary, and take over the ship as a Confederate prize.

But now he was concentrating on survival. McGuire had already been swept once over the side of his vessel into the turbulent sea after a massive swell had hit the *Raven* and slammed it into the side of the two-master that was their quarry. Quick thinking on the part of seaman Bill Baker had saved McGuire's life, as Baker snatched the soggy seaman with a boat hook from the frothy black water into the relative safety of their tiny craft. Fortunately, since no Union sailors had appeared to peer over the deck railing, it seemed the din of the storm had drowned out even the noise of this unwelcome encounter between the two vessels.

But in the meantime, the rudderless *Raven* had been swept around to the same port side of the ship where John and his crew were waiting for the waves to subside before boarding. The *Raven* was lashed securely to the *Swan* to prevent any further damage to the boat or harm to the crew, although both boats were once again dangerously close to the swaying hulk above them.

John felt a tugging at his peacoat. Turning around he saw that it was little brother Willie, hair matted to his head by the pounding rain. John crouched down into the bow of the boat so as to keep his balance and better hear what Willie had to say.

"Captain Beall, the men are ready to board!" Willie shouted into John's ear.

John cupped his hand and gestured for Willie to come closer so that he might respond. The wind was blowing at John's back and would carry his voice. But persistent, recurring problems with his one severely wounded and often infected lung made it impossible for him to yell or shout. A normal speaking voice was the most he could muster.

"Very well, Willie. It doesn't look like the weather is going to improve much. And the longer we are tossed about, the more likely that we'll be discovered by the ship or destroyed by the waves."

Willie nodded approvingly.

"Prepare the men to board," he simply ordered.

John could not hear Willie's reply, but he could see the grin of approval on Willie's face in the dim light coming from onboard the ship.

According to plan, Willie tapped the man in front of him on the shoulder, and gave a single thumbs-up sign. The signal was passed from one man to the next in the *Swan* and then to the *Raven*. Willie heaved a single rope ladder over the ship's side railing. He was a big, strapping lad, and had put on considerable weight since his bout two years previous with dysentery. Baker, also young and strong, pulled a soggy rope ladder from the bottom of the *Raven* and did likewise.

Grappling hooks on the end of each rope bit firmly into the rail overhead. The schooner continued to pitch and sway in the wind and waves to an erratic rhythm. The *Swan* and the *Raven* were pulled closer to their prize by the umbilical-like lines, and the men prepared to clamber up the ladders.

John, as captain, and McGuire would go first, even though sudden and immediate death may await them at the top of the ladders. But that was the way John felt it should be. After all, they were supposed to lead the men entrusted to them. And it was that unflinching bravery and dedication to principle that resulted in the unswerving loyalty by his men to him.

As Willie steadied the twisting hemp, John put his left foot on the rope rung, pulled himself up and began the climb to the top. The little boat heaved and bobbed below him as he continued his climb.

John tried not to look beneath him as he climbed up the ladder, two Colt Navy revolvers tucked into his belt. Swells slammed him and the ladder into the side of the ship in an unpredictable syncopation characteristic of the sea, bruising his hands and causing them to become increasingly numb from the pain. Lightning had now begun to flash behind the bulbous clouds overhead, illuminating the two bare masts amidships. Steel grommets holding lines and sails banged incessantly against the schooner's masts and railing, muffling any noise being made by the men in the little boats below.

John reached the top of the ladder, panting and gasping for each now-painful breath. He grasped the railing tightly with his left hand, pulling one of his pistols from under his belt. "Got to be tough," he said to himself, shaking off the familiar pain from his lung and the unfamiliar agony in his hands, which were already beginning to swell up around the battered and bruised knuckles. He looked to his right, and saw that Ed McGuire was also just under the railing. He nodded to McGuire, and hauled himself over the railing and onto the deck of the enemy ship, as McGuire did likewise.

* * * * * * *

Grizzled old Tom Smith had a reputation around Mathews County, Virginia as an outspoken Confederate sympathizer. Nearly bald and toothless, he had earned the grudging admiration of many young men from the tidewater county for his fiery speeches against all things Yankee on the County Courthouse steps. He also earned their respect for the way he single-handedly had kept his tender daughter Lizzie out of their clutches. Word around the county was that the untimely death of his wife fifteen years ago from pneumonia had transformed the docile tobacco farmer and part-time oysterman into the assertive character he now was.

John Yates Beall met old Tom soon after the capture of the schooner *Alliance* on that dark and stormy night several weeks past. He and his men had taken the *Alliance*'s crew by complete surprise, since nobody except for John and his brazen compatriots would have dared challenge the inclement weather. John had hoped to save the ship as a Confederate prize, but the tidal rivers of the peninsula, as well as the Bay itself, were soon choked with federal gunships, sent as word of the *Alliance*'s capture made its way to the War Department in Washington. So John and his men scuttled the ship, after loading several wagonloads with booty and prisoners for delivery to Richmond, and returned to the tiny *Raven* and *Swan*.

Hot pursuit by a massive force of three regiments of Union cavalry and infantry, augmented by one battalion of artillery dispatched by frightened Federal officials, had forced Beall's Confederate irregulars to lay low. Word had come to John from one of his men who knew the town that Old Tom would provide them with refuge.

Smith's plantation straddled the tiny peninsula between Chesapeake Bay and the Piankatank River. Just beyond Smith's estate was the Dragon Swamp, a primeval bog infested with all sorts of slimy and slithery creatures. John and his men had melted into that overgrown web of vines and trees after filling the *Raven* and the *Swan* with sand and burying the both of them for later retrieval.

Earlier, federal troops advancing down the single road through the swampy peninsula had been detected by Bennett Burley, a brash young Scotsman serving picket duty. Burley had just arrived in Matthews from Richmond, where he had been asked to join John's operation. Burley carried papers to Beall indicating that President Davis himself was most anxious to test the torpedo Burley had designed. And the Chesapeake Bay was a virtual cornucopia of inviting targets.

Based on Burley's reconnoiter, John moved his men out of the protective cover of the swamp, just ahead of the advancing federal troops, into a dense stand of trees on the Smith farm. He planned on retrieving the boats under cover of darkness, and then making a nighttime watery escape from the tightening noose of an immense Federal patrol, which was closing ever tighter.

As dusk approached, the smell of freshly baked apple pie wafted out through the open windows of the Smith estate. Like moths to a flame, John and his men were drawn inexorably to the smells that reminded them of their homes before the war.

John told his men to wait for him under the big oak tree in the front yard, now speckled with ginger, sienna and amber colored foliage. He rapped three times on the brass lion's head that acted as a front door knocker. The lithesome Lizzie Smith opened the door just a crack and peered around the corner.

"Oh, it's you, Captain Beall," she said sweetly. "I thought for a minute it might be the infernal Yankees."

"No, ma'am, it's only a few sons of the south, hoping for a little piece of pie before we move on. I don't expect we'll have a chance to partake of any decent home cooking for some time after tonight."

"Well, come on in then, captain. And bring your men in, too." Lizzie wiped her hands on her apron, which was covered with little splotches of flour. She opened the door widely, and extended her hand to invite John inside the spacious house. Lizzie had already lit candles for the evening, since oil was no longer available, and the soft muted amber glow behind her reminded John of Martha. He smiled at the thought of his betrothed.

John waved a hand over his head to his men, indicating that they should come inside the house, too. After the men had all entered, they stood together awkwardly in the front hall, waiting for further directions. Lizzie turned to John and asked, "Do you know how close the Yankee troops are, Captain Beall?"

John stroked his straggly goatee, looked pensive, and responded, "Not really. All I know is that one of my men, Mr. Burley here," he said, gesturing toward the squat Scotsman, "spotted the Yankees a few miles up the road toward Mathews Court House, headed this way. They appeared to be taking their time as they moved through the swamp, afraid of rebel snipers in the trees, I expect," John said.

"Well, captain, I wouldn't be too worried just yet," said Lizzie sweetly, as only southern women can do. "Daddy was out doin' evening chores just an hour or so ago. Seems the Yankees have set up a picket line right outside our gate," she said, apparently nonplussed.

Clearly audible gasps arose from John's men.

Lizzie grinned and winked at John "But Daddy said they won't be movin' onto our property," she continued. "Y'all have plenty of time for a piece of pie, not to worry. But I wouldn't wait too long. Daddy was talking with one of the soldiers, real friendly like, who said there's thousands of Yankee soldiers looking for you in three or four counties hereabouts. Eventually they'll come scoutin' for you here."

"Captain, we'd better be going right away, don't you think?" The question had been asked by Bill Baker, a brave soldier under fire, but still inflicted with impetuous youthful behavior, as far as John was concerned.

"No, Bill, I think we'll be much safer here, at least for now. The Yankees haven't set foot yet on Mr. Smith's farm, so there's no immediate danger. And we'll have an easier time of it after it gets dark." John peered out the open window at the giant crimson globe of the setting sun, sinking slowly into the horizon over the unbroken stand of trees in the Dragon Swamp and the Union forces. John's men nodded their heads knowingly. Their captain was right. Bill Baker also nodded his head in silent agreement.

John knew he needed to speak with old Tom soon. The Yankee picket line was barely a mile distant. Despite what he had said to his men, he knew they were in deep trouble, and the prospect of escape from the tightening Federal noose looked bleak. But maybe Smith would have some ideas on back ways around the picket lines so that they could retrieve their boats and escape to safer territory.

"Where is your father, Miss Smith? I should like to speak with him," said John.

"He's finishing up his chores, I believe. Although I really don't know why. Them Yankee soldiers are probably gettin' pretty hungry by now. We won't have a pig or chicken left after they set foot on our farm."

Lizzie sighed solemnly. But then a stoic smile crossed her lips, as she realized she had eighteen hungry Confederate men in her house, to whom she had promised some fresh baked apple pie. Why stop with the pie, she thought? Better to feed these men of the south than those damnable Yankee invaders.

"You men come on into the kitchen," Lizzie said to John's assembled troops, "but be sure to leave your muddy boots by the door. I don't want a mess in my house. I'll fix you up a real good supper before you move on."

The band of privateers looked at each other, hardly believing the good news. A real meal! No more moldy biscuits! Patting each other on the back, they chatted amiably as they moved in pairs into the kitchen to await the feast about to be set before them. But John Yates Beall was increasingly concerned, as he spied the flickering lights of Union campfires in the encroaching dusk.

* * * * * * *

Thanks to Robert McFarland, the old Indian scout turned newspaper editor turned volunteer Confederate privateer, John Yates Beall and his men managed to sneak through three successive Union picket lines that night, after a full meal at the Thomas Smith farm. McFarland had volunteered to John that he thought they could thread their way through the lines and back into the Dragon Swamp, and indeed they did. Tales of this brazen escape from under the noses of the Yankee pursuers quickly spread, of course. The Federal gunboats, soldiers, cavalry and artillery left the area after several more days of half-hearted searching for the notorious Captain Beall.

During October and November, John and his crew had captured, miraculously without incident or injury, over a dozen U.S. government transports, sloops and schooners carrying supplies southward down the Chesapeake in support of the Yankees' peninsula campaign. Poorly armed and small in number, his irregular force succeeded primarily through surprise and sheer bravado.

But John still had not yet realized his ultimate goal, capture of a Union war vessel. He tired quickly of the cat and mouse game with the Federal gunboats, and wanted to inflict some serious damage, especially after hearing of how Federal soldiers had lynched Sands Smith, Tom's younger brother, in retribution for Beall's escape.

Bennett G. Burley, the Scotsman sent by Confederate War Secretary Seddon, had become increasingly close to John. The son of a Glasgow master mechanic, Burley was not only intelligent and mechanically inclined; he was totally fearless. Despite what John perceived as Burley's lower class upbringing, the man had a certain panache, an obvious bravado, that compensated for his sometimes-simplistic solutions to problems. It was these characteristics that captured John's attention.

In spite of his growing relationship with Beall, Burley had been unable to get John to agree to try out his torpedo on one of the captured transports. John argued that he did not want a huge explosion attracting a lot of unwanted attention. He preferred to quietly scuttle the captured ships and let them drift until they filled with water and sank. But John had promised Burley that he would allow him to test the explosive device when they found an appropriate Union war vessel.

And now that John's plan for capture of a Union warship was finally underway, both men were as excited as little children going to visit a favorite aunt in a faraway city. John's blueprint called for his trademark late night capture of a Union schooner, from which a surprise attack could be launched on a Union warship.

Late on a mid-November night, while safely ensconced in a thicket by the Accomac County shore, John surveyed the Bay with a telescope he had appropriated for himself as a souvenir from the *Alliance,* his band's first and most daring exploit. Dim moonlight revealed a large two-master that fit the bill; it had two little tenders that could be used to transport his men to the gunboat, his ultimate target, sitting less than a mile distant. He would take that schooner and launch his next operation from there.

It was a bitterly cold, blustery night. The air had a bite to it. It numbed every piece of exposed flesh in seconds. Mother Nature was sending a clear signal to all warm-blooded animals that winter was at hand.

John was particularly uncomfortable. He had come down with a catarrh, his first serious illness since recovery at Runnymede a year and a half previous. His bronchia were inflamed, and he had begun to cough again, starting once more the cycle of painful, weakening spasms he hated so much. But this time, he had his laudanum handy, and the coughing and pain were mercifully under control.

Although the weather was an enemy to his personal health, John used it as his ally in battle, as he always had. This kind of weather sent most other men to seek shelter from the elements in the protection of a warm cabin below decks, effectively surrendering control of the sea to the vigilant, to seamen like John and his men.

With the element of surprise as in their past successful exploits, John and his little band once more captured another Union schooner. Now it was time to concentrate on the bigger prize – capture of a Union warship.

"Mr. Edmondson," Beall called after making sure his new prisoners from the captured schooner were securely squirreled away below decks.

"Yes, Captain," Edmondson responded promptly, spitting out the fresh plug of chaw that he had put in his mouth. Sam Edmondson was a tall gangly young man of about twenty from the Eastern shore of Maryland, and he knew well the waters on the eastern side of the Chesapeake Bay from his years of fishing and oystering with his father. Edmondson also knew that his captain appreciated prompt response to his orders, but didn't much care to have a man drawl through a mouthful of tobacco and saliva.

"Mr. Burley and I have been talking," John wheezed, "and I think that it would be better to move the *Swan* and the *Raven* to one of those little coves over there along the shore." He gestured across the bow of his latest prize to the dim gray mass that represented the shoreline a mile distant.

"Our little craft, as humble as they may be, are still considerably more attractive than these Yankee rowboats," John continued, his voice raspy, "and even a bunch of dim-witted Yankees might be able to spot the difference. Take a few of the men with you, and row over to one of those coves. Stay put for the day there, and come back right after dark tomorrow."

"Yes, sir, captain," snapped Edmondson. He had learned that it didn't pay to question Captain Beall when he issued orders. He always had things well thought out; that was how they had been able to not only avoid capture, but also avoid any kind of casualties over their months-long spree on the Bay.

What Edmondson didn't know was that his captain had decided to defer till tomorrow night his plan to slip up on the Yankee gunboat and use Burley's torpedo. And Burley required calmer seas to make sure the torpedo hit the target just right.

Bundled up in heavy woolens against the frigid wind and frozen waves, Sam Edmondson and five others of Beall's command slipped over the side of their captured merchant ship, three each into the *Raven* and the *Swan*, bobbing below. As the little boats moved farther away from the schooner, they bounced up and down like tiny marionettes on a string, the men pulling on the oars in a constant battle with the elements. John peered into the gloom, assuring himself that the men were safely away. Satisfied, he made his way to the captain's quarters below to map out one more time the plan to use Burley's torpedo on the target warship, tantalizingly close, yet still so far away.

* * * * * * *

"Fantastic!"

Union Brigadier General Henry H. Lockwood could barely contain his glee. After months of frustrating pursuit of John Yates Beall and his pirates, the entire band of Chesapeake Bay marauders was finally his.

"Let's hear the details of your capture of Beall and his pirates," Lockwood ordered. He motioned for the young officer standing in front of him to sit in the very official-looking high-backed dark leather chair beside the huge walnut table, which the General had decided to use as his desk. Certain privileges attached when Lockwood was appointed commander of the First Separate Brigade of the Eighth Army corps. One of them was the right to appropriate the building of his choice for his headquarters. General Lockwood had chosen the well-appointed, two-story brick home of Peter Browne, a physician turned rebel officer, for his headquarters in the tiny eastern shore burgh of Drummondtown, Virginia.

Lieutenant John W. Conner, company B, First Eastern Shore Maryland volunteers, sat down uncomfortably in the chair designated by General Lockwood. He had just come in from the field and his uniform was still wet and muddy. Icicles, frozen to his droopy brown mustache and ringlets of hair hanging over his collar began to melt and run down his ruddy face. A sludge of sand, water and mud oozed from his boots as he stood at attention in front of the general, leaving a tell-tale puddle on the antique Persian rug covering the floor. But that didn't bother Lockwood much, since the rug belonged to the previous resident, that damned rebel doctor.

"Cigar, Lieutenant?" inquired Lockwood jovially. It seemed to him like an ideal time to celebrate.

"No thank you, General, I don't smoke," the stoop-shouldered lieutenant drawled deferentially.

"Very well," Lockwood said. The General opened a box conveniently located on the desk beside him and took out a thick, black cigar. He rolled it under his nose, so that the full, deep aroma of the aged tobacco filled his nostrils. He removed a tiny black pocket knife from the upper breast pocket of his tunic, flicked open the single silver blade, and cut a tiny tip off the end of the cigar.

As Lockwood leaned over to light the cigar from a candle flame burning beside him, Conner cleared his throat, to remind the General that he was still waiting to proceed with his story. The General took a deep draw on the cigar now firmly clenched between his teeth, and waved his hand toward Conner, a clear signal to the junior officer that he could begin to recount the tale of how the infamous pirate John Yates Beall had been captured.

"Well, sir, we got word from a fisherman that he thought there might be some rebels in boats in one of the creeks. Seems he spotted them about noon yesterday. There were several men in these two skiffs, one painted black, the other white. The fisherman asked who they were, and they said they were on a hunting trip. That old salty dog didn't believe 'em, he told me, because he couldn't see how two men could run the boats by themselves. We suspected right away that it was Beall, because the description the fisherman gave us of the two boats matched up with what we already knew they were using."

"Excellent, very good. Give me that old man's name, and I'll see that he gets a reward," Lockwood said. He was beaming at the irony of how an old fisherman and a young lieutenant had been the undoing of the wily Beall and his crew.

Lockwood leaned forward in his chair, so as to savor every word of the capture. Without thinking, he drew deeply on his cigar and exhaled in the direction of Conner. The gangly lieutenant with the droopy mustache coughed slightly, but knew better than to say anything.

"Who did the old coot report this story to anyway?" Lockwood asked.

"He reported it to my captain, who dispatched me and about twenty men to take the two rebels in the boats and any others we might find. We had been camped out on shore protecting the wharf while one of our gunboats was tied up for wooding. So we got the fisherman to guide us to the inlet where he had seen the two men and, sure enough, they were still there. It was just about dark, and I think they were a little surprised to see us. One of the rebels readily admitted that he was part of Beall's command. We captured four more men who had hidden themselves ashore, on the little island where their boats were tied up."

"But what about Beall? Was he among them?" Lockwood inquired eagerly.

"No, sir, he was not. But we were able to convince one of the younger men, if you know what I mean, of the value of telling us about Beall's whereabouts." A wry smile crossed Conner's face.

"And where was the pirate captain?" asked Lockwood.

"It seems that he and another half dozen or so of his men, all officers apparently, were onboard a little schooner they had captured night before last. Once we knew where he was, we simply sent out men in a couple of boats, surrounded the ship and demanded that he surrender or be blown out of the water. He surrendered."

"So we captured all of Beall's command, with nary a shot?" Lockwood asked incredulously.

"Except for a few shots over the heads of the rebels on the island, that's correct." Conner, still overwhelmed by briefing a general first hand, sat stiffly in his chair. Except for a slight nervous twitch of his right foot, he appeared perfectly calm and collected.

"This is tremendous, just tremendous!" Lockwood boomed. He got up from his chair and walked, arms clasped behind his back, around the desk. Standing beside the young lieutenant, he grasped his hand and firmly shook it. "Congratulations, son, to you and your men. This is splendid news."

"Thank you, sir," Conner said meekly.

"And so where are Beall and his pirates now?" Lockwood asked, letting go of Conner's hand and returning to his official side of the desk. Lockwood casually wiped the wet grime acquired from Conner's palm on the side of his trousers and remained standing, glancing out the beveled glass window behind him.

"They're in the Drummondtown jail," replied Conner through his still wet mustache, "but they can't stay there long. It's much too small. And we're still in enemy territory, so it's probably not safe to hold them here too long."

"I quite agree," the General responded, nodding his head curtly, half-distracted by activity in the muddy street outside and the wharf beyond. "I'll cut orders for you to carry back to your captain. Custody of these pirates will be transferred immediately to you personally to transport them to Baltimore for trial and ultimate disposition."

The midday sun shone brightly through the huge window just behind General Lockwood. The beveled glass split the rays into tiny rainbows and cast them over his shiny, hairless dome. The General took a handkerchief out of his left rear trouser pocket and wiped off the tiny beads of perspiration forming on his temple.

The General turned and faced the young man with the muddy uniform and droopy mustache. "Lieutenant, just what do you think of Beall and his men? I mean, do you think they are pirates, or are they soldiers just like you and me?"

"Well, sir, that is an easy question for me. Those men are lower than dogs, and should be hung immediately!" Conner suddenly lost his composure, and his face grew red with rage as he remembered anew how a band of renegade rebel raiders had burned down his parents' home just last month. Beall was no better than those savages!

"I couldn't agree more," Lockwood replied. "We need to send a message to the South that this illegal, piratical activity will absolutely not be tolerated." Conner wagged his head firmly in assent, but said nothing.

"Lieutenant, as I said, I'm going to detail you and your company to provost duty for the purpose of guarding the prisoners while in transport. And as far as I am concerned, I'd like to encourage you to create as many enticements for those dogs, as you call them, to escape. You know what happens to prisoners trying to escape, don't you?" Lockwood looked Conner straight in the eye, to make absolutely sure the young man understood what he was saying.

Conner didn't flinch. "Yes, sir, they are shot on sight."

"That's correct, Lieutenant." A thin smile crossed the general's face, as he took a piece of paper from his desk and began writing orders for Conner to carry back. Orders that, if everything went as he expected, would result in a fitting end for Beall and his band. I'll have the last laugh, he mused, as he savored the demise of the pirates who had embarrassed him so much the last few months, and who had made him the butt of innumerable jokes by superiors and subordinates alike.

* * * * * * *

John Yates Beall sat huddled with his men in a corner of the main cabin of the old steamer, which had been impressed into service and modified for use as a Union gunboat. The polished pine floor was cold against his backside, and uncommonly hard. But there was little John could do about that; they had been ordered by their captors when they boarded the gunboat to remain seated, unless it was necessary to leave the cabin and use the head just around the corner in what used to be the purser's quarters.

76

Shortly after coming aboard and prior to the order to be seated, John walked around the tiny cabin. He peered out the portholes and determined that it might be possible to take over this little ship. It appeared that only a token force of Union soldiers had been assigned to the boat on guard duty. And, except for two armed sentinels just outside, all of the weapons appeared to have been stacked neatly on the main deck just beyond the cabin door and armed sentinels.

"Look, men," John said, "if we don't make our escape now, before this boat docks at some Yankee prison camp, we very likely will end up tried by the Yankees and hanged as pirates. I realize there are no guarantees to this thing. I know this is a risky proposition."

"What's your plan, captain?" inquired Bill Baker, the same young man who had questioned the wisdom of having supper at Tom Smith's with Union forces just beyond the gate. John could now always count on Bill to ask what the plan was.

"It's very simple. We will overpower those two soldiers standing guard just outside the door. Using them as shields, we will grab the stack of weapons they've left for us, and then demand the captain turn over control of the boat or face a battle and the certain death of the two young guards. Then we'll make our escape by sailing across the bay, back to mainland Virginia and safety."

A firm baritone voice with a Scottish brogue responded immediately. "I agree 100 percent with Captain Beall," said Bennett Burley, soldier of fortune and torpedo maker extraordinaire. "We all know these bastards. Don't you remember how they treated poor, old Sands Smith?" A few muted "uh-huhs" came from the men. "They not only hanged the old boy, in front of his wife and all seven of his daughters. They riddled his poor, lifeless body with hot lead, just to make a point. And what was that point? That rebel lives ain't worth a damn!"

Burley paused to collect his breath, his face growing beet red from a combination of the brisk winter breeze blowing into his face through the open cabin door and his own self-generated intensity over the prospect of escape. "What makes you think they're going to treat us any better? In fact, what makes you think that, when we're conveniently away from shore, they won't shoot us and throw our lifeless bodies overboard? What's more, I have no doubt whatsoever that Captain Beall's plan is workable." More heads nodded in approval at the logic of the brash and bold Scotsman.

John remained silent, carefully studying the faces of the men he had come to know so well over the past few months. They've been a brave lot, he thought, willing to give anything a try. But they had never been faced with this kind of a test before. This test required men amenable to collectively, not individually, making the ultimate sacrifice, if necessary.

"Shh," John warned, holding his index finger to his lips. "We've got to keep the volume down. Whatever we do, we don't want to draw the Yankees' attention to our little conversation here." The cabin grew quiet, once again filled only with the muffled sounds of the paddlewheel churning up the azure waters of the Chesapeake.

"How do the rest of you men feel?" John inquired softly. He had learned at Runnymede from General Williams, what now seemed so long ago, that there are two key ingredients to being a successful leader. One, bravery inspires bravery; if you want your men to be brave, inspire them by your example. And two, give your men a chance to be heard; they may not agree with what you decide to do, but they still will take some ownership in the decision.

Lieutenant Ed McGuire, his red shock of unruly hair blowing in the stiffening breeze, spoke up. He was cautious where John was brazen; compromising where his captain was demanding. "Permission to speak freely, captain?"

John nodded his concurrence. He had learned that he needed a man like Ed McGuire around to temper his enthusiasm. He did not want to be surrounded by complacency; he believed it was important to have every theory, every plan, tested before being implemented.

"I don't think it's a good idea," he said simply. "Captain, I'm worried about that company of Maryland volunteers that got on the boat with us. I know some of their weapons are stacked up outside, but for all we know, there could be dozens of them waiting on the upper deck just above for us to attempt to escape. So they could shoot us down like dogs, just like they did with Sands Smith." McGuire, always straight to the point, smiled as he realized he had used the same Sands Smith incident that Burley had used to take the opposite position. They both knew that the death of Sands Smith had had an enormous impact on their little band, but most especially on Captain Beall.

"Yeah, Captain, do we know where those fellas are?" inquired one of his men. "I don't wanna be no duck in a shooting gallery." Some of the men nodded their agreement.

"Lieutenant McGuire's right," chimed in another. "Those Yankees could be on the upper deck above us, muskets at the ready, just waiting for us to try and escape." More heads nodded in concert.

John raised his hand to quiet the group. He had heard enough. Although he had asked for their input, he was disappointed that these men would now be so unwilling to undertake what appeared to him to be an exercise with acceptable risk, in exchange for their freedom. He stood up, crossed his arms firmly and said to no one in particular, "Why are you so unwilling to risk something, anything for your freedom? Do you really think this group of Maryland scallywags has some sort of grand plan to execute us?"

John paused. The men avoided his glance and stared at the floor or vacantly into space. Any chance to inspire them to take that chance to escape had vanished into the briny mist. He knew the orders his captors had given called for him to stay seated, but he walked over to a porthole, alone, where he peered though the smoky glass at the dim outline of Virginia, and freedom, slipping away with the miles.

6

NOVEMBER 27, 1863
NEAR RINGGOLD, GEORGIA

"Oh God, NO! Stop, Stop! Please don't cut any more!" The piercing cry of the young infantry colonel lying on the makeshift operating table filled the ramshackle old farmhouse.

Four burly Irish surgeon's assistants, all of whom curiously had well-developed handlebar mustaches to match their equally well-developed forearms and quads, held the writhing man down on the plankboard and sawhorse surface, as the Confederate field surgeon resumed cutting off the mangled stump of the man's left leg, just above the knee. The surgeon had applied a tourniquet, fashioned from the belt of one of the patients he had lost, around this patient's thigh. But the colonel's constant twisting and turning in agony had managed to work it loose. Although the tourniquet was still nominally in place, reduced pressure caused blood to squirt methodically from the severed artery onto the hapless aide assigned to hold down that quadrant of the man's torso. The surgeon reached across the table, pulled on the tourniquet and stanched the flow of blood to an acceptable trickle.

"Why in the hell don't you do something?" a frustrated Charles Cole raged. "For God's sakes, can't you see how much pain he is in?" Charles had not worked long at his brother's pharmacy in Memphis, but even he knew that patients undergoing an amputation under normal circumstances would be heavily sedated or anesthetized. This patient had not been.

The surgeon turned to Major Richard J. Person, second in command of the Fifth Confederate Infantry, and ordered, "Keep that soldier away from me. The amputation is difficult enough without this distraction. And I've got other patients I'll have to tend to today." Indeed he did, for a dozen men squirmed helplessly in pain or had already passed out from loss of blood outside on the half-frozen muddy morass, awaiting their turn to have one or more limbs sawed off. Major Person pushed himself behind the surgeon, gently nudging the distraught Charles Cole away from the table, back toward the far wall.

It was a gruesome enough job being a field surgeon under the best of circumstances. But since the bloody battle of Chickamauga two months previous, essentially all medicines and bandages had been used up. Amputations were being done routinely this day without the benefit of any painkillers or clean bandages.

Mercifully, many men not already unconscious or in shock soon lost consciousness after the first few pulls of the blade of the surgeon's saw. The best the surgeon and his staff could do for bandages was to take the soiled uniforms from soldiers they couldn't save, rinse the carnage and remnants of battle from them in the muddy little stream flowing through the back side of the postage-stamp sized farm clearing where they were encamped, and then tear the clothing into serviceable strips for bandages.

The surgeon wiped his brow with his bloody apron, and turned to resume his grueling task. The young colonel with the flowing jet back hair and grime-covered beard had passed out from the unbearable pain, making the balance of the doctor's job so much the easier.

"Charles, why don't we step outside. There's really nothing we can do for Jamie now except entrust him to God's care and the good hands of the surgeon," Major Person said soothingly, gently taking Charles Cole by the elbow and steering him toward the door.

Charles would not be budged. "NO way in hell," he responded indignantly. Ever since joining the Fifth six months ago, he had been a constant companion to his brother Jamie. Except, of course, for the hospitalization obtained for him through Jamie's intercession, just after the carnage at Chickamauga Creek.

Charles had been experiencing chronic digestive tract difficulties, symptomatic of dysentery. But so had many other men, North and South. There would have been no bodies to fight the war if all of the sick soldiers were put in a hospital. So, unless the symptoms were serious, men were expected to cope with their discomfort as best they could.

But Jamie knew Charles' problem was more his intense fear of combat than dysentery. Jamie could hardly send Charles packing when the going got tough; that was unthinkable. It would send entirely the wrong signal to all the rest of the men in the regiment, who would continue to be expected to fight and die on command for the cause. But a brief rest in the hospital, away from the sights and sounds of combat, would do wonders, he reckoned. And so Jamie had convinced the regimental doctor to send Charles to the hospital for a few weeks' stay.

Charles rejoined his unit just as General Bragg's army commenced to lay siege to Union forces in Chattanooga from the surrounding mountaintops. Then, unbelievably, Missionary Ridge fell to Union General Grant's Army of the Cumberland, after a surprise frontal assault into the face of the Confederate defenders. Two days had passed since that debacle. Yankees half-heartedly pursued Bragg's dispirited ragtag rebel remnants southward through the Chickamauga and Pea Vine valleys.

The rebels finally halted their retreat and dug in on Taylor's Ridge, just beyond Ringgold, where they hoped to stop the advance. Taylor's Ridge was a massive, rocky outcropping covered with dense underbrush and a well-developed forest. Jamie had been injured just one hour previous as the Federals commenced the battle by pouring artillery fire to the southern defenders.

"Major I'm staying right here until I know that Jamie is all right," Charles reaffirmed emphatically. "And I don't really give a god damn what you order me to do!" he said, his voice rising both in volume and pitch. Charles resented the pious attitude of this Southern blueblood; he had ever since Jamie had first introduced them. His feelings of resentment rose further when Person lectured him about the evils of alcohol, after Charles and some of the enlisted men had helped themselves to homemade corn liquor discovered behind a barn alongside Chickamauga Creek.

At the sound of the commotion behind him, the surgeon turned to face the feuding pair. "Look," he said icily. "This distraction not only bothers the hell out of me. It also puts this man's life in jeopardy," he said, pointing with a bloodied hand toward Jamie. "Every minute I waste means more lost blood. So if either of you really care about the patient, you will leave me to do my job. And go do yours." He stared long and hard into both men's eyes, just to make sure they got the message.

Charles jerked his elbow from Major Person's grasp, turned on his heels and stormed out of the house, stepping over and around the wounded.

Cole was really not a major problem, thought Major Person, so long as Jamie was around to keep him under control. But it looks like there'll be a battle with him from now on, at least until Jamie resumes his command. Person sighed deeply and said, "I'm sorry, doctor. The man is distraught because it's his brother you're operating on."

The surgeon harrumphed an unintelligible acknowledgment, and resumed his grisly duty. Person made his way gingerly through the maze of bodies outside the makeshift hospital and left in search of Charles. As he closed the door gently behind him, one of the wounded let loose with a blood curdling scream before taking his dying breath. Person grimly went on his way as the cascading sounds of cannon volleys suddenly stopped.

* * * * * * *

It didn't take Major Person long to find Charles Cole. Having observed him over the last six months, he knew that in times of stress, Cole would do one of two things: get sick or drink. Walking through the open flap of Cole's tiny tent, Person observed Charles crumpled on the ground with his head flung back and a jug to his lips. Out of the corner of his eye, Charles noticed that his self-appointed nemesis had entered his quarters. He put the jug on the ground and snarled at Person, "What the hell do you want?"

"Charles, I think we ought to have a little talk," replied Person calmly. The sounds of soldiers returning to their encampment from the firefight down the hill filled the air outside the tent. Person closed the flap behind him, not only to keep out the nippy wind that whipped around the tent tie-downs, but to keep out prying eyes as well.

Richard Person reminded Cole of a younger version of his father. Both were tall and square-jawed; both had magnificent heads of hair. And both were self-centered, self-righteous persons to whom Charles was nothing more than an ant. Or so he felt. Person's invitation to "have a little talk" brought back vividly to Charles' mind the last conflagration he had had with his father nearly two years ago over Tess Maloney. He fumed in drunken anger at the thought.

"You're my superior officer. I guess there's not a whole hell of a lot I can do about it. Now that you're in here, you might as well say what's on your mind," Charles droned in a monotone.

"Very well, but before we begin, I'd like to ask you to join me in a word of prayer for your brother, Jamie." Major Person had been an elder in his church before the war started and, though not a minister, possessed a good command of the language of prayer.

Charles said nothing. Person remained standing, or more accurately stooped over, his head bumping against the top of the sloping canvas. He clasped his hands together and closed his eyes shut tightly, unable to observe that Charles had used this opportunity to grab the jug of corn squeezings on the ground and take another long pull. Wiping the froth from his beard onto the sleeve of his muddied tunic, Charles sat impassively as Major Person sought divine intervention.

"Dearest Heavenly Father, we come to Thee this day to ask that Thou wouldst extend Thy divine healing power to embrace our friend and brother, Jamie Cole. Lord, Thou knowest that Jamie has been true and faithful to Thy Word, and that he has sought in all things to do Thy will. We humbly beseech Thee to wrap Thy loving arms around Jamie to take away any pain and to restore him to full health. In Jesus' name we pray, trusting always in Thy will. Amen."

Person opened his eyes, just in time to see Charles reach for the liquor for one more pull. The pious major erupted at the sacrilege taking place right before his eyes.

"Now see here, Lieutenant Cole, I have half a mind to write you up for court martial! I have been ordered to overlook all of your past indiscretions, at your bother's insistence, I might add. But your conduct today has been disgraceful. At the field hospital," Person continued, his voice rising as he remembered the scene that had taken place just minutes before, "you disobeyed a direct order from me to leave."

"I beg your pardon," Charles intoned sarcastically, "you never gave me a direct order to leave; you only encouraged me." He stared with icy black eyes at Major Person, who returned the frozen gaze.

"And then I come here into your tent and find you drinking. You know very well that the penalties for drunkenness during battle are quite severe," said Person.

Charles pushed himself up off the muddy ground, weaving only slightly, and stood toe to toe with his protagonist. The overwhelming fumes of alcohol combined with sweat and mud forced Major Person back a step.

"Wrong again, Major," Cole smirked, "You'll recall, I am sure, that the firing stopped just as we were leaving the field hospital. If you'll look outside," he said, gesturing toward the front of the tent, "it seems as though the day's battle is over. And I didn't start drinking until *after* the battle."

Major Person's anger was fast approaching the boiling point. He gritted his teeth, as he always did when his anger was mounting, and both fists were clenched shut so tight that his skin turned white around the knuckles. He momentarily considered giving Charles a good drubbing, but put the thought from his mind as soon as he realized that then he, not Cole, could find himself in front of a court martial.

Upon further reflection, he also recognized that Cole was technically correct. While Cole's behavior had been disgusting and probably insubordinate, it was certainly not shocking enough under these circumstances to get the attention of his superior officers. But, knowing Cole as he thought he did, he felt that, unfortunately, Charles would give him plenty of opportunities to find something worthy of court martial.

"Lieutenant Cole, I am going to overlook your insubordinate behavior and disrespectful attitude today," Person said. "I know Jamie's being wounded has had a profound impact on all of us." "But," he stated as emphatically as he could, "I will be watching you carefully from now on. If you step out of line in the least bit, I swear before God Almighty that I will do everything, EVERYTHING, in my power to insure that you suffer the most severe penalty available."

Major Person poked his index finger forcefully in the air in Charles' direction, just to make certain that the squat, black-bearded man in front of him got the message. "Do I make myself clear?" he asked.

Charles snapped off a limp salute and smiled thinly. "Yes sir, Major. You certainly do." Person wheeled sharply on his heels, pushed aside the tent flap and marched back outside, leaving the tent exposed to the bitter late November air.

"That son of a bitch," Charles thought as he moved to reclose the flap and shut out the nippy wind. "Here we go again; this bastard Person is every bit as bad as my old man back home. He thinks he can lord it over me, does he? God damn it, I'm every bit as good as he is, and I don't wear that fake Jesus-loving, book reading snobbishness around on my sleeve, either. I'll show him, and every other one of these god-damned bluebloods, what a real man can do."

Charles nodded his head in satisfaction at his decision. "I'm going to get the hell out of here just as soon as I know that Jamie is better," he thought, "and show these bastards just who Charles Cole is."

Charles bent over to pick up the half-empty container of liquor lying on the ground. He extended his fingers but could not quite reach the jug. Disgusted, he kicked it across the tent and stormed the few feet to the tent flap. He pushed it aside and, muttering obscenities under his breath, make his way up the muddy wagon path to the hospital to check on Jamie's condition.

7

APRIL 1864
MEMPHIS, TENNESSEE

"So, Charles, how are things with the Fifth?" inquired Jamie Cole. The now-disabled Confederate veteran was seated at the breakfast table, sipping his first steaming cup of morning coffee. His stump of a left leg was elevated and rested on one of the straight, high-back chairs about the table. Jamie's wound had become infected after the amputation, and the healing process took much longer than he thought it would. He found, though, that keeping the stump elevated reduced the throbbing sensation he was still feeling.

"About as you might expect," Charles responded unenthusiastically. He rubbed his bleary eyes, stretched out both arms, and let out a gaping yawn. Charles was not about to tell his brother, the wounded, ribbon-bedecked war veteran, that things had been absolutely rotten since Jamie had been shipped home on extended leave to recover from his battlefield injuries. The encounter that Charles had with Major Person on the day Jamie was wounded was merely the prelude to what turned into a living hell for the reluctant young officer.

When Major Person assumed command as Jamie's successor, he made good on his promise to Charles that his every move would be watched. He struck upon a masterful plan to keep Charles at bay by making him his executive officer. This was a job that consisted mainly of performing ministerial functions Person detested doing. At first, Charles towed the line and conformed to Person's rigorous and unwavering standards. There was little else he could do. But he also remembered the promise he made to himself to slip away from the unit at the first available opportunity. Although he believed he was no less fearless than anyone else in the unit, he hated the life of a soldier. The constant battle against the elements, chronic hunger, grayback ticks, fatigue, boredom and occasional sheer terror was not what he had in mind for himself.

And so, when he could take it no more, he deserted, sneaking his way through the lines back to Memphis, where he knew the Confederates no longer had authority. He had arrived at his brother's door last night after dark, and was mercifully invited in by his sister-in-law, Amanda. Jamie had already gone to bed.

Charles pulled out a chair from the table and plopped into it. His once-bloated frame had firmed up considerably under Major Person's reign of terror. He now was more muscle than fat, and he had noted a perceptible increase in the attention from the ladies in the small little towns he had walked through on his way back to Memphis, even as dirty and bedraggled as he was.

"How about a cup of coffee, Amanda?" he croaked, his voice reflecting the grogginess of the early morning, pre-caffeine hours. The glowing globe of early morning sun stretched over the horizon, and robins had already begun to peck in the moist ground outside the kitchen window in search of juicy little worms and grubs.

Amanda Cole, who had been standing over the kitchen sink rinsing dirty dishes, poured a steaming cup of java into a large earthenware coffee mug and set it down on the table beside Charles. She too had noticed a change in Charles, but was still wary of him. He was her husband's brother, though, and so she kept her peace.

"It sure is great to see you again, little brother," Jamie said, his eyes twinkling. He reached across the table and slapped Charles on the back. Charles smiled weakly.

"So what are you doing back in town, Charles? It's really pretty dangerous to be crossing back and forth between the lines. Did Major Person give you leave, or what?"

"Well, sort of," said Charles. "Actually, I have been detailed to special service on behalf of the Confederacy." On the road from the field to Memphis, Charles had thought long and hard about his cover story to explain to Jamie how he had managed to show up on his doorstep unexpectedly, when the rest of the regiment was engaged in the defense of Atlanta. And then it came to him. Special service, espionage. Yes, that would be it. It would certainly explain his presence, and there would be no way for Jamie to check on the veracity of the claim. If Jamie started asking questions, he could always say he had been sworn to secrecy and dodge any inquiry. It was a perfect cover for a Confederate deserter. And what's more, it would give his rabid rebel brother some reason to be proud of him.

Jamie lifted one eyebrow quizzically. He knew perfectly well that "special service" was a term euphemistically applied to espionage and similar dark pursuits. He knew it was dangerous work, and he had trouble believing that his brother Charles, whom he thought he knew well, would be willing to risk his life on behalf of a cause to which he was, at best, a late and reluctant convert. But then he looked at his little brother, deep into his shiny black eyes. Yes, he saw it there. Charles had changed. Coincidental with the firming up of his body, Charles' inner person appeared to have taken on a new and multifaceted dimension, an intensity of spirit, that Jamie had not noticed before.

In fact, what Jamie didn't see was that his brother's soul was burning with revenge. He hated damned patrician gentlemen officers from the South. He hated the way Major Person and others like him had made his life a holy hell. He detested them and everything they stood for.

"Well, Charles, I know that you can't talk about your assignment, but let me tell you I'm very proud of you. And Amanda is, too, aren't you, honey?" Jamie turned his head, just to make sure that his wife responded properly to the cue. "I sure am," she replied dutifully, not missing a stroke in her swipes across the dirty dishes.

Jamie leaned across the table, and gestured for Charles to come closer. "I already know all about your assignment, Charles," he whispered, and then winked.

"You do?" responded Charles, trying hard not to look startled, but with just a tinge of curiosity in his voice.

"Yes, it's all round town. At least in rebel circles."

Charles was perplexed. How could his brother know what his special service was, when in fact it was nothing more than a fabrication? "Well, you know I can't talk about my detail," he said, in the most authoritative voice he could muster. "But why don't you tell me what you think it is? If so many people are aware of it, then perhaps I should report that fact to my superiors, so that the plan can be changed, and necessary protections made for my safety, and for that of others."

In fact, Charles intended to do just the opposite. If he got enough information, he just might be able to pass it on to Union forces, in exchange for federal greenbacks.

"Of course, Charles," responded Jamie with a wink and a smile. "Excellent idea." He took a sip from his coffee mug, making a face when he realized the brew had turned cold and bitter. "Amanda, honey, would you mind leaving Charles and me alone for just a few minutes? We've got some business to discuss."

Amanda was more than happy to leave the kitchen. She had finished her chores there, and had plenty of other things to do. "Certainly, dear," she said, stooping to brush a kiss across her husband's cheek as she exited through the swinging kitchen door.

When Jamie was sure that his wife had left the room, his face conveyed the most earnest look Charles had ever seen in his brother. Must be something really important going on here, he thought. The Federals should pay big bucks for this.

"I really shouldn't be talking about this with you, Charles," said Jamie. "I mean, information about Confederate spying and sabotage should be closely guarded."

"I understand perfectly," said Charles coolly. His curiosity was piqued, and he needed to find out what was going on now as much to satisfy himself as to possibly convert the information to cash. "And that's why you need to tell me everything you know, just to make sure the operation has not been compromised."

Jamie exhaled heavily, a tangible sign of relief. "Yes, you're quite right, Charles." He paused for a moment, looking pensive, then continued.

"As I understand it, the Confederate Congress has appropriated $1 million for the establishment of a rear guard action against the Yankees, operating out of Canada. The general plan, quite simply, is to take the war to the Yankees' back door, to attack Union shipping on the Great Lakes, to free our officers and men being held in Yankee prison camps, and to lead a popular revolt in the Midwestern states against Lincoln's tyranny. This would, of course, break the back of the Yankee war effort, and they would be quick to sue for peace."

"Well, so far you are right on track," said Charles. He really had no way of knowing, of course, but this kind of grandiose plan sounded like something politicians would cook up. And the $1 million did catch his interest. There might be a way to latch onto some of that money, too. "But how is this plan to be put into action?" Charles asked.

"President Davis has already selected a number of men to carry out this activity. I understand that a cavalry officer from General Morgan's command is en route here now to begin recruiting for the operation. I also understand that a number of other junior officers from Kentucky and Tennessee have been recruited to follow. Men like you," said Jamie, a proud smile on his face. The coincidence was too great to overlook. Charles fit the bill. Why else would he be here at his door, thought Jamie, fit and trim for the first time in years?

"Correct again," Charles lied. Jamie was believing just what he wanted to believe. "But tell me, how do you know all this?"

"Very simple, Charles. Because that officer I spoke about, who is leading the military operation out of Canada, passed through here on his way north. A Confederate network has been established, where men on missions for the South swing west through to Memphis, then north to Chicago, before finally turning back east, toward Canada. And this house, right here, is part of that network."

"This officer – what's his name?" Charles was pressing his luck, asking so many questions for which he had no answers himself. But Jamie was so caught up in being part of the story that he did not notice.

"Hines, Thomas Hines, I believe it is," Jamie responded. He pulled out a tobacco paper and his tobacco pouch and began rolling a cigarette.

"I've got to admit, you sure do have the straight story," said Charles. He took a cigar out of his breast pocket, and allowed Jamie to light it as they sat together at the kitchen table. "I'm sure that, as you can readily understand, you must keep this information absolutely confidential. Especially now that the damned Yankees are occupying this town, you really can't be too sure who you're talking to," he said, grinning slightly as he caught the irony of what he had just said.

"For my safety, as well as for the safety of all the others involved in this plan," he continued, "I've got to have your word that you will tell nobody about this." Charles took a drag on the smoldering black cigar, exhaling the pungent smoke toward the ceiling.

"You most certainly do, Charles," said Jamie, nodding his head in approbation, "you have my word on it."

Charles stood up, pushing the chair across the plank wooden floor with the back of his legs. "You'll excuse me, now, Jamie," said Charles. "I've got to go out and get some supplies for my trip north."

"Fine, Charles," Jamie responded. "How long will you be staying with us?" he asked offhandedly.

"Just a few days, I think. Long enough to get rested up a bit," Charles said, as he headed for the back door leading off from the kitchen.

"Be careful, Charles. The Federals are constantly on the lookout for southern men to question," Jamie warned sternly. He knew his brother was aware of the presence of Yankee troops in the city, but he just had to make sure that Charles was reminded of the danger.

"Thanks for the warning, big brother," said Charles, with a smile and a wink. How ironic, Charles thought, that a year ago almost to the day he was in jail, under the provost marshal's control. And now he was going there voluntarily, with the prospect of dollars instead of jail time as the end result. Closing the door behind him, he drew another drag on the cigar, flicking the ash nonchalantly as he walked down the path to the back gate and the street beyond. It had not occurred to him that he might be recognized as the belligerent drunk who just a year ago had threatened to kill the guards.

* * * * * * *

Charles Cole had been kept waiting for nearly an hour before a private ushered him into a cramped little nook that served as the office of Major Thomas N. Hook, Assistant Provost Marshal for the City of Memphis. It was an unusually hot and humid day for April, and the tiny window that served as the only source of light and fresh air for the Major's room had been flung wide open. The clump of horses' hooves on the cobblestone pavement below mingled with the mumble of pedestrian traffic to provide a kind of low level, almost soothing, background noise. Despite the open window, the stagnant air scarcely moved and the humidity seemed to cling to every pore like a damp rag.

The private merely brought Cole to Hook's open door, with not even an introduction, and left him there. Hook was seated at his desk. His head was bent low as he pored over the mountain of papers in front of him.

Even though seated, the Major's ample frame was obvious to Charles. A balding man of at least 50 years of age, the heat and humidity were clearly bothersome to Hook. The top buttons of his tunic were undone to allow at least a modicum of air to reach his skin. As he continued to read the papers in front of him, the Major constantly dabbed a handkerchief at his luminous dome, where beads of sweat formed incessantly, intent on running down his forehead and into his eyes.

Charles cleared his throat, in an attempt to attract the Major's attention. Hook seemed oblivious to everything but the paper he was studying intently. Cole cleared his throat a second time, this time louder and longer, and moved a step into the room. Hook looked up over his wire-rimmed reading glasses in Cole's general direction. "Yes?" he scowled, obviously incensed at the distraction from whatever project he had been working on.

"Major Hook, I was informed by your secretary that I should take up my business with you," Cole said, somewhat intimidated by the Major's brusque manner.

"And who are you?" snarled the Major, dabbing at his forehead. A bead of a sweat rolled down over his eyebrow and onto Hook's glasses. "Damn it!" he swore. He tore the glasses off his face, wiping both lenses carefully with the same handkerchief he had used to trap the offending perspiration. The lenses cleaned as best he could, Hook put the glasses back on his nose, carefully slipping the frame over each ear.

"Captain Charles H. Cole, sir, late of the Fifth Confederate Infantry," replied Charles, and . . ."

"Cole, Cole," said Hook. "That name sounds familiar. Have we met?"

Despite the heat, Cole felt himself breaking out in a cold sweat. Oh my God, he thought, has he placed me? If he does, he won't believe a word I say. The thought belatedly occurred to him that he should have used somebody else's name.

"No sir, I don't believe so," said Cole. That answer was indeed truthful. He had never actually met this man, although it certainly was possible that Hook had seen his name on the prisoners' roster. Cole trusted the man's apparent short attention span and his own gutsiness to pull him through.

Hook accepted Cole's response at face value and inquired no further. Obviously agitated, Hook moved the conversation onward. "If you're here to take the amnesty oath, you've got the wrong office. That could all have been done by my secretary without need to see me," Hook said.

"Sir, I certainly am interested in taking the amnesty oath, and I did discuss that with your secretary. As I explained my other business to him, in very general terms, he thought it best that I mention the other matter to you. He said I could sign the amnesty oath on my way out," Cole said.

Major Hook put down his pen, removed his reading glasses, and leaned back in his chair. It was the first time he paid anything more than superficial attention to the young man standing in front of him. Hook thought he was a pretty good judge of character; you had to be to work in the provost marshal's office. Most of the people he dealt with had one lie or another to tell, or some sort of cover story, in vain attempts to explain the offenses that brought them to the attention of the provost marshal in the first place.

The man standing before him was obviously in good physical condition. Despite his own infirmities, Hook recognized a good body as an outward sign of a disciplined mind. There was also a certain intensity, an aura of sorts, that seemed to envelope Charles Cole. This was obviously a man who bore listening to, Hood concluded.

"Please sit down," he said, gesturing toward a single hard wooden chair in front of his desk. Cole said down, dutifully.

"Very well, Captain Cole, what have you got on your mind?" Hood asked, after Charles had seated himself.

"Sir, I happen to have information which I believe would be invaluable to the Union. Being a Pennsylvanian myself, I am quite interested in doing what I can to see that the Union is preserved," Cole said.

"But I thought you said you were a captain in the Confederate army," said Major Hook, poking the air emphatically with his finger. Hook was confused. What was a Pennsylvanian doing in the rebel army?

"That's correct, sir," explained Cole. "I found myself here in Memphis after the war started, working for my brother, a local pharmacist. Unfortunately, he has strong rebel tendencies and was appointed a colonel in the unit. He asked me to join him."

Cole paused, and observed that Major Hook was studying him intently. "Sir, he is my brother, my very closest friend. I really had no choice," insisted Cole. "And now that he has been disabled," he continued, "my personal obligation to him is no longer binding."

He had carefully crafted his answer to avoid telling Major Hook that he had not joined the Confederates until *after* he had served in the Union Army, until *after* Memphis had been restored to Union control, and until *after* he had served time in this very building, in the jail just one floor below.

"Yes, yes, I can see how you could find yourself in such a situation," responded Hook, nodding his head in agreement. "And how is your brother now?"

"He's back in Memphis, sir, recuperating from the amputation." Cole bit his lower lip. "I think his fighting days are over."

"I'm sorry about your brother. But please, continue."

Cole now spoke forthrightly, without hesitation, for he had rehearsed this part well.

"During my stay in the rebel army," he said, "I acquired secret, very valuable information. This information could save thousands of Union lives. And it could make you a hero." He paused, to observe if the import of his statement had sunk in. It had. Major Hook now leaned his massive frame forward in his chair, intent on learning how information from this Yankee turned rebel officer could make him a hero.

"Major, before I continue, there are several preliminary matters we need to discuss."

"Yes?" responded Hook quizzically, dabbing at his sweat-soaked brow with his now-damp handkerchief.

"Well, sir, I have sacrificed considerably to acquire this information," said Cole. "I put my life at substantial personal risk during my time with the rebel army. And if word ever were to leak out that I was the one who betrayed the biggest rebel espionage and intelligence operation of the war, the prospects for my continued good health would be nominal. Quite bluntly, sir, I would be a dead man. I am willing to take that risk, on behalf of my country, but I believe it only fair that I be adequately compensated for it."

Hook's face screwed up in obvious displeasure. The provost marshal did pay for good information. But usually just nominal amounts, never more than a hundred dollars and usually much less, for nominally valuable information primarily of local interest only. Cole's introduction sounded like the entrée to a price tag considerably higher.

"Captain Cole, I recognize your concerns," said Hook. "And I am sure that, if what you are about to tell me is true, you will have the deepest gratitude of the United States Government. And I will see what I can do, I promise you that. But I obviously cannot bind my superiors to anything firm and specific until we have an opportunity to evaluate the validity and value of the information. I am sure you can appreciate that."

Cole tried to hide his disappointment. This was not going to be as easy a task as he had first supposed. Still, the prospect was there for a big payoff. And, as the options raced through his mind, what choice did he really have? He could hardly say, now that he had come this far, that he had reconsidered, and decided to keep his information to himself. That was a guaranteed way to turn a potential profit into disaster. It was a buyer's market, and Cole knew he would have to continue to abide by the rules established by the buyer, in this case, Major Hook.

Cole then proceeded over the next hour to tell Major Hook all about the Confederate operation planned out of Canada, as told to him by his brother Jamie, with appropriate embellishment, of course, where necessary. He informed Major Hook all about Thomas Hines, and passed on what he had heard about the intended Confederate objectives. He continue to protect his brother Jamie, and attributed all of his information to cavalry officers in General Morgan's and General Forrest's commands with whom he had had some acquaintance.

Hook listened with growing attention to Cole's fantastic story. By the end of the hour, the Major was convinced of Cole's *bona fides*, and decided this story must be shared with the provost marshal himself, who would make the decision about what to do next.

As Cole concluded his narrative, Hook lumbered out from behind his chair, extended a hearty handshake, and asked him to return in three days, at which time he thought he would have a decision from the provost marshal regarding the request for cash. Hook bellowed for his secretary, the same young private who had earlier brought Cole to Hook's office. Cole followed the young man in the blue uniform to the provost marshal's front office, where he read, swore to and signed an oath of loyalty to the United States of America.

* * * * * * *

Charles Cole sat waiting nervously on Major Hook for only a few minutes this time before being ushered into his office by the Major's secretary. It had been a difficult three days for him. While making up tales to Jamie about the special service he was about to undertake for the Confederacy, he really was waiting on the payoff, from the very forces that Jamie detested, for his betrayal of the Confederacy.

Cole didn't give a damn about either side of the conflict, but it did trouble him that he had deceived his own brother. Jamie was the only person who had accorded Charles even the slightest degree of love or respect. But, Charles convinced himself, it would destroy his relationship with Jamie to admit that he was nothing more than a common deserter. And so he continued to live and propagate the lie.

Little did Cole know that over the last three days, a plan had been evolving, under the aegis of Major Hook, to convert Cole from a rebel deserter to a Union agent. Upon authorization by the provost marshal, his immediate superior, Hook had fired off a wire to the War Department in Washington, seeking confirmation of the basic facts of the plot as revealed to him by the anomalous young Confederate officer from Pennsylvania. It was common knowledge that spies and agents worked freely on both sides, and if what Cole said was true, the War Department would certainly be aware of at least some of it by now.

They were. Lafayette C. Baker, head of the United States Secret Service, confirmed by return telegram that there was no value to the Union in Cole's information. But if Cole was as connected with rebel affairs and personalities as he appeared to be, he might make an ideal candidate to worm his way into the confidence of the conspirators, Baker wired. See if you can convince Cole to go to Canada, concluded Baker.

"Captain Cole, how good of you to come by," effused Major Hook as Cole was ushered into his office. "Please have a seat." The mound of paperwork that Cole had to peer over the last visit appeared to have been moved, and he was able to fully observe the pear-shaped Major Hook. Cole chuckled inwardly as he sat down in the Major's sole visitor's chair. Hook wouldn't last a day in the field, he mused. No wonder they've got the old fart sitting behind a desk.

Major Hook leaned forward, his arms folded on the desk in front of him. Unlike the last visit, when Hook seemed to scowl on the slightest provocation, the rotund Union officer seemed to be in a genuinely jolly mood today.

"I'll get right to the point," said Hook. "I have checked with our sources, and find that the information you provided during our last visit was already widely known. So, I'm sorry, but we won't be able to do anything by way of compensation."

Cole bit his upper lip and gripped the arms of the chair so tightly that his knuckles turned white. He resisted the temptation coursing through him to cuss out the son of a bitch and storm out of the office in search of the nearest tavern. Intuitively, he sensed that Hook was not through with this conversation. He had been too polite, too bubbly to convey news that he had to suspect Cole would have difficulty taking. Just sit still and keep your mouth shut, Cole cautioned himself, and see what the old boy has to say.

Hook noticed that Cole was not pleased with his report. Nothing unexpected there. But the final test was yet to come, he thought. Let's see how he responds to Mr. Baker's suggestion.

"Captain Cole," Hook continued, "I have been impressed with your command of this subject, and your willingness to work with the government. I have communicated my impressions of you not only to the provost marshal here in Memphis, but also to officials at the highest levels in Washington. I believe there may be a way that we can work together. Are you interested?"

Cole relaxed his grip on the chair. His mind raced as he tried to anticipate what Hook as going to suggest. Perhaps there will be a way to salvage something here anyway, he thought. There may still be a shot at making some money out of this deal, and showing those damned rebel dandies a thing or two.

"What exactly did you have in mind?" Cole asked. His deep black eyes conveyed intensity and sincerity, which Hook found irresistible.

"The government would like you to offer your services to the rebel leaders in Canada. All the while working for us, of course," said Hook.

Cole hoped his jaw had not dropped perceptibly. They are asking me to be a spy? He could hardly believe his ears. And then the reality hit him; it felt like a huge lead weight had just dropped on both of his shoulders. I could get killed, he thought. That spy business is dangerous work. But then Cole remembered what Jamie had said about the $1 million that the Confederacy was using to bankroll the operation. This may be a way to tap into both sides. A sly grin crossed his face as he thought about the prospect of getting paid by the Union to steal from the Confederacy. An ideal situation. It is worth the risk.

"Major Hook, I believe we may be able to work something out here," he said.

"Excellent, excellent!" Hook responded enthusiastically, as he grasped Cole's hand and shook it up and down for a seemingly endless number of times.

Hook proceeded to describe the general plan, which would initially require Cole to return to Philadelphia to await further instructions. But the rebel charlatan had trouble concentrating on the words spilling from the mouth of the rotund assistant provost marshal, as his mind continually returned to images of stacks and stacks of gold, and then greenbacks, piled up to the sky.

8

JUNE 1864
COLUMBUS, GEORGIA

Martha O'Bryan had been depressed for nearly two years. Horribly, deeply, incessantly, incurably depressed. It had been that long since she had last seen her beloved John. Her affianced had been faithful in his letter writing to her, until inexplicably his correspondence had suddenly ceased about six months ago.

But now, as she stood amidst the crowd gathered at the train station in the sweltering Georgia midday heat that hung like a dense fog over the platform, her mood was dramatically different. Her fortunes had reversed, and now Martha was not just happy, she was ecstatic.

She tightly clutched an icon of her rapture in her delicate little glove-bedecked hands. Oblivious to the throng of people milling about her and the intense sun beating down overhead, she lovingly removed the letter from its well-crinkled envelope, to read it once more. Since the letter had first arrived a week ago at the home of her widowed Aunt Mildred, with whom she was now staying, Martha had read and reread the letter for what seemed at least a thousand times, until she could repeat each word, each nuance, every inflection, as though John were speaking to her himself.

She read the letter yet again:

My dearest Martha,

I am so glad that I now know where you are! In these troubling times, it is difficult to keep track of where loved ones may be, but thankfully I received a brief note from Mrs. Williams as to your current whereabouts.

Oh, how I have missed you, my love! Until my exchange a few months back by the Yankees, after having been captured by them on the Chesapeake November last, I had been unable to write to you. I know how you must have worried when my letters stopped coming, and it caused me grievous pain. But all is well now, and I am safely back in Virginia.

It was a harrowing experience while I was in the custody of the Federals, I daresay. But God, in whom I have placed custody of both my mortal and eternal existence, saw fit to protect me from all danger and return me unharmed to the bosom of liberty.

And now, my love, even in this time of great turmoil and distress, I am able to tell you that we will soon be reunited. I will be leaving within the week by train from Richmond to come to you.

Although we have been apart for so long, you should know that my every thought has been of you. It has pained me to not experience your love, your little laugh, the way you make me glad to be alive. The thought of seeing you again has sustained me during our time apart. But now I look forward to the moment when I may once more caress your gentle face and smother you with hugs and kisses.

All my love,
John

Martha's heart had leapt for joy when she got the letter last week. John is safe! He is coming to join me, and we will never be parted! She had already begun to make inquiries with her aunt's parish pastor to determine when they might be wed.

And so, even though she did not know the exact day when he might arrive, she had faithfully dressed in her Sunday finest and driven down to the station every afternoon in her aunt's fancy surrey. Each day, she saw trains arrive from the north, bearing scores of wounded and dying men, the bitter fruit of war. The faces of the men, who in age were no more than boys really, were innocent no more.

For some months, Confederate casualties were being transported from the battlefields to the hospital facilities in Columbus. These poor souls were quartered all over town. Even the Court House and two saloons on Broad Street had been equipped and were now overflowing with wounded warriors of the South. The horror of war had spread to this quaint river town, although still far removed from the killing grounds.

Martha tried her best to ignore the horror and the agony reflected in the men's eyes; they reminded her too much of John when she first met him that day now more than two years ago at Runnymede. She wanted to be the first image in her darling John's vision when he alighted from the train, not more graphic reminders of war and suffering.

She was stunning, as she had been for each of the last four days. Despite the oppressive heat, Martha wore a full fluffy white linen dress, with dainty lace gloves and gleaming ivory-colored shoes. The willowing crinoline hoops underneath her dress made it look as though she literally floated with every step. Her hair fell gracefully from her face in gentle curls, softly framing the delicate contours of her face. She wore a lime green sunbonnet and matching parasol, which accented her mischievous green eyes. She was, in essence, the paragon of femininity.

Suddenly and unseen, from somewhere deep within the throng of men and women milling about the platform, a high-pitched female voice cried out, "the train is coming! I see the train!"

Martha hastily, yet lovingly, replaced John's letter in its envelope and tucked it up over the top of her dress, where she lodged it between her two firm breasts. She had fantasized ever since receiving this letter about what married life would be like with John. And although they had each foresworn premarital sexual relations, she nonetheless could not help thinking about the time when John would take her for his own. Having John's letter so close to her heart, tucked away in that valley of soft feminine flesh that men find so compellingly fascinating, gave Martha shivers of delight and expectation.

The plume of gray-black smoke from the smokestack of the belching behemoth appeared just over the treetops, a precursor of the train's arrival. Although Martha could not yet hear the train's whistle, she knew from the past four days of waiting, that the engine would come into view as it rounded the bend just past the ammunition factory.

Leading to the heartland of the South, safe from Yankee intrusion, the rail line not only served as the means of moving Confederate wounded to the hospitals; it had also become a lifeline of hope for Southerners seeking to avoid the advancing Union juggernaut. For those persons with money enough for a ticket, the train was the vessel to continued life more or less as they had known it, and hope that the war would end soon.

For John Yates Beall, the train was a means to escape, at least temporarily, the horrors of war. It was also the means by which he would be reunited with his beloved Martha.

Slowing to a crawl, the train pulled into the crowded station. John was in the last of the four passenger cars, having been lucky enough to buy his way on board at the last minute. He had been travelling from Richmond for over a week. The train stopped at every little wide spot in the road, and he had to transfer more than once. He was anxious to see his Martha again, the sooner the better. What's more, travel via the rails was becoming increasingly erratic. And so, when he could get a seat on a train, he took it, regardless of whether he would have preferred to travel at a more leisurely pace, where he could rest and bathe properly.

John's face was haggard and drawn. Unable to sleep except in brief fits on the crowded, noisy and hot train, large black bags had developed under his still brilliant blue eyes. The lines of his mustache and chin whiskers had gotten lost in the accumulated stubble of at least four days growth of facial hair. He had not had a change of clothes for even longer. The usually white, starched shirt he wore under his black frock coat had become a dingy gray from the accumulation of cinders from the train blowing through the open window by his seat and sticky perspiration. He had changed his collar and cuffs a few days back, so that at least part of his attire would be relatively fresh, but they were all now dirty, too.

The incessant, infernal sun beating down on the tin roof of the car had caused him to perspire to the point of dehydration. He had also developed another catarrh, and his old familiar pains had returned. Thank God for laudanum, he thought, tapping his coat pocket which contained his ever-present bottle of the magic elixir. Yes, the trip had taken its toll on John, and he knew it.

But it was all worth it. Ever since his capture on the Chesapeake, John had dreamed of nothing else but seeing his Martha again. Although he would have preferred to arrive in a bit more grand fashion in Columbus, where Martha was residing with her Aunt Mildred, he knew that her love for him would overcome the momentary unpleasantness over his appearance and any unpleasant body odors.

Even before the train stopped, a mob of anxious and frazzled travelers crowded past John, as he reached for his valise in the rack above his seat. Rather than fight the mad rush to exit the train, John waited until the way was clear and then walked to the front of the car. He was in no mood, and was frankly too tired, to fight the herd mentality.

Finally able to exit, John stopped at the top of the step before alighting. He squinted as his eyes adjusted to the bright outdoors and then peered onto the platform for any sign of Martha. Since he had been unable to tell her when he would be arriving, he had no expectation that she would be there. Yet, deep in his heart, he wished that she would be awaiting him, ready to fling herself into his arms in an instant.

"John! John!" The cry was carried to him as though on wings of an angel, like a voice in the wilderness must have sounded to John the Baptizer. He knew instantly that it was Martha. And then he saw her, running down the now half deserted platform, her dazzling white dress billowing in the breeze. In the excitement, she had dropped her parasol, and her lime green sunbonnet bounced precariously with every step.

John's heart beat so fast at the sight of Martha that he thought he would faint. But then, all of his fatigue, his illness, his discomfort vanished into the miasma. Drawing on that well of energy that resides deep within every soul, he ran toward her, until they were both in each other's arms, their lips locked in a seemingly eternal embrace made all the more powerful by the nearly unbearable separation they had each endured for so long.

* * * * * * *

A few dusty blocks down the street from the train station stood the Perry House. A grand dame of an establishment, in the best traditions of the South, the Perry House was considered to be "one of the largest and most commodious Hotels in the interior of the whole country" according to a newspaper ad. But the scourge of war, even when conducted at a distance, had not been particularly kind to the Perry House. The challenges of the war years had been borne with some difficulty. Parts and paint were in short supply, as were workers to operate and maintain the place. It still exuded a sort of gentle ambience, though, much like that of an aging yet kindly dowager. Fortunately, the kitchen had not suffered, as local, fresh produce could still be had.

Despite the multitude of war refugees flooding into Columbus, few stayed at the Perry House, because it only accepted gold or Yankee greenbacks; it had stopped accepting Confederate notes over a year previous. It was not beyond John's reach, though, since he had wisely converted much of his available cash to gold at the start of the war. The hotel was also only a short ten-minute stroll from Martha's Aunt Mildred. It was the logical place for him to stay.

After a hot bath, a shave, and a long nap in his room at the hotel, John changed into his one remaining clean set of clothes, while he sent the others out to be laundered. Never a dapper dresser, John's taste in clothing ran toward basic black, English conservative styles. During his time in England a decade ago, where he had resided with his Grandfather Yates, John had acquired an interest in all things English, including plain, basic gentleman's clothing. Except for physically demanding labor at Walnut Grove, John dressed pretty much the same wherever he went: starched white shirt and cuffs, black cravat, black waistcoat and trousers.

Martha came back for him about 6:00 p.m., to take him to meet Aunt Mildred. They had had little time to talk after John's arrival; he was so insistent that he get checked in to the hotel and to clean himself up and rest a bit. Martha had hoped to discuss her plans for the wedding with him, but decided to wait until after supper. She asked her Aunt Mildred, a gabby soul to say the least, to avoid the subject until she had a chance to discuss it first with her betrothed. Always willing to accommodate her favorite niece's every request, Mildred had agreed.

Mildred had become a widow six months ago, having lost her husband, like many others, to the ravages of war. Martha was dispatched by her parents to Columbus not only because they wanted her safely out of the range of Yankee guns and sex-starved Yankee soldiers, but also because they felt that having her stay with her aunt would help ease Mildred's pain, too. And they were right. Although in her late 40's, Mildred was not so old that she had lost touch with her youth.

Mildred beamed widely as Martha introduced John to her. "So nice to meet you, young man. Martha has told me so much about you. You're quite a hero, I understand." John grinned sheepishly, but said nothing. This woman was not the least bit shy, and John admired people who spoke their minds. Mildred was somewhat hefty and her wavy, long hair was flecked with streaks of silver among the black. She did not strike John as an enfeebled old woman. Quite the contrary, in fact.

Mildred turned to Martha, grabbing her by the elbow and guiding her around the side of the house. "You kids come around back onto the veranda. It's a little warm today, so we'll have supper outside," said Mildred. She had not allowed the opportunity to question the thought that any other arrangement was possible. John grinned knowingly and winked at Martha, who appeared radiant, almost angelic. John followed along behind the two women as they made their way to the back of the house, chatting and laughing like two prepubescent girls.

Despite privations otherwise caused by the war, Aunt Mildred was still able to provide regular, wholesome meals. She raised her own vegetables and chickens on her little plot, and it was from her own produce that tonight's supper would come.

Mildred continued her nonstop friendly banter throughout the delightful supper of chicken stew, piping hot biscuits and fresh buttermilk. She was insatiably curious about everything in John's life, his family, his home, his exploits on the Chesapeake, his time in the Yankee prison, his views on the conduct of the war.

His family connection was of particular interest to Mildred. An avid local historian, she was aware that one of the founders of Columbus was Elias Beall. "Are you any relation to Elias Beall of Virginia?" she asked. "You know, he was one of the five commissioners who first settled our little town."

"Well, ma'am, I didn't know that," John answered politely. "I may very well be related to him, if you say he came to Georgia from Virginia." The truth of the matter was John really didn't know much about his father's genealogy, but that was hardly something you would say to someone so captivated by history. Especially if that person was Aunt Mildred.

Martha sensed that John, ever polite, was unwilling to admit that the barrage of questions had tired him. So, as the sun was sinking over the rooftops of the little townhouses and cottages of Columbus, she was able to drag him away from the table and from Aunt Mildred by suggesting that John may want to take a walk with her. Never a stupid woman, Mildred got the message that the two of them wanted some time alone. "Go ahead," she said, as though she had been invited to join the pair, "I've got my chores to do yet before dark."

As they walked back toward John's hotel, arm in arm, the exertion of the trip and stress of the day finally caught up with him, and he began to cough spasmodically, his face turning a deep crimson from the strain. It had been over two years since Martha had last seen John, and she assumed perhaps somewhat naively that John's lung injury had fully healed. Obviously it had not.

"Are you all right, honey?" she asked, her voice quivering with concern. Unable to answer because of the coughing spasm, John leaned against a fencepost along the road. Martha held tightly onto his arm, as if to brace him up against the onslaught. He reached into his coat pocket, pulled out a smallish brown bottle filled with fluid. He pulled the cork, then put the bottle to his lips. Leaning his head back, with some difficulty, he took a couple of swigs of the elixir. In a moment, the coughing had stopped, and he was able to resume speaking again.

"There's nothing to be worried about, my love," John said hoarsely, as he noticed the anxiety still in her eyes. "I occasionally still have these coughing spells. Damned Yankee minie ball in my chest." Martha was unconvinced, as John seemed breathless after every phrase. "See how much better I am already?" he asked, his voice growing noticeably stronger. "The laudanum deadens the pain and smothers the cough. It is truly a miracle of modern medicine."

"Can you go on?" Martha asked, her voice filled with concern. John stood tall and erect, until his back was ramrod straight.

"I surely can," he replied. "I'm sorry to have frightened you. It looks much worse than it really is." He didn't know whether to believe himself, but hoped that Martha would.

Together, hand in hand, they continued their stroll to the hotel as the last glimmers of light faded from the sky, stopping as necessary so that John could catch his breath. Martha decided she would wait until tomorrow, when he was stronger, to discuss the wedding with John. After a long, luxurious kiss goodnight outside the hotel, she waved good-bye to John and returned to her Aunt Mildred's, still wondering about the true state of John's health. Martha put that, too, out of her mind until some later, more convenient, time.

* * * * * * *

"Darling, I've missed you so!" said Martha as she greeted John the next morning in the hotel lobby. John's blue eyes twinkled with delight at the sight of his fiancée. He put both arms around her snowy white shoulders and kissed her lightly on the cheek. He coughed lightly, but otherwise showed no signs that his respiratory system was giving him any problem this morning.

"Is that any way to greet the woman who will be the mother of your children?" Martha teased. She knew that John was shy about public displays of affection. The long, passionate kisses they had exchanged at the train station and hotel yesterday had been the exception, not the rule.

John returned her playful banter. "There'll be plenty of time for that later," he said with a naughty wink. A shiver of delight ran down Martha's spine at the prospect of passionate, physical, interminable love with this man of her dreams, now here in her arms, so close to her, yet . . .

"How about some breakfast?" he asked, returning her from her dreamy trance. "I hear this hotel cooks up some mighty fine meals." Bowing slightly, in an exaggerated mimicry of southern high society, he extended his right arm to her. They sauntered off blissfully in the direction of the dining room.

Throughout their breakfast, the conversation was light. John asked well-meaning questions about Martha's parents, now in Yankee-occupied Nashville. Martha asked John probing questions about his exploits on the Chesapeake, which John relived in every glorious detail.

After the plates had been cleared away, John gently took Martha's hand in his, and stared lovingly into her eyes. No words were necessary. What better time, Martha thought, to discuss the wedding with him.

"John, do you remember that church we walked by on the way to the hotel last night? The white framed one with the lovely tall spire?" Martha asked innocently. "That's the First Presbyterian. Aunt Mildred is a member there."

"I certainly do remember it, even though I was feeling a bit poorly. Although, in fact, the simple magnificence of the edifice invigorated me," he said, nodding his head in appreciation.

"I agree it is a magnificent structure. And Aunt Mildred will be delighted at your remarks. She's been a member there since she was a little girl. She was baptized in that church and married my uncle there." She paused as she remembered that a memorial service for her uncle had also been held in that church after receiving word that he had died and been buried on the field of battle. "I've been attending there ever since I arrived in Columbus. The pastor is a wonderful, God-fearing, compassionate man. You'll really find him to be an inspiration when you meet him later today."

John looked puzzled. "But darling, it's only Friday. What's the occasion to meet with your pastor – what's his name again?"

"Stiles. John Milton Stiles."

"Pastor Stiles, thank you," said John, "on a Friday?"

"To discuss our wedding," Martha said, watching John's face carefully for his reaction to the news that she had initiated wedding plans.

Now John realized what Martha had done. And he knew that he had little choice but to tell her now that would be impossible, at least within the timetable that Martha probably had in mind. He squeezed her hand firmly but gently and looked deep into her eyes, as green as the first shoots of grass in springtime. The intensity of her love, her devotion to him, was a continual source of amazement. He hated what he had to do, but he had no choice. He struggled to maintain his composure, carefully observing what appeared to him to be his own shocked countenance reflected in her eyes.

"We need to talk about that, my love, but this is not the place to discuss it," John said. She still didn't understand what John was trying to tell her.

He needed privacy to discuss with her why he couldn't marry her now. Not just because he feared that she would break understandably into uncontrollable tears, embarrassing herself in a way that she would later regret. No, he needed privacy because what he was about to share with her was a matter of utmost secrecy to the Confederate government.

Even though he had been instructed by none other than Confederate War Secretary Seddon himself to not discuss his assignment with anyone until he arrived at his new duty post, he knew he had to let Martha know. Otherwise, he feared she might leave him. Forever. The thought of that prospect was ghastly – and totally unacceptable. And the risk that Martha would inadvertently mention the incident was practically nil. So he would tell her.

But where? A public restaurant was obviously not the place to discuss state secrets. Neither was Aunt Mildred's; as much as he liked the woman, he was concerned that the gabby widow might overhear and unwittingly retell part of the conversation. It was certain that even here in Columbus there were people who could not be trusted. If John's mission were to become known to the enemy, not only would his own life be endangered, but that of possibly thousands of good men at the same time. And then it occurred to him. He would invite her to his room.

"Martha, sweetest," John intoned seriously, "I need to share information with you of some considerable sensitivity to the Confederate government. The utmost privacy is called for. Would you come to my room with me so that I may discuss this with you?" He coughed slightly, then reached into his coat pocket to make sure the laudanum was there in case he should need it.

John thought Martha might be scandalized by the prospect of going to his room unescorted. It was common knowledge that, other than family members, only ladies of the evening would ever dare enter a single man's room alone. But Martha could detect by the serious expression John wore on his pale face, and by the little beads of perspiration forming where thinning brown hair met his forehead, that John was terribly serious

Martha nodded, unable to think of anything to say that would seem appropriate under the circumstances. Neither of them said anything more as John paid the check and escorted Martha up the winding staircase in the grand lobby to his room on the second floor.

* * * * * * *

Martha sat nervously on the edge of one of the two elegant Queen Anne chairs that filled the bay in John's room. The wispy filigreed lace curtains danced in the fresh morning breeze. She observed the frantic activity taking place in the street below. Funny, she thought, it looks so normal. But men were suffering and some were dying awful and gruesome deaths just a hundred miles or so from here. Yet you couldn't tell by the looks on faces of the people below, trying to get on with their lives as best they could under the circumstances.

John occupied the seat opposite her. They were close enough to touch each other if either of them leaned forward even the slightest. John seemed tense and nervous to Martha, perhaps mirroring the edginess she herself was feeling.

John coughed, a bit deeper than earlier in the morning. Stress seemed to make that happen. His face twisted ever so slightly, just enough to reveal the nagging pain deep in his chest. He reached for his pocket again, pulled out a bottle, tugged the cork free, and then took a long swig. He put his handkerchief to his mouth and spit into it. Appearing now somewhat better, and the cough and pain under control for the moment, he prepared himself to tell Martha why they could not at this point in time fulfill her life's dream and be married.

"Martha, you know how much I love you, don't you?" She smiled sweetly, happy for the verbal reaffirmation from John of what she well intuitively knew in her inmost thoughts. "This pains me terribly to say, my darling, but I believe it would be best if we not be married for a few months more."

Tears welled up in Martha's eyes, and she dabbed at them with her dainty little lace kerchief. John could not help but notice that Martha was dejected, but knew that he had to continue with the whole story, for then she would clearly know why he could not marry her now.

"What I am about to tell you must go no farther than this room," he continued sternly. "Not to Aunt Mildred, not to your parents, not to anyone. If the information you are about to learn were to fall into the wrong hands, my life and that of thousands of other sons of the South could be compromised."

"I understand," said Martha in a soft, tinny voice. She was working desperately to keep her emotions in check.

John arose from his chair and paced back and forth across the suite, as he pondered how best to share the details, holding his hands alternately behind his back or tugging at his beard and mustache.

""Martha, soon I must go to Canada – very soon, actually," he finally said. "President Davis himself has directed me to undertake a mission which, if successful, will result in an early end to the war and freedom for our country," he said. "Nothing less than the future of the Confederacy is at stake."

Martha felt numb. "My goodness, that's a lot to take in. I had hoped you would stay here with me till this cursed war is over. But I understand the need to respond to the clarion call of duty." She paused, then continued. "If you must leave, John, couldn't we still have our wedding before you depart?" she offered hopefully.

"I'm afraid I can only stay a few days more. My mission must get underway as soon as possible."

Martha looked crestfallen as she came to grips with the reality that even the thin hope she had that they could be wed before he left would not be realized. She nodded her head, more in silent understanding than in agreement, then let it fall ever so slightly to her chest.

"Martha, my mission is quite simple, and I want you to be aware of why I must leave so soon," he continued. "I will be commanding the Confederate Navy on the Great Lakes."

Martha jerked her head up in astonishment. "But that is all Yankee territory! You won't even be close to any southern states."

John smiled knowingly. He knew Martha was a quick study. That was one of the reasons he had found her so captivating, so compelling a partner. Still, she didn't have enough information yet to grasp the intricacies of the plan. Nor did she have the reason John could not commit to support her for the rest of his life – it just was too risky a venture for him to be able to do that.

"The South doesn't have any sailors that far north, does it?" she continued. "And where will you get the boats?" Martha furrowed her eyebrows tightly, betraying her intense worry.

John bristled slightly at Martha's open and obvious concern about the plan, one that he believed would be the salvation of the South. He took one look at her eyes, though, and knew that his sweetheart's criticism was not directed at the efficacy of the plan. She was a bright girl. She had to suspect that others were also considering all of these questions she was raising out loud and in her own mind. Rather, she was afraid she was going to lose John again. Prison at best. She shuddered to think of the worst possible outcome – that she would lose John forever, much as her Aunt Mildred had lost her own man to the war.

John walked back to the chair next to Martha and sat down. She had buried her head in her hands and was silently sobbing. Gentle waves of curls swept over her face, hiding the tears somewhat that had begun cascading down both cheeks. John leaned over and touched her gently on the shoulder. The feel of her silky soft skin awakened yearnings deep within him that John had not had for a long, long time.

"Martha, look at me," he said gently. She raised her head. Little rivulets of tears streamed down her face. Her eyes were already

110

red from crying. She tried her best to put on a smile, but her lips trembled and tears still flowed freely.

John had never seen her like this before. What should I do? he thought, frantic at the prospect that he had caused so much grief for one whom he loved so much. He took both her hands in his and leaned over to her. He whispered in her ear, "I love you more than life itself. Say the word and I will stay here with you forever."

"Oh, John!" she whimpered. "I love you so much! I can't bear the thought of being parted from you again. Ever," she said emphatically.

Martha stood up and went to the window. She reached through the open window and pulled in the shutters, carefully latching them so that they would not blow open in the breeze.

"What are you doing?" John asked.

Martha extended her hand to John, motioning him to stand up, and said simply, "Kiss me."

Did he dare dream what was about to happen? John stood compliantly, suspecting but not yet willing to admit that Martha was about to change his life forever.

John wrapped his arms around Martha and placed his lips on hers, gently at first, thrilling once again at the touch of his beloved. Martha kissed him back, hard. A primal overwhelming force deep within began to overtake him. He felt his self-control fading with each passing second. He pulled his mouth away from hers and panted, half convincingly, "No, Martha. We can't do this. It's wrong!"

But Martha would not be deterred. She didn't care what people thought. She began undressing John first, starting by removing his jacket and shirt, then moving lower. Somewhere deep inside her soul she also sensed that God would understand that this act of utmost intimacy was the ultimate expression of love between a man and a woman.

* * * * * * *

It had been nearly a week since John and Martha had first made sweet, sweet love in his hotel room. John had asked her to forgive him for breaking his covenant to remain chaste until they were wed. But over time, as his knowledge of her body grew with each succeeding encounter, and as he began to appreciate the fear she had that he might never return, he also rationalized that God would forgive him this indiscretion.

John had already stayed longer than he knew he should. But he cherished this time with Martha so much, it was becoming harder by the day to think about what, in his heart, he knew he must do. He knew that the entire Canadian operation must be organized and undertaken as soon as possible so as to have maximum impact on the upcoming U.S. Presidential election. Reports from the battlefield indicated to even the inexperienced eye that things were going badly for the South. The lifeblood of the South was draining away daily. If the Confederacy were to be saved, this operation must be commenced sooner than later.

In fact, he already felt guilty for not going to Canada immediately after approval of the plan by Secretary Seddon. Then, as now, he was pulled in a classic tug-of-war between love of country and love of a woman.

Since telling Martha this morning he must leave on the afternoon train, she had been in a sullen mood. He had whispered before their first lovemaking that he would stay with her forever, if she asked, and he meant it. Still, Martha had known in her heart that John could not easily keep such a vow, not when so much was at stake, and still be the man of deep principles and convictions that she treasured so much.

And so, she was not surprised when John had asked her concurrence in his decision that he must proceed on with his mission. She had argued feebly that he had already given so much of himself to the conflict. He had nearly been killed at Bolivar Heights, he had nearly been shot after capture on the Chesapeake and then confined in irons to a Yankee prison camp, she reminded him. But, even as much as he loved her, John believed with all his heart that the South's last gasp hope of freedom rested on the success of this operation. And he knew he was the best person, perhaps the only person, to make sure that it was carried out properly. Grudgingly, Martha had agreed, and so she prayed in the morning that God would spare her beloved John just one more time. She would repeat that prayer every day until the war was over and John was safely back in her arms.

As they stood at the tracks, hand in hand, waiting for the arrival of the train to Macon and points north, John stared through the mid-day haze toward the steeple of the church where Martha had believed, and desperately wished, they would be wed. Pure white, the steeple rose to a point topped by a simple cross in a leaden sky. We will be wed in that church some day soon, he hoped, perhaps even as early as this winter.

A distant high-pitched whistle announced the arrival of the train. Thick, gray-white puffs of smoke belched form the stack as the train creaked into the station, grinding to a halt. Few passengers were on this train, as it was headed north and closer to Federal positions.

John and Martha stood on the platform as long as possible, clutching each other's hands tightly. John was wearing his traditional conservative garb. Martha did not feel like this was an occasion for high society fashion. But the simple plaid muslin dress with a pattern of coral and white still looked ravishing on her.

Thunder began to rumble in the distance, and lightening flashed ominously on the horizon, hardly the proper setting for a cheery fare-thee-well.

"All aboard!" the conductor bellowed, and John knew it was time to go. He grabbed his one valise from the platform. But before he boarded, he would have to say good-bye to Martha. He knew she felt they may never see each other again, and it was important for her to know how much she meant to him, and how hard he would try to keep his promise to return to her. He also wanted her memory of this parting to be one she would cherish in her heart forever if the worst happened to him. He had rehearsed this scene in his mind over and over.

"Martha," he said tenderly, "I must be going now."

She began to sob gently.

"Please don't do that," he said, in a feeble effort to keep her from completely breaking down. "I will return to you as soon as possible. God has protected me before, and He will not take me home to Him until He is ready. I know that everything will work out for the best. Just remember how much I love you. And pray for me every day, as I will for you. You will be in my thoughts every waking moment."

He leaned over to her and lifted her chin with his one free hand. He gave her a long, tender kiss. "I love you," he said simply, sweetly, clutching her hand. John then clambered up the three steps into the train. Martha started weeping uncontrollably.

The conductor lifted up the steps as the train lurched its way down the tracks. John leaned over the open half-door of the passageway, thirsting for every second with Martha in his sight.

At first, she stood there, simply sobbing. She hadn't wanted that to happen; she wanted to be strong for him. She momentarily gained control of herself once again. "I love you, John Yates Beall!" she yelled, as loud as her wispy voice could muster.

"I love you too, Martha O'Bryan!" John responded in kind.

Martha started walking down the tracks as the train pulled farther from the station, and then she broke into a trot as it picked up speed. "Please don't go! Please don't go!" she screamed, over and over again, waving her lace kerchief in the air in John's direction as she chased the train down the tracks in an ultimately futile effort to be with him for every possible second.

Tears welled up in John's eyes as he realized how much he loved this woman, and how much his departure was hurting her. It would have been kinder to her to have never met, he thought for a moment. But then he realized how much they both were destined for each other at this moment in time, no matter what the future had in store for either of them. John waived back gamely, pretending not to hear her plaintive cries of despair.

Martha finally had to stop running as she approached the end of the platform. The last car of the train pulled past her.

Seconds later, when the train steamed around the bend, John's last image of Martha was of her futilely chasing the train down the track and sobbing, convinced that she would never see her fiancé, her lover and best friend, alive ever again.

PART II: THE PLAN

"I hereby direct you to proceed at once to Canada, and there to carry out the instructions you have received from me verbally, in furtherance of the interest of the Confederate States of America which have been entrusted to you."

– Letter dated April 27, 1864 from Jefferson Davis to Jacob Thompson, Confederate Commissioner in Canada

9

JUNE 16, 1864
SPRINGFIELD, PENNSYLVANIA

The message was cryptic. Charles Cole held the telegram in his hand. It had been delivered just minutes before to his father's home. The words were written in a flowery scrawl by some clerk in the telegraph office and said simply: "Sales Meeting with Mr. Carrie. 16 June, 4:30 p.m. Rittenhouse Hotel. Your presence appreciated." To a casual reader, the message appeared to be simply an invitation to attend a business meeting. But use of the code name "Carrie" in the telegram was the key that had been agreed upon between him and Major Hook in the Provost Marshal's office before he left Memphis. And there was sufficient innocence to the message that prying eyes would not suspect anything out of the ordinary.

Cole was now flushed with excitement. His special Canadian assignment, and access to the $ 1 million that Richmond was using to front its operation to the north, was about to begin. This enthusiasm for the mission had not come to him immediately. As he mulled over his new assignment on the way back from Memphis, he had been distracted by the risk associated with his role of double agent. And there was also the prospect that, for whatever reason, he may get to Canada and be rejected by the Confederate authorities, cutting off his access to the cash.

Cole still couldn't put out of his mind the very real prospect that, if he played his cards right, he would leave Canada for parts unknown, his pockets flush full of greenbacks. Maybe I'll head out west, he thought. Buy me some land and settle down. Raise cattle, play poker, drink cheap red-eye whiskey all day, and make me some little Coles. Or maybe even better, buy some land cheap and sell it to immigrant settlers who have no idea what kind of God-forsaken country the high plains can be in the summer. Texas, maybe, where the plains go on for eternity and nobody knows, or cares, about your past. And where it's not a sin to have a little fun drinking, or with women, or preferably, both.

Thank God the telegram finally came, he said to himself, closing the door as the messenger left for his next stop. I couldn't have waited much longer, he thought, sighing deeply. The last few weeks he

117

had spent in his father's home had been, at best, less than cordial. And the frigid atmosphere between them had deteriorated in the last few days, despite what Cole thought had been a valiant effort on his part to at least keep things civil between them.

Then, with a start, Cole realized that *today* was the 16th of June, the date of his meeting with his union contact who would give directions for the start of his mission. It was already 10:00 in the morning, and he had just gotten out of bed. He needed to make arrangements, and make them quickly, to travel the dozen or so miles from Springfield to the scheduled appointment at the Rittenhouse Hotel in Philadelphia.

He hastily rolled a cigarette as he pondered the logistical implications of the meeting. He found a match in the little brass decanter on the top of the massive walnut sideboard by the front door, struck it on his heel, and held the flickering orange flame just underneath the cigarette as he drew on it.

In his younger and more innocent days, his father had taken Jamie and him into Philadelphia on a fine spring day, just to show them what a big city looked like. Always one to take the grand road where it was available, Father had taken them to the Rittenhouse to dine. Cole could still picture the grandeur of the dining room, from the multiple crystal chandeliers, sparkling light reflecting off each facet like hundreds of miniature rainbows, to the crisp white linen tablecloth and sparkling silver service.

He smiled dimly as he remembered the better days of his early childhood. Maybe if this deal pans out, he thought, I'll be able to live the high life again soon.

Cole's mind returned to the immediate problems of making it to the city in time for the meeting. He had no funds and no means of transportation. His mother and his father both were gone, although he would have been reluctant to have to try and explain his situation to them anyway.

And then he remembered. Mother always kept a $20 gold pieced tucked away in her bedroom, just so that she would always have money available in an emergency. She was not very creative when it came to seeking hiding places, and from past observations, Cole knew that he would find the money behind the armoire in her bedroom upstairs. He stubbed out his smoldering cigarette on the hall floor and bounded up the stairs to his mother's night chamber, in search of the double eagle that would start him on the first leg of his greatest, and most profitable, adventure.

* * * * * * *

118

Cole tapped his foot impatiently. He had already rapped three times on the door to Room 144, the last time hard and persistently. The front desk clerk downstairs had informed him that, yes, Mr. Carrie was in his room. Cole himself saw that the room key was not in the little pigeonhole behind the clerk, so he knew the clerk had not made a mistake. He pulled his pocket watch from the breast pocket of his waistcoat. The time read exactly 4:30. That was the time set by "Mr. Carrie" for the meeting. Where was the son of a bitch? His ruddy face began to grow red with anger and impatience.

He was just about ready to go back down the hall to the lobby to inquire again regarding the whereabouts of the mysterious Mr. Carrie when a strong baritone voice boomed from behind the door: "Who is it?"

"Mr. Carrie, this is Charles Cole. I'm here for the sales meeting." A well-dressed, middle-aged couple on their way down the hall to the lobby looked inquisitively at Cole, but said nothing as they moved past him. Cole tipped his hat at the lady, smiled graciously, and pretended nothing was out of the ordinary. I hate having to scream from the hallway, he thought.

"Just a moment, please, Mr. Cole," said the disembodied voice. "I'll be with you momentarily."

Cole could hear the seconds pound away in his head. After what seemed an interminable wait, the door opened quickly, so quickly in fact, that it startled him. "I'm Mr. Carrie," the man said. "So glad you could come. Won't you please come in?"

The man Cole believed to be Mr. Carrie stepped back from the door just enough so that he could drink in the ambience. Even from the hallway, Cole could observe that the room was plush. In fact, it was a suite. Directly in front of him, in the middle of the room, a massive round mahogany table was situated. Beams of light from the late afternoon sun filtered through the window beyond and danced on the glassy polish that covered the table. Four equally massive highback chairs were placed equidistant around the table. In the middle of the table, a small but tasteful arrangement of ruby red roses filled a delicately shaped vase.

"I'm terribly sorry," Mr. Carrie said. "I hope I haven't kept you waiting. I was just in the bedroom and didn't hear anyone knock."

"That's quite all right," Cole smiled. He knew that it was important for him to establish a good rapport with this man, and he was not about to tell him that he had been kept waiting in the hall, pounding on the door. "I'd only just arrived. I hope I'm not too late."

Mr. Carrie glanced at the mantle clock on the fireplace to his right. 4:35 it read. "No, you certainly are not too late," he said. Cole had remained standing in the hall, and Mr. Carrie repeated himself, "Won't you please come in?" Cole bowed slightly to indicate his assent and entered the room. He waited as Mr. Carrie closed the door and followed him to the far side of the room, where several sofas and overstuffed chairs had been gracefully arranged about an oval shaped, powder-blue Persian rug. Mr. Carrie extended his arm, inviting his guest to sit in one of the chairs, and then took a place on the sofa opposite him.

Mr. Carrie made an instant impression on Cole, as he did on everyone when they first met him. In fact that was his strong suit: first impressions. He was respectably tall and handsome, square-jawed and with wavy, neatly trimmed hair the color of amber. Deep-set blue eyes highlighted his clean-shaven face. He smelled heavily of perfumed soap, probably rose-scented, and had the floral aroma of a man who spent hours bathing every day. Cole guessed the man must be in his mid-30s. He was certainly not the type of fellow you would associate with being involved in special service. In fact, he looked like a respectable, well-to-do businessman, which is, of course, one of the features that made him so successful.

Carrie crossed his legs gracefully and smiled disarmingly at Cole. It was the kind of smile designed to make a guest feel more at ease, and it was having its effect on Cole, whose stiffly-carried body now relaxed into the plushness of the cushy chair in which he was seated.

"Mr. Cole," Carrie began, "I believe that complete and total openness and trust between business partners is extremely important. And don't let anyone fool you. What we are about to enter into constitutes a business relationship, albeit a very unusual one dictated by the times."

Where is he headed? Cole wondered. What is it he expects of me now? Calm down, he told himself. Everything will be revealed in due time.

"As you know, you have been selected to provide information on the specific plans and extent of the Confederate operation in Canada against the United States Government. It will be dangerous work. Even a single mistake could be fatal."

A cold chill shot down his spine. Cole knew the work would be dangerous, but he chose to focus on the financial windfall associated with the venture, rather than the risks. He stared at the massive oil painting over the fireplace and concentrated on the vibrancy of the purple lilacs, which seemed to explode from the canvas, highlighted in the work.

"You will not know whether the people you come in contact with can be trusted or not. You will be totally on your own. After our meeting today, you may not communicate with me directly, even though you will see me from time to time. Before we go any further, are you prepared to accept that?"

"Yes," Cole said firmly. He opened his mouth to speak again, but Carrie had already started to talk.

"Good, then, let's get down to business," Carrie said. "I believe I can trust you; you have an honest look about you." Good! Cole thought. Now we're getting somewhere!

"First, I believe you should know something about my role here. My real name is not Carrie; it's Hyams. Godfrey J. Hyams. That 'Carrie' name was used because the Provost Marshal did not want my name known to you until we were sure that you would be with us. When we next meet again, it will be in Canada. I will be introduced as the assistant to Jacob Thompson, one of the three Confederate Commissioners to Canada. It is imperative that you not indicate that you have ever seen me before in your life. To do so will result inevitably in our swift and untimely deaths. Is that clear?"

Cole had been taking in everything Carrie, or really Hyams, had been saying. He could hardly believe it. Here was a man who was a Southern gentleman of the highest order, the kind he had grown to despise in the rebel army, who was obviously very highly connected with powerful people in the Confederate establishment. The man's bearing, his manner of dressing, spoke volumes about the man's background. But then why was he betraying everything he represented? Cole considered at first whether he should ask that question, but then thought better of it.

He would never know the answer to his question. In reality, however, Godfrey J. Hyams was a rising, albeit egocentric, star in the rebel realm. He was generally a pretty smooth politician, the kind of good old boy with a flair that Southern men would vote for. At the start of the war, he was serving as mayor of Little Rock, Arkansas.

But Hyams also had been openly critical of some of the prominent Arkansas men appointed to rebel commands, all of whom were political rivals. These men had utilized their own considerable political pull to make sure that, despite his intense courting of military appointment, Hyams was passed over by Richmond. After months of excuses, he deduced the nature of the conspiracy, and at that point decided he would do everything he could to bring down the Confederacy. All that motivated him was revenge, pure and simple.

"Mr. Cole?"

Cole did not realize that he had not responded to Hyams' question. "Oh, yes, I'm sorry. Of course, Mr. Hyams, I understand fully. As far as the Confederate authorities are concerned, I have never met you. But," Cole said, "if you are already on the inside, so to speak, of the Confederate operation, then why do you need me? What could I possibly find out that you would not already know?"

"Excellent question, Mr. Cole. It shows you're the kind of fellow we need." Hyams leaned forward, his face filled with intensity and sincerity. "We need you because Mr. Thompson really doesn't get much into the details. If he doesn't know them, then I don't either. And," Hyams said after pausing momentarily, "we need to know the specifics of the plan, so that lives can be saved."

Cole nodded quietly.

"Now," Hyams said simply, "let us talk about the logistics."

In the back of his mind, Cole wondered when the talk would turn to money. Even though he had grand designs on pilfering as much of the Confederate Canadian bonanza as he could, he could hardly be expected to finance the whole operation out of his own pocket. Especially since his own pocket was nearly empty.

"Mr. Hyams, I don't know if anyone has made you aware of this or not, but I am hardly a wealthy man. I understood Major Hook in Memphis to say that I would be in the Federal employ. And it certainly will take some money to make it to Canada in the first place, as well as…"

"Please, Mr. Cole!" Hyams boomed with a voice like crusty molasses. His face grew a deep scarlet color, and the veins on his neck literally throbbed with anger. Cole was experiencing directly some of the rage that had created enemies behind the scenes for Hyams back in Arkansas. "I am quite aware of the need for adequate financing! I have been authorized, assuming you agree to continue on this mission, to offer you a $200 advance for travel and other initial expenses, plus $100 dollars in gold for each month that you are in our employ. And, of course, that will be in addition to whatever compensation you acquire from the Confederates in Toronto."

Hyams' temper subsided as quickly as it had flared up. Actually, he was glad that Cole had pricked his anger. Now he had a chance to see how the bearded, steely-eyed Charles Cole would respond under pressure. Cole had passed the test with flying colors. He had not flinched so much as an eyelash at Hyams' outburst. In fact, he was still sitting there coolly, apparently unperturbed, although, unknown to Hyams, just beneath his skin Cole's blood was boiling like molten magma pressing way against a fissure in the earth's crust.

"Well, thank you, Mr. Hyams. That is quite generous," said Cole. He was seething inside at the lecturing this snob had given him. But he knew, even before knocking at the door of the man's suite, that he would have to keep his temper under control to ensure continued involvement in the program. And so, he had sat there and listened to Hyams' raving.

"I just wanted to make sure there were no misunderstandings before we got into the details of the operation," Cole said. His voice was nonthreatening, but conveyed just enough steely determination to impress Hyams.

A smile as sweet as a choirboy's crossed Hyams' thin lips. He looked almost cherubic. "Well, then, let's get down to business, " he said, as though the flare-up had never happened.

* * * * * * *

Hyams had invited Cole to dine with him at the Rittenhouse that evening. Cole begged off, citing as his phony excuse a need to return home to take care of his aging mother, which on reflection now seemed incredibly lame. But in fact, Cole was concerned about just one thing. Alcohol. Liquor would certainly be consumed at dinner. And he had to avoid that, at least for now.

The last thing Cole wanted to do, for he had come to know himself well over the last few months, was to allow the drunken Charles Cole to emerge to meet Godfrey J. Hyams. That could have destroyed any chance to make this plan work. The inebriated Charles Cole was hardly the kind of man to whom any government would entrust anything. Charles Cole the sot was, at best, a bullying oaf. And at worst . . . . Well, best not to think about that.

Oh yes, Cole now knew himself well. He smiled inwardly at how he had managed to present exactly the right picture at exactly the right time. He would have a drink when he got home, though. Just a small one. To celebrate.

The sun was melting into the horizon in front of him as he headed the rented carriage down the Springfield Road. The air was alive with chirping crickets, barking dogs and high-pitched squeals of playing children. These noises of early summer wafting on the gentle June breezes were interrupted only by the steady clomp-clomp of the old chestnut mare's hooves and her occasional snorting as she struggled against the occasional inclines in the road.

Into this idyllic setting Cole rode. If he had not just come from this meeting with Hyams, the war would be the furthest thing from his mind. But he had met with Hyams. And Hyams had given him plenty to think about.

He would have to pack immediately and head to Canada. Just as well, though, he thought. He had grown weary of even being in the same room as his father. God, how he hated that man. The time he had spent in his parents' house had reinvigorated within him the motivation to get out, once and for all. In fact, if it hadn't been for the fact that Major Hook had ordered him to wait there for further instructions, he would have left long ago.

Holding the reins gently in his right hand, Cole reached into his pants pocket and retrieved the gold Hyams had advanced him for the trip north. The gold pieces glinted in the palm of his hand, reflecting the rays of the setting sun. It wasn't as much as he would like, at least compared with what he expected to milk out of the Confederate Canadian operation later on, but it was one helluva good start.

Hyams promised him that $50 would be transferred to an account in his name upon receipt of each of his biweekly reports, to be mailed to a post office box in Washington. And this was in addition to anything the Confederates paid him. Yes, things were definitely starting to look better.

And who is this Vallandigham fellow anyway that Hyams was telling him to meet? Cole wondered. Hyams had said Clement Vallandigham was a good friend of Commissioner Jacob Thompson in Toronto; a recommendation from him would grease things considerably. Helluva good politician, too. But he doesn't know squat about anything related to military affairs.

Just tell Vallandigham you're an escaped rebel prisoner from Johnson's Island who rode with Forrest, Hyams had said. Tell him you want to free your buddies or do anything to fight the Yankees. He'll give you a glowing recommendation on to Thompson. And then you're set, Hyams had told him. Hyams had given Charles enough information about General Forrest's exploits and the situation at the prison camp for rebel officers at Johnson's Island in Lake Erie so that he could tell a believable story. But no one would check anyway. That was one of the flaws of the Confederate operation, Hyams had said. Too sloppy, or too stupid; didn't really matter which one.

Yes, this was going to be a piece of cake. Just a few months of this and I'll be set for life, Cole mused. That would show his old man. Yes, indeed, it would. The magnitude of the total change in direction of his life was nothing short of amazing, Cole thought. The prospects for the future excited him, and he was anxious to get on with it.

"Giddap!" he cried to the old mare as he snapped the reins. She snorted and snapped her head back, but plodded on down the road at the same pace, not nearly in as much of a hurry as the young man sitting in the surrey behind her.

Cole sighed deeply. "Goddamned old nag! If you were mine, you'd be headed for the glue factory yet tonight!" But the swaybacked mare ignored the harsh tone of the ranting behind her, leaving Cole muttering in frustration.

10

JULY 1864
WINDSOR, CANADA WEST

The room was sweltering. The thin wisp of a late afternoon breeze trickled through the open window, causing the lace curtains to dance occasionally in the breeze. But the air bore so much humidity that it provided scant relief. A steady stream of perspiration rolled down the young man's forehead into a thick orangish forest of beard, where it disappeared.

John Wilson Murray already had sat at this window for hours today, as he had done for the better part of the last few weeks. He was prepared to venture out to follow the short man with a black beard and a bowler when he left the residence of Clement Vallandigham, former United States Congressman from Ohio, Copperhead leader, and Confederate sympathizer in exile. The Vallandigham house was located conveniently just across the quiet residential street from his observation perch.

Murray shifted his weight in the hard wooden chair, then wiped his sleeve across his sweaty brow. He recognized this behavior as a sign of boredom. Even for a veteran of the tedium of long sea voyages, this watching and waiting taxed his endurance. Over the years since he left his home in Edinburgh as a teenager to answer the siren call of the sea, he had learned that patience was a virtue. One that few men ever acquired. Except him.

Actually, as he thought about it, Murray's instructions from his captain were simple. Observe Vallandigham's house, and await Charles Cole's arrival. Then follow Cole and watch for any signs that might indicate betrayal. He had been given a good physical description of Cole, and he had been easy to spot. He wasn't sure why he, of all people, had been selected for this task, or why Captain Carter himself had assumed responsibility for keeping an eye on Cole. When he had asked Carter, in command of the U.S.S. *Michigan,* the captain was mum. Except to say that sources within the rebel organization itself suspected that Cole was planning some mischief involving his ship.

Yesterday, soon after Cole had strolled up to the wide oaken door of the Vallandigham residence in exile, and pulled on the brass lion's head knocker, Murray donned his natty brown frock coat, the color of chocolate, and waited just inside the doorway of the guesthouse where he was staying. He waited for Cole to leave, so that he could follow him and learn where he was staying, and perhaps be able to observe Cole's traits for signs of incipient personality and character flaws.

He had already learned a lot about Cole. Being a seaman of some experience, Murray knew about the temptations of alcohol and women. Both could betray you as easily as both could attract you. Alcohol relaxed your guard and loosened your lips. And to women also, it seemed, much was said that shouldn't be.

As he sat the previous night in a corner of a tiny tavern slowly sipping a beer, it became obvious to Murray that Cole could not be trusted. Cole swilled down one shooter of whiskey after another. He became increasingly tempestuous, with whitecaps of anger boiling inside of him, threatening to overpower all other emotions. Cole had damned near gotten himself killed, too, when he put his hand, uninvited, on the quite bountiful breast of a young stevedore's girlfriend. Only the quick intervention of the tavern owner, concerned about damage to his establishment from another all too frequent brawl between drunken seamen, had saved Cole from serious bodily harm.

In the tavern, Murray had overheard Cole bragging through an alcoholic haze that he was a good friend of Vallandigham, and that he was going to have lunch with him again on the morrow. And Cole had been true to his word. Promptly at 12:30, a rejuvenated Charles Cole sharply rapped on the knocker at the Vallandigham residence, and was promptly ushered inside.

Now, some five hours later, Murray sat numbly at the window of his boarding house entranceway, still watching and waiting. He had learned yesterday that there was no need to be in a hurry; the hours he stood downstairs waiting for Cole had seemed to be interminable. And then when Cole finally did leave the Vallandigham residence, he sauntered down the street at a leisurely pace, apparently oblivious to everything going on around him.

Sounds of laughter caught Murray's attention, reactivating his senses. The frivolity was coming from two men in the doorway of Vallandigham's residence. He recognized one of them; the short, moderately rotund body with the black beard and the bowler hat, perched jauntily to one side. Cole.

The other man was middle-aged, tall and distinguished looking. His face was clean shaved, except for a well-groomed growth of facial hair that followed his jaw line from ear to ear. The man carried himself with the bearing of someone who perceived himself to be a great and noble leader. Even from this distance, Murray could observe his deep-set eyes; they conveyed an intensity of purpose. Murray had not seen the man before, but suspected it was Clement Vallandigham himself.

Murray felt the tension inside himself mount as he observed the two men, chatting amiably, walk down the street in the general direction of the city center. Obviously under the influence of the older man, the two moved at a brisk pace. Cole was picking up his stubby little legs as fast as he could, struggling to keep up with his taller and older companion. Murray knew he would have to hurry, or the two men would be gone before he even had a chance to get behind them.

Quickly tugging his frock coat off the back of the chair with one hand, Murray grabbed his cravat from the bed behind him with the other. He pulled the coat on and struggled with the cravat as he hurried out the door and down the stairs. Murray sensed something important was about to transpire. He couldn't lose Cole now.

* * * * * * *

John Murray was proud of himself for the manner in which he had avoided detection as he tailed the two men for blocks down the street. This was no easy task for a broad-shouldered man towering over people at 6 feet 4 inches, with orangish-red hair and a full beard. But Cole and the other man had been so engrossed in their own conversation that they paid little attention to the massive red-bearded hulk following just a half-block behind them. When the two men reached the Hyrons Hotel, Murray lingered just a moment, peering at the display in an adjacent men's clothing store window, before strolling on in behind his targets.

The Hyrons Hotel dining room was well into serving the first seating of the evening when Cole and his companion arrived. The lobby of the genteel hotel was quiet. No ungentlemanly behavior was allowed under any circumstances, in true English fashion.

Cole and his dinner companion were already conversing with the head waiter, a hunched over, shriveled prune of a man, when Murray pushed his way through the heavy oak and brass door and entered the lobby. It was not difficult for Murray to overhear their conversation as he lingered nearby, checking his pocket watch for the arrival time of a nonexistent companion. Murray's acute senses of sight and hearing had been among the factors that led to his being detailed to this special duty.

"Is there any way that we can be seated now?" Cole's companion asked politely, with increasing insistence in his voice.

"I'm quite sorry, sir," the old waiter sniffed in his best English snobbishness. "Service has already commenced for the 5:30 seating. I am afraid that it is impossible to accommodate you gentlemen until the next seating."

Murray was close enough to the two men to observe the little veins on the back of Cole's neck start to pop out. His skin was turning as red as a well-pickled Harvard beet. Before he could explode a verbal cannonade all over the waiter, the other man firmly but gently grasped Cole's arm. The touch had a hypnotic effect on Cole, and his body noticeably relaxed.

Sighing deeply, the other man said, "Very well, then. When is your next seating?"

"Seven o'clock, sir," the waiter croaked.

"That will do. We would like dinner reservations for your next seating."

The waiter went to a delicately carved oak table, with filigreed grape vines etched into the legs, just beside the entrance to the dining room, removed the fountain pen from the inkwell and proceeded to write.

"Let's see. Party of two. Seven o'clock. Yes, that will be fine. May I have your name please, sir?" the shriveled up old waiter intoned in a nasal voice.

"Vallandigham.   V-A-L-L-A-N-D-I-G-H-A-M.   Clement Vallandigham."

As the old waiter struggled to write down the long and complicated name, Clement Vallandigham and Charles Cole proceeded across the lobby to the hotel bar, where they obviously intended to pass the next hour or so before dinner. Neither cast an eye in the direction of the tall, bearded man with the orangish-red hair standing in silence just a few feet away from them.

* * * * * * *

Murray decided it would be better if he not make himself too conspicuous, even though he was dying to hear what in the world the famous Clement Vallandigham could be discussing with the stubby alcoholic with the hot temper. Of course, he knew that Cole would be checking in with Vallandigham, perhaps even getting instructions from whatever mission he was on, and the like.

But Murray had to admit to himself that he was more than a little surprised last night in the tavern when Cole announced to the world that he was going to see Vallandigham again. And as he pondered how the day had gone, he had to admit that he also was

130

puzzled by how long Cole had stayed inside Vallandigham's house this afternoon. What in the world could they have been talking about that would take that long? And now, here was Charles Cole, having drinks and dinner with the best-known rebel sympathizer in North America.

Murray easily made a reservation for the 7:00 dinner seating. He also managed to make arrangements with the waiter to be seated at a table adjacent to the one where Cole and Vallandigham would be escorted. Unlike the two Americans he was now following, however, he knew how to get his way with the crusty old English codger. A yarn from his repertoire of tall tales of the sea as a British sailor, and a few shillings discreetly slipped into the old man's palm, had assured that John Wilson Murray would accomplish his objective.

Murray bought a newspaper and sat on one of the plush sofas in the lobby, just off the dining room, to while away the next hour. He waited until after Vallandigham and Cole had been called for their seating before strolling toward the front of the dining room to await his turn to be seated.

He listened carefully during most of the evening meal, but only observed the usual pleasantries being exchanged between Cole and Vallandigham, until the dinner was winding down.

"Mr. Vallandigham, I must say that I believe the time you have spent in assisting me will be of great benefit to our cause," Murray heard Charles Cole say between mouthfuls of lemon pie.

"Thank you very much, Mr. Cole," responded Vallandigham. He sipped on his cup of coffee, waiting courteously until Cole was finished with his meal before lighting up his after-dinner cigar.

As Cole pushed away the plate, Vallandigham continued after igniting the stogie. "The men in Toronto to which I am referring you can assist you greatly. I must admit, though, that when you first showed up yesterday on my doorstep unannounced, I was more than a little concerned about just how much information to share with you."

Vallandigham took a long drag on the cigar, and paused, pensive, before continuing. "But your description of the abominable, criminal conditions of the prison camp on Johnson's Island – a topic with which I am more than a little familiar as an Ohioan – confirms everything I have heard about that abysmal hell hole."

"I certainly understand your apprehension, Congressman." Cole smiled inwardly as he remembered how Hyams had instructed him to play to Vallandigham's ego. It was working. Vallandigham puffed out his chest at the mention of the word "Congressman" like an old Rhode Island Red rooster parading around the barnyard.

"But I knew you were the only person who could help me," he continued. "Why even before I made my escape from Johnson's Island, it was common knowledge around the camp that you would help escaped Southern officers either make their way back home or to operations against the Yankees."

"You know," Cole said, leaning forward over the table toward Vallandigham, "I would be willing to do just about ANYTHING to give back to those damned Yankees some of what they dished out to me." Cole's tone got considerably more angry. "The bastards! The colonel's dog lived better than we did!" Cole pounded the table with his fist for effect. Vallandigham was impressed with the vigor of Cole's expression, for it conveyed to him a certain comfort level in what he was about to do.

"Mr. Cole, I am confident that you will have every opportunity to rectify the situation," said Vallandigham.

Murray noticed that the tone of the self-assured man's voice had taken on an air of modesty. Murray chuckled to himself. How easily people can be persuaded to do things they would not otherwise be inclined to do through nothing more than simple flattery, he thought.

"As we discussed this afternoon, I believe there may be a place for you in the office of Jacob Thompson, one of the Confederate Commissioners to Canada. Commissioner Thompson is a personal friend of mine of long standing. We go back a long way, to the time when we served in the Congress together. I will leave it to Mr. Thompson, of course, to determine what he has in mind for you."

"Of course," Cole responded forcefully. "I have no doubt that Mr. Thompson will be every bit as helpful as you have been."

"You should make your way to Toronto as soon as possible, Mr. Cole," said Vallandigham. "Commissioner Thompson is in immediate need of good men."

Vallandigham took another sip from his coffee. "Stop by my residence at 8:00 a.m. tomorrow morning," he said, putting the cup back in the saucer with just the tiniest of a jiggle, "and I will have a letter of introduction for you to present to Commissioner Thompson. There's a train to Toronto later in the morning. You should be on it." Vallandigham took another drag on his cigar, and then flicked the dead embers on the end onto the floor.

Cole's eyes shifted toward the floor. "I'm sorry, sir, but I, well. . ."

Vallandigham knew exactly what Cole was trying to say. "I understand, Mr. Cole. I will advance you the cost of the train ticket to

Toronto." Vallandigham clasped his hand over Cole's as if to seal the deal.

Murray smiled at Cole's ruse. Pretty convincing, he thought. If Vallandigham only knew that Cole had enough money to go on a drinking binge last night, he might want to reconsider his offer.

"Thank you, again, Congressman," said Cole. "You have no idea how much I appreciate this."

Cole and Vallandigham pushed back their chairs and removed the linen napkins from their laps. As they made their way to the front door of the hotel, John Murray's eyes followed, making sure they both left before leaving the hotel himself. No need to follow them; Murray knew everything he had to. It would take him very little time to get ready to follow his quarry. Just pack and get down to the train station in time to purchase a ticket on the 10:00 train to Toronto. But first he had a few administrative items to attend to.

* * * * * * *

The telegraph office remained open day and night. This was a particularly slow evening, though, and the young clerk had dozed off in his swivel chair. It had been a long day and there was only one hour to go before the shift change at 10 o'clock.

"Young man," said the deep bass voice, with just a tinge of Scottish brogue. The voice was not too loud, but just loud enough to awaken the clerk from his dreamy slumber.

The clerk awoke with a start, as his eyes focused on the huge man with bright orange beard and curly red hair standing over him. He jolted backward, the hard wooden wheels digging into his side as he fell.

John Murray threw back his head and laughed at the sight of the boyish wisp of a clerk sprawled on the floor. The clerk wanted to do something horrible to his protagonist, but thought better of it as he sized up the massive hulk of a man.

"Here, let me help you up," Murray said, still chuckling over the sight of the young clerk. He extended his beefy right hand, effortlessly hoisting up the boy from the floor into an upright position. The clerk adjusted his cravat and eyeshade, cleared his throat, and squeaked "Thank you." There was really nothing more that he could say, without risking an insult to this customer, and possibly imminent bodily harm to himself.

Murray walked back around to the customer side of the counter. "I have a wire I would like to send," said Murray. He removed a carefully folded piece of paper from his inside breast pocket and handed it across the counter to the clerk. "It is most important that it go out immediately."

"Certainly sir," the boy said. Some of the squeakiness had gone out of his voice as his pulse returned to close to normal, but he still was not quite sure what to make of this unusual man. He counted up the number of words, and made a notation on his ledger of the charge.

"I'll need to read it before you leave, sir. To make sure that I have read your message correctly."

"I really don't believe there should be a problem. But of course I'll wait."

Picking up the paper on which Murray had written the message he wanted sent, the clerk noticed that his customer was probably correct. The handwriting was smooth and flowing; it would not be a problem to decipher. Still, he better make sure. The message read:

> *Jno. C. Carter*
> *Commander, U.S. Steamer Michigan*
> *Buffalo, New York*
>
> *C. met with V. En route to Toronto tomorrow. Appears C. may be involved with Johnson's Island. C. not to be trusted. Am following to Toronto. Will wire you from there with further reports. Please advance funds as discussed.*
>
> *J.W. Murray*

The clerk nodded his head as he finished reading the message. Yes, quite clear, he said. The red-bearded Goliath of a man paid for the wire and left, still chuckling as he remembered again the clerk lying sprawled on the floor.

* * * * * * *

**Aboard the U.S.S. *Michigan*
Buffalo, New York**

Commander Jack Carter, United States Navy, had already taken breakfast in his cabin, as was his custom. The *Michigan* was tied up at the pier so that prospective recruits could be given a tour of the ship. Carter hated this duty; it was unfathomable to him that a sea captain with his thirty-odd years of experience would be reduced to being a glorified tour guide. He sighed, knowing that, indeed, his involvement in the war effort would be reduced to that unless something dramatic happened. He had recently come to believe that such a turn of events now was frankly possible.

Carter had returned to his review of the list of new recruits from this Buffalo trip when a knock came at the door.

Ensign James Hunter, officer of the watch and one of Carter's most trusted subordinates, entered, and saluted crisply.

Carter returned the salute. "At ease," the commander said softly. Hunter relaxed and assumed a more casual pose.

"Telegram just arrived, sir," Hunter said, placing the distinctive Western Union envelope on the captain's desk. "It's from Mr. Murray."

Carter pulled open his upper desk drawer, and retrieved his reading glasses. He hated to wear the damned things, but recognized that diminished vision was to be expected when you hit your 50s. "Wait just a moment, Mr. Hunter, while I see what Mr. Murray has to say."

Ensign John Wilson Murray had been detailed to tail Charles Cole as soon as Carter had been informed in a wire from his old friend in the Memphis provost marshal's office, Major Frank Hook, that Cole would be involved with the rebel plotters. Theoretically, at least, Cole was to be a Union agent. But, of course, you could never be too sure with someone like Charles Cole.

Commander Carter read the wire quickly, and then re-read it, just to make sure he had grasped it correctly the first time. Yes, their suspicions appeared to be well founded. Thank God he had Murray on the scene to keep an eye on Cole. He congratulated himself. Pretty good for a washed-up old salt pulled out of retirement, he thought, to be keeping up with all this spying nonsense.

Carter removed the reading glasses, and placed them gently on the table. "Just as I suspected, Mr. Hunter. Prepare to sail," Carter ordered. "We're going to Johnson's Island."

"Very well, sir!" Hunter barked. He stepped backwards out of Carter's quarters, closing the door gently behind him. He bolted up the stairs to make immediate preparations to get up a head of steam. Within a few hours, they would be sailing up Lake Erie to Sandusky Bay. There, nearly 3000 rebel officers, the cream of the Confederate military crop, languished in the Johnson's Island prison camp, a mere twenty miles from Canada and potential freedom.

11

JULY 1864
TORONTO, CANADA WEST

The massive limestone façade of the Queen's Hotel glistened, jasper-like, in the crisp morning sunlight. A gentle breeze off Lake Ontario barely ruffled the three immense red, white and blue Union Jack flags fluttering over the hotel entrance as Charles Cole made his way through the front door. A bellman in a snappy, military-style uniform, complete with gold epaulets and matching braid, bowed ever so slightly and opened the door for Cole to enter the regal hostelry.

Looking back over his shoulder as he headed toward the grand staircase, even Cole was overcome by the beauty of the view. He had never been a sentimental type of fellow. Still, it was impossible to overlook the charm of the city. Large gray and white gulls circled over the emerald-green water of the lake, occasionally diving to pick up pieces of bread cast by romantics strolling arm in arm along the pier. Fishing boats that docked there at night were gone, of course, but colorful small skiffs and sailboats filled the horizon. It was an idyllic scene.

Cole shook off the growing pleasurable feelings caused by the delightful view. He was here on business. Although he was more comfortable than when he had first been ushered two weeks ago into the presence of Jacob Thompson, the Chief of the Confederate Mission and the South's man-in-charge of special assignments out of Canada against the North, he knew that he was still walking on thin ice.

True, Thompson had been considerably impressed by the glowing recommendation that Cole had cajoled out of Thompson's old friend, Clement Vallandigham. So impressed, in fact, that Cole was immediately handed the assignment of surveying the defenses of Union cities on the Great Lakes. Thompson was very demanding, and Cole knew that if he was not satisfied with his report, he might as well plan to beat a hasty retreat back across the border, tail tucked between his legs and missing out on the opportunity to rake in some of that Confederate gold.

It was to present his report on the Great Lakes survey project given him by Thompson that Cole had returned to Confederate Headquarters at the Queen's Hotel. Before heading up the red-carpeted stairs to the Confederate Mission's suite of offices and living quarters on the second floor, Cole stopped at a mirror. He needed to look his best. He agreed with one thing his father, with whom he seldom saw eye to eye, had told him as a young man. Appearance is important. Which is probably why Cole had not cared much before about how he looked. To rebel against his father. But those days were behind him now.

He adjusted his bowler hat, tilting it jauntily to the side so that it had just enough of an appearance of sophistication to be noticed. He adjusted his cravat, making sure the bows of shiny black silk were of equal length, and then brushed his hand lightly over his beard as he leaned closer to the gigantic gilded mirror that graced the front hall. This would be the wrong time, he felt, to leave part of his breakfast in his thick black beard, where it would surely be noticed.

When Cole reached the Confederate offices, he was ushered immediately into Jacob Thompson's personal office. He removed his black bowler, setting it carefully on the edge of the short, oval-shaped, onyx-colored table that occupied the space between two large sofas in front of the marble fireplace. Cole chose not to be seated, and stood behind the farthest sofa, by the window. He now allowed himself the luxury of once again drinking in the dreamy tranquil scene on the lake below, his arms clasped loosely behind his back. He had only been standing for what seemed like a few seconds when Jacob Thompson entered the room.

In some respects, Thompson was an impressive looking man. Tall and broad-shouldered, his presence filled the room. But the rest of his physical appearance was not quite so impressive. There was a certain angry scowl to his face, and he appeared to be perpetually frowning. He also seemed to be a man very much in a hurry. His frock coat was rumpled, and there was a little grease spot on his white shirt, probably from the morning's breakfast. His hair had a wind-blown, unruly sort of look. Both eyes were bloodshot and tears welled in them regularly. The tears were a function, Thompson had told Cole when they first met, of his allergies.

But Cole's initial impressions of quirkiness vanished as soon as Thompson opened his mouth.

"Charles, Charles, how good to see you again!" Thompson boomed, grabbing Cole's right hand in both of his bear paw-like hands, pumping furiously. "It surely is a lovely day outside, don't you think? I know a young man like you could certainly think of plenty of other more interesting things to do on a day like today," he said with a wink. "Why, even an old man like me can."

138

Cole wondered just what Thompson meant by the term "old man." Although Thompson was definitely older than he was, probably in his mid-fifties judging by his appearance, he certainly wasn't that old. But there was little opportunity for Cole to interject his remarks on this subject. Chugging along like a train coasting downhill, Thompson kept up the nonstop chatter.

"Well, then, let's get down to business," Thompson continued, "so you'll have a chance to enjoy this splendid day." Thompson led Cole by the arm to one of the two huge sofas that faced each other in front of the fireplace, by the table where Cole had left his hat. Draped above the fireplace was a gigantic Stars and Bars, complete with gold fringe on all sides. Large paintings of Jefferson Davis and Robert E. Lee, living icons of the Confederacy, hung on either side of the rebel flag. There was no mistaking that this room was the epicenter of Confederate operations in Canada.

"So, what have you found out?" Thompson queried.

"Quite simply, sir, the Union has pretty much ignored the defenses of its cities on the Great Lakes."

As Charles Cole began his report on the task given him by the Confederate Commissioner two weeks earlier, Thompson abruptly abandoned his ebullient politico mannerisms and was well into the serious role of high-ranking Confederate official.

There were few men in the South more dedicated to the rebel cause than Jacob Thompson. That is precisely why Jeff Davis had given him this most important assignment, as Chief of the Confederate Mission to Canada. Even partial success could turn the upcoming election in the North away from that diehard Lincoln in favor of a more conciliatory Peace Democrat. $1 million of increasingly scarce greenbacks from the Confederate Treasury, safely deposited by Thompson in a Canadian bank to fund all of these schemes and machinations, admittedly helped expand Thompson's already expansive attitude concerning aggressive action against the North.

"What makes you say that, son?" Thompson asked, his face now riveted intently on every word Cole was to say.

"Sir, perhaps I should describe how I carried out the task you assigned to me a couple of weeks ago, when you asked me to research the defensive capabilities of the Union's Great Lakes ports. Then I believe it will be a little clearer why I have come to the conclusion that I just presented to you."

"Go on, Charles."

"I decided that the best way to learn what you asked of me was to see it with my own eyes. I know you said you were interested in just getting a general picture, which could be obtained through judicious use of publicly available information in the library and such. But, from my own experience, such information is filled with inaccuracies. So I took the train to the major cities – all the way to Chicago, in which you said you had a special interest. I checked out the port and defensive capabilities myself first-hand."

Thompson was impressed with the initiative Cole appeared to have taken. In the two weeks since he had assigned him this task, which was admittedly a dry run to see what he was capable of, Thompson had heard nothing from Cole. Absolutely nothing. Thompson thought at first he had another slick-talking, do-nothing sycophant on his hands. It appeared he had guessed wrong.

"I've written a full report for you, Commissioner, with all the salient details," Cole said. He reached into his pocket and pulled out a buff-colored envelope stamped with red sealing wax. The envelope barely had a three-dimensional look to it. Thompson guessed three or four pages were inside.

Cole gently slid the envelope across the table to the Commissioner. "Thank you," Thompson said. He removed a handkerchief from his trousers and dabbed at the corners of both bloodshot eyes. "Damned allergies!" he muttered under his breath. After replacing the handkerchief, Thompson pulled a pair of half-glasses from his inside breast pocket and tucked each wire rim carefully behind the appropriate ear before he commenced reading.

While Thompson read the report, Cole labored to hide his nervousness. Thompson was obviously reading for detail. It seemed to Cole like ages before Thompson gently laid the report down in front of him on the table. A smile stretched across Thompson's face. He had obviously liked what he had read.

"Charles, this is excellent!" Thompson gushed effusively. "I wonder, would you mind sharing your report with some of my staff this afternoon? I believe there will be a lot of interest, and I would like to give them the opportunity to ask whatever questions they may have. I also have some ideas about other projects in which I believe you can serve the South. There might be some danger. Would that particularly trouble you?"

Cole grudgingly knew he had ridden this horse this far. It was hardly the time to get cold feet, even though so far he had managed to repress the thought of danger. The overriding interest in getting his hands on some of the Confederate money had been effective in that effort. And, of course, if he got caught in any inescapable danger, he

140

could always flip back to the Union side, although their measly $50 every other week was hardly what he had counted on.

"If there is anything, sir," Cole finally said, "ANYTHING at all I can do to assist I would be most honored. Although, naturally, my main interest is in working to free our men from that miserable hell hole on Johnson's Island."

"Excellent, Charles."

Thompson leaned back in his chair, self-satisfied, his hands clasped together across his chest. He peered out the window toward the lake for just the briefest of moments. His thoughts collected, he said, "Can you meet with us at 2:00 this afternoon?"

"Yes, indeed."

"Good, I'll look forward to seeing you at 2:00. You can enjoy the rest of this beautiful morning anyway." Thompson winked one weepy, bloodshot eye at Cole, and then escorted him to the anteroom. As they entered the room, Thompson's personal secretary, Walter Cleary, was engaged in an earnest conversation with a thirtyish man with a short Van Dyke beard, thinning brownish hair and light, steel-blue eyes. Dressed in black, the man appeared to Cole to resemble an undertaker, or perhaps a banker, more than anything else.

Cleary broke off his discussion as soon as he noticed his boss. "Captain Beall is here for his appointment, Commissioner," he said, motioning toward the man with which he had been so intently engaged in conversation.

"I'll be with you in just a moment, Captain," Thompson said to his somber-looking visitor. What kind of first impression was this man making, Cole wondered. "Mr. Cleary, could you see if you can arrange accommodations here this evening for Mr. Cole? That is all right with you, isn't it, Charles?"

"That's very kind of you, sir. Yes, that's fine." Cole grumbled to himself at the thought of trudging back to pick up his valise from the boarding house he had checked into last night. It will be better accommodations, though, he rationalized.

On his way out the door, Cole noticed that the man Walter Cleary had called "Beall" received, somewhat awkwardly, the same ebullient greeting from Thompson that he had received earlier on his arrival. Strange man, this Thompson, strange man. But he does control the purse strings, he thought. Shaking his head, Cole headed to the lobby to inspect the bar, just for a moment, of course, before heading to pick up his bag from the boarding house.

* * * * * * *

"John, my boy! How are you? I heard all about your exploits on the Chesapeake before I left Richmond to sail up here. Way to give those damned Yankees hell! I knew you had the ability to lead and inspire men the first time I set eyes on you down at Runnymede. Do you remember that time?" Thompson put his arm around John Yates Beall's shoulder as he ushered him into his office.

"I certainly do, Commissioner," John responded. Those days in Pascagoula, when he first met and then fell in love with Martha, were as clear in his mind as the moment they happened.

The thought of Martha brought back that bittersweet feeling he always had when something, anything at all really, triggered a remembrance of his fiancée. This was even more true over the last month, as he made his way ever northward to Canada, crossing from Virginia into Union territory.

As he travelled ever closer to Toronto, he knew that with every passing mile he was moving farther and farther away from Georgia and his Martha. He shook off the thought; there was nothing he could do now to change the course he was following. He could only trust in God Almighty and apply his best efforts to do what he could to end the war as soon as possible. Then he and Martha would have that wedding in the little white church. And in grand fashion, too.

Thompson reached for his humidor and pipe, but then remembered John's lung injury, and sat down on the sofa opposite without the tobacco. He could tolerate tobacco better himself when not being bothered as much as he was now by his allergies. His eyes were itching so much now that it was just barely tolerable.

Thompson mentally sized up John, and thought he looked pretty good, especially considering he'd spent the last winter in a Yankee prison camp.

"Walter gave me the letter that you brought in for me to read yesterday," Thompson said, running a hand through his hair. "As you are very much aware, I too am familiar with the general instructions given to you by President Davis and the Confederate Congress to develop a Confederate Navy presence on the Great Lakes. And, considering your past experiences on the Chesapeake, I must say, I think you're on to something with your proposal to run a privateering operation out on Lake Huron. It would be months before the Yankees were able to get anybody up there to go after you."

An awkward silence filled the room, as John waited to hear Thompson's response to his proposal. From his inside breast pocket, Thompson pulled John's proposal letter. He unfolded it and skimmed it briefly before continuing.

"And I agree with your analysis," the Commissioner said, "that it would have a tremendous impact on morale and could be the final straw that brings down the Lincoln presidency. Of course, we all want that more than anything. That damned railsplitter is so intractable, he won't negotiate at all. He and his abolitionist cabinet will accept nothing less than complete and total capitulation of the South. That is something he will NEVER get!" The thought of Lincoln's insistence on restoring the Union and the flagging Confederate prospects had elevated Thompson's decibel level and his face turned a brilliant shade of violet.

Thompson rose from the sofa, walked over and stood in front of the fireplace, his arms crossed. So far, John had said nothing. Thompson provided little opportunity for him to interject himself into the conversation. And he certainly agreed with everything Thompson had said. No disagreement there, no sir, none whatsoever.

Turning to John, Thompson beckoned him to come stand beside him. John got off the sofa, and walked over to Thompson. "See that out there?" Thompson said, taking John by the arm and pointing in the direction of the azure blue waters of Lake Ontario, stretching into a milky white haze on the horizon.

"Yes sir, I do. That's Lake Ontario, I believe."

"Correct. And not more than 40 miles on the other side of that lake is the vulnerable, unprotected underbelly of the enemy. Besides the expanse of water, do you know what else stands between us and the Yankees' rear?" Without giving John a chance to answer, Thompson said, "Absolutely nothing. Nothing, that is, except for one little thing."

"What's that, sir?" John was curious. Where was Thompson taking this conversation?

"The U.S.S. *Michigan*. Only Union warship on the Great Lakes. The only one the Yankees will ever be able to have on the Lakes. To get another here, they'd have to sail up the Saint Lawrence, through Lake Ontario and then take the Welland Canal around Niagara Falls. The British will never let the Yankees sail one more armed warship, let alone a flotilla, through Canada like that. You know what that means John?"

John knew perfectly well what that meant. "It means, sir, if the *Michigan* can be taken or captured, then the South can control the Great Lakes and the Union rear from Canada," he said. "If we had our own warship, of course."

Thompson nodded. "Of course," he said. "We're working on that right now. But first, we have to put together a plan, and a special team of trustworthy, competent, fearless men to take over the *Michigan.* Sound like something you might be interested in?"

Jake Thompson knew perfectly well that John would be interested. The privateer idea was a sound one, and John certainly was no novice to the enterprise. But the *Michigan* plan was one hell of a lot more important. And with winter coming on early that far north, the Lake Huron option had little time to be put into effect.

"I think it's a splendid idea, sir," John said. "But there's just one small problem. Both President Davis and War Secretary Seddon gave me verbal orders to report to you regarding the Lake Huron idea. We hadn't discussed doing anything else, and I certainly don't want them to believe I have disregarded their orders."

"Don't you worry about that, John. I'll take care of that. And starting right now, I'm modifying the orders you received in Richmond," Thompson said. "As Chief of the Confederate Mission to Canada, I have that authority. This is all contingent, of course, on your agreeing to assist us in our plan to take the *Michigan.* So what do you say?"

The idea had only been broached within the last few minutes. Yet John's mind was whizzing with possibilities. Think of it! Capturing the only United States warship on the Great Lakes! That would bring the war to an early end, that's for sure. The population of the lake cities would be in a state of panic, all across the enemy's rear flanks. A few well-placed shots from one of the ship's cannons into Yankee lake transports wouldn't hurt the cause, either. He was getting more excited by the second.

John finally relaxed. He always seemed to be more cool and calm when he had the admiration and support of his superiors. And Thompson was asking him to be responsible for no small feat. Yes, he would do it. The tension dissipated like the mist on the great lake just beyond. John's eyes twinkled again, and the corners of his thin mouth turned up in that truly unique way that made people who saw it believe that John was the warm-hearted, caring individual he really was.

"Sir," John said enthusiastically, "I would be honored to assist you in whatever way you deem most appropriate. I look forward to running the Stars and Bars up on the *Michigan*'s mast, and the sooner the better, I say!"

Thompson made a fist and pumped it down hard once, then twice, in victory. "Tremendous, John! I am confident that you will not be disappointed!"

"So, what do we do next, Commissioner?"

"What we do next, John my boy," Thompson said, "is get together with some of the other key players." Thompson paused for a second, taking the handkerchief from his back pocket, and dabbing carefully at each weepy eye again. He rubbed the handkerchief back and forth across each eyelid to provide at least momentary relief to the itching, and he continued talking.

"I'd like you to come back after lunch, say 2:00, and meet with some of the other people who are going to be involved," Thompson said. "We'll see if we can arrange some of the details of the plan then. Is that all right with you?"

"Yes, sir," John replied.

The handkerchief now returned to his back pocket, Thompson extended his hand to John, who grasped it firmly and shook it. "Two o'clock it is, then," Thompson said.

"Two o'clock," responded the man in black, who now chatted amiably as the most powerful Confederate official in Canada walked him to the door.

* * * * * * *

John Yates Beall was more curious than surprised to see the same short, chunky man with the black beard and bowler sitting in Walter Cleary's office. This was the same fellow he had seen Thompson escorting out of his office that morning. The man sat by himself in an overstuffed chair just beside Cleary's desk. He put down the newspaper he was reading just long enough to say a curt "hello" to John.

The man smiled that remote, existential sort of smile that people use when they know they should appear to be friendly, but really haven't the slightest interest in carrying on a conversation. Of course, it could also be that the man didn't speak much because of the alcohol. He reeked of gin, and a musty aura of stale cigar smoke hung over him like a dense fog. John could smell it as soon as he entered the anteroom occupied by Walter Cleary. Himself a teetotaler, John had quite a nose for alcohol. He could smell it a mile away, although as loaded up as this man was, there was no need for a sensitive nose to be able to spot it.

John nodded politely, and started to speak to Walter. He found Walter Cleary to be a very engaging fellow. Cleary shared John's interest in philosophy and French revolutionary history. Other than his dear Martha, there was no one that could carry on with in conversation better than Walter.

Ah, yes. Martha. It seemed that everything reminded John of his fiancée. He had never believed a man could be so incomplete without the presence of the woman he loves. But now he knew. He missed her terribly, so much that he found it difficult to keep himself focused on whatever task was at hand. But there was nothing he could do about that now. He would just have to try and struggle through each day as best he could. Each day brought him closer to the reunion with his beloved and to that big church wedding John had promised a weeping Martha before he left Columbus.

The grandfather clock standing inside the Commissioner's office chimed out the hour in sonorous tones just as Thompson opened the door and stepped into the anteroom. John could see that two men were already inside, seated at one of the three commodious chairs which flanked the two sofas.

"Come on in, gentlemen," Thompson said. John graciously waited for the black-bearded man to push himself up out of his seat, grunting and groaning with effort. He managed to keep himself surprisingly steady as he entered the Commissioner's office. Must have had years of practice, John thought.

"Mr. Cleary, would you inform Mrs. Davis that I would like to see her, please?" Thompson asked. Cleary was already on his way out the door to locate the lady when Thompson added, "You may escort her directly into the meeting after you've found her. She will be expecting you. I believe she said she would be in the tavern." Thompson closed the door behind him.

The two men already inside rose as John and the inebriated man in the bowler entered.

"Let me introduce everybody," Thompson said, dabbing at his weepy right eye with his handkerchief. The mysterious short, bearded man, past the point of being concerned about etiquette, introduced himself first to John, then to the others. "Charles Cole," he said somewhat sloppily, thrusting his right hand out to each of them in turn.

Thompson introduced the other men as General Thomas Hines, his military operations assistant, and Godfrey J. Hyams, special assistant in charge of couriers. John was impressed that such a weasel-looking little man like Hines could be a general. Not only was the man short but also very thin. He also had those droopy basset hound kind of eyes and big ears to match. Hard to imagine this fellow in command.

The thirtyish man who fit the classic Greco-Roman command profile was Hyams. Reasonably tall, with wavy blonde hair and intense midnight-blue eyes and a clean-shaven face, Hyams was an imposing figure of a man. He also smelled of rose-scented soap.

146

John had already formed an impression about Cole, and it was not a very good one. How a man could come into a meeting like this, at this hour of the day, reeking of liquor, showed, at best, a strange lack of sensitivity. Cole's beady black eyes darted back forth from one side to the other, creating an impression of untrustworthiness and suspicion. John marveled at how much the alcohol had changed the man's very persona. When he had seen him earlier in Thompson's anteroom, Cole had a commanding presence. He carried himself well, and his dark eyes twinkled. But this was a totally different person now in the room. John wondered if Thompson had noticed the difference.

The men sat around the black onyx table in front of the fireplace and exchanged general pleasantries. All of them except Charles Cole, that is. He sat impassively on a sofa by himself, chewing away furiously on a monstrous cigar, alternately spitting out bits of tobacco in the general direction of the floor and exhaling little ringlets of silver-grey smoke toward the ceiling.

Although every window facing on the lake was open, the curtains were not even twitching; no air at all was moving. The midday stillness was oppressive and hung heavy over a body, like a sweat-soaked shirt on a man's back. John wished he could get up and move closer to the open window and what little fresh air there was, but the exigencies of the situation required him to sit and endure the foul tobacco smell.

The rancorous odor also had begun to irritate his lungs and John felt an increasingly biting tickle rise deep in his chest. He knew from experience that the tickle could turn to a deep, bloody cough, which would start the lung spasms all over again. He might, of course, ask Cole to give up the cigar. But that would only remind Thompson, and perhaps the others, too, of the frail condition his lungs were in. And that might send him packing back to Virginia, his mission unfulfilled. So tough it out, he told himself, tough it out. He gently tapped the pocket of his frock coat, unnoticed by the others. Yep, the bottle of laudanum, his ever-present help in time of trouble, was there. Just in case, of course.

If Thompson had noticed that Cole had been hitting the bottle, his face didn't show it. He smiled politely as the men talked back and forth, from time to time contributing something himself to the conversation. Eventually, he rose from the sofa, clasped his arms behind his back, and paced in the narrow space between the fireplace and the black onyx table. John noticed that the Commissioner had put on his ponderous face again. He always did that when he had some serious business to attend to.

147

Thompson cleared his throat. All eyes turned in his direction. "Gentlemen," he said, "we are about to embark on a mission which I believe, which President Davis believes, can bring about a swift and successful end to the war. I have spoken about certain elements of this mission with each of you. But now it is time to pull all of the pieces together."

"As you know," Thompson continued, his pace quickening, "the Yankee prison camp on Johnson's Island now holds nearly 3,000 of our officers, the crème de la crème of our military operation. No less than six generals are currently confined in that wretched place. Mr. Cole, who recently escaped from the Dantean nightmare, tells me that, under orders coming directly from Secretary Stanton himself, the rations provided to our men have been reduced to the point where even the commander's dog has ended up in somebody's mess pot!"

A subdued smile crossed Charles Cole's face, as he found it especially amusing that Hyams, a Union spy in this den of Confederate plotters, was hearing the same information he had passed on to Cole as part of his cover story. And as instructed by Hyams just a month ago in Philadelphia, Cola had not shown even the slightest sign of recognition when introduced to him by Thompson.

"Those gallant men on Johnson's Island are not only being treated shamefully, especially for officers and gentlemen. They are being slowly starved to death. And we shall do something about it!" The fire was rising in Thompson's voice. The Commissioner paused, dabbed at both eyes with a handkerchief he now carried clutched in his fist, and then continued.

"God has smiled on our valiant cause. We know that the only United States warship on the Great Lakes, the 16-gun steamer *Michigan*, is now stationed off Johnson's Island. The Yankee strategy, such as it is, is to protect against any rescue effort to free our officers. What they have really done is given us the chance to not only free the men, but the opportunity to take over the *Michigan* at the same time."

Thompson stopped his pacing perfectly under the Stars and Bars and said firmly, "Gentlemen, with the help of almighty God, we shall do so! And soon!" Thompson's right arm, balled fist at one end, made a mighty swipe through the air for emphasis.

"Here, here!" Hyams said, jumping to his feet enthusiastically.

General Hines also rose to his feet, applauding.

Even John Yates Beall, never comfortable with exuberant displays of emotion, rose to his feet, applauding politely.

Charles Cole let out a war whoop, and danced up and down in a wobbly sort of way behind the table, nearly colliding in his inebriated state with Thompson himself. Cole pulled a fresh, fat, black cigar out of his shirt pocket, found a match in his trousers, and struck it on the side of the onyx table. John grimaced at not only what to him was Cole's excessive inebriated enthusiasm, but the casual way in which a fine piece of furniture was used to provide fire to the cigar.

From the door to Thompson's anteroom came a knock, hollow and deep. In all the excitement, nobody had noticed the knocking, but Walter Cleary entered anyway.

Cleary turned and smiled at someone behind him, nodding his head. Thompson finally noticed that Cleary was at the door. "Is Mrs. Davis out there with you, Walter?"

"Yes, indeed, sir. But she's just a little under the weather."

"Makes no mind," the Commissioner said, gesturing for Cleary to show the woman in.

As Annie Davis entered the room, a sudden gentlemanly silence overtook the men standing around the fireplace. All eyes were turned toward the door as a petite, well-proportioned woman with long, silky, chocolate-brown hair strode forcefully, yet gracefully, into the room. "Commissioner, you wanted to see me?"

"Yes, indeed, Mrs. Davis. Yes, indeed. Come right on in!" The woman's eyes focused on the Confederate flag, and she almost tripped over the table before finally stopping just short of Thompson.

As Annie Davis stood silently beside him, Thompson proceeded to explain primarily for the benefit of Cole and Beall, who had never met her, that Annie's late husband had served Virginia and the Confederacy valiantly as an officer under General Pickett. That he had died in the charge at Gettysburg. That the widow Davis, following the example of service inspired by her late husband, was serving the South as a courier under Godfrey Hyams, crossing through the lines to deliver messages between him and Richmond. And that now Annie Davis was going to embark on her most challenging and dangerous mission yet.

With no fanfare, and with no hint of the impact of what he was about to say, Thompson escorted Annie until they were face to face with Charles Cole. With a wry smile on his face he said simply, "Mr. Cole, I'd like to you meet your wife."

* * * * * * *

"So, what's the matter, Captain Cole? Never been married before?" Annie's spirited, cat-green eyes flashed jovially, and the one little dimple on her left cheek reflected the humor she saw in this whole situation.

149

But Charles Cole was not amused. He said nothing at first. He was still shell-shocked at the pace at which everything had progressed. Like an out-of-control wagon rolling downhill, dragging the horse with it. And he was the horse.

Thompson had had a good laugh, that's for sure. Imagine, introducing a complete stranger to you as your wife! Not that Annie was undesirable. Far from it. The woman looked good, real good. So good, that she didn't need to wear any kind of makeup. Her skin was flawless, milky-white, except for he cheeks, which showed just a little bit of peach. Beautiful woman! And sexy, too. There was something about her sensuous eyes, her full red lips, and come hither personality that Cole found not only attractive but also compelling. Yep, if he was going to have to spend a lot of time with this woman, whose cover was that she was Cole's wife, he couldn't have asked for a better choice.

Not only was Annie attractive. She shared some of Cole's other interests. Like liquor. Cole could smell it on her breath. She had been sitting down in that tavern at the Queen's Hotel, all by herself, in the middle of the afternoon. Just sitting. And drinking. Cole's kind of woman.

Annie appeared a little reluctant to take on this assignment from Thompson. And Cole could understand that. Not only would it be dangerous. She would also be spending a lot of nights in Cole's room, if her cover story was to have any validity at all. But when Thompson said he was writing out a draft to Cole for $60,000 in gold to fund his operation, well, her whole attitude changed, swiftly and dramatically.

Cole almost didn't get the Sandusky assignment. It was the plum, of course. Sixty thousand dollars, more than he could imagine, in cold, hard cash. To entertain the *Michigan* officers. To bribe its crew. To buy weapons. No, he almost didn't get the assignment because Thompson was afraid someone in Sandusky, where the *Michigan* was now stationed, would recognize him as an escaped prisoner. But Cole assured Thompson that nobody in the town would recognize him, because he obviously never went there when he was a prisoner. And none of the men at Johnson's Island would recognize him, either, because he hadn't been there long enough to get acquainted, so to speak.

But to appease Thompson, Charles said he would cut his hair, and shave off his beard (which he didn't really intend to do), and that seemed to settle things. Of course the fact that Cole purportedly knew the area better than anyone, since he had actually been inside the camp, and his loquacious personality, which would allow him to pierce confidences, were the real reasons he was selected. That Beall fella

150

hardly seemed the right man for the mission, since hard drinking and garrulous behavior were so much a part of the assignment.

Shortly after they left the hotel, Annie said, "Here, this is the bank office. The Commissioner said they would be able to give us some sight drafts." Cole was getting more nervous and uncomfortable by the second. Here was this complete stranger, lovely as she was, so directly involved in what he considered to be his own personal affairs. But that was the way Thompson had ordered it.

Annie was to accompany him to the bank and, although any sight drafts could be made out to Cole, *she* would hold this one. In different circumstances, he would have been more than a little incensed that Thompson didn't trust him, or so it seemed. But Hyams had spoken up, when he could see Cole was perturbed, and might blow his own shaky cover. Hyams said it was standard procedure. A man caught with $60,000 cash would be immediately suspect, he had said. Where Annie was going to put the money, no man would have the courage, or the audacity, to check. And Cole had to admit the wisdom of taking all precautions to avoid being shot by the North as a spy.

Cole opened the massive brass door to the bank, doffed his hat at Annie, and smiled. Maybe this wasn't so bad after all, he thought. I can get used to this.

Cole was so preoccupied with the money, and Annie, and everything, that he had not really noticed a man had been following them since they left Thompson's hotel. A hulk of a man, with curly red hair and a fiery orangish-red beard. The man waited discretely until Cole and Annie had entered the bank. Opening the door for an older woman, he then entered, his inquisitive eyes searching immediately for Charles Cole.

12

It was a week since Charles Cole had last seen Annie. He thought he might miss her, since she was not only an accommodating drinking companion, but also a woman with a voracious sexual appetite. He found both very much to his liking. The sun had barely set over the horizon that first day in Toronto before the two of them were intertwined in an alcoholic swirl of lovemaking. The trail of drinking and sex, sex and drinking had continued as Cole and Annie made their way to this bustling little city on sheltered Sandusky Bay. Soon after they had first checked into their suite at the West House, on the glistening Sandusky waterfront, Annie had received a telegram stating that her mother was gravely ill. This coded message from Hyams in fact directed Annie to return to Toronto, and she had left immediately.

As a matter of fact, Charles did miss Annie. But he soon found that as a wealthy oil promoter for the Mt. Hope Oil Company with oil and gas leases around the fantastically famous Drake discovery well in Titusville, Pennsylvania – which was the cover given him by his Confederate superiors in Toronto – he had no trouble at all in finding friends. Especially female. The war had sucked up all of the city's most eligible young bachelors, and Cole soon found himself surrounded by ladies. Very lovely ladies. And so thoughts of Annie quickly moved to the back of his mind.

It had been a hell of a week. He decided early on that he was not going to let that rebel $60,000 just sit around moldering in a bank vault somewhere. And so every night he was partying away, and when there were dances, he found himself twirling around the dance floor of the West House ballroom with the most beautiful Midwestern girls, the crème de la crème. They sort of reminded him of Pennsylvania women, to which he was most accustomed. They were so fresh and innocent, with milky white skin, flaxen hair, and well-proportioned figures, like that Maloney girl back in Springfield who told her daddy that Cole had raped her.

During the day, to keep his Confederate handlers back in Toronto thinking that he was doing something in exchange for the $60,000 they advanced him, he had been meeting with the well-hidden rebel sympathizers in the strongly pro-Union community. Although he disliked having to put on this front, he did so anyway. You could never be quite sure that these Copperheads didn't have their own instructions to keep an eye on him. Cole had done just enough, no more, to keep anybody in Toronto or Richmond from getting suspicious.

Tonight was the last chance he would have for a while to live an uninhibited life, flitting from one female to another like a bee bent on accumulating the most honey. There was a telegram in his box at the hotel this morning from Annie. She would be back in Sandusky, arriving on the noon train tomorrow. And then Cole would move back into that comfortable, pleasant niche with Annie. But first, he had his sights set on one special young lady. One who passed him a seductive, flirty little smile last night. A young twentyish woman, she was closely guarded by an older gentleman who hovered over her protectively. The thrill of the hunt drew Cole to her. The challenge of conquering the unconquerable. He would have that girl tonight. Yes, Winifred March, the lovely lass with the winsome look in her eyes, would be his.

* * * * * * *

The trail of Charles Cole had been easy for John Murray to follow. Cole made no pretense to try and disguise his moves. And he seemed to pay no attention whatsoever to things going on around him. Continually distracted by alcohol and the ladies, he had not noticed the Scotsman with the flaming red beard following him, always at a discrete distance, of course.

But it was difficult for Murray to learn very much of the details from a distance. It was not often that he had either the need or the interest in getting close to Cole and his new lady companion, the one Cole called "Annie." But when the two of them arrived in Sandusky, well, that presented a whole new range of opportunities. Murray could use his vast circle of friends in the city to keep an eye on Cole.

And since Cole was now in Sandusky, he certainly warranted closer watching. Conditions had admittedly gotten worse for the rebel officers confined on Johnson's Island, due to Secretary Stanton's orders to cut rations and close the sutler's shop. Rumor had it the prisoners had been reduced to eating rats and even the camp commander's dog. The likelihood of some sort of trouble being stirred up increased as the men confined there grew more desperate. And, of course, the *Michigan* was now positioned just off Johnson's Island, its sixteen guns pointed at the narrow entrance to the channel into and out of Sandusky Bay.

Initially, Murray had not been too worried about Cole. He seemed to be a pathetic case. But when the red-bearded Scotsman learned that Cole had been meeting with well-known rebel sympathizers in the city, warning flags went up in Murray's head. Although he had been able to keep a pretty good eye on Cole's movements, Murray had not been able to find out much of what Cole might be up to. Not until he noticed Cole paying particular attention to Winifred Marsh did he have a hope of getting on the inside of Cole's plans.

Miss Winnie, as she was known around the Sandusky social scene, was a bit of an oddity. It wasn't her physical appearance that attracted curiosity. Nothing wrong there. In fact, Miss Winnie was the envy of the homegrown ladies in the community. Tall and graceful as a gazelle, she exuded charm, poise and a soft femininity that captured the hearts of the regular army men posted at the cannon battery out on Cedar Point, the officers and crew of the *Michigan* and even the young, but still handsome, limbless men who served in the invalid corps assigned to guard the rebel prisoners on Johnson's Island, just a few miles across Sandusky Bay from the city.

Miss Winnie was an oddity because she was from the south. Louisville was her home. As soon as she opened her mouth, the words dripped from her velvet-smooth lips like honey, and every bit as sweet. Even the most rabid Yankee soldier couldn't help but get just a little excited at the prospect of a relationship with the woman, relationship being broadly defined to include even a passing glance.

Murray decided he could use Miss Winnie's obvious charms to some advantage. He had noticed that Cole, like every other man in Sandusky with any testosterone in his system at all, was particularly attracted to her. But Murray held the trump card. He had become well-acquainted with Miss Winnie's uncle, George Marsh, local haberdasher *par excellence* and a fellow poker aficionado like Murray.

The little bell hanging over the Water Street storefront tinkled lightly as John Murray entered the shop. "Geo. Marsh & Son" was barely legible in the weather-beaten sign hanging outside next to the door. Twenty years of gale force winter winds from Canada had done that. George had planned on replacing the sign when his son Robert took over the business. But then Robert got killed at Shiloh, and George lost interest in lots of important and unimportant things. Subconsciously, he had decided he would let the sign molder and fade, just like the memory of the only son he ever had.

It was a typical late summer Saturday morning in Sandusky, hot and oppressively humid. Beads of salty liquefied humidity rolled down Murray's forehead, gathering into droplets on his bushy red eyebrows and dripping onto his cheeks. George Marsh, usually somber-faced and completely businesslike when dealing with customers, came up from underneath the broad wooden counter, where he had been looking for his scissors to cut the string on the hatbox he was wrapping for the cranky old man drumming his fingers on the countertop. A measuring tape was draped casually around Marsh's neck, like it belonged there.

Although he would never admit it, business had been bad for Marsh since the war started. The dapper young men who had formed his main customer base were now wearing Union blue and kepi caps.

"John, John my boy! So good to see you!" Marsh peeped in the high squeaky voice that had become his trademark in Sandusky. "I'll be with you in just a moment." The sight of his friend and poker partner, John Murray, put new vigor into Marsh's activities.

"Take your time, George," Murray said nonchalantly. "I'll just be lookin' around the store some. May need a new pair of trousers here in a while."

After Marsh had finished with his customer, he came out from behind the counter. "Well, John Wilson Murray," he chirped. "What can I do for you today? A new pair of trousers, you say? I've got some fine wool in this week; make an excellent pair of trousers for the fall and winter. Not too far away, you know."

"Well, in all honesty, my friend, it's not a pair of trousers that I'm most interested in now."

Marsh was puzzled. "But you said. . ."

"Yes, I know what I said," the Scotsman interrupted. "But I couldn't speak about the real purpose of my visit while you had a customer in the store."

"There's no one here now, John. So why don't you quit playing games and tell me what you've got on your mind," barked Marsh.

Murray could tell his friend was just a little upset that he was not going to be buying anything today. Maybe things were even worse with Marsh's business than they seemed, he thought.

"It's about Miss Winnie."

The sour look on Marsh's face disappeared like the dew on the meadow in the hot morning sun. A sly grin moved the corners of Marsh's mouth upward. "I was wondering when you would come to me about her," Marsh said. "Every other eligible man in town has been clamoring for her attention. You might as well throw your hat in the ring, too."

"No George, it's not like that," Murray said. "This is serious business concerning your niece. It's a matter of some importance to the Union."

"Now wait just one minute, John! I know you are aware that my niece comes from the south. Are you suggesting . . ."

"Heavens no, George!" Murray interjected. "I'm not suggesting Miss Winnie is anything but the honest, straightforward, fun loving young lady that she appears to be."

"Good! I'm glad we got that straight!" Marsh said. He started to relax again, and his voice moved back down to the lead tenor range it normally occupied. "But what is it that you want with my niece?"

"George, I'd like her to do nothing more than she's been doing since she got here. Just talking to all of the young men who are interested in making her acquaintance. With a slight difference."

"What's that?" asked Marsh, now more confused than threatened.

"I'd like her to inquire and find out anything she can about one man."

"One man? Why just one man?"

"Because the government has reason to believe the man in question may be a rebel saboteur," Murray said calmly.

"Jesus Christ!" Marsh swore. He seemed to be about to faint, but righted himself. "Right here in Sandusky! Is there any danger?"

"Absolutely not," Murray lied. "I will not be asking your niece to do anything that would put her in any danger whatsoever. And I'll not let her out of my sight while she is with this man."

Marsh paused while he pondered all of this, staring at the cobweb up on the ceiling by the picture window. "All right, I'll let you speak with her. She'll have to decide for herself whether she will help. But I have obligations to Winnie's parents. If she decides to get involved, I'll have to be involved, too. Deal?"

"Deal," Murray said.

"Good. When would you like to speak with her?"

* * * * * * *

George Marsh closed his haberdashery shop at noon, like he did every Saturday. Since Murray had been concerned about discussing Charles Cole with Miss Winnie in a public place, Marsh invited the Scottish seaman turned sleuth to sit in the cool shade of his back yard, surrounded by the delicate beauty not only of his niece, but also of the summer roses that flourished under his tender care.

157

Marsh's wife had died of the fever that swept the town six years previous and, with the sacrifice of their only son to the fires of war, he had been lonely. Marsh found that puttering around in the yard and getting rich, sandy soil under his fingernails was a far better way to endure the solitude than just sitting and moping. And, it gave him a sense of accomplishment to see the magnificent results of God's handiwork.

As soon as he walked in the door for lunch, Winnie could tell by the way his bushy grey eyebrows were furrowed that something was troubling Uncle George. Her curiosity was piqued even more when he told her he wasn't interested in the fresh corn and snap beans that she had prepared for lunch. That was really unusual, because Uncle George loved fresh summertime produce. But she had learned since coming to stay with Uncle George at the start of the war that if he had anything to tell you he would, whether you wanted to hear it or not. And that if he didn't want to tell you anything, no amount of prying would change his mind, only make him more determined to say nothing.

Winnie was clearing off the luncheon dishes when, at about 1 o'clock, she heard a knock at the front door. She went to answer it. There, on the other side of the screen door stood a big burly redheaded, orange-bearded man dressed in a Union Navy officer's uniform. She had seen this man before, she knew, but couldn't quite place him.

"Miss March?" he asked, tipping his officer's cap ever so slightly. "I am Ensign John Wilson Murray, from the United States warship, the *Michigan*. I'm here to see your uncle. Is he available?"

"Certainly, sir," Winnie responded. She opened the screen door, and the sailor with the slight Scottish brogue entered. "I'll tell him you're here." She still wondered what this man could possibly want with her uncle. She concluded he must need some special item of clothing for the big ball tonight. Uncle George was well known in town for opening his store back up, after he had closed it, so that a customer could meet some emergency need. And she surmised that business being so slow made him even more customer-oriented that he had been before.

Winnie found her uncle in the sunroom, where he was taking a nap. It was then that she learned from Uncle George that Ensign Murray was there not just to see her uncle, but her too. "Take him to the gazebo," he said, rubbing his eyes wearily. "I'll be right there."

Winnie returned to the foyer, where she had left Murray standing, hat in hand. She thought about asking Murray right there what in the world he wanted, but thought better of it.

She led him through the kitchen out the back door to the spacious and immaculate green lawn. In the center of the expanse was George Marsh's gazebo, shining pearly white in the midday sun. The fragrance of honeysuckle and roses growing up the trellises that encompassed all sides of the structure permeated the air with a powerful perfumed scent and shaded the interior from the harsh afternoon sun.

After showing Murray around the grounds, Miss Winnie left him by the gazebo and excused herself to the kitchen to make some tea. When she returned, Murray and her uncle were engaged in a lively conversation, which promptly stopped when she entered the garden gazebo.

"Winnie," her Uncle George said seriously. "Mr. Murray here is an officer on the U.S.S. *Michigan*, as you know. He told me this morning that there was a matter he thought you might be able to assist him with. I believe you ought to hear what he has to say and decide for yourself if what he is asking is something you would be willing to do. All right?"

"Certainly, Uncle George," she answered respectfully. "Some nice cold tea, gentlemen? Mr. Murray, the water is ice cold – it comes from the spring at the back of the property." Winnie offered the glasses to the two men, filling each with the cool amber brew.

Murray cleared his throat and set the glass of tea on the table in front of him. "Miss Marsh," he said, "what I am about to say to you must not pass your lips to anyone else. It concerns something which I believe you and you alone can do to assist the Union cause."

Winnie drew a sharp breath. No wonder Uncle George was so tense when he came home! Imagine, a Kentucky girl, right here in Sandusky, being able to do anything that could affect the outcome of the war!

"Will you give me your oath before Almighty God that you will not reveal the conversation we are about to have with anyone else?" Murray asked. Winnie nodded silently.

"Good!" Murray exclaimed. "Now let's talk about how you can help us apprehend a Confederate spy and saboteur."

* * * * * * *

The night was perfect for dancing. A thunderstorm late in the afternoon has cleansed the air and a cooling breeze floated through Sandusky off the lake. The large dining room on the second floor of the West House, which was converted to a spacious ball room after the last seating of the evening had taken place, was already starting to fill to capacity with dancers even before the red-orange evening sun had sunk into the violet western horizon. Ladies young and old had begun to ogle the few eligible men, almost all of whom were outfitted in crisp Navy or Army uniforms.

Charles Cole loved to dance, primarily because by definition it got him close to women. The touch and smell of softly scented and powdered feminine flesh aroused the hormonal-driven animal lurking just beneath a paper-thin veneer of civility. He had arrived early, just like he had for the past week, to size up his intended conquest for the night. And of course, the ladies were likewise looking him over, too, he knew. And that didn't bother him one bit.

Then he saw her. That woman again. The one with the sultry look who had such a smile. Not that her smile was her best feature. Her finely developed female form was obvious even underneath all of the padding that women were obliged to wear. But it was the smile that had caught his attention and so captivated him.

The woman was in the company of an older gentleman, a man in his fifties or so. He appeared to be her father. That would make the conquest even tougher. But Cole was not in the least bit intimidated. He knew how to work these old men.

Cole walked across the ballroom floor, past the bar's well-stocked shelves containing everything from fine Kentucky bourbon to Ohio wine and Tawny Port. His eyes focused on the woman, who was engaged in conversation with three other young women, all of them attractive. The old man stood to the side of the young people, seemingly uninterested in whatever it was they were talking about. Feeling Cole's gaze, the young beauty turned her head and cast a captivating, slightly toothy smile. Cole smiled back. The old man drew closer to his charge, so that he was right next to the lady by the time Cole reached her.

"Good evening, ma'am," Cole said, doffing his hat and bowing ever so slightly. "Please don't think me forward, but I just had to tell you after observing you on the floor last week, you are a wonderful dancer." Cole had really turned on the charm, which he was quite capable, and quite experienced, at doing.

"Thank you, Mr. . . ."

"Cole, Charles Cole."

"Mr. Cole. You are too kind." Funny, Cole thought. She speaks with a Southern drawl. What in the world is she doing here in Sandusky, Ohio?

The orchestra struck up the first tune of the evening, a lively two-step. Better press now, Cole thought. "May I have the pleasure of

160

this dance?" he asked, bowing ever so slightly, his mouth and eyes locked in a deceptively pleasing smile.

Miss Winnie consented, and off they went, whirling around and around the dance floor. The first dance led to a second, the second led to a third, and the two of them, transfixed in each other, had become a thing.

Winnie was thrilled to the point of tingling to think that she was actually dancing right here with a rebel spy and saboteur. Of course, as they engaged in small talk between numbers and as they danced together, Charles Cole never admitted any such thing. He was an oil developer from Pennsylvania, he said, here in Sandusky trying to raise money from well-heeled investors to drill some oil wells near Titusville. He certainly didn't sound like any rebel spy. Winnie was confused until she realized that, of course, the very best spy is the one who doesn't look or sound like one.

After the third dance, Winnie began to fan herself. Cole noticed that little beads of sweat were beginning to form on her nose, and suggested they retire to the punch bowl.

The instructions she had received in the afternoon from Ensign Murray continued to resonate in Winnie's head. "Convince Cole that you are a southern sympathizer," Murray had said. "As a native of Kentucky, you could convince Cole of this without arousing his suspicion. Tell him how distraught you are about the pending execution on Johnson's Island of your fellow Kentuckian, John Nickell. And then just see where it leads."

"So what do you think of Sandusky, Mr. Cole?" Winnie asked, as she sipped the cinnamon-laced punch that her would-be suitor had poured for her.

"Lovely town," Cole said, the ever present smile still creasing his face. "But until I met you tonight, I didn't realize just how lovely."

Winnie knew Cole was trying to flatter her and blushed. She knew how to deal with men. But flattery still got her attention, even coming from this man whom she inwardly detested. Although she was from a state with strong rebel sympathies, she was an ardent Unionist. Because of that, Cole's platitudes passed over her like water over a duck's back.

"That's nice of you to say, Mr. Cole. Although I really don't feel lovely. In fact, I feel downright ugly."

Cole was puzzled by the lady's comment. How could beauty personified feel ugly? He was uncomfortable with this situation, and decided to say nothing.

"It's just dreadful," she drawled on, tears welling up in her doe-like brown eyes. "Those petty Yankee tyrants out there on Johnson's Island are going to execute another innocent man in just five days! Haven't you heard?"

"No ma'am," Cole lied. "I really don't pay much attention to politics."

"Politics? This isn't about politics. It's about justice! All poor John Nickell did was fight for what he believed in. And now they're going to hang him as a guerilla!"

The talk about hanging spies made Cole's blood run cold. What if the Yankees caught him while he was making contact with these Copperheads? The only man who could really vouch for his Yankee bona fides was Godfrey Hyams, who for all intents and purposes was a high-ranking rebel leader. Cole felt the little hairs on the back of his neck start to tingle. Color drained from his ruddy red face. His stomach began to churn, and he felt the acrid, metallic taste of vomit welling up inside him.

"Miss Marsh," Cole said, his ever-present smile now gone. "I'm afraid I'm feeling a tad under the weather. Would you excuse me, please?"

Even before the last words had crossed his lips, Cole made a mad dash out of the room, leaving Miss Winnie holding her punch glass, her mouth agape. And across the room, Ensign John Wilson Murray wondered what in the world had gone wrong with the plan.

13

SEPTEMBER 1864
BUFFALO, NEW YORK

The weather was uncommonly hot and muggy for early September. Crisp breezes, swept over the Arctic tundra and icy waters of Hudson's Bay, were yet to come. But John Yates Beall still felt a chill as he sat in his train compartment, squinting through the soot-smudged window. "Safe!" he realized. "I'm safe!"

John's chill disappeared as the train slowly but inexorably picked up speed, moving out of the yard and onto the seemingly endless clackety iron ribbon. The train would gradually wind its way along the sloping south shore of Lake Erie and on to Sandusky, away from the immediate risk at the border crossing from Canada into the United States.

John's innate concerns for his safety probably were not warranted. The border guards obviously never suspected that John was a Confederate agent, about to lead one of the most brazen rebel schemes of the war. John looked, acted and sounded every bit like the British subject he pretended to be. Those years in England with his grandfather had indelibly imprinted upon John certain English mannerisms and speech patterns. He also favored the conservative dress of English gentlemen. And his own patrician upbringing in Virginia had bestowed upon him a certain air that radiated aristocracy. So it was perfectly understandable how John Yates Beall had easily convinced the American border guards that he was a British subject, en route to Cleveland to conduct a periodic inspection of one of the foundries that produced goods for his company back in England.

The tension gradually dissipated with the passing miles, and John felt the taut muscles in the nape of his neck gradually relax. He leaned his head back on the silky black cushion behind him, closed his eyes, and dreamt of Martha. His lovely Martha! How he loved her so! It had only been a few brief months since she faded from view on the train platform in Georgia, waving frantically at him, as though somehow that might encourage him to abandon his dangerous mission and return to her. He still could see her face in his mind's eye, her auburn hair, up in that little bun like she always wore it, her button nose, her round green eyes, that mischievous crinkly smile.

Even though he missed Martha dearly, he had become increasingly excited about and preoccupied with what had become known at Commissioner Thompson's Confederate headquarters in Toronto simply as "The Plan." As though it were the only plan. In just a few short weeks, John would spearhead a surprise military action at Sandusky designed to liberate thousands of Confederate officers from the hellhole of Johnson's Island, and take over the 16-gun U.S.S. *Michigan* in the process. The war would end soon thereafter, he hoped, and then he could be reunited with Martha, never again to part.

With all the able-bodied men stoking the fires of the Union war machine, the ribbon of steel winding along the lake was in obvious need of repair. A sudden bump-bump-bump, as the train rumbled over a particularly bad stretch of track, jolted John out of his subconscious netherworld. Instinctively, his hand moved to the inside breast pocket of his frock coat, where he had hidden a tiny single-shot derringer. Yes, it was still there, right next to his ever-present bottle of laudanum.

John was embarrassed about packing a weapon normally carried by women. A Colt Navy revolver was more his style, a weapon that radiated power and masculinity along every inch of its polished steel barrel. But it was impossible to conceal such a gun, and Commissioner Thompson had insisted that he have at least some capability to extricate himself from a jam if the need arose.

Thompson had been particularly insistent.

"Now, John," he said, patting the young Virginian on the back, "I wouldn't normally ask one of my men to carry a weapon at all when crossing the border. But if the Yankees find those greenbacks on you, you'll be done for. You need to have some way to get out of a bad situation. Because if you can't, that $25,000 would not only fall into Yankee hands, but we would not be able to go forward with the plan."

Ah, yes, John thought. The Plan. His compatriot Charles Cole had insisted on the $25,000 to bribe the officers of the *Michigan* and at Johnson's Island. This was in addition to the $60,000 that had already been advanced to him before he left Toronto. Cole had just reported to Thompson that, on his signal, the *Michigan* officers would all simply vanish. Pay those damnable Yankee crooks their bribe money, and they would turn their backs. A rebel flag would be hoisted above the *Michigan*, and the Confederate prisoners on Johnson's Island would be freed. It was that easy.

John recalled the simple coded message carried from Sandusky to Toronto in Annie Davis's petticoat: "Preliminary plans in place. *Michigan* can be ours for $25,000. Prison defenses weak. Guards compromised. Send cash via messenger as soon as possible. Cole."

John was there with Thompson when Annie delivered Cole's message. There was never any doubt that Thompson would send the greenbacks. It was just a matter of making sure every detail was in place. "After all, you and Cole have to meet anyway to work out the details," Thompson reasoned out loud, "so I might as well send you now." Over Annie's protests that she deliver the cash to Cole, and despite the risk of Beall being captured, Thompson was not about to part company with that much cash without confirming that the plan was ready to go forward. So John Yates Beall found himself on a train to Sandusky, 250 hundred-dollar bills sewn into the lining of his frock coat.

Sitting alone in his compartment, John closed his eyes, put his arms behind his head. Beatific visions of Martha floated across his mind's eye again, and thoughts of the Plan faded like the haze that blended into the blue-green horizon over Lake Erie.

* * * * * * *

Sandusky, Ohio
Two Days Later

John had asked for and received a luxurious corner suite in the West House. The vacation season was over, and the hotel was more than anxious to accommodate this obviously well-to-do businessman with the British accent and mannerisms.

After checking in, John was escorted by the porter to his room. He tipped the man handsomely, as would be expected of a man with sufficient affluence to afford such a suite. Opening his valise on the walnut-grained canopy bed, he pulled back the eggshell-colored Irish lace curtains on his north-facing window. John could see through the late afternoon haze the silhouette of Johnson's Island rising from the greenish-grey water of Sandusky Bay. The clatter of horses' hooves on the cobblestone bricks of Water Street mingled with the cries of gulls, fishmongers and deck hands on the pier below. The scene reminded John of the Chesapeake waterfront burghs he had come to know and love so well. The view of Johnson's Island, though, served as a stark reminder that John was here for a reason. And a very important reason at that – but it was not going to be a Sunday picnic.

John carefully pulled the curtain and shuttered the window. He went to the oval wall mirror by the hall door and adjusted his cravat before heading down to the dining room, where he was to meet Charles Cole for dinner.

165

Cole was waiting for him at the door, a glass of champagne in one hand and an alcoholic glaze in his eyes.

"John, old fellow!" Cole bellowed. He slapped John on the back, hard. Cole's champagne sloshed over the side of the tulip-shaped goblet, dribbling down the back of his palm onto the ruby-red carpet. The other dinner guests queuing outside the entrance to the dining room pretended not to notice the tipsy black-eyed man in the jaunty bowler. "I'm so glad to see you! I was beginning to worry that you might have forgotten about our dinner engagement." A wry smile crossed Charles Cole's face.

John knew exactly what Cole meant. Cole was concerned about the money – the $25,000, which John had removed from the lining of his frock coat and carefully put into the brown kid leather envelope he was now clutching at his side.

"Nothing to worry about, Mr. Cole," John said formally. That old feeling was coming over John again, the one he felt when he first met Cole in Canada. A certain uneasiness that defied definition. "I just had a few things to do in my room before venturing down for dinner."

"I hope you're hungry, Mr. Beall. This place has absolutely the best mutton chops in the Midwest." Cole had detected John's detachment and reverted to the more formal "Mister Beall." But Cole would only make a slight accommodation to proper manners. He slapped John on the back once more, smiled that unnerving smile, and gently pushed the Virginian toward the starch-shirted maître-d.

Charles Cole was right. The mutton chops were delicious. Served in a delicate sauce flavored with hints of mint and basil. John could hardly believe that such a relatively small town – what was it, only 4,000 people? – so far removed from the culture of the east coast could have such a sophisticated menu, so elegantly prepared. The magnum of champagne ordered by Cole was empty by the time dessert was served. John, being a teetotaler, had abstained, which seemed to make Charles Cole all the happier.

"Shall we take a walk along the waterfront?" Cole inquired after finishing off the last crumbs of chocolate cake on his plate, using his index finger to sweep up the last bit of frosting. "There's a nice breeze blowing in off the lake, and the view is magnificent." He was smiling that wicked smile again.

Now there was one thing with which John couldn't quarrel; the view was magnificent. Besides, he was not about to pass $25,000 in cash to Cole in a room full of people. Better to do it away from prying eyes.

166

The two men left the dining room, after John had charged the meal to his room. He observed that, except for his overly gregarious greetings, Cole seemed not to be the least bit affected by the substantial quantities of alcohol he had consumed, except for a slight increase in swagger. One whole magnum of champagne! The thought of consuming that much alcohol was repulsive to John. More important, he wondered how anybody who was so much under the influence of alcohol could keep his head straight when the time for battle came, as it most certainly would.

Older couples, whose lives focused so much on each other, walked along Water Street, oblivious to the two men who had now stopped by Pier 17 at the end of the boardwalk. The sunset over the western waters of Sandusky Bay and the Catawba Peninsula beyond, was indeed magnificent and was the main attraction of the evening. The sun had grown into a fiery red balloon on the horizon, leaving wispy pink and purple clouds behind as a reminder of its ever-fleeting brilliance as it seemed to sink below the surface of the lake.

From a distance, hovering under a gas lamp farther up Water Street was another figure, out of earshot but not out of sight. A young man in a Union Navy officer's uniform, his full orangish-red beard glowing every bit as bright as the setting sun, lurked there. John Wilson Murray tried to appear nonchalant, but was immensely curious about what was transpiring at the end of Pier 17. He had been following the two men ever since they left the West House. Murray knew something was happening. This was the first visitor that Cole had had since arriving in Sandusky over a month ago. The rebel plan must be moving forward. Murray noticed nothing, nothing that is except the passing of a leather envelope from the stranger in black to Cole.

* * * * * * *

John Yates Beall spent the next day just walking around Sandusky, hoping to ascertain the strength and positions of Union defensive forces in and around the lakefront city. Cole had tried to dissuade him. "No need for that, Mr. Beall," the black-bearded man said between bites of ham and eggs for breakfast that morning. "Nothing but a few old men and cripples. Why don't you just go on back to Toronto, and leave this operation to me?"

John felt the anger well up within him. Had Cole completely forgotten why I am here? he thought. We're supposed to work out the details of the Plan, for God's sake! Maybe I was a little too hasty, he thought, turning the money over to this rascal before meeting with the local Copperheads Cole says he recruited to assist in the plan. Maybe Cole needed a little reminding.

Fighting to maintain his composure, John gently replaced his coffee cup in the saucer in front of him, and leaned forward over the table, until he was less than six inches from Charles Cole's flushed ruddy face. "Perhaps I should make one thing clear," John said stonily. Cole stopped chewing and looked up. John's steely gaze had the desired affect.

"Yes, please do," said Cole, trying hard not to appear too intimidated.

"General Thompson has given me very specific instructions, *very* specific," John whispered though clenched teeth. "He has given me complete authority to determine whether to proceed with this plan. If everything is not in place to my satisfaction, I am authorized to terminate the operation. And *you*, Mr. Cole," John said, his index finger poking Cole's egg-splattered linen napkin dangling from his neck, "if you do not cooperate fully and completely, I am also authorized to take whatever measures I deem necessary to deal with you."

Cole stared at John in shock. His mind was filled with unbridled rage. For Christ sake, this man is my subordinate, he fumed. I'm in charge of this operation. That aristocratic son of a bitch should be doing what I say! How dare he talk to me like this! Cole thought. But John's message was not lost on Cole. If he didn't play along, Cole knew he would be forced to give back the money Beall had just handed over. The thinly veiled threat of trouble if he didn't cooperate also caught Cole's attention. Better to humor the man. Just a few more days and I'll be long gone with their money, he mused, and then they can yell and fume at whoever else they damn well please.

"Now, Mr. Beall, we really don't have a problem here." Cole's voice was velvet soft and sweet as wildflower honey. "Please don't take offense. I only thought you might want to get back to Canada so that you can start making final arrangements."

"Perhaps you've forgotten, Mr. Cole, but we still have to meet with your volunteers." The tension was out of John's voice, but just barely.

Cole had completely forgotten about the volunteers. During dinner last night, they had talked about the role these local rebel sympathizers could play. Beall and he had both agreed that they were an important source of manpower, but had left open just what they could do that would support, rather than hinder, the plan. Beall wanted to meet the men to be able to gauge for himself, and Cole had said a meeting could be arranged. In fact, he had promised to get the men together this evening. Thank God, Cole thought, that I actually made contact with these folks. And thank God that I know that the Knights of the Golden Circle are meeting tonight.

"You're quite right, Mr. Beall. I had forgotten. I still need to arrange for you to meet with my volunteers. But it should not be a problem. I am sure we can do it this evening." Cole stressed the word "my" just a little, to impress upon John that he still had an important role to play. But otherwise, Cole was a paragon of sincerity.

"Very good, then," John said calmly. "Make the arrangements."

Charles Cole resumed wolfing down his breakfast, as though nothing had happened, while John Yates Beall pondered what new problems this encounter with Cole had created. He had a funny feeling about the man sitting across the table from him. Maybe it was his shifty, beady eyes. Maybe it was his boisterous, drunken conduct. Maybe it was the insincerity of his grin. Whatever the reason, he didn't trust Charles Cole. Not one bit. He hoped the meeting tonight would assuage that feeling. But he was becoming increasingly pessimistic that it would.

* * * * * * *

"Mary, have you seen my English book?" Amanda Roberts was flipping furiously through the jumble of clothes on and under her bed, with no luck. Her roommate and best friend since childhood days, Mary Stephens, had her nose buried in another of an endless stream of novels. Mary loved to read. Any book was fair game for her. But especially historical novels. She loved reading about people's lives in other places and times, and dreaming that she was there. Anywhere would do. Because anyplace was better than here in boring Sandusky, Ohio. Although, upon reflection, Mary had to admit that even Sandusky was an improvement on her parent's dairy farm in nearby Perkins Township.

"MARY!" Amanda hollered.

Mary twitched noticeably. Amanda had really shouted loudly this time. It did get Mary's attention. She threw the book down on the floor.

"What is the matter?" she echoed back.

"I can't find my English book!" Amanda snapped. "Have you borrowed it again?"

"Don't be silly," said Mary. "There's nothing in any old textbook of yours that I want to read."

"But I can't find it anywhere!" Amanda's lower lip began to quiver, a sure sign that she was about to cry. Mary could see her best friend was perturbed. She was sorry she had shouted back at her. She should have known better. Amanda always was the sensitive type. So sensitive that Mary was surprised that she was willing to live on her own in Sandusky to be able to go to high school. Although the fact that her best friend Mary was there sure made it a lot easier. Amanda would never have gone to Sandusky alone.

Mary Stephens and Amanda Roberts were two pert seventeen-year old farm girls from neighboring Perkins Township. Their homes were just a few miles to the east, but a whole generation away. The two teenagers went everywhere together. They did everything together. They were inseparable. Both were exceptionally bright, too. And so they had done what was unthinkable for farm girls: they went to high school. Since Perkins Township education stopped at the 8th grade, a move to Sandusky was necessary. The transition to independent living had been made much easier by sharing this room, just a few blocks from the school.

"If I can't find my English book, I'll just die," Amanda whimpered. "I have to find it! We've got our first test tomorrow. I'll be lost if I don't study for it!"

Amanda collapsed on the bed, buried her head in the middle of still-unfolded dresses and dainties from the laundry, and began to sob uncontrollably.

"Come on, Amanda, there must be something we can do. Don't just lie there and cry! Let's take control of the situation!" Mary was a take-charge kind of person. "Isn't there someone that we could borrow the book from?"

Amanda pulled her head from the bed, dabbing at her eyes. Then a little smile crossed her face. "Bobby!" was all she said.

"Bobby?"

"Yes, Bobby Harrison. He only lives around the block on Washington Street!"

"Isn't he the fellow who's kind of sweet on you?"

Amanda's eyes twinkled again. "Of course," she said. "Why do you think I want to borrow it from him?"

"Well, let's head on over there. It's not too late," Mary said cheerfully. She was already done with her homework and, besides, she was interested in Bobby, too. Although she certainly was not going to tell Amanda that right now.

The girls decided that, although it was dark outside, it was still warm enough that they could venture outdoors without a cape. Amanda

170

was back in good spirits once more, now that her crisis was about to be resolved, and she and Mary chuckled and teased each other as only teenage girls can do. They headed out the door of their second floor room and onto the landing leading to the stairway down to the main hall.

Mrs. McGuire's boarding house, where they had their room, was an imposing old structure. It covered two city lots and went three stories tall. From the widow's walk, above the third floor, you could take in the whole city below and the bay beyond. Johnson's Island, hugging the north side of the bay, was clearly visible, as was the warship, the *Michigan*.

Most of Mrs. McGuire's boarders were men. Travelling salesmen, mostly, and most of them middle-aged. They were people passing through town, and looking for a place to stay that not only was cheaper than the West House downtown on the waterfront, but which had all the conveniences of home. Molly McGuire mother-henned all of her guests, and consequently had no shortage of boarders. Despite the predominance of men, it was the presence of Molly McGuire that drew the two girls to her boarding house. Or more accurately put, it was what convinced the girls' parents to let them stay there.

Mary closed the door behind them, and moved toward the staircase, which led down to the parlor and the massive oak front door with the leaded glass window. At the top of the stairs, Mary stopped dead in her tracks. Amanda, who was trailing right behind her, bumped into her and nearly pushed her down the stairs.

"What did you stop for?" Amanda asked, obviously annoyed.

"Be quiet!" Mary whispered sternly. Although there really was no need to whisper. A steady hum of male voices seemed to rise on the blue-gray smoke of their cigars up the stairs.

"I've seen that man before," she continued, pointing to a short, somewhat rotund man with a black beard and beady black eyes to match, "and I don't want to see him again!"

Her words dropped from her mouth like grease onto a hot griddle. The man, impeccably dressed with a neatly-tied cravat and a jaunty bowler perched on his head, had just entered through the hall. He was talking with John Robinson, one of Mrs. McGuire's guests. Behind the short, dark man, through the doorway and onto the front porch, was a growing crowd of men that, based upon their dress, came from various stations in life.

"Who is he? I don't recognize him," Amanda asked innocently.

"That's the man who tried to rape me!" Mary's eyes shot sparks, white-hot, like fusillading cannonades on the Fourth of July. She would not speak that man's name, although she knew it – Charles Cole. It would somehow taint her yet again to let his foul name cross her fair lips.

"Oh, my God!" Amanda said. "You never mentioned anything about that before. When did this happen?"

"Never mind!" Mary snapped. The feisty farm girl was not about to be distracted by Amanda's sniveling.

"Please, Mary. Let's go back to the room. I'm afraid what he might do if he sees you. I can do without the English book." Amanda peered meekly though the tobacco-induced cloud at the object of Mary's hatred.

"Absolutely not!" Mary shot back. "I am not going to let that man take control of my life. That's exactly what he would like to do. And I'll be *damned* if I'll let him."

Amanda had never heard Mary use any kind of swear word before, not even the relatively benign "D" word. Never in their 17 years together. That was not the way her strict Lutheran parents had raised her. Amanda knew Mary was greatly perturbed.

The crowd streamed from the parlor and the front porch into Mrs. McGuire's sitting room. What luck! Mary thought. The heating register in their room was just above the place where the men were gathering below. By opening the register just a little, she would be able to hear everything. The grates would obstruct her view somewhat, but with luck, she might see something.

"That man can't be up to any good at all. What in the world is he doing here, of all places?" Mary pondered aloud. Intuitively, she felt down to the very center of her bones, that if that man were here, some sort of shenanigans would be going on.

Mary and Amanda moved back down the hall to their room. Unknowing fear, anger and curiosity had been tugging at Mary's emotions over the last few minutes, although it seemed like an eternity.

Then Mary breathed a pent-up sigh of relief, as she realized that the man had not seen her. And she would hear everything that was going on in the parlor downstairs. This time, Amanda would be her witness. This was not going to be like her last encounter with Charles Cole, no siree, where it was his word against her. If that man said or did *anything* at all suspicious, this time he was going to pay!

* * * * * * *

The day dawned cool and crisp. Fingers of steam rose from the waters of Sandusky Bay as the warm aqua-colored waters of Lake Erie met the cool dry air blowing across it. Gulls swooped for minnows breaking the surface, or sat on the tops of pier posts, simply waiting and watching. To the residents of Sandusky, it was a typical fall day. Although the bite in the air was a precursor of the howling winds, driving snow and freezing sleet of January, it was a welcome relief from the dog days of August which, thankfully, were now behind them again for another year.

But to John Yates Beall, this was anything but a typical day. This was the day when the Plan had come together.

As he stood at the platform awaiting the train back to Toronto, the morning sun shone brightly upon his face. It was a sign, John thought. *The brightness of the day shines like the glory of our cause. The good Lord has looked with favor upon this mission.* He nodded to himself, content.

In the distance, a train whistle blew. John ticked off the elements of the Sandusky end of the Plan in his mind, one more time, just to make sure he had not overlooked something. The Plan was in motion. If anything needed to be revised, or reconsidered, this was his last opportunity. Once he was on the train back to Canada, it would be too late.

The volunteers. Cole had marshaled the forces of the Knights of the Golden Circle, and John was convinced that, although their numbers were small, they were generally men dedicated to the Confederate cause. All they really had to do, Beall convinced himself, was to row out to the *Michigan* after Cole had drugged the crew members that hadn't been bought. They could certainly hold the ship until he arrived with the real sailors, the ones that Bennett Burley had recruited in Canada. And, despite the row he and Cole had earlier, John was now determined that Cole could accomplish his part of the plan.

The date was set. There was no turning back now. The *Michigan* would soon be theirs and the men on Johnson's Island freed. John and his crew would escort the weak and the sick to Canada and safety. The bulk of the Johnson's Island contingent would then take over the arms of their captors and be carried across the bay to the mainland by more local Copperheads with boats. The liberated rebel officers would then fight their way, if need be, south to the Appalachians. That should be a relatively easy task, they had agreed, since the Union's rear line was notoriously poorly defended.

As a final precautionary measure, John would send a coded telegram to Cole on the day for execution of the Plan, to confirm that the rebel contingent was set to make their water-borne surprise incursion, courtesy of a lake steamer. And Cole would then call his own Copperhead crew together to implement their end of the plan.

Nothing should go wrong. Everything had been arranged. Within a week, thousands of Confederate officers would be free. John would be captain of the only warship on the Great Lakes, in essence in charge of the Great Lakes operations of the Confederate Navy. The *Michigan*'s 16 guns would command the Union's attention. And the Stars and Bars would be fluttering from the mainmast.

* * * * * * *

Charles Cole removed the pile of crumpled telegrams from his valise. It wasn't much of a hiding place, but he didn't expect that anyone would be going through his room anyway.

"Waiting to ship your goods. Please confirm your Order. Mr. Carrie." The message was the same on each wire he had received. The only distinguishing feature was the date on each one. Cole knew he was being reminded that he had not filed his biweekly reports with his Union contact for nearly two months.

Cole's lips turned up in a sneer, and he laughed out loud. Guffawed, in fact. Who the hell cares about some damned silly report now? He thought. In another week, he mused, I'll be gone. I've got the $25,000 from Beall, sitting safely in the Mt. Hope bank account. Plus the other money that I was able to finagle from Annie that I stuck temporarily in the damned bank up in Canada. As soon as the Canadian funds can be transferred to Sandusky, I'll be out of here. As far away as possible.

The real catch was that Annie was back. Cole was still attracted to her. It would be hard for any man not to be attached to an attractive woman that could drink and make fiery, passionate love like she did. But it would be tough for him to sneak away too soon. Annie was dedicated to the cause. And she seemed to be paying extra special attention to him since she had returned from her last trip to Toronto. Cole was just a little bit concerned about whether Annie would pull that derringer out from her bloomers and use it on him. Patience, man, patience, he told himself.

Cole tore each sheet of yellow paper bearing Mr. Carrie's message into half, then half again. He piled the pieces in a neat pyramid in the large clear glass ashtray sitting on the lamp stand near the door. He removed a packet of matches from this pocket. Lifting his left shoe from the floor, he drew the matchstick across the sole.

The square little stick glowed red on the end, and then, with a tiny puff of grey smoke, erupted in a violent orangish-blue flame. Cole put the burning match to the pyramid in the ashtray. He smiled with satisfaction as the flame crept, slowly at first, up the side of the paper mound, then erupted into a miniature inferno.

Cole pulled a cigar from his breast pocket, and leaned over the flame to light it. He took one deep draw, then two more in quick succession, until he was sure the stogie was lit. Picking up his bowler from the bed, he primped himself in the mirror hanging on the back of the door, first adjusting his hat, then looking for lint on his frock coat. As the burning papers curled up into a little pile of smoldering black ash, Charles Cole opened the door, closed it gently behind him, and then headed toward the hotel dining room where Annie was already waiting for him.

* * * * * * *

"Sis, you've just got to believe me!" Mary Stephens paced up and down the kitchen floor like a caged lion, already convinced that even her own family would not now believe her.

Julia Stephens could see that her teenage sister-in-law was perplexed. But what was she to do? Only 21 years old herself, she hadn't much experience in dealing with this sort of thing. War plots and Confederate sabotage right here in Sandusky, Ohio? Who would ever believe that such events might transpire in this sleepy little town!

This was the kind of thing that she needed Vincent for. He would know how to deal with this. The young girl with fire in her eyes was his own sister. He was older and more experienced at life generally than she was.

But her Vincent was a lawyer with the Treasury Department in Washington, where he would almost certainly stay until the war was over. That was how Vincent Stephens served his country. Blind in one eye since birth, and at the advanced age of 40, he had been rejected by the volunteer army. Like all of the Stephens clan, though, he was a fierce Union man, and insisted on making this sacrifice for his country. After all, he had reasoned, it was the least he could do when so many young men were dying for their country.

"Mary, honey," Julia cooed, "I never said I didn't believe you. I'm just trying to tell you that other people may find this story really hard to believe."

"What's so hard about it? There are thousands of rebel officers right out in the bay! The government must believe there's a reason to be concerned about something, or they would never have sent the *Michigan* there in the first place."

"I know, dear," Julia said as calmly as she could. She knew the girl had a point. "But there are all of these soldiers at Johnson's Island, and on Cedar Point. And there's all those guns on the *Michigan*. I just can't believe that a bunch of men are going to row out to a warship of the United States Navy, climb aboard unnoticed, and take the ship over in the middle of the night. Besides, what would they do with it?"

Mary Stephens sensed that, once again, nobody would believe her, even if Amanda had backed up her story. But that was unlikely. Her best friend had hastily packed her suitcase and hired a carriage this morning to haul her home to her parents. Amanda had been scared to death. Literally. Mary's talk about rape had frightened her. But it was the fact that rebel saboteurs were operating right in Sandusky . . . . That was just too much. She had cried all night. It would be safe back with Mamma and Papa. So that's where Amanda went.

"Sis, I'm not suggesting that you or I have to do something about this all by ourselves," Mary protested. "All I'm saying is let's do *something*. Let the provost marshal check it out. What could it hurt?" Mary knew that her story would only hold water with the authorities if the wife of a prominent lawyer, such as her brother Vincent, backed her up.

"Fair enough, Mary," Julia responded, sighing heavily. She got up from the table and put her arms around her sister-in-law. Even though Julia was a few years older than Mary, she was a petite little thing, barely reaching five feet. She just came up to Mary's chin. "As soon as your brother comes home from Washington in a few weeks, we can discuss it with him. He's got all of those connections in the capital, you know. He'll be able to get some immediate attention directed to this."

Mary could hardly believe her ears. She grabbed Julia by the shoulders, and pushed her away.

"But I told you, they're planning to make their move next week! We can't wait until Vincent gets home! That will be too late, much too late!" Mary's fists were clenched tight, and the skin showed white where her fingernails were pressing into her hands.

"Are you sure, dear? Something's going to happen next week?"

"Absolutely," Mary said emphatically, nodding her head in affirmation. "I heard them say so last night."

176

"Very well, then," Julia smiled hesitantly. "I've got a friend who's an officer on the *Michigan*. Ensign Murray. I'll speak with him, and see what he thinks. Is that all right?"

Mary was not so sure that an ensign would be able to do much of anything. But at least he was on the ship that the rebels had targeted. He would certainly have a better idea what should be done next.

"Alright, but I want to be there with you. I want to make sure nothing is left out," Mary said.

14

It had been a long time since John could relax. Although he was loath to admit it, the tension associated with developing the Plan had taken its toll. Especially in having to deal with Cole. John was still not entirely comfortable with putting his life – and those of the men Bennett Burley had recruited for the mission – in the hands of Cole. But at this point, everything was set. John consoled himself with his unshakable certitude that everything was now in God's hands.

John was snapped back to the reality of the moment by a rapid tap-tap-tap on the end of his bamboo fishing pole.

"Pull, man, pull! Pull the bloody line in! You've got to set the hook!"

Bennett Burley had dropped his own pole on the dock and reached across to Beall's.

"Don't you know anything about fishing, captain?" Burley shouted. The shouting really was not necessary; it was a calm day. No wind to speak of. But the winter's chill was fast approaching, and John could already feel it in the air. It was chilly, and a northwesterly breeze kept the waters choppy.

John felt that all too familiar tightening deep in his chest. And the beginning of just a tickle in his right lung that, if things developed as they usually did, meant that John was in for another spell of hacking and coughing, spitting up blood, and gasping for air, much like a fish out of water. That little brown bottle of laudanum that accompanied John everywhere was his only relief.

Burley set John's pole onto the dock. Hand over hand he hoisted the dripping wet line out of the murky water. The line dashed haphazardly left, then right, constantly tugging, as the fish on the line made what would ultimately be a futile effort to stay below the waves and away from the inevitable terror about the surface. The battle ended quickly enough, for the tiny perch was hopelessly outdone by the Scotsman, who knelt grinning on the dock.

At the end of John's line was a feisty yellow perch, fighting ferociously, yet hopelessly, for its life. It was only a fish, but its eyes conveyed the terror of its own personal torment as Burley grasped it firmly about the middle, removed the hook from its mouth, and threw the flopping fish into the pail where it joined the 20 or so of its cousins already caught.

"You will recall, Mr. Burley, that this was your idea, not mine, to go fishing. I really don't care much for this sport." John had tried hard to enjoy these few hours of relative solitude, where the tensions of the moment could be forgotten, where he might be able to escape the checking and rechecking of details of the Plan, running through his own mind. And he had to admit that, to his extent, this trip to the Windsor City Dock had been a worthwhile expenditure of time.

The Scotsman guffawed. "That may be so, Captain Beall. But sometimes facing our own phobias and fears is the best way to overcome them. Wouldn't you agree?" Burley reached into the bait bucket. His hand darted around the water until he had cornered a tiny, wiggling minnow. Burley held the little baitfish behind its head, and ran the barb of the hook from its jaw though the front of its head, just between its two eyes.

"That was a mighty nice perch we pulled in, captain. Here," he said, handing the pole back to John, baited and ready, "there's plenty more to be caught."

John sighed, and took the pole. He gently lowered the line into the water, watching the helpless minnow swim to its inevitable doom as the dinner for a hungry perch waiting under the dock.

Burley was absolutely correct, of course, and John knew it. The only way to overcome a problem is to look it square in the eye. Good advice, John thought. Especially when it comes to the Plan. Forget about whether the details will work out. Forget about whether Cole will perform as scheduled. Just plow ahead. Trust in God to see that everything works out as He would have it. Yes, that was the answer.

John barely noticed the tapping on the end of his line, as yet another perch succumbed to the temptation to go for the minnow on the hook.

* * * * * * *

The wide ribbon of water known as the Detroit River was all that separated the Village of Windsor from the City of Detroit, on the north side of the river. It was a quirk of geography, not lost on Southerners who found themselves in the undesirable position of being separated from home by hundreds of miles of Yankee territory, that Union territory was north of them. What had been a sleepy little town before the war had come alive with intrigue. Local merchants had prospered greatly as rebels, Copperheads and even skedaddlers moved across the placid river, often under cover of darkness.

Many of the hotels and boarding houses of Windsor were fast being turned into virtual Confederate strongholds. As had been the case in the military and social order from which they came, groups and classes tended to be attracted to areas and places that reminded them of home. The Southern aristocracy found the Windsor Castle House very much to their liking.

The very name – Windsor Castle – conjured up images that the more-established Southern expatriates found impossible to resist. Regal. Elegant. Sophisticated. Exclusive. Extravagant. And it truly was all of these. The imposing red brick structure was located at the edge of town, just where the streets turned to dusty country roads and grassy lots turned to forest. In fact, it was really an English country estate. The mansion, imposing in and of itself, was surrounded by an English country garden, complete with manicured boxwood hedges, and appropriately placed statuary of Greek goddesses, nymphs and such. The gracefully aging stone statutes were covered with a fine green patina, nurtured in part by the perpetual dampness carried in year round off the Detroit River.

For John Yates Beall, now a guest in Room No. 1, the Windsor Castle House triggered special memories. Back in his room after the fishing expedition with Burley, he peered through the open window of his room at the lush gardens beyond. Recollections of teenage years he had spent in England with his Grandfather Yates cascaded gently from the past into the present. The time with his grandfather had been idyllic. They had spent most of the time just travelling the English countryside. The faces and voices of all those innumerable relatives to whom he had been introduced by his grandfather as simply "your American cousin" were clearer than they had been for years.

But even these memories, pleasant though they were, could not and would not obliterate the reason John was here in the first place. It was now just a matter of days until the Plan was to be executed. And there was still much to be done.

Burley had come to Canada after a daring escape through the sewers from Fort Delaware, a Union prison camp some forty miles below Philadelphia. After being reunited with his old captain in Toronto, he was tasked by John with the job of recruiting rebel refugees for the Plan.

Burley worked with a vengeance in finding the best crew available. He had scrounged up the twenty brightest and best, Burley said. Men of action, all battle tested. And a few with seagoing experience.

John would decide for himself tonight. Not that he didn't trust his old comrade with the lilting brogue. He had no doubt, no sir, that the men Burley had selected would do. And since the Plan was really quite simple, it was bound to succeed. So long, that is, as Cole didn't botch things up in Sandusky.

The thought of Cole and the possibility of trouble brought a sudden, but not unusual, tightening in John's chest, and a tickle in his bronchia. He tried hard to suppress the cough welling to the surface. But he knew, based on the renewed frequency of the attacks, that only the contents of a special little bottle could keep things under control. He fumbled in his pocket for the laudanum. It wasn't there! In a near panic, John then spied the brownish bottle on the writing table where he had left it. He lunged for it, and removed the cork with his teeth. Spitting the stopper out onto the bed, John threw back his head, and let the soothing liquid deliver relief down his gullet.

* * * * * * *

Sandusky, Ohio
Near Johnson's Island
Aboard the U.S.S. *Michigan*

Captain Jack Carter furiously paced the bridge. Back and forth, back and forth he moved. It was only about eight good steps in one direction before he had to turn around and march back in the direction from which he had come. His hands were clasped firmly behind his back, and his eyes were riveted to the polished planks of flooring, worn smooth by incessant pacing of the aging warrior that commanded the only American naval vessel on the Great Lakes.

The day had dawned bright and warm. But as is often case on the Great Lakes in autumn, the weather was fast changing. A cold wind was blowing over the shallow waters of Lake Erie, and white caps, frothy like well-beaten egg whites, appeared everywhere. The temperature had dropped ten degrees in the last hour. And it was likely to drop at least another ten before the Canadian cold front settled in.

The white painted hull of the *Michigan,* bobbing fitfully at anchor, cast a skeleton-like appearance over the Johnson's Island landing, as low-lying moisture-laden black clouds scuttled across the sky.

The only concession to the weather that Captain Carter had made was to pace the deck even faster. He knew that young sailors expected to look to their commander to lead and inspire them. He didn't want to be their father figure. Or even worse, their grandfather figure. He wanted to be their leader.

"So, Ensign Murray, what is this important message you've got?"

The wind whistled through the curly red beard and hair of Ensign John Wilson Murray, whipping it across his face in one direction, then another, as he paced the deck with his captain. Murray had not had time to change from civilian clothes he had been wearing ashore. The message he got was too damned important for that. If what he had learned was correct, precautions needed to be taken immediately.

"As you know, captain, I have been keeping a watchful eye on Mr. Cole. Really hadn't been much to watch, actually, since he arrived in Sandusky. The man appeared to be doing little more than swilling down champagne and eating mutton chops at the West House dining room. He did make an occasional visit to some well-known rebel sympathizers. I have followed him all around for quite some time now. But all I ever was able to attribute to him before was some vague talk about taking over the *Michigan*. It seemed unlikely to me that the rebels would ever get organized enough to pull anything off. Especially with people like Cole responsible for setting things up. Up until now, there was hardly anything that would give a cause for alarm, sir."

"Yes, of course. I know that, Mr. Murray. Ensign Hunter has been faithfully delivering your reports. It seems that all this Cole really did was swindle the rebels out of some of their filthy lucre. Nothing wrong with that, though, is there?"

"No, I guess not, sir," replied Murray dutifully. "It's that much less they've got to spend on their war machine, such as it is."

"Anyway, please continue, Mr. Murray. You didn't come out to the ship just to repeat what Ensign Hunter has already conveyed to me. No, that wouldn't be it all, would it?"

Carter stopped his pacing at the end of the bridge. Grasping the railing, he peered through the netting, which enveloped the main mast of the ship like some giant spider web. Just a few short miles across the bay, the steeples of Sandusky's churches pierced the gloom of the leaden sky.

"Sir, I am somewhat hesitant to report to you what I have heard. Not just - - -"

"Now, Ensign," Carter interrupted, "you wouldn't be standing here if you didn't intend to report, would you? And why in the world would you be 'hesitant,' as you put it, to keep your commanding officer apprised of matters that may affect his command?"

Murray shuffled his feet, uncomfortable with the question. "Well, sir, it's because I'm not sure how much weight you're willing to give to the story of a teenage farm girl. I know I am having difficulty grasping this myself."

"Teenage farm girl. What teenage girl? What are you talking about, Ensign? I am becoming very confused. I believe your orders were to keep Mr. Cole under close scrutiny. Whatever in the world has a teenage girl got to do with that?"

Murray cleared his throat. The wind was picking up even more now, making it increasingly difficult to hear. "Mary Stephens, sir. The girl's name is Mary Stephens." He now had to shout to be heard over the howl of the wind through the rigging.

"Yes?" Commander Carter's brows furrowed together in anticipation.

"You see, sir, Miss Stephens overheard an entire meeting presided over by Mr. Cole. A lot of men were there."

"How many is 'a lot,' Mr. Murray?" Carter inquired thoughtfully.

"She wasn't real clear on the number, sir. She wasn't in a good position to be counting them. But Miss Stephens said she thought it was well over two dozen fellows, sir."

Carter said nothing, but nodded his assent to continue.

Murray hesitated for a moment, then went on. "In seventy-two hours, a rebel invasion force is supposed to be coming from Canada to capture the *Michigan*," Murray gestured pointedly at the deck of the ship beneath their feet, now rising and sinking in the storm-induced swells, "and to free the rebel officers we are holding right over there," he said, nodding in the direction of the prison camp on Johnson's Island.

The pitch of the wind blowing through the rigging climbed to a high-pitched howl. The wind had changed direction and now the ship was undulating in the oncoming swells. Despite the noise of the storm, there was a deafening silence. Carter grasped the railing tightly with the increase in ferocity of the wind.

"Jesus, Mary and Joseph," Carter mumbled under his breath, shaking his head in disbelief. "I never thought they would be brazen enough to try it."

"What's that, sir?" Murray shouted over the wind.

But Carter was not listening to the young ensign next to him. His mind was too preoccupied with the magnitude of what appeared to be on the horizon for him and his crew. If it was action he wanted, it appeared he certainly was going to get it now. In spades.

"Jesus, Mary and Joseph," he mumbled again. "Jesus, Mary and Joseph."

* * * * * * *

Windsor Castle Hotel
Windsor, Canada West

The Windsor Castle's private dining room was filled with a smorgasbord of men. Most were young, in their twenties. Most of them were from Virginia and Maryland, spiritual kinfolk of John Yates Beall, whose chair at the head table was as yet unoccupied. The men came in all shapes and sizes. But their one unifying bond – besides the fact that they were all fiercely dedicated rebels – was that they all had a certain steely glint in their eye that signaled fierceness and independence. It was this characteristic that Bennett Burley had spotted in them, and which attracted his interest. It was the sheer power of Burley's persuasive personality that drew the men into the Plan.

A huge man with a flowing, jet black beard and long, straight hair down over his shoulders tapped Bennett Burley on the shoulder, as he stood making small talk in a corner with two of his recruits. "So where is this Captain Beall? You said he'd be here by now." The man tripped, just a little, as he leaned into Burley's face. Even though, as a Scotsman and a sailor Burley was accustomed to strong drink, the odor of stale alcohol was overpowering.

Burley recognized the man who now peered down at him through glassy eyes, his eyelids drooping from the accumulated weight of too many beers. William Byland was his name. An oysterman from the Eastern Shore. Tough as nails. But overly fond of his booze, even for a fisherman. Byland was most fond of beer, of which there was plenty tonight. The men were drinking especially heavily, since Burley had banned all tobacco to protect Beall's fragile lungs.

The Scotsman pulled a pocket watch from his breast pocket. Tenderly opening the lid, he stared at the timepiece, totally composed, or so it seemed. 8:00. Captain Beall was supposed to have arrived a half-hour ago. Burley closed the pocket watch, and returned it to his pocket. "Captain Beall will be here momentarily, Mr. Byland. Just go get another beer. By the time you've finished it, you'll be ready for Captain Beall." Burley winked good-naturedly at the tree of a man, who then ambled off toward one of the tapped kegs of beer in the corner of the room.

Actually, Burley was worried. He had left Beall in his room three hours ago under a big eiderdown comforter, headed for a laudanum-induced sleep. Beall had had another of his coughing spells. Burley had witnessed these bouts before. They were all bad. But this one appeared to be worse than any of the others. If it were any other man, the Plan would be postponed until the leader's health had improved. But not John Yates Beall. He insisted that everything go ahead as planned. One way or the other, he would see this through, Beall had assured him.

Burley was about to excuse himself to go roust Captain Beall when a palpable hush rippled through the gathering. Burley turned his head toward the door. There stood Captain Beall.

"Good evening, gentlemen. My name is John Yates Beall. Won't you all please be seated? We've got a lot of work to do yet tonight." John strode briskly to the chair at the head of the table, pulled it out, then seated himself. Ramrod stiff, his very presence exuded authority. The crisp black suit and sparkling, starched white shirt, accented with a dark navy blue cravat, created the perfect picture of a man in control.

The men moved swiftly to their seats, taking their mugs of beer with them. Some of them pushed the dirty plates and glassware toward the center of the table, making little clinking noises. A few of the men talked to each other in subdued tones as they seated themselves. But otherwise, the room was silent.

John cleared his throat, and the background clinking and talking stopped. "On behalf of President Davis and the Confederate States of America, let me extend thanks to all of you for agreeing to join us here this evening." John's voice sounded hoarse, Burley observed, but conveyed a vitality and fire that came from deep within his soul. "I know why we're here, and so do you. Tonight . . ." John caught his breath, and fought back the rasping feeling rising in his chest. "Tonight, we lay the final plans for a military operation." John paused, caught his breath again, and then continued. "An operation which I am totally convinced will tip the scales in favor of the cause of freedom for the South."

"Here, here!" A couple of voices from around the table cheered lustily.

"As Mr. Burley has undoubtedly informed you, you men shall be part of an elite vanguard force. Our primary objective is simple, we shall capture the Yankee warship, the U.S.S. *Michigan*."

The men had indeed already been apprised by Mr. Burley of the objective. The enticement of what seemed to be an easy bounty posted by the rebel government for capture of the *Michigan* had been Burley's single greatest inducement in attracting his force.

John reached for a glass of water on the table in front of him and took one slow sip, then another.

"And we shall in the process liberate thousands of our brethren being held prisoner on that dungeon of a prison called Johnson's Island!"

More cheers and whistles erupted from around the table. John motioned for quiet.

"Although I am confident of success, let me remind you all that there is considerable danger involved in this venture. And to a certain extent, the outcome depends on you." The excitement that had been building now seemed to dissipate, as the men contemplated what failure might mean for them.

"Unfortunately, there are Yankee spies and sympathizers all about us. That is no revelation. The North knows very well that men and women of the Confederacy are here in Canada. You are all men who have either been driven from your homes, or who have escaped from Yankee prisons. And for this reason, I must insist at this time that each and every one of you give me your solemn oath. . . that the details to be discussed here this evening shall go no further."

There was general nodding of agreement among the now stern-faced men seated about the table.

"If any of you have difficulty with this requirement, you are invited to leave now, with no recrimination or retribution whatsoever." Nobody moved. None of the men had any intention of leaving.

"Very well, then." John gestured toward Bennett Burley, who was standing against the wall, observing the entire scene. "Mr. Burley, will you join me, please," John said, his voice growing even firmer. Burley nodded, and moved to a chair next to John's.

Seated just to the left of the young captain, one of the other young Virginians recruited by Burley listened carefully to the plan details, which followed. Very carefully. He, too, had decided that this adventure could mean money. But he had come up with a more sure way to get it. He had an appointment in Detroit later this evening. With the provost marshal.

* * * * * * *

Detroit, Michigan
Later that Night

"Do you hear that knock, dear?" Louisa Hill poked her husband gently in the ribs. A fitful sleeper in the best of circumstances,

187

she had grown even more tense as the war years dragged on. Her husband, Lt. Col. Bowdoin Henry Hill, had acquired a lot of unusual late night callers. He had told her it was part of his job as the provost marshal. To keep the military peace and protect the nation's borders, with rebels swarming like mosquitoes just across the river in Windsor, it required that he adjust his schedule to conform to the needs of his informants. That was B.H. Hill's job – to recruit, utilize and reward informants, persons who would betray the rebel cause, for the proper remuneration of course.

Hill's eyes fluttered open. "What did you say, dear?" he moaned. Actually, Hill suspected the reason for the wakeup. Another rebel at the door. These visits had grown increasingly frequent since the fall of Atlanta three months ago. Although he could understand that these rebs could read the inevitable handwriting on the wall about the South's impending doom, he couldn't figure out just why these fellows, most of them ragged and dirty, had to make their appearance at his door in the dead of night. He gave up wondering about this and simply concluded that, like cockroaches, certain creatures prefer to do their business under the cover of darkness.

"I said I heard a knock at the door," she replied. Louisa Hill pushed the quilt that had been covering her toward the foot of the bed, then threw her legs over the side. She fumbled in the dark on the lamp stand, found the box of matches, and lit the coal oil lamp.

B.H. Hill squinted in the dim light and sighed. "I guess I better find out who's there," he said. He reached over to the chair next to his side of the bed, got his nightshirt off the chair and pulled it over his head. It had turned frosty cold in the bedroom, since the cold front moved through in the afternoon, and Hill was reluctant to leave the comfort of his bed. But there was duty to be done and, by God, he would do it.

Louisa was disappointed that B.H. had put the nightshirt on so quickly, for she liked drinking in the view of his body in the flickering amber light of the coal oil lamp. She marveled at her husband's ability to still sleep completely naked, every single night, no matter what the weather or the occasion. He said it was so that his skin could breathe. Louisa surmised that it was for more mischievous purposes. She welcomed his advances, even though she and her husband were both approaching middle age.

The knocking came at the door downstairs again. This time there was no mistaking the sound. There was definitely someone at the front door.

Hill walked around to Louisa's side of the bed, picked up the lamp and walked to the window. Yep, there he was. A shadowy figure was outlined in the dim light of the street lamp outside their window. It was impossible to see who it was, what with the light so bad. To further disguise himself, the man had the wide brim of his hat pulled tightly around his face.

Hill threw open the bedroom window, and the cold air of the outside world rushed into the room, instantaneously changing the temperature from cool to cold. Hill admitted to himself that he was glad that, in addition to the usual requirements of modestly, he had put that nightshirt on to at least keep some of the chill off.

"Heh, you there?" Hill shouted out the window. The man below looked up, but did not utter a word.

"What is it you want at this ungodly hour?" Hill bellowed. He had a clear view of the street below, and nobody had apparently been tailing this character on his door stoop. He didn't know what time it was, but he knew from the deathly stillness that is was late, very late. Middle of the night most likely.

The man shifted his head slowly in the direction of Hill's window. "Sir, I have come with information of the gravest importance," he drawled in a syrupy Virginia accent. "But I would prefer to discuss my business with you in a more circumspect situation, if you don't mind." Ever polite, the man now tipped his hat toward Hill, then lowered his head gently again.

"Very well, sir," Hill responded haughtily. "I shall be down shortly."

Hill pulled his head back inside, then closed the window gently, but firmly. Her part of the job completed, Louisa had already crawled back in bed, tossing and turning in a futile effort to find just the right part of the bed to induce a prompt return to sleep. As he headed toward the bedroom door, the flickering flame of the lamp illuminated the time on the ticking wall clock. Two o'clock in the morning.

"This had damn well better be important," Hill mumbled to himself. "I'm getting awfully damned tired of this bullshit!" he said under his breath. "Two o'clock in the morning! Unbelievable!"

Below, the man fidgeted, his bladder filled with beer from the Windsor Castle House. He knew he should relieve himself now, while he had the chance. Glancing over his shoulder to make sure nobody could see, the man urinated as inconspicuously as possible on the wall of Hill's home. Now relieved, he knew he could go on for a time without any interruptions. The man was quite sure his discussion with

Hill would take some time, for he had something very important to say. All for the right price, of course.

15

It had been a particularly profitable week for the *Philo Parsons*. Except for a one-day reminder that Old Man Winter was waiting outside the door, the weather had been conducive to leisurely cruising on the lake. Balmy temperatures and billowy clouds floating lazily across the sky had returned, drawing greenback-bearing passengers aboard the posh side-wheel steamer for a last cruise before the weather turned sour. It was almost incidental that the route took the ship from Detroit down Lake Erie to Sandusky, on the south shore of the inland sea.

Walter O. Ashley, the ship's clerk, was secure in the ship's office on the upper deck of the *Parsons*. He took off his eyeshade and sighed deeply. He had grown to detest Sundays. It was the only day that the ship didn't sail. And so it was during the sailing season that every Sunday – a day set aside by the Lord for prayer and reflection – that all decks were scrubbed down, toilets cleaned until they glistened, food brought aboard by the box and cartload, and preparations made for the next week's sailings.

It was also on Sunday that Ashley was expected to reconcile the books for the previous week. This part of the job he liked, because a portion of the profit was his. This week in particular, he was glad he owned a piece of this floating money machine. Three roundtrips had generated nearly two thousand dollars in fares and sundry sales. Not a bad return on an initial outlay of $16,000 for the boat. It was especially good for this late in the season. Captain Atwood, principal owner of the little enterprise, would be quite pleased.

The Ingraham calendar clock on the wall above Ashley's roll top desk ticked steadily. Its pulsating, hypnotic beat was warm and soothing. Ashley wheeled himself back in his chair and noticed the time. Six o'clock. "Damn!" he said to himself with a start. "Late for dinner again." The missus would be mighty peeved. She didn't much like the fact that he was never home during the week, but she could deal with that. She insisted, though, that Sunday evenings be devoted to her. Ashley had given up trying to explain that once the sailing season was over, he would be home for months on end.

"Hullo, there! Anybody on board?" The voice drifted from the dock through the open porthole just to the left of Ashley's desk. The clerk peered out the porthole toward the dock below. There stood a short little man, draped in a navy pea coat with a wool cap pulled tight over his head. His hands were thrust into his jacket.

Ashley strode out the door and cupped his hands to bellow back to man on the dock. "The ship doesn't sail until tomorrow morning, sir. 8 o'clock. It's on the sailing schedule there in front of you," he yelled.

The man in the pea jacket looked up toward Ashley and nodded. "Yes indeed, sir," the man shouted back. "I am well aware of your ship's schedule. Friends sent me to see if special arrangements could be made for our group for tomorrow's sailing," The man's deep, baritone voice, resonating with a thick Scottish brogue, stressed the word "group."

Group, Ashley thought. Multiple fares! What a great way to start what may be the last good week of sailing! "How many in your group, sir?" he inquired.

"There'll be about twenty of us, captain," the pea coat-clad man responded.

Without hesitation, Ashley roared back. "Very well, sir. Come aboard. I'll be right down."

Ashley hobbled out of the ship's office, gimping down the deck to the stairwell, favoring his clubfoot. The man in the pea coat sauntered slowly toward the gangplank, where he waited patiently for Walter O. Ashley, ship's clerk and part owner of the *Philo Parsons*.

* * * * * * *

"Well, Mr. Smith, I trust you have some more information for me?" Lt. Col. B.H. Hill rubbed his hands together in anticipation.

"Yes, sir, I do," the man who called himself Smith squeaked. Even though they were safely ensconced inside Hill's commodious house, Smith still fidgeted nervously, fearful that one of his rebel compatriots might somehow discover him warming himself in front of the proverbial fire of the Union provost marshal, the ultimate symbol of Yankee military authority. "Could I have something to drink, sir?" Smith blurted out, "I'm mighty parched."

"Pardon me, son, I've forgotten my manners," said Hill. Hill's soothing, fatherly voice was betrayed by his cold, black eyes. The eyes finally settled on Smith, who looked down at the floor.

Hill walked to the door and called for Louisa. "Darling, would you please bring us some hot coffee, please?" He turned and asked, "Is coffee alright, Mr. Smith?"

Smith nodded, and fidgeted again in the hard wooden chair, his bottom crisscrossed by the cane webbing that formed the seat. Little did he know that Hill had picked that chair deliberately. All of his informants sat there, precisely because it did make them fidget. It gave them an indication early on who was in charge. He was.

Hill walked back to the sofa across from Smith, sat down, crossed his legs, and looked at Smith. "Now, where were we?" Hill scratched his short-cropped salt and pepper beard pensively. That was done for effect, too. People said he looked like General Grant, and Grant was never impetuous. "Oh, yes, you were to have gotten more information on this silly plot to invade Ohio from some of your friends, weren't you?"

Smith bristled, sat bolt upright in his chair, and leaned forward until his face was only inches away from Hill's. "Sir, I don't believe for a minute that this plot is silly. Anything but, in fact. It appears to be well thought-out, and the leaders of the operation are brave, dedicated, and intelligent men. It is personally sanctioned by none other than Jeff Davis himself," he said. "I don't believe it would be wise to underestimate the seriousness of this operation." Smith had leapt to defend the nobleness of the mission, temporarily forgetting that he had come to betray it.

Smith was proud of himself; he too could play this little mind game. If Hill didn't think the plot would amount to anything, there'd be damn little compensation. And that, of course, was the reason Smith was sitting here in the first place, for the money. The fact that the war appeared to be a lost cause helped soothe his conscience, too. In fact, he had convinced himself that by sitting down with the enemy, he was actually saving the lives of all those long-suffering rebel officers imprisoned on Johnson's Island, who would certainly die if this foolhardy attempt to break them out were really true.

"Well, why don't you let me be the judge of that, Mr. Smith," said Hill.

"To begin with, when was the last time you met with the plotters?" Hill inquired. The interrogation was underway.

"Just this afternoon, sir," responded Smith. "As far as they know, I'll still be heading south down the lake with them tomorrow morning." Smith paused, as Louisa Hill brought in the silver tray bearing two flowered English china cups and a large pot of coffee. She

193

set them down silently on the table between the two men, and left the room as quickly and quietly as she had entered it.

Smith reached under the wide band of his hat, which lay on the floor beside him and retrieved a small, white object. "They gave me this here ticket," he said, handing it to Hill.

Hill retrieved his reading glasses from his left breast pocket, and balanced them carefully on the bridge of his nose. "Good for one passage – Amherstburg, Ontario to Sandusky, Ohio. September 19, 1864." Hill read the flowery handwritten inscription, which filled the blank spaces on the pre-printed ticket.

"And there are twenty of them in this rebel band?" Hill inquired. That was the number Smith had provided him during that late night meeting yesterday. Smith nodded in the affirmative.

Hill whistled softly under his breath. This was big, really big, he thought. Assuming of course, this rebel scum could be trusted to carry out what they threatened. Past experience with these Southern turncoats had been disappointing. The information they provided him was usually worthless, or worse, flat out wrong. Most of these plots and plans were idle bar talk of dreams. But this time it somehow seemed different; this seemed real. It was hard for Hill to put a finger on just why. Maybe it was the ticket. That's a lot of trouble to go through for an idle fancy or work of a dreamer.

Hill pushed himself up off the sofa, walked to the window and looked out on the street, down to the very spot in front of his house where he had first spotted Mr. Smith. He clasped his arms behind his back authoritatively.

"Very well, Mr. Smith," Hill said. "Let's go over the details of this rebel plan, as it was told to you, and then we'll be done."

* * * * * * *

Sandusky, Ohio
Near Johnson's Island
Aboard the U.S.S. *Michigan*

Captain Jack Carter had come to detest receiving telegrams. They only spelled trouble; they never contained even a scintilla of good news. Just yesterday, one had come to him, asking that he inform one of his crewmen of the death of his mother. And now Ensign James Hunter, his officer of the day, stood hunched in the doorway of his cabin, holding in his left hand the distinctive yellow envelope that signified the arrival of yet another wire. More bad news.

Carter sat bent over his writing desk, reviewing the previous day's entries in the ship's log. "What have you got for me there, ensign?" barked Carter, barely glancing up. His eyes were bloodshot, and ugly gray-black circles had started to form under his eyes.

Ever since Ensign Murray had reported the distinct possibility of an impending invasion by rebels from Canada, Carter had slept little. He felt it was his duty to remain ever vigilant, to be prepared at a minute's notice to lead his men into battle against the rebs.

But Carter was ready. He had cancelled all shore leave. He had dutifully informed the War Department in Washington. He had alerted the prison commander at Johnson's Island to be on alert for any unusual activity by the prisoners that might signify a rebellion in concert with the anticipated invasion. All he could do now was wait, since he didn't know if the threat was real or, if it was, precisely how and when this invasion was supposed to take place.

Hunter ducked under the transom, pulled his shoulders in, and stepped through the narrow doorway into the captain's cabin. Hunter looked every bit the hardworking farmhand that he had been before the war. He saluted stiffly. "It's a telegram, sir. The clerk who delivered it said it came in over the wire marked 'urgent.'"

Carter sighed. He absolutely hated getting these wires. "Very well, mister. Let me have it. Just wait a minute while I read it."

"Yes, sir." Hunter handed the wire to Carter, then backed up a step toward the doorway in the cramped little room. The captain adjusted his little half reading glasses, opened the yellow envelope with his index finger and read the enclosed message:

> Have information that force of 30 rebel pirates departing Monday a.m. from Windsor aboard steamer *Philo Parsons.* Destination Sandusky. Pirates working with Charles Cole, rebel agent in Sandusky, to capture your ship and attack Johnson's Island prison. Urge utmost caution and immediate preparations to repel.
>
> B.H. Hill, Lt. Col.
> Provost Marshal
> Detroit

Carter re-read the wire, then laid it gently on his desk. He removed his reading glasses, pulling the frames off one ear, and then the other. He laid the lenses on top of the missive that promised to change the whole character of his war effort. At this point, Carter didn't

195

know whether to be scared or excited. He wanted action, and it appeared he might get it. He had come to feel like a eunuch of a sailor and officer, just sitting here pulling guard duty, and mixing it up a bit with Johnny Reb would surely be an improvement.

But even though he had more information about the nature of the rebel force, this Charles Cole character was still a wild card. Was Cole really working with the rebs now? Just a few days ago, Ensign Murray had brought the report that Cole was actively involved in a plot just like the Provost Marshal had described.

None other than Lafayette Baker himself, head of the Secret Service, had instructed Carter to keep close tabs on Cole. Even though Cole was supposed to be in the employ of the Federals, he had now been judged to be untrustworthy. This confirming wire from Detroit seemed to confirm that suspicion, and in spades.

Instinctively, Carter knew what he must do. "Mr. Hunter," he said, his voice now firm with the conviction of command. "There is nothing that we can do this evening. But I want you to assemble the men on the forward deck at 6:00 a.m. sharp. No excuses. Make sure the cook holds up breakfast until after the assembly. I want everybody, and I mean EVERYBODY, out there."

Hunter surmised that the telegram was important. Captain Carter had been acting a bit strange the last day or so, since the giant Scotsman John Wilson Murray had spoken with him. Carter had been pacing the deck frantically – even more than normal – pausing frequently to scan the horizon for some unknown object. Or he sat locked in his cabin in full dress uniform, polishing his steel sword until even the tiniest glint of light observed the wrong way could blind a man.

"Yes sir, captain," responded Hunter dutifully. "But what about Ensign Murray. He left the ship again yesterday and is not aboard. Would you like to send a launch ashore to retrieve him?"

Carter grasped his forehead in his hand, massaging out the tension headache building rapidly in front of his eyes. Damn! Hunter was right. Murray wasn't on board the ship; he wouldn't be here for the assembly. Carter had sent him back to Sandusky, after first hearing of a specific rebel invasion plot, and had ordered him to stick even tighter to Cole than he had before.

Murray needed to be informed. And Cole needed to be watched even closer. I'll send another officer ashore, Carter thought. Yes, he had the man. Charlie Eddy. Loyal, hardworking, although rather strange. But "average" wasn't what the situation called for.

Murray could handle that end of it. Loyalty was what was required. That was the key word. Loyalty. And Eddy was plenty loyal to Carter.

"I'd like you to see to it that you and Ensign Eddy see me in my quarters immediately after the assembly is concluded tomorrow morning, Mr. Hunter."

"Is there something we can do now, sir?" the ensign asked curiously.

"No, not really," Carter said. "We won't be in any real danger until tomorrow afternoon at the earliest." Carter knew that the boat wouldn't get to Sandusky until late the next day. But they would be ready for them. The gun crews would be drilling all day, the boiler room would have a good head of steam up, and he would double the posted lookouts.

"It's likely I'll have the two of you go ashore tomorrow in search of Mr. Murray."

"Very well, sir." Hunter snapped off another crisp salute. He backed out of Carter's quarters, pivoted and headed below decks to the engine room.

PART III: SEPTEMBER 19, 1864

"We want 3 dozen hatchets, also 4 grappling hooks."

– Letter dated September 14, 1864 from J.Y. Beall to an unnamed friend in Canada

16

ABOARD THE *PHILO PARSONS*
IN LAKE ERIE, OHIO

"You know what, Fred?"

Fredrick Hukill had nearly dozed off. The lazy midday sun had lulled him into a state of nearly catatonic relaxation. Actually, it was more like a state of suspended animation. But of course he could count on old Al Skinner to keep him from getting too lackadaisical. Hukill lifted his hat from his face – which had blocked the glare of the sun from his eyes – opened one heavy eyelid and turned his head toward Skinner. A frown momentarily creased Hukill's face, but just for a second or two. He wasn't going to let anything destroy the magnificence of this day. Not even his nervous, hyperkinetic old friend Al Skinner.

"What, Al?"

"Well, you see, Fred, it's like this." Skinner twitched his head to the right, his right shoulder arcing in unison. But Hukill didn't notice. Skinner had had these nervous tics for as long as he had known him. And he had known Al for a very long time indeed, since they grew up together on the same tenement street in Cincinnati over fifty years ago. "This day is just too perfect."

Hukill raised an eyebrow skeptically.

"What do you mean, too perfect?"

"Well, I really can't put my finger on it. I mean, who could ask for a better day, right? Nice warm sun. Just enough breeze to keep it pleasant. Nothing to do but sit on this here deck chair and enjoy the cruise."

"That's right, Al. Who could ask for more?"

Skinner continued his chatter before Hukill could replace his bowler hat over his face and return to his nap.

"See, it's always like this with me," Skinner rattled on. "Whenever something is going real good, ya know, something happens to mess things up. Remember that time when we were over in Baltimore, Fred? Remember that?" Skinner's right elbow flailed out, and a little whooping sound, barely noticeable, escaped his lips. His tics grew more dramatic as he got more excited.

Hukill nodded. Old Al was really wound up today, tighter than a clock spring. Best let him work it out of his system, he thought. He'd heard Old Al tell this story about the Baltimore riots for what seemed at least a hundred times, maybe more. It had been probably the most exciting thing that had happened to Skinner in his entire life.

"There we were, right downtown," Skinner said, "just trying to do a decent day's business, you and me. Darned good day it had started out to be, too. We was a-sellin' everything from ball peen hammers to limb saws like they was goin' out of style." Skinner nodded his head in agreement with himself. His left eyelid fluttered as fast as a hummingbird's wings, then stopped just as suddenly as it had started.

"Darned good day for a couple old hardware salesmen, yes indeed," Skinner continued. "But do ya remember how that day ended, Freddy? Do ya?"

Fred Hukill sighed. "Yeah, Al. Riots."

"Riots? Riots, you said? A hell of a lot more than riots! Those damned rebel scallywags in Baltimore were attacking Union soldiers. Can you imagine?" Both Skinner's shoulders arced upwards, first his right, then the other.

"Well, Al, those folks who see things from a Southern perspective may view that event completely different." Hukill now assumed the professorial role, one to which he had become accustomed over the years of his friendship with Old Al. The man didn't have all his wits about him most of the time, and when he did, it wasn't for long. Old Al didn't appreciate the subtleties of 1861 political and military strategy, such as it existed. "Al, those riots were started because some damned fool politician masquerading as a general decided it would be a good idea to march 8,000 fully armed men through the streets of Baltimore in broad daylight when tensions were already running high."

Skinner's face flushed beet red. The pitch of his voice had risen at least an octave as the thrill of the memory coursed through his veins. "It's an American city. And it was American soldiers. They had every damned right to be there! Those rebs shouldn't have done it. They should've just left 'em alone." Skinner's right wrist shook violently for a second, then stopped.

Hukill knew the game was up. When Old Al's story got to this point, he had run out of steam. All he knew was that it was wrong for the rebel-leaning citizens of Baltimore to attack those federal troops moving through their city in 1861 on the way to the defense of Washington. He really didn't need to know any more.

"You're right, Al. They really shouldn't have done that." Hukill replaced his bowler over his face, and stretched out his feet on the polished maple deck, hoping against hope to be able to resume his nap.

"And sir, what do you think about that?" Hukill heard Old Al speaking, but it wasn't to him. Or to himself, either, which Old Al also was prone to do with increasing frequency. No, his old friend and business partner Al had struck up a conversation with a total stranger. That was why he was such a successful salesman. Wasn't anybody that could escape Old Al's grip, once he set his mind on talking to you. You'd buy something just to be able to have an excuse to leave the store.

"Are you addressing me, sir?" The stranger spoke with a lilting British accent. Fred Hukill took the bowler off his face once again, to see who Old Al was bothering this time.

The stranger looked pleasant enough, really. He had a very congenial face, with a wispy beard that he was now tugging. His thinning brown hair matched the wispy beard. But the man was dressed like some damned undertaker, all in black. The man's pleasant demeanor contrasted with the harshness of his conservative black attire. It somehow didn't seem to fit him just right.

"You betcha!" Skinner responded, his left eye twitching wildly for several seconds.

"Now, Al," Hukill interjected, "this man may not even have heard our conversation. And if he did, he probably doesn't know much about what went on in this country three years ago."

The stranger in black smiled. "That's quite all right, sir. But actually, you are indeed correct. I don't know much about what transpired in your country."

Hukill arose from his deck chair, gently pushing Old Al behind him. Undaunted by the snub, Skinner muscled his way around to Hukill's left, placing himself between his friend Fred Hukill and the stranger.

"So, mister, where ya from?" Old Al barked.

"I am originally from England, but I've spent the last several years in Canada," the stranger said. "Never been to the States before."

"Well then, stranger, let me be the first to welcome you to our country," Skinner stuck out his right hand, pumping the stranger's proffered hand in a vise-like handshake. "Land of the free, home of the brave." Skinner had forgotten the national anthem had been written during a war with Britain, where this stranger said he was from.

"Why, have we left Canadian waters yet?" the stranger asked.

"We most certainly have," Hukill responded. "Come here, I want to show you something," he said. Hukill took the stranger by the arm and led him gently to the deck railing.

"See that?" Hukill said, pointing to a dim grey outline rising from the horizon.

"Yes."

"Those are the Erie Islands. American soil," said Hukill, now proud to play the role of tour guide for his foreign friend. A thin smile crossed the stranger's lips. Hukill continued, "Name's Frederick Hukill, from Cincinnati, Ohio. My friend here's Al Skinner."

The stranger bowed ever so slightly. "Pleased to make your acquaintance, gentlemen. My name is Beall. John Yates Beall."

* * * * * * **

The *Parsons* stopped in succession at each of the Erie Islands as it made its way southward to its terminus in Sandusky. To most of the passengers, the islands had blended together into an amorphous blur. They were all so close together geographically, and the routine was the same at each one. Each stop involved little more than tying up temporarily at a dock and exchanging bags of mail with the local postmaster and also unloading cargo generally consisting of day to day provisions for use by the islanders. At every stop, a handful of passengers disembarked, valises in hand.

The only variation to the routine occurred at Middle Bass Island, where Captain Atwood had left the boat. Middle Bass was where the Captain made his home; he always got off here. DeWitt Nichols, Atwood's young protégé, would handle affairs on board during the last few miles between Middle Bass and Sandusky.

Fred Hukill had barely noticed the comings and goings of the passengers and crew. The time had literally flown as he and his new friend, John Yates Beall, carried on a lively and protracted conversation. Beall was typically English, Hukill had concluded, well versed in the arts, history and culture. It seemed to Hukill that the Napoleonic era held a particular fascination for Beall, which helped explain why their conversation had been so spirited. Hukill was engrossed with the same subject.

"Obviously, Mr. Hukill, Napoleon's strength lay in the way he so brilliantly fused tactics and strategy into one grand design, wouldn't you agree? Consider, for example, how he lured the allies into that poorly conceived attack at Austerlitz by creating the illusion of weakness and indecision." John Yates Beall had not had such a lively conversation in months. While professing to be British, he nonetheless

204

threw himself into promotion of Napoleon as a master battle strategist and tactician.

Fred Hukill, leaning against the deck railing, nodded his head in polite disagreement. "Certainly, Mr. Beall, no one can dispute Napoleon's brilliance as a general. But I believe you have overstated the technical aspects at the expense of the political. It was only because his enemies were unwilling to make war offensively and fervently, from which affliction Napoleon did not suffer, that he succeeded. The allies simply didn't much like to fight. And that allowed Napoleon to seize the initiative." Hukill groped in his coat pocket and found the cigar he was looking for. He licked the twig-sized stogie to seal the wrapping, then bit off the tip.

Deep within the bowels of the side-wheeler came a rumble, followed by a loud, short blast.

"Leavin' Kelleys Island," Al Skinner chimed in. It was the only opportunity he had had to say much of anything since his best friend Fred Hukill had gotten so engrossed in the Napoleon discussion with the British-sounding John Yates Beall. "Won't be long now. Next stop's Sandusky. And not a minute too soon, if you ask me."

"Where did you say we are?" John Yates Beall had perked up his ears and showed a keen interest for the first time today in something Skinner had to say.

"Kelleys Island, didn't ya hear me? Kelleys, I said." Both of Skinner's eyebrows twitched erratically. "The sooner we get to Sandusky the better, I say. Yes indeed. Something funny's goin' on here. Yup!"

"Oh, shut up, Alfred!" Hukill hardly ever referred to Old Al by his full, formal name. Nor did he treat him so brusquely in the company of strangers. But his whiny little friend could grate on your nerves, and often did. Hukill had learned to live with that. It seemed though that Old Al had upset his new friend, Mr. Beall. You could see it in the stranger's eyes. They had a sort of distant look. Hukill patted down his pockets, looking for a match to light his cigar. No luck.

"Now, Mr. Hukill, let's hear him out," Beall interjected. "He's obviously distressed about something. Isn't that right, Mr. Skinner?"

A broad smile crossed Skinner's face. It was the first time that Beall had spoken directly to him since he and Fred had first met this stranger over two hours ago.

"You bet I'm distressed. Have you fellas seen what's goin' on here? Something fishy, I say, somthin' fishy." Both of Skinner's pinkies began to twitch, and the left side of his face contorted into a grim smirk. And then this tic passed.

"Like what, rebels taking over the boat?" Hukill's voice dripped with sarcasm.

"Could be, Fred, could be." Skinner nodded his head enthusiastically. "Come over here a second, both of yous. Come on," he said emphatically. Skinner was only a couple of feet away. Hukill and Beall looked at each other, grinned and stepped over to Skinner.

"Come closer, gents, come closer." Skinner's voice was now not much more than a hoarse whisper. He motioned with his hands for them to lean in even more.

"There's a whole bunch of fellas ridin' with us today that are up to no good," he croaked. "Look over there, by the stairs."

Hukill and his English-sounding friend looked in the direction of the staircase leading down to the main cabin below. That was where the ladies on the trip had gathered. Five men stood huddled together, on the staircase speaking in apparent furtive tones. They admittedly presented a less than favorable first impression. The men stood around a huge chest they had lugged aboard at Amherstburg, back in Canada. The chest was wrapped with two course strands of fraying, dingy rope to hold it together. "See 'em? See those guys?"

Hukill spoke first. "You mean those kind of scruffy looking men?"

"You see 'em! You see 'em!" Skinner shouted, ecstatic. The men below looked in his direction. One tipped his hat and smiled a toothless grin. The men returned to their whispered conversation. "Could be rebs! They could be rebs!" Skinner whispered hoarsely.

Beall guffawed. "Now Mr. Skinner, whatever in the world would make you say that? Those men may not be bank presidents. May even be skedaddlers, trying to slip back home to visit family. But they look perfectly harmless to me."

"They got that look in their eyes, is all I can say. I seen it before. In Baltimore. Remember Baltimore, Fred? Remember those damnable rebs?" Skinner's left elbow failed out, nearly hitting his new friend in the ribs, and then let out yet another small, involuntary whoop.

"Now, Al, let's not bore Mr. Beall with that Baltimore story." Movement to Beall's left caught Hukill's eyes. A short little man, overdressed for the weather in a navy pea coat, approached Beall and tapped him on the shoulder. "Mr. Beall, may I speak with for a moment?" the man said, his voice dripping with a Scottish brogue as thick as haggis.

John Yates Beall turned to face the Scotsman. "Ah, business again, gentlemen," he said. "Excuse me while I have a few words with my associate." He bowed gracefully, then strolled leisurely with the

Scotsman in the direction of the stairway to the parlor below decks. As he passed the "skedaddlers" at the foot of the stair, the men stopped their conversation, and several of them nodded politely to Beall.

"Somethin' funny goin' on here, Fred," Skinner said, as his right ear twitched. "Somethin' ain't right!"

"I know, Al," Hukill sighed. You're the only thing funny around here, he thought. Poor Old Al! Getting stranger by the day.

* * * * * * *

Beall and Burley sat huddled around a tiny round table in the main cabin of the *Philo Parsons*. A passenger, just embarked at Kelleys Island, sat there with them, nervously glancing around the room. He was a massive man, wearing a suit that noticeably fit him much too snugly. Rolls of pasty skin lopped over his shirt collar, a noticeable pink line above his collar signaling his discomfort. The only thing that seemed to fit him right was his mismatched floppy straw hat, which he kneaded nervously between his fingers.

John extended his hand. "So good to see you again, Mr. Robins - - -"

"Ssshh!" the man hissed. He held a stubby index finger to his lips and scowled. Dirt was lodged beneath the nails of the man's hand. "Please don't speak my name aloud, captain! Ain't nobody 'sposed to hear my name, that's what I was told."

John had come across many a strange bird in the last few years. And now, on the very same day as his encounter with Al Skinner, here was yet another. This was not a good sign.

Burley had done his best in recruiting men for this expedition, but it was impossible to have an army of saints, John knew. Drunks, philanderers, men filled with blood lust and those seeking to escape the drudgery of their own banal existences – they all wore Confederate gray, just as John imagined was true in the Union army, too. But this mountain of a man sitting next to him was different. He was strange, no question about it. His size, mannerisms, manner of speech, darting eyes – all suggested a man definitely out of the ordinary. But the man was not one to be feared. He seemed to John like a huge child. Maybe that was what made him seem so strange.

John smiled at the man-child. Thank God this was only a messenger he was dealing with. If the fate of the mission hinged on this one person, John knew he would have just continued on to Sandusky, found Cole and told him the Plan was off, and hopped on a train headed back to Toronto.

"Certainly, I understand," John whispered. "You're quite right. It is not necessary that we use our names. You never know who's going to be walking by. Perhaps it would better if we went to a more private part of the boat," he suggested. Burley, who had leaned forward over the table to better hear the conversation, nodded his head in half-hearted agreement.

A broad smile broke out across the bulky man's face. "Oh yeah," he said, "that sounds real nice. I ain't never been on a big ole boat like this one before. You can give me the tour."

"Well then, let's go for a little stroll. My friend and I," John said, nodding in Bennett Burley's direction, "have gotten to know this vessel quite well since we came aboard this morning. And I expect we may get to know it even better as the day goes on."

John led the way as the three men meandered out of the parlor and walked leisurely toward the stern of the boat, looking for a place where passengers had not congregated. The men said nothing until John nodded to them to stop. They were standing just behind the big paddle wheel. The wheel was churning in rhythmic cadence, propelling the boat across the expanse of inland sea towards Sandusky. There was no view, since the wheel towered even above the hurricane deck. And the slapping of the water over the wheel tended to muffle conversation. Most people preferred to be elsewhere.

"I believe this is as good a place as any to get some privacy," he said. "How does it suit you Mr. R. It is alright if I call you Mr. R, isn't it?"

"You can call me that, yes siree. But we can't talk now; we ain't gone around the whole boat yet," the big man in the small suit whimpered. "You said you would show me the whole boat!"

John sighed, and glanced at Burley, standing just to his left. Burley was trying hard to suppress a laugh, although John thought the situation was anything but funny. After all, this man carried the final word from Charles Cole as to whether John's mission would proceed, or whether he and his men would disembark at Sandusky and dissipate into the vapor, each man making his own choice about whether to head home through Union lines, or to sneak back into Canada.

"Mr. R, I promise you, I will give you the grandest tour of this boat, even including the captain's quarters, if you like. I'll even see that you get a nice, big glass of sarsaparilla. Would you like that?" John's voice oozed sincerity. The man-child nodded eagerly.

"But first, I just need to know if you brought us a message from Mr. Cole."

Mr. R glanced around them, up and down the deck. Clumps of people stood peering over the railing at the distant but discernible landmass on the horizon. About twenty feet away from them, toward the stern of the boat, a couple threw pieces of old bread in to the air. Their two tots squealed with delight at the aerial acrobatics of dozens of gulls diving after the tidbits.

"I do have a message for you," Mr. R whispered, just barely loud enough to be heard above the wheel. "Mr. Cole sent me this morning to tell you that everything is in order. He said to tell you he will be waiting for you at the ship." John knew what that meant. Cole was going ahead with his plan to take over the *Michigan*. "He said you should wait off the Marblehead lighthouse until he fires a signal flare, after dark." The big man smiled smugly, proud of himself for remembering the entire message.

But for John, the message from Cole had a new and complicating wrinkle. There had been no discussion of waiting until dark. It was only four o'clock. When did it get dark this time of year anyway? Seven o'clock at the earliest? That was a good three hours away. And here they were, barely an hour out of Sandusky. John needed time to think, but there was none. The *Parsons* had to be taken over soon, and then he would decide what to do next.

"Thank you, sir, thank you very much," John said. He grabbed the big man's lumpy fist with both hands and shook them. "Now, if you will just return to the parlor for a few minutes, Mr. Burley and I would like to talk. We'll be along shortly. . ." Mr. R was about to protest, but John continued, ". . . and then give you the grand tour of the *Parsons*."

John groped in the pocket of his frock coat, and retrieved a quarter. "Go ahead and have that sarsaparilla while you're waiting on us." He pushed the quarter into the man-child's hand, who wandered off to the main cabin where the bar was, whistling happily all the way.

* * * * * * *

"So, Fred, why hasn't your old pal Mr. Beall come back to talk, huh? Seems mighty uppity to me. He don't really care much for ya after all, does he? Just talked cause ya had 'im boxed in, didn't he?"

If Al Skinner wasn't his wife's brother, a damned good salesman, and a lifelong childhood friend – not necessarily in that order – Fred was convinced he would have punched him out by now. His nonstop chatter would drive any ordinary person over the edge. But he knew that was really difficult for him to engage anybody in a meaningful conversation. In casual conversation, people shied away from Old Al soon after being exposed to his nervous twitchings and whoopings.

"Al, don't you remember? Mr. Beall said he had some business to take care of with that Scottish gentleman. Who knows how long that would take. And he didn't promise to come back and pick up with us again. Anyway, he's only been gone a few minutes," Fred sniffed.

"Yea, but you two was gettin' on just fine. Talkin' about that Napoleon fella, for God knows what reason." Both of Old Al's arms twitched at the shoulders, so that he looked like a chicken trying to take flight. "If I was you, I'd at least try to find him, so you can get his address. Find out where he's stayin' in Sandusky, at least. Maybe we could have dinner with him tonight, before we head to Cincinnati in the mornin'. Although if he's as snooty as I think he is, he'll be much too busy with his friends to find time to fit us into his busy schedule."

Hukill suspected Old Al may be jealous of his ability to carry on erudite conversation, but in his own way, Hukill tried to help out his best friend. He nodded his head in agreement.

"Well, Al, that's an interesting suggestion," Hukill said. "Dinner with Mr. Beall would be pleasant. We'd at least have something else to talk about besides hammers and C-clamps. I'll be willing to bet he's a well-travelled man. Certainly, he could tell us a lot about his home in England. Remember how much you've always wanted to go to England, Al?"

Al Skinner's deep-set violet eyes sparkled. World travel was his major interest, and something about which he could carry on a conversation. Not that he had any personal knowledge. Hard to be a world traveler when you're just a hardware salesman. But Al Skinner devoured any and all books on the subject. He could actually carry on a decent conversation, at least for a little while, about the pyramids at Giza or the dikes of Holland with equal enthusiasm.

"Yeh, England. He would know a whole lot about England, wouldn't he? Why didn't I think of that?" Skinner paused momentarily, removed his hat and scratched the bare pate at the top of his head.

A high, loud, tinny sound suddenly filled the air. Al jumped, startled by the unexpected noise. "What's that, Fred? Damn near scared the hell outta me!"

The noise came again, this time in two short bursts. A whistle, Hukill thought. That's what it was, a whistle. But a whistle for what? He rose from his deck chair, his big cigar still firmly clamped between his teeth. He walked to the railing, where other passengers stood, pointing.

There it was. Another boat, a side-wheeler just like the *Parsons*, except about only half as long, and with a single deck. "Island Queen" it said on the side. "See there, Al," said Hukill. "That whistle came from that boat over there, the *Island Queen*. It was just letting the captain know he's there, so we don't run into him," Hukill said reassuringly. "Or maybe, he's just greeting us, you know, like strangers passing each other on the road wave to each other." The *Queen* must be headed into the same dock at Kelleys Island that the *Parsons* had just left.

Hukill grabbed Old Al gently by the arm, leading him toward the stairs to the deck below. "Come on, Al, let's go see if we can find Mr. Beall, see if we can extend him that dinner invitation you suggested."

The five seedy men who had been standing by the staircase the whole trip had not moved. Hukill was not sure whether he really wanted to have to work his way around them or not. It wasn't that he was afraid of them, really, at least not here on this boat. They just were people you generally tried to avoid, from the lower elements of society, or so it seemed. Maybe they were just folks down on their luck, or skedaddlers who had gone to Canada rather than be forced into the Union army, like Mr. Beall had said.

A familiar figure, dressed in black, came up the stairs. Good! Hukill thought. No need to look for Mr. Beall now. We've already found him. Their new friend stopped at the top of the stairs, glanced at Hukill, and smiled a pleasant, disarming smile. But Beall had stopped, right there, where the seedy men were. What on earth was he doing there? Hukill mused. One of the scruffy, dirty-looking men snapped to attention, and saluted Beall.

Old Al tugged at Hukill's sleeve, hard. "Fred, did you see that? What is Mr. Beall doin' with those scallywags anyway? What did that one fella salute him for? I don't like it one little bit. No siree, not one little bit." Old Al let out a whoop, and his head twitched violently back and forth, like some erratic pendulum on a clock.

"I don't know why, Al," said Hukill, now frozen in his tracks. "But I don't like it, either."

17

ABOARD THE *PHILO PARSONS*
4:15 P.M.

"Captain Beall, those two friends of yours are actin' mighty funny. Don't you think we should wait for a minute till they move on? They could sound an alarm or somethin'." William Byland tossed his flowing coal-black hair over his shoulder and momentarily halted removing the bindings from the battered black trunk in front of him. Four comrades surrounded him so that no passenger's peering eyes might see the contents of the weathered old box when it would momentarily be opened.

John Yates Beall, his hands clasped Napoleon-like behind his back, had noticed Hukill and Skinner staring at him and his men. But he had concluded those two were no threat and dismissed their apparent interest in him. By the time those two figured out what was happening, he reasoned, Confederates would have control of the *Parsons*. "Proceed, Mr. Byland," he said calmly, "the time for action is upon us."

The last knot undone, Byland pulled the cord from the trunk, wrapped it in a coil and shoved it into his trousers. "Mr. Byland," Beall ordered, "would you kindly notify the other men that arms are available for distribution?"

"Yes, sir, captain." Byland snapped off a salute and moved crisply up the stairs to the hurricane deck, where twenty more of Beall's men were waiting.

* * * * * * *

DeWitt Nichols loved this part of his job. Every time Captain Atwood stepped off the boat at Middle Bass Island, Dewitt Nichols, first mate on the *Philo Parsons*, became DeWitt Nichols, captain of the ship. DeWitt knew that he was destined someday to become captain in his own right. After all, his namesake, DeWitt Clinton, was largely responsible for the Erie Canal, through which much of the northeast's freight traffic had moved for decades since it opened in 1825. What more fitting tribute than for DeWitt Nichols himself to become a steamboat captain? And after just a few more years' apprenticeship, he would have his own boat.

Nichols' enjoyment of his sense of authority, and of his ultimate destiny, was interrupted by a sharp knock on the door behind him. He took his hands from the wheel and turned to see a tall, brown-haired man, dressed in black, standing inside the door to the pilothouse.

"I'm sorry, sir, but passengers are not allowed inside the pilothouse," Nichols declared. His deep baritone voice usually overcame people's first reaction to his compact frame. The authoritative voice, plus the stern look in his eye (which he had mastered from years of practice in front of a mirror), usually conveyed sufficient authority that people obeyed his orders. But this man didn't budge. He had a cool, calm demeanor that Nichols immediately found chilling.

"Are you the captain of this boat?" the tall man asked.

"No sir, I'm the first mate. And as I said previously, I must ask that you please step out that door. It's a company rule, no passengers in the pilothouse. I'm sorry," Nichols stated politely, but a bit more firmly. He had learned from his apprenticeship under Captain Atwood that it is wise to avoid upsetting the passengers. An upset passenger will never return to pay another fare, especially when you've got competition. An upset passenger will tell all his friends about the bad experience. This was bad for business and detrimental to the bottom line. So be strong, but polite; that was the operative rule he had learned.

The tall man had not budged. "You do have charge of the boat at present, do you not?" he asked. The features of the tall man's face were immutable, chiseled as in stone.

Nichols was trying to be polite, but this passenger was unlike any he had encountered before. What on earth did he want?

"Yes sir, I do." Nichols said, his voice betraying his irritation. "But I must ask you again, sir, to please leave the pilothouse, *immediately*."

"Of course," the tall man said, his lips pursed in a forced smile. "But I have a matter of grave importance to the safety of your boat that I must discuss with you. Would you step back here for a minute?"

Something of "grave importance to the safety of the boat?" Good God, what was he talking about? Nichols wondered. If something happened to the *Parsons*, he could lose his job. And then he would never, ever become a steamboat captain. His dream would cascade into obscurity like wastewater from a bilge pump.

Little droplets of cold sweat began to bead on the top of Nichols' forehead and the nape of his neck. He had to get to the bottom of this quickly, before whatever was the problem got completely out of control.

"Very well, sir. But couldn't you please tell me what this is all about? If safety of the passengers is in jeopardy, I need to know immediately," Nichols pleaded.

"It's a bit complicated," the tall man in black said coolly from just beyond the door, "but I assure you no one is in any immediate danger."

The boat was in deep enough water, and there was no other traffic visible on the lake for miles. The wheel could be unattended for a moment. Nichols sighed nervously, locked the wheel in place, and stepped through the pilothouse door.

Seemingly from out of nowhere, a band of five fierce-looking men surrounded Nichols. His heart leapt though his throat. Robbery! These men were about to rob him! And all the passengers, too! Nichols felt his stomach turn upside down and inside out at the thought. He would lose his job for sure.

Nichols lost all pretext of bravado. "What do you want?" he peeped meekly. Although he was not really sure that he wanted to hear the answer.

"My name is Captain John Yates Beall," the tall man in black said, "and I am a Confederate officer. I am seizing this boat in the name of the Confederate States of America, and you are my prisoner."

Nichols jaw dropped and froze where it landed. Confederate? CONFEDERATE? I must be losing my mind! Nichols thought. The closest damned rebels are five hundred miles from here.

"These are some of my men," the rebel leader continued. "There are twenty of us on board, all well-armed. If you follow our instructions, no one will get hurt."

In a sudden, totally irrational burst of inspiration, Nichols knew he had to get free. The captain kept a pistol under the pilot wheel. If he was able to get to it, he might be able to stop this madness. Or at least be able to tell Captain Atwood that he had tried to prevent this piracy.

Nichols darted in the direction of the pilothouse door, but before he could get more than two steps, a big burly man with the longest black beard he had ever seen wrestled him to the ground. Two of the big man's comrades hoisted Nichols back onto his feet and held his arms in a vice-like grip behind him.

"That was most unwise, sir," Captain Beall said. "I am afraid that now I will need to confine you more closely. Tie his hands!" he ordered. The man with the long black beard pulled a length of rope.

Nichols recognized the distinctively frayed binding as one that had earlier been around the big trunk brought aboard by men who now, in hindsight, were obviously rebels. Nichols' hands were swiftly and firmly tied behind him.

The rebel leader reached under his long black frock coat and pulled a long Colt navy revolver from the waist of his trousers, holding it to the back of Nichols' skull. The cold steel barrel glinted in the late afternoon sunlight, momentarily blinding the young mate.

"Now, sir," Beall said authoritatively, "you must pilot this boat as I direct you. It is not my intention to harm you – or anyone else on board – but I will do what I must for the safety of my men and the integrity of this mission. Are you willing to cooperate?"

Nichols was once again frozen in fear. The rope which bound his hands behind him had been tied much too tight. His wrists begin to tingle, a sure sign that circulation was being cut off. "Yes sir, I am," Nichols chirped. "But I will need my hands to pilot the boat. I give you my word as a gentleman that I will do as you instruct me."

"Very well," the rebel captain said smugly. He nodded to the black-bearded man, who quickly unfettered the very same hands which he had just moments before bound. "If you please, I would like you to run down the lake and lie off Marblehead."

* * * * * * *

Click. Click. Click.

Walter Ashley didn't recognize the sound of pistol hammers being locked. He had so little experience with such things. Then it all happened so fast. Three men instantaneously surrounded him, the cold steel of their navy sixes pressing into his skull.

"Get into that cabin or you're a dead man!"

Ashley closed his eyes tight, in a vain effort to wish away the surreal experience now surrounding him. Maybe this is all just some strange kind of a dream. But how could he be dreaming? he wondered.

"Damn it, I said move!" the voice drawled into his ear. "Move your ass by the count of three or the gulls will be fighting over your splattered brains for supper!" The voice paused briefly, then began counting. "One. Two."

Dream or not? Ashley opened his eyes. Nope, no dream. One of the men was standing right in front of him, the icy barrel of his revolver pressing into the skin on Ashley's forehead. The man was so close to the clerk's face that Ashley found it impossible to focus on the man's features. But he could not overlook his foul smelling breath. Strangely, it reminded Ashley of his beagle back home in Detroit.

216

The words came with amazing swiftness to Ashley. "Please gentlemen. I will do whatever you want. Just don't hurt me!" His hands went up to indicate his total surrender. Tears began to form in his eyes as the thought struck him with brutal force that he might never again see his darling wife. I'm too young to die, he thought. Only twenty-eight. And then in an instant he realized the paralyzing fear of imminent death that hundreds of thousands of young men, north and south, had been forced to confront over the last three years. A fear that he had been fortunate enough to avoid because his clubfoot kept him out of the army.

Walter Ashley gimped his way into his tiny office. The three men followed, slamming the door behind them.

* * * * * * *

Fred Hukill had never in all his years seen anything like this.

He had just been minding his own business, enjoying a relaxing trip on his way home, courtesy of the lake steamer *Philo Parsons*. And a damned fine trip it had been, too. The weather was crisp and cool in the morning, but had become modestly warm by the afternoon. And he had relished the conversation with Mr. Beall. But now men were running everywhere, brandishing hatchets and pistols wildly, like Indians on the warpath. Shots and screams grew in volume and number into a virtual cacophony of anarchy.

Although he hated to admit it, Hukill knew exactly what was going on. Pirates were taking over the boat. And it seemed his new friend John Yates Beall was their leader.

"Fred, Fred, Fred! What d'we do? I'm scared, Fred. I want out of here!"

Hukill's old friend Al Skinner sat whimpering on the deck, curled up tightly into a ball like one of those little insects you find when you lift up a board that's been on the ground for too long.

Hukill squatted on the deck beside his companion. Old Al was so frightened that the nervous tics had been replaced by an incessant rocking motion, back and forth, back and forth. "It's alright, Al," he said, patting him gently on the shoulder. "We're not in any danger. These men are under Mr. Beall's command. Whatever it is that he's up to, I'm sure he'll see to it that nobody is hurt. We should just stay calm," he said, as much for his own benefit as for Skinner's, "and stay out of harm's way."

* * * * * * *

It was always noisy in the engine room of the *Parsons*. Gargantuan boilers throbbed with seemingly unbridled power as steam was generated and forced over the turbines. Giant grinding, creaking crankshafts delivered power to the wheel that propelled the 233 tons of boat, plus accumulated passengers and freight, through the turquoise-colored waters of the Great Lakes. The rhythmic clunk of wood being thrown into the fiery steel boiler punctuated the pulsating machinery sounds.

Yet for James Denison, engineer of the *Philo Parsons*, there was a predictable, almost tranquil, quality to the sounds of the ship. But different, alien noises were added to the mixture this afternoon. On the main deck just above him, Denison now heard the sounds of boots moving back and forth. Not really moving, more like running. And then there were the screams. One shrill voice in particular was so piercing it made his blood run cold. And now more screams and gunshots!

Denison's first thought was to remain in the relative safety of the engine room. It was a place he knew even better than his own home. He was comfortable here. But what if there were some catastrophe on deck? Improbable as it seemed, what if the boat was sinking? He could be trapped here below, holding his breath as the cool lake waters would at first lap at his feet and then rise around him and over him. He shuddered at the premonition that he might fight the rising water eventually at first, holding his breath as long as he could, but then, almost willingly, take water into his aching lungs.

Still torn with indecision, James Denison removed his apron, hung it neatly on one of the steam gauges, and climbed up the ladder to the trap door overhead. The door opened underneath the rear stairs, so he knew he would be safe from anyone running above as he clambered onto the main deck.

"You there! Stop in your tracks or you're dead!" A hostile voice with a distinct southern twang rose out above him. Denison froze instantly, knowing now intuitively that he would have been better off to stay in the engine room, wreaked by doubts and fears than to be shot dead in his tracks.

Standing on the stair above him was Michael Campbell, the impetuous young pilot on the *Parsons*. Campbell stopped midway up the steps, but just momentarily.

"Go to hell!" he said. The pilot spat and bounded up the stairs, taking them two at a time. So the order to stop had been directed at Michael Campbell, not at him, Denison reckoned.

Crack! Crack! Crack! Two pistol shots, then a third, reverberated through the chilling air, and then intensified as the echoes bounced off the stairs, decks and walls of the boat. Denison could see that Campbell had stopped dead in his tracks, just as he had reached the hurricane deck above. God, was he hit? Denison wondered.

"That's it! We gotcha now!" a sardonic voice from above said. "Now just move that Yankee ass of yours down those stairs to the hold with the rest of your buddies!" Laughter erupted as two men pushed Campbell, stumbling, down the stairs.

Denison was about to retreat back to the safety of the engine room when he felt cold, hard steel being shoved into the small of his back. "We got us another one, boys!" the reb behind him drawled. "Don't try nothin' funny there, pal," the voice snarled, "or I'll ventilate ya right here and now!"

Denison glumly shuffled down the deck to the main hold, the barrel of the revolver pressed deep into the bare flesh of his back, prodding him along.

* * * * * * *

"I told you they'd find us, Fred. You heard me, didn't ya? Now we're gonners. We're all gonners! God help us!"

Fred Hukill carefully, tenderly lifted the crumpled, whining heap lying on the deck of the *Parsons*. It seemed to Hukill that his special charge, Al Skinner, was just so much dead weight. Listless, no response at all. Like heaving a big old bag of potatoes onto a wagon from a muddy, rain-soaked field. Skinner was a beaten man.

Hukill saw movement from the corner of his eye, but by the time he realized the danger, it was all he could do to try to deflect the impending blow. A steel-pointed toe of a heavy boot found its mark just under Hukill's rib cage, knocking the wind out of him. Hukill gasped for one pained breath, then another. He winced in agony and fell back against the railing.

"Get up there, you damned whimpering old fools!" the voice said. "How many times do I have to tell you to move along!" Hukill peered through pained-wreaked eyes into the barrel of a Colt revolver. The man at the other end was one of the scruffy men he had warned his friend Mr. Beall about. One of those people whom Beall had assured him were harmless. Hukill grimaced not only at the pain but also at the betrayal of the man he had assumed was a friend.

"What seems to be the trouble here?" A familiar voice penetrated the buzzing in Hukill's ears. Mr. Beall!

"Oh my God, Mr. Ross! What in heaven's name have you done to these men?" Beall's voice quivered with anger at his subordinate. The man stood there, silent, with a blank, sullen expression on his face.

Hukill grabbed ahold of the railing and lamely attempted to pull himself up. Beall tucked his pistol into his trousers, and squatted down beside the gasping man. "Mr. Hukill, I am terribly, terribly sorry!" the rebel leader said tenderly, his voice filled with what seemed to Hukill through the pain to be genuine sorrow.

Hukill thought he saw Beall's eyes glisten almost to the point of tears. "Many of my men have been victimized by the war, and I know they must find it difficult to keep their rage under control. Please accept my apologies. I will see to it that this man is appropriately disciplined."

Hukill nodded.

"Mr. Ross!" Beall snapped. "You will see to it that both of these men are escorted into the main cabin and made comfortable!" With that, Beall turned and moved smartly to the steps leading to the hurricane deck and the pilothouse.

Beall's subordinate mumbled a weak "Yes, sir." Ross put his rather massive arms under Skinner's shoulders and attempted to lift him from the deck. "Harrumph," he grunted, as he struggled against the near-dead weight. Skinner could be lifted onto his feet but getting down the deck to the main cabin and through the hatchway would be another matter. Ross glanced over his shoulder, but could see none of his compatriots.

"I believe I am better now," Hukill wheezed. "May I help you with my friend?"

Ross shot an icy stare at Hukill, then shrugged his shoulder. "If you want," He sneered, "jes' so ya don't get me in no more trouble."

The two men half lifted, half dragged Skinner to the main cabin, where all of the other fifty-some civilian passengers were already huddled. Many of the thirty or so women and children had been separated from the male passengers. The complete total silence in the room was punctuated only by the occasional whisper between friends and fearful sobbing of some of the ladies. Twenty or so men armed with pistols and hatches stood guard about the cabin, occasionally ordering the passengers to stop talking. Hukill and Ross took Skinner to one of the vacant velvet-padded benches and gently laid him down on it.

"Ladies and gentlemen!" a baritone voice boomed. A short little man with a light brown mustache had climbed onto a piano stool at the front of the cabin to speak. There was a sort of no-man's land between him and the fear-numbed passengers huddled in the back of the cabin. Hukill recognized him as the Scottish man who had pulled Mr. Beall away on business, just before all the shooting and screaming began. Beall was not standing next to the Scotsman, but occupied one of the cabin doorways. The late afternoon sun streamed in behind Beall, making it seem as though the presence in the door was that of an apparition rather than a human.

The furtive whispering ceased.

"I want to assure you that we mean no harm to any of you." Muffled sobs continued unabated. "If you will bear with us just one moment, everything will be made clear." The Scotsman nodded to Beall, who stepped sprightly from the doorway to the front of the room. The Scotsman hopped off his stool and shoved it back under the massive upright piano.

"Thank you, Mr. Burley." John Yates Beall stopped, gazing into the eyes of some of his captives before speaking. His heart moved into his throat when he saw his glances returned with fear. He knew the mission was the right thing. But he had to return theses people's lives to normal as soon as possible. They were noncombatants and should not have to be subjected to this.

"Ladies. Gentlemen." Beall smiled his warmest smile. "I am terribly sorry if we have inconvenienced you in any way. I assure you that it is our intention to inflict absolutely no harm on any of you. We ask only that you cooperate with us so that we may speed things along."

A voice rose from one of a group of four men standing protectively around women who appeared to be their wives. "What's all this about, anyway? Are you pirates, or what?" one of them asked boldly.

The man's wife shushed him, but he stood his ground, feet spread wide apart and arms crossed defiantly.

"Sir, let me get to the point," Beall responded. "We are not pirates. We are Confederate soldiers and sailors, and we have taken custody of this boat in the name of the Confederate States of America."

Moans, sobs and cries rose louder, like a tidal wave, from the assembled captives.

"Please, please!" Beall shouted. He felt an irritating tickle rise deep within his chest, an ominous sign of the recurrence of trouble caused by the Yankee minie ball he still carried around in his lungs.

A loud bang exploded from Burley's pistol, and the crowd grew silent again.

"We intend to put you all ashore in just a few hours. You are in no danger whatsoever; you need not fear us!" Beall said firmly. "We are Christian gentlemen, and we mean you no harm."

"Now, I must ask that you cooperate with us in just one more detail," Beall continued. "You can understand that we must ensure that no weapons are in your possession. This is a safety precaution for all of us. Let me start with the ladies. Do any of you carry any weapons whatsoever, any knives or guns?" One frail, thin hand crept up meekly; a single-shot derringer was gripped between two gloved fingers.

"Would you please retrieve that weapon from the lady, Mr. Burley?" The Scotsman strode over to the woman, a rather dour-looking middle-aged aristocrat wearing much too much makeup. Burley bowed politely and took the pistol, without a word, holding it delicately between thumb and forefinger.

"Unfortunately, as for the gentlemen, I am afraid that it will be necessary for us to physically search each of you individually. Will the gentlemen please line up along the far wall there?" he said sweetly, pointing to the port side of the boat where ten of his men were gathered.

"This will all be over very quickly, I assure you," Beall said, as the men began shuffling from one side of the cabin to the other. He left as abruptly as he entered, striding through the cabin past the gathering line of male passengers. He was eager to return to the pilothouse for a glimpse of the biggest prize of his life, the U.S.S. *Michigan* and its sixteen guns, the only Union warship on the entire Great Lakes. Tonight, he was determined, it would be his.

* * * * * * *

Not even an hour had passed since Captain John Yates Beall and his men had swept through the *Philo Parsons*, taking complete and total control of the steamer. Everything was proceeding exactly as planned, and John was ecstatic. All of the passengers were under guard in the main cabin. The forward deck had been cleared of pig iron and other cargo to make room for the most seriously wounded that would be liberated from Johnson's Island. The boat's crew – but for the mate, DeWitt Nichols – had been safely locked up in the forward hold, and John's men were performing their functions. And now, here he was, mere minutes away from his first glimpse of the biggest prize of his Confederate military career, the U.S.S. *Michigan*.

John stood stiffly beside the mate, peering intently across the water, concentrating on memorizing every landmark. The outline of the Ohio lake coast was now clearly visible through the late afternoon haze. Directly off the starboard side of the boat, a tall white monolith rose on the horizon into the turquoise sky. The Marblehead lighthouse, John knew. He had purchased a map of the lake during his trip several weeks previous to meet with Cole in Sandusky. The map was carefully folded and tucked inside his frock coat pocket, should he have any need to refer to it.

And then, suddenly, there it was. The *Michigan*. It looked just like when he had first spied it from his room at the West House in Sandusky. Its three masts ascended from the azure sea like a tiny stand of denuded trees. The black top of the roundish stack was visible too, but no smoke curled from it. The *Michigan* was at anchor.

"Mr. Nichols, your glass, please."

Without a word, the mate pulled his telescope from its case beside the wheel and handed it to his captor. John peered reverently through the lens at the great white ship anchored inside Sandusky Bay. There would not be much room to maneuver, only about a mile or so between Cedar Point and Sand Point, two sandy spits of land jutting out into the lake. But that should not be a problem since the *Parsons'* pilot would know the waters well. Once the *Michigan* was theirs, and the invalid and sick rebel officers had been liberated from Johnson's Island, there would be no need to be in a hurry. Who was going to chase them anyway, if the only warship on the Great Lakes was under his control?

Reluctantly, John removed the piece from his eye, and handed it back to Nichols.

"Thank you, Mr. Nichols," John said. "If you will, kindly turn back up the lake toward the islands."

"But, but, why do you want to go back there?" Nichols stammered. "I thought you was after the *Michigan*."

"Why we are following this course is my business for the time being," John said calmly. "I will let you know everything you need to know in due course, if and when it becomes necessary." There was certainly no need for this Yankee to know they would have to just cruise around until dark; that Cole's directive, as communicated by Mr. R, had been to wait for his signal rocket from the *Michigan* after dark before entering the bay.

Nichols stared sullenly at Beall, spat on the floor, and then cranked hard on the wheel, changing the course of the *Parsons* once again.

18

SANDUSKY, OHIO
MIDDAY

"Goddam it, woman!" Charles Cole spat out the words, as though some pesky gnat had gotten stuck to his tongue. "I told you fifteen minutes ago that we had to leave *NOW* if we wanted to catch the 1:40 train." His gold plated pocket watch glinted in the midday sun as he jerked it from his vest pocket. Cole popped open the cover and stared intently at the second hand, as though the gaze of his eyes would freeze time where it stood. He snapped the cover shut, and put the timepiece back in his pocket. He resumed pacing back and forth between the door and the bed, where Annie Davis was frantically shoving everything from pantaloons to bonnets into the two huge flowered valises spread open on the bed.

Annie was trying to hurry. But, of course, she could hardly be blamed for not being ready. When Cole had come back to their room, reeking of alcohol, she was still asleep in bed. She had pulled the soft, downy cover completely over her head to protect herself from the cool breeze wafting through the open window of their room. One thing she had insisted upon when they checked into the West House over a month ago was just that. She needed a room with a pleasant view, and a room with a favorable breeze, she said. The cooling vapors blowing off Lake Erie were essential to make the dog days of August tolerable. But now it was the latter half of September, and the once pleasant and consoling wisps of air flowing through their window and about the room had taken on a distinct chill.

"Charles, I'm moving as fast as I can," retorted Annie, still as naked as when she had crawled, or rather when Cole had pulled her, from the bed. She was struggling with the hangover from last night's binge in the West House bar. Her head was like a gigantic overstuffed fuzzy yellow ball, and she had no desire to move at all. "But you can hardly expect me to be dressed and to have packed everything in these bags in just 15 minutes," she continued. "I am a lady, and these things take time." As she bent over the bed, her long, soft, chocolate-brown hair flowed over her ample bosom. She had done it intentionally. Cole always became aroused when she allowed her hair to wash gently over

225

her milky white breasts. His arousal always had a way of dissipating his anger, which came over him like a prairie thunderstorm in early spring.

She lifted her head and shook back her hair. Her breasts undulated gently. This should have been enticing, very enticing. But Cole continued his silent pacing. He had apparently not even noticed her nakedness.

"What's the big rush to catch the train today anyway? Can't we leave on one later in the day, or maybe even tomorrow?" Annie asked. "I mean, this is all so sudden."

Cole clenched his teeth. His hand curled instinctively into fists that he pounded against each other. He was bothered by the insolence of this woman, and frightened by the prospect of being trapped in Sandusky while the authorities were interrogating Beall's rebel raiding party. 'What the hell am I waiting for?' he thought. 'I don't need this damned woman anymore. I'll just leave her behind, what the hell.' This was wishful thinking, he knew. It wasn't so much that he needed Annie. With all the money he had stashed away, he could buy all the female attention he needed.

She just knew too much. If he were to skip out on her now, she could be upset enough to go straight to the provost marshal and spill her guts about Charles Cole, rebel provocateur. About Charles Cole, who had stashed rebel payoffs in banks in Sandusky, Toronto and Philadelphia. That would not only result in the federals cleaning out at least some of the accounts before he could; it might even lead him to a most unwelcome appointment with the hangman. 'Yeah' he decided, 'I'll dump her alright. But not until I've cleared out all those bank accounts and move someplace where they'll never find me. South to Florida maybe. Or Texas. Or California.

"This whole conversation is pointless," Cole said coldly, his dark eyes glowing like fiery coals. "I'm going down to the train station to see when the next train is. I'll be back within the hour. Make sure you're ready to go then. No excuses." He would tell her later, after they were safely on the train headed east, about the reason for leaving Sandusky so hurriedly. He didn't know just yet what the reason was that he would tell her, but he was sure he would come up with something believable. He was real good at that. Making up stories to tell women was his specialty. That and enjoying top shelf Kentucky bourbon or fine imported French champagne.

Before Annie could answer, Cole turned on his heels and went out the door, slamming it behind him as he left.

* * * * * * *

226

Even though the breeze off the lake was cool, the midday sun radiated penetrating warmth through the woolen uniform of Ensign James Hunter. In any other situation, this was the kind of day a man of the sea lived for. The temperature was cool, but nonetheless pleasant. The azure sky was filled with fluffy white, cotton-ball clouds, and just a slight breeze rippled the surface of the bay. But Hunter was not on a pleasure trip. He was on a mission where the real scent of danger hung in the air like the smell of burning leaves in autumn. He had experienced this feeling before, when he served on the gunboat *Port Royal* off the Virginia coast. That seemed like eons ago, but in fact had only been just a handful of months.

Since the dawn assembly, Captain Carter had dispensed strenuous workouts throughout the entire morning to the entire crew of the *Michigan*. Ammunition was stacked, weapons were cleaned, drills were run. Even though he was exhausted, Hunter stood tall in the bow of the barge as the four bone-weary *Michigan* sailors pulled it through the waters at a steady clip. The ship's flags fluttered from the stern. Hunter now could actually see the details of the faces of people standing on the dock. It was a matter of mere minutes before they were ashore in Sandusky. He put his hand on the cold wooden butt of the revolver he had tucked into the waistband of his breeches. Danger was an exhilarating feeling, but he had to admit it was a lot less worrisome to know that you had a weapon to deal with the fear. Reassured, his attention returned to the details of the city dock, which loomed ever larger in front of him.

A voice squeaked behind him, barely noticeable over the rhythmic splash of oars hitting and leaving the water in unison. "Jim, do you have any idea where we'll be able to find Mr. Murray?" It was Charlie Eddy again.

Hunter chuckled to himself. Charlie Eddy had never really expressed much interest before in going ashore. The macho drunken behavior of Eddy's fellow officers was often directed at him. Eddy was a gaunt and nonassuming man, with the most beautiful waxed handlebar mustache Hunter had ever seen; it fairly glistened.

But Captain Carter liked him and, more important for this mission, trusted him. Charlie Eddy would do anything for Carter. The captain was his protector, and treated Eddy like a son. Once, after being pummeled in his bed by unknown, unseen comrades in the dead of night, Carter had ordered a mid-night assembly on deck. He bellowed and stormed about like a bull elephant, and made it crystal clear that if so much as one thin hair on Ensign Eddy's balding head was ever touched again, all shore leave would be cancelled for a month. Ever since, Eddy had been left alone. And did anything Carter asked him.

Hunter scrunched his massive frame down in the bow seat as the boat neared shore. "Well, Charlie," he said, "it seems to me like the best place to start would be the West House."

Hunter tapped his corncob pipe on the side of the barge, and the half-spent tobacco and ashes fell to the water, where it was caught up in the swirling vortex left by the next oar hitting the water. Hunter took a pinch of fresh tobacco from the pouch in the pocket of his uniform and tapped it into the bowl. "Ensign Murray was supposed to stick to Cole like glue, so it shouldn't be too hard to find him."

The lanky officer struck a match on the side of the launch and held the smoldering flame above the charred bowl of his pipe. "Last time I saw him," Hunter said, drawing deeply on the pipe between phrases, "Murray told me Cole has been spending most of his waking hours the last few days running between the bank and the West House bar."

Eddy nodded nervously.

"And," Hunter continued, "most of his nights screwing his brains out with that big-breasted, green-eyed wench that he keeps around."

This kind of talk bothered Charlie Eddy. He always suspected it was part of the whole sailor machismo, although not something that he would do normally. So he just nodded in tacit, if not full-hearted, agreement.

"Although it shouldn't be any trouble finding Mr. Murray," Hunter said. "We should be able to spot that beard and flaming red hair of his a good distance away."

As the barge came alongside the pier reserved for *Michigan* boat traffic at the foot of Water Street, the coxswain leapt from the boat, line in hand, to tie the vessel up to the dock. Even before it was secure, Hunter clambered over the sailors' clattering oars onto the rickety wooden dock, almost slipping on the slimy green algae growing in a depression in one of the planks. Eddy, ever cautious, waited until the oars were all stowed so that we wouldn't trip over them.

"You men stay by the barge at all times," Hunter commanded. "Do not let anyone near it, and guard it with your very life if need be."

The Union sailors all muttered "Aye, aye."

"Mr. Eddy and I should return within the hour, perhaps sooner. You must be ready to make way immediately upon our return, with or without our prisoner. Is that understood?"

Without even waiting for a reply, Hunter strode down the dock, Eddy struggling to keep up with the brisk pace.

The dignified brick hostelry known as the West House was just a block away. It would not be long now, Eddy knew, before they would either have their man or be in the thick of it somehow. His heart raced, and his breath came in labored, quick little gasps.

* * * * * * *

Jim Hunter had been right, as usual. Murray was easy to find. They just strolled into the West House bar, busy even for mid-afternoon on a weekday, and there he was. Even through the musty, dusky haze of the smoke-filled tavern, they had been able to spot him. He was dressed in nondescript civilian work clothes, but the red hair and beard made him a cinch to pick out. Murray was sitting at a table in the shadows, just a few steps from the bar but nearly invisible in the murkiness.

Light trickled in when the door to Water Street was opened. But otherwise, the only light was provided by a few sputtering oil lamps hanging over the bar and at various spots around the room. Ever cautious, Hunter approached Murray, who still had not noticed him. The Scotsman was staring intently at the door to the lobby, oblivious to the goings on around him. Eddy hung back, his feet literally frozen to the floor. The fear had risen from his gut to his throat as soon as he entered this haven of machismo. The foul taste of bile coated his tongue.

It was only when Hunter started dragging a chair across the wooden floor to sit at Murray's little round table that the red-bearded officer turned his head. Murray said nothing; he merely scowled at Hunter, who proceeded to sit down anyway.

"What's the trouble, John? Is there something wrong?" Hunter croaked the words out, barely audible above the hum of chatter from the men scattered around the bar.

"I sure as hell hope not, lad!" Murray snarled. "Just stay out of my line of sight to the door there." He picked up his near-empty glass of beer, filled it from a pitcher on the table, and blew off the head of foam. "Cole just went to the toilet, and I want to keep him in my sight when he comes back."

Hunter nodded his acquiescence. Looking toward the door where he had left Eddy standing, he motioned for the gaunt little man to come join him. Eddy, ever uncertain and hoping against hope that he had misconstrued Hunter's gesture to join them, pointed his finger at himself, as if to say "Who, me?" Hunter nodded, and beckoned Eddy again, this time more emphatically.

Sheepishly, Eddy crept across the room, wary as a cat in a room full of rockers. There were no more chairs at Murray's little table, and Eddy was not about to risk a controversy by taking someone else's. So he just stood there. It was a most awkward situation.

Hunter cleared his throat, as if to get Murray's attention. "John, things are breaking quickly. The captain sent me and Eddy here," he said, nodding his head in the other officer's direction, "to arrest Cole and bring him back on the ship immediately." He paused, waiting for some kind of reaction from the redheaded Scotsman. "We'll need your help, of course."

Murray took a long, slow sip of his beer, and then set the glass down on the table. The little bubbles of white foam on his moustache vanished as he wiped his coat across his lips. "I don't think that would be a good idea, just yet."

Hunter was startled by Murray's response. "What?" he shouted. The background chatter of the patrons stopped momentarily. Hunter felt all eyes in the barroom riveted on him. He lowered his eyes and his voice. "Don't you understand?" he whispered, leaning over the table. "Captain Carter has sent us here under orders. We are to arrest the man and bring him back to the ship for questioning."

"Well, if you can wait just for a few minutes or so, laddie," Murray said, "we'll have more evidence on him than you can imagine. He'll be hangin' from the yardarms by daybreak if we give him just a little more room and a wee bit more time."

"Good heavens, what for?" Eddy peeped.

Murray smiled sweetly at the gentle man. "So we can let him finish tryin' to bribe me."

Horror struck Eddy. Instantaneously. His already tender innards felt as though somebody had stuck a dull knife into him and twisted, slowly. Goodness, he thought, I surely hope they don't plan on me being involved in this thing! This was a lot more than Eddy thought he was getting into when the barge pulled away from the *Michigan* on this mission.

The darkness in the room was pierced momentarily when the door off the lobby opened, just long enough for a patron to enter the bar. It was a dark-featured man with a thick black beard, and, even in the gloominess of the barroom, noticeably piercing black eyes. His bowler hat was cocked slightly askew, as though he had bumped unknowingly into a wall just enough to affect the angle. The man looked around, squinting through the ribbons of smoke swirling about the room. His eyes fixed on Murray, and a smile came across his face.

"Charlie, I'm afraid you'll have to pull up another chair," Murray said apologetically. "It seems my mate here has taken your seat."

"No problem," the man said. "No problem at all." Spotting another seat just to the right of the rickety chair, he pulled it up to the tiny table. Hunter scooted closer to Murray not only to make room so the man could squeeze in, but also because there was something about this character that frightened him just a little bit. He wanted to keep himself as far away from this person as possible.

"Charlie, say hello to James Hunter and Charles Eddy, officers on the *Michigan*."

The man smiled, stuck out his fist and introduced himself. "How do you do, gentlemen," he said. "My name is Cole. Charles Cole."

The moment of awkward introduction was quickly overtaken as Charles Eddy passed out, hitting the scuffed wood floor with a leaden thud.

* * * * * * *

"I'm glad to see you've recovered from your malaria attack," said Cole, as he fanned the face of Charlie Eddy with his hat.

A shaken Eddy nodded weakly in response. "I should've known better to leave the ship when I was feelin' so shaky," he said, his voice barely above a whisper. Grabbing ahold of Cole's arm for support, he pulled himself up off the floor, and plopped himself into the chair that, just moments before, Cole had pulled over to Murray's table. Cole, Murray and Hunter all hovered over him, like protective parents over their fledgling. Both of Eddy's hands came up slowly to his waxy mustache, to make sure every twisted hair was in place. It was.

James Hunter marveled at the spunkiness of his fellow officer. Quick thinking on John Murray's part had concocted the malaria cover story. Eddy was dead to the world when all this transpired. But now, apparently having shaken his initial jitters, Ensign Charles Eddy had fallen right into his role as a traitor and fellow traveler and co-conspirator with a rebel spy.

Finally the other men pulled up chairs and sat down at the little table. "Bartender!" Murray bellowed. "Two more glasses and another pitcher!"

When the frothy brew arrived, Murray plunked down another quarter. With the hands of an expert, he filled each glass just full enough so that the foam could rise ever so slightly above the lip.

Murray struggled to his feet. "Cheers!" he toasted, then threw the cold beer down his gullet. Cole and Hunter followed suit, while Eddy cautiously sipped from his glass.

As Hunter refilled the glasses, Murray spoke.

"Charlie, as I told you earlier, it was not just me who had an interest in working with you. There are some others in this with me, including these two," Murray said, nodding in the direction of Hunter and Eddy. He leaned over the table, and motioned for all of the men to come closer. "Now, frankly, I don't really want to know what it is that you're about with the *Michigan*. Just tell us what you want us to do. And," he whispered, "we'll need to have you make an advance payment. Just for expenses, mind you. Three hundred apiece."

Charles Cole could feel the confining walls of a trap close about him. He was damned close to making it out of town. He had even managed to check out of the West House, and had made arrangements for Annie to accompany their bags to the train station. But then this Murray fellow came up to him, introduced himself as an officer aboard the U.S.S. *Michigan*, and said he wanted to talk with him.

What was Cole supposed to do? He had no choice but to hear Murray out. He and Murray had gravitated to the bar, where Murray proceeded to offer, with absolutely no prodding necessary, to deliver the *Michigan* into Cole's hands.

How did Murray know that Cole had an interest in the ship? Even having to ask the question indicated to Charles Cole that he may be in some danger. Only a few local people – all members of the Knights of the Golden Circle – were supposed to know. Cole felt somewhat better when Murray volunteered that he had heard something might be in the works from Dr. Stanley, a prominent and outspoken local Copperhead. Cole remembered Stanley was one of those present at the meeting with Beall a couple weeks back at Mrs. McGuire's boarding house.

Cole grudgingly acknowledged to himself that he would have to play along. These men knew too much. They could take him directly to the authorities if they wanted to. He knew he was about to be fleeced for $900. But what choice did he have? None.

Cole sighed deeply. "Very well, gentlemen," he said flatly. "You'll have to accompany me to the bank so that I can make a withdrawal."

"Then let's be on with it," Murray said. He winked at his fellow officers, confident once more that the trap was about to close around this rebel scum, Charles Cole.

* * * * * * *

The three *Michigan* officers and Cole stood just outside the bank on the plank boardwalk. Charles Cole pulled his pocket watch from his vest, looked at the time, and quickly closed it back up. Four o'clock. Although the sun still shone brightly, it had already begun to sink into the western sky. Nervously he tapped the shiny toe of his black leather riding boot on the sidewalk. He had intended to be out of town on a morning train with Annie and his money; if only he hadn't bumped into Murray!

Murray clinked the 30 ten dollar gold pieces in his hand and hefted them, just to hear the jingle and feel the bounce. Too bad he would have to turn this money over to the captain eventually, since it was evidence of Charles Cole's traitorous crime.

"So now you've each got your thirty pieces of silver," Cole sneered. His initial fear had transformed itself into anger as he considered over and over again in his mind how he could have avoided parting company with $300 to each of these men. He was even more frustrated when he thought that he only had to make this payment just to get rid of these fools.

"It wasn't silver," Eddy corrected. "It was gold." As soon as the bank teller had shoved the coins through the window, just a few brief moments before, he had quickly put the payoff money in the brown leather pouch he carried with him wherever he went. Usually, it held only a handkerchief, wax for his moustache, the key to his trunk and assorted coinage. Never gold, and never money in this amount.

"Now, Mr. Cole, I can't understand why you're so upset," Hunter said. He pulled on his corncob pipe. As he exhaled, the breeze off the lake carried the smoke upwards where it quickly vanished. "You should have expected to make some sort of investment. It would take more than one person, you know, to pull off what you want."

"If you say so," Cole said. "I'm just not sure what it is each of you is going to do to help."

"Well, Mr. Cole, we have thought it all out," Hunter said, as he peered down at the man in front of him. "We have a plan. Let us share it with you."

"Perhaps this evening, gentlemen," Cole said. "But I must be getting back to the hotel. My wife will be wondering what happened to me."

"This won't take but a few minutes," Hunter insisted. "We can explain our idea to you on our way back to the barge. Anyway, we can't wait until later. There is a window of opportunity tonight to deliver the ship to you, if you'll be ready."

Taking Cole by the elbow, Murray said, "Come on, Charlie. I think Mr. Hunter's right. You at least ought to hear what we've got to say. If you don't like it, just say so. Or if you want to discuss it some more later, we can come back this evening."

Without even waiting for a response from Cole, Hunter steered Cole down Water Street, in the direction of the pier where the *Michigan* barge was waiting, just a few short blocks away. Murray walked on Cole's other side, and Eddy followed a few steps behind, nervously twirling his moustache.

Hunter proceeded to lay out the "plan" to take over the *Michigan* as the four men made their way ever closer to the barge. Of course, it was not really a plan at all. In reality, Hunter was making it up as he went along. But if he had had to do it, it really was not a bad plan at all. It sounded credible. Hunter told Cole he had the night watch, so Cole could come on board after the crew had retired for the night. Murray would secure the weapons locker, and Eddy would take control of the engine room. There were six others of the crew who had agreed to assist them, Hunter said, and they would corral the rousted crew and officers into the forward hold. It would all be over in a matter of minutes.

"I like it," Cole said, shaking his head emphatically. In fact, if he had even a remote interest in taking over the ship, this plan would work. How could you lose when it was others doing the dirty work for you? But Cole was not interested in taking over the *Michigan*. What he was interested in was getting the hell out of town as soon as possible, before the shooting started. And while there was still money left in his bank accounts. There was little money left now in his Sandusky account, thanks to the day's $900 withdrawal for these bastards. But over $50,000 sat waiting, gathering dust, in the other bank accounts he had set up in Toronto and back in Philadelphia. "I guess all we have left to agree upon is the time. What would you suggest, Mr. Hunter?"

"Our watch starts at 10:00, so any time after that would be fine."

"Excellent, Mr. Hunter. I'll be there."

The four men had reached the foot of the pier, where the *Michigan*'s barge sat bobbing peacefully. Hunter nodded, and the four sailors untied the boat, and hopped aboard.

"It's been a pleasure meeting you. And you too, Mr. Eddy," said Cole. He shook hands with each of the officers, and turned to leave.

"NOW!" Hunter shouted.

Before Cole could even turn his head to see what was going on, Murray had grabbed both of his arms and yanked them behind his back. A sharp pain shot from Cole's shoulders down to his fingertips, as he felt muscles pop in each shoulder. He was enraged. Cole twisted out from Murray's arm lock with an agility that startled even him, and he dashed up the pier. His heart raced, driven equally by the pain and by the prospect of escape from danger. He had only run a few steps, but already his lungs ached as he pumped his arms in a futile effort to extract just a little bit more energy from his abused body.

And then, totally unexpectedly, the footrace came to a halt as Charlie Eddy, who had taken after Cole immediately, literally flew through the air, his arms flailing in front of him just enough to trip Cole up. As Eddy lay on the pier, Cole tumbled and turned like a snowball rolling downhill, his battered and bruised body finally coming to a halt just inches from the wheels of an oncoming carriage on Water Street.

Hunter and Murray, who had been trailing the swift-footed Eddy, lifted Cole's semi-conscious form from the street and dragged him back to the barge. Moments later, a shaken but proud Charlie Eddy stood watch over his prey as Hunter and Murray guided the barge through the glassy bay waters back to the U.S.S. *Michigan*.

19

Aboard the U.S.S. *Michigan*

Inside Captain Carter's cramped cabin, Cole's accusers had gathered, squeezed inside the tiny box of an officer's quarters like pickles into a jar. At first, Carter had balked at the prospect of conducting the interrogation in his own quarters. Amazingly, even after all these 20-odd years aboard various and sundry ships of the United States Navy, Carter had been able to hide his claustrophobia from his men and fellow officers. He still didn't like close quarters at all; his irrepressible feelings on the subject had unfortunately never changed.

But Carter realized there was no choice here. He could hardly conduct a decent interrogation anyplace else aboard ship, although the galley had seemed like a good prospect at first. He decided against it when he realized this could be a long, dangerous evening. The men need their evening chow, since it was conceivable that they would not have a decent meal for a full day, or maybe more. And so, Cole had been half-dragged, half-shoved through the war vessel into the captain's own quarters.

Cole had only been aboard the *Michigan* for a scant five minutes, but already he was sweating profusely. Hunter had shoved him onto a tiny stool against the cabin wall. "You no good, rotten son-of-a-bitch!" the massive ensign howled. "We gotcha now. Ain't no way you'll sabotage this ship, by God. As a matter of fact, you little worm," he sneered, "you'll be lucky if you see the sunrise with all your pieces in the same place they are now! Come to think of it," Hunter continued, "you'll be lucky to see sunrise at all!"

At this, Hunter threw back his head and laughed heartily. It was a deep, satisfying laugh. Carter, of course, could not join in. It would be inappropriate for a man of his station to engage in this type of intimidation of a prisoner, even when the prisoner was as loathsome as Charles Cole, the man who would have turned the *Michigan*, his ship, into a rebel raider of some sort. The other men in the crowded room had no such compunctions, and they joined Hunter in mocking the quivering man in front of them. Even the usually reserved, wispy

Charlie Eddy had joined his fellow officers in this exercise of male machismo.

Cole began whimpering and muttering some indiscernible nonsense into his fine bowler hat. Then, predictably, the hat was filled with reddish-brown vomit that erupted from Cole's churning stomach, up through his esophagus, escaping over his tonsils through his heaving mouth with explosive force. The pungent, acrid smell of undigested food, alcohol, bile and stomach acid was joined by the unmistakable odor of urine. A small, almost imperceptible stream trickled down the chair leg and formed a small puddle on Captain Carter's prized Oriental rug. It was a blue Tabriz, a souvenir from Persia that he had picked up in a North African bazaar ten years ago.

The roiling laughter, which had escalated as Cole lost control of his bodily functions, came to an abrupt halt. "Gentlemen!" Carter barked gruffly. "That will be quite enough! You are officers in the United States Navy! And Navy officers do not – I repeat – do NOT – treat their prisoners in such a fashion! Now," he said, "step back and give that man some room to breathe!"

Carter's orders had their intended effect. Cole's tremulous convulsions began to diminish to the point where they were soon no more than mere trembling and sniffling. Carter's officers had also suddenly acquired a more serious demeanor. Although he did not condone their behavior, and never would have planned it this way, it dawned on Carter that perhaps he might now be able to really learn something from Cole. The shadow of a man in front of him was almost certainly an inveterate liar, and everything he said had to be taken with a grain of salt. But, judging by the way Cole kept his eyes fixed on Carter like some puppy dog waiting for his master to dispense another treat, it seemed that the rebel spy might think his only way out was to please Carter. The alternative – which Carter decided he would make amply clear to Cole – would be to let Hunter and Murray conduct the interrogation on their own. Cole certainly wouldn't want that.

Carter smiled gently at Cole. "Sit up there, Mr. Cole. We've got a lot to do, and a very short time to do it. I want you to make yourself comfortable, at least as comfortable as you can be under the unfortunate circumstances in which you find yourself. These gentlemen here," he said, waving his hand in the direction of Hunter, Murray and Eddy, "are officers on this ship. But I am in charge. And I will be asking the questions. Unless," he paused, "I am having difficulty getting answers. In that case, a different approach may be warranted. Do I make myself clear, sir?"

Cole was sitting sloppily in the chair, with his feet jutting out straight in front of him, and the backs of his heels dug into the deck floor. The space from the middle of his back to his posterior looked like a perfect isosceles triangle. Already a beaten man, Cole simply nodded his understanding.

"Very good, then, Mr. Cole. Very good. You've made a wise decision. Now, let's start with just a few simple questions, shall we?"

And with that, the interrogation of Charles Cole began. At precisely this same time, not too many miles away out on the lake, John Yates Beall and his men had already taken command of the lake steamer *Philo Parsons* by force.

* * * * * * *

4:30 p.m.
The West House Hotel

By now, Annie Davis was used to this kind of indifferent treatment from Cole. Although they had been together only since meeting for the first time just a few months ago in Toronto, she had come to know him quite well. She felt she almost had come to know as much about Cole as she knew about the traits, the likes and the dislikes, of her poor deceased husband.

Charles Cole, she had quickly learned, was a man who, on the one hand, insisted on strict conformance by others to his demands. On the other hand, he totally refused to apply the same standards to himself. Cole's insistence that she get packed immediately, followed by his disappearance for hours while she sat, increasingly frustrated and impatient, in their room at the West House, was typical of him.

Finally, though, she could bear it no more. She had been sitting in this increasingly lonely and stuffy room for over two hours. She had not heard or seen anything from Cole since he stormed out. She sighed deeply, but knew what she must do. She had done it before, more times already than she cared to remember. She would have to go find Cole. Most likely, he was down at the bar, and well on his way to getting completely and totally inebriated. Cole could swill down any kind of alcoholic beverage with the best of them. In fact, she reasoned, there was even a distinct possibility that he had already passed out for the afternoon.

As she glided gracefully through the spacious lobby of the West House, resplendent in a lacy dress of light yellow muslin, she felt once again the eyes of the men she passed riveted on her every step. Were they mentally undressing her? She had once wondered. Were they focusing on the uplifted peaks of her more than adequate bosom? What lurid thoughts filled the minds of all these men, young and old alike, when she entered their lives, even if only for a few fleeting seconds? Annie had since learned to ignore their stares, and to disregard her own concerns about what men were thinking. If anything, she was flattered. And besides, right now her mind was on other things, like the whereabouts of the missing Charles Cole, her lover and, she never forgot, her responsibility. If she was able to find him in time, it was still possible to get him sobered up enough to board the last train heading east in a few hours.

"Why, Mrs. Cole, you certainly look lovely this afternoon, if you don't mind me sayin' so."

Leroy Sullivan, working the afternoon shift at the desk of the West House had a fixation on Annie Davis, just like most every other man that ever met her. He never let an opportunity pass to engage her in small talk of some sort. Although Annie thought his boyish flattery was cute, he was hardly her type. Well over 70, Sullivan was hunched over and withered up, like some over-ripe prune plum hanging on a tree that never got picked. He attempted to cover his advancing age by coloring the few thin hairs atop his head and then drawing them, strand by strand across his shiny pate.

Annie drew her fan up to her face, moving it coyly back and forth. "Why, Mr. Sullivan, you are much too kind," she said. "But I shan't refuse your compliment, sir. There'll be a day in the future, I'm sure, when such lovely expressions from men will come with increasing infrequency."

Sullivan chuckled. Actually, it was more like a cackle. "I doubt if that day will ever come, ma'am. Not for you, anyway. You've got class."

"And a big bosom too, eh, Mr. Sullivan?"

The old man's ears burned bright red with embarrassment. He knew it was true, and so did Annie. But in his day and age, such talk was confined to the bedroom when it was whispered in your lover's ear in a moment of passion.

"Mr. Sullivan, you've been here for the last few hours or so, haven't you?" Annie asked innocently. The embarrassed desk clerk was more than happy to change the topic of conversation.

"Yes ma'am, I sure have. Been here since about noon." He looked pensively at the ceiling, while scratching his clean-shaven chin with the blunt end of the registration pen. "11:45, to be exact."

"Well, maybe you can help me then, Mr. Sullivan," Annie continued. "My husband Charles left the room about 1:00 or so, and I haven't seen him since. To tell you the truth," she said, "we had a bit of a squabble, and I'm afraid he got rather angry with me."

"Well, Mrs. Cole, that happens, you know. Happened to me most every day while my late wife Sarah was still around, God rest her soul. Nothing to be ashamed about, though. Not at all." The old man's eyes glistened ever so slightly at the thought of his wife of nearly fifty years, who had died of pneumonia the previous January.

"So did you see Charles?"

"Yes, ma'am, I did. He went into the tavern about 1:00 or so. Stayed there for a spell, over an hour, I reckon, before he left." The old man's brows furrowed up as he tried to figure out how to finish telling the story.

Annie could see something was troubling the old man. He must have seen something unusual, or worse, some bad turn of events involving Cole. Damnation! She thought. What kind of trouble had Cole gotten himself into this time?

"And then, Mr. Sullivan, did you see Charles when he left the tavern?"

"Yes, indeed," the old man said. "He left the tavern about 2:00 or so."

"Two o'clock? He certainly did not come back to the room, since I've been there the whole time. Did you see where he went?"

"Well, Mrs. Cole, I can't say for certain where he went. All I can tell you is what I saw. Your husband left the tavern in the company of three officers from the *Michigan*. And ma'am," Sullivan continued, "it may be none of my business, but it seemed Mr. Cole was pretty unhappy to be leaving with those men. And they didn't seem none too friendly toward him, neither."

Annie knew instantly what Cole's involvement with the *Michigan* officers meant. Although he had made contacts with certain men aboard the *Michigan*, Cole had gone out of his way to avoid fraternizing with them. They were going to turn their ship over to him, he had told her, so they didn't dare be seen in his company socially. It would compromise the integrity of the mission, he said.

It seemed obvious to Annie that Cole was now in trouble, that the mission was in trouble. Why else would three officers from the *Michigan* have made contact with him? And why had Cole not returned to her? "I'm sure it's nothing, Mr. Sullivan," Annie replied coolly. "They probably just decided to go to another tavern." She smiled politely, and turned to go back to her room to think this through.

As she entered the familiar surroundings of their room, which had become the closest thing to home she had known since leaving battle-scarred Virginia, her mind was whirring. Annie's eyes were drawn immediately to the two packed valises. They stood as silent witness to the dilemma she faced. Should she leave? She quickly reasoned that it was best for her to stay put. Cole may not actually be in trouble, in which case her departure could jeopardize the mission. And if he was in trouble, he may need her to be here to help him in whatever way she could. Annie knew this approach had its risks. She was a spy, too. And the Yankees weren't averse to dealing harshly with women in times of war. It was even conceivable that they might hang her.

* * * * * * *

5:00 p.m.

The rap, rap at the door was so faint that Annie didn't hear it at first. Standing on the other side of the room, she had been peering intently at the activity on Water Street below, straining for some sign of Cole. It was only when a second, more persistent round of rapping came that she realized somebody was at the door.

Annie moved with a quick, cat-like stride to the door. Opening it, she was unsure whether to be surprised or disappointed. It wasn't Cole on the other side. It was Abraham Strain.

She barely knew Mr. Strain. She had only met him once before; it was several weeks ago when she accompanied Cole into Strain's hardware store down the street a few blocks, right next to the bank. Cole had introduced her, and Strain had politely acknowledged her existence. He only stuck in her mind for two reasons.

First, Cole told her later that day that Strain was a leading and loyal Copperhead, and said could be counted on in any time of trouble. Cole said that about very few people, since he had so little confidence in anybody but himself.

The second reason Annie was able to remember Strain was because of his eyes. His eyes were the color of robin's eggs and, in some peculiar fashion, nearly hypnotic in their effect on other people. They were such an unusual color and intensity that nobody ever forgot them.

Strain stood there, nervously fingering his hat, waiting for Annie to speak.

"Mr. Strain, isn't it?" was all she said. Her countenance was polite but, under the circumstances, anything but beatific.

"Yes, ma'am, it is. I'm afraid I've got some bad news for you. It's about Charles."

242

Even with the expectation that whatever business Strain was on was not good, Annie was still taken aback to hear the obvious. She said nothing, but gripped the door tightly in apprehension of what she would hear.

Annie forced a strained, polite smile. She momentarily considered inviting Strain into the room, but thought better of it. She didn't think it was appropriate for him to see the packed valises. "Please be direct, Mr. Strain. I do need to know about my husband, and I am strong enough to handle whatever it is that you are going to tell me," she said.

"I can see that, Mrs. Cole," said Strain. "You see, ma'am, I've got the hardware store next door to the bank. A little over an hour ago, I saw your Charles walking with these three officers from the *Michigan* out of the bank. I know they were from the ship because two of them were in uniform, and I'd seen all three of 'em around town before.

"I was sweeping the front of my store," he continued, "and I saw the whole thing. Your husband was obviously very unhappy to be with those damned Yankees, and they were havin' to kind of push him along. They were headed in the direction of the pier where the *Michigan*'s barge had tied up."

Strain swallowed hard and took two deep breaths. He was clearly frightened, and even the furtive movements of his normally hypnotic, flashing eyes betrayed the fear.

"Please go on, Mr. Strain. What happened to Charles?"

"Well, these officers started pushing him into the *Michigan*'s barge. He tried to get away, but they caught up with him and threw him in the boat. Last I saw, they were headed out to the *Michigan* with your husband along as their prisoner."

It was as Annie suspected. Cole had been found out. She needed time to think about what her next move should be.

"Thank you, Mr. Strain. I appreciate your promptness. Leave it to me; I'm sure Charles will be all right."

Strain nodded but still stood sentinel in the doorway. "I'm sure he will be, ma'am. But we've got another problem, and I'm at a complete loss as to what to do about it."

"And what is that, sir?"

Strain looked up and down the hall nervously. When he was sure it was clear, he continued, but spoke quickly and in a hoarse whisper. He leaned forward, cupped his hand and croaked in Annie's ear. "What about the Plan? Are we still going ahead tonight? Should the men still be gathering to go out to Johnson's Island to transport prisoners?"

Annie knew, of course, about the Plan. At least about the general nature of it. Cole had been sent to Sandusky to scout out the defenses in and around Johnson's Island and to recruit local rebel sympathizers to help ferry freed prisoners to the mainland. She knew, too, that John Yates Beall would be bringing soldiers over water from Canada, and that they would be the shock troops of the Plan, taking over the *Michigan*. But she didn't know when all this would happen. In fact, she thought that when Cole was encouraging her so forcefully earlier in the day to get packed and get ready that the mission had been postponed or cancelled for some reason.

Now the full magnitude of the situation flashed across her mind. She could see that Cole had no intention whatsoever of fulfilling his part of the Plan. He was trying to skip out of town *before* things got hot. And he was perfectly willing to abandon to the hangman not just Beall and his men, but local supporters as well. He was just going to leave them to stumble into God knows what.

Instantly, Annie knew what she must do. It was her duty to protect these men from the traitorous Charles Cole. "No, Mr. Strain," she said, "in light of these circumstances, the Plan will be postponed. You will see to it that the other men are aware too, won't you?"

"Yes, ma'am, I certainly will. You can count on me."

Good, she thought. At least there's one man I can count on. But what about Beall and his men coming down from Canada? If Cole was performing as she expected, by now he had spilled his guts about even the most infitesimally small aspect of the Plan. The Yankees would know everything. And if Strain and the locals were set for tonight, that must mean that Beall was already on his way. Something needed to be done immediately to warn him. That much was for sure, she knew. And Annie also knew that, somehow, she alone could save Beall and his men.

Annie stepped back into the room and nodded politely to Abraham Strain. "Thank you so much," she said to him sweetly, "for the news. I know it was difficult for you to bring me such bad news about my husband, but at least now I know what I must do."

Abraham Strain tipped his hat and left to go warn the others as Annie Davis returned to her room to ponder on the best way to warn Beall that his life, and those of his crew, were in grave danger.

* * * * * * *

7:00 p.m.
Aboard the U.S.S. *Michigan*

"Turn up the lamp, there, Mr. Murray. My eyes aren't what they used to be."

Captain Carter's vision was affected not only by the lowered intensity of the declining rays of twilight, but also by the strain imposed on his eyes by squinting for the last hour as he wrote and rewrote Charles Cole's confession.

"Now, Mr. Cole, I'm going to read back to you this statement. I want you to listen real carefully to what I'm reading, because I'll be asking you to sign the statement if you agree with it, and, of course, if it's factually accurate. Are you ready?"

Charles Cole sat hollow-eyed on his tiny stool and stared vacantly at the reflected light from the lamp dancing ott the walls.

"Mr. Cole," Carter said louder and stronger, "I said, are you ready?"

Cole nodded weakly.

Carter cleared his throat and began to read from the two crinkly pages of paper in his hand.

> "I, Charles H. Cole of the State of Pennsylvania, and late of the 5th Tennessee Infantry of the rebel army, hereby make this statement of my own free will and volition.
>
> "In the spring of 1863 I was working in Memphis, Tennessee. While there, I was coerced against my will by my brother, a Confederate officer, to join the rebel army.
>
> "In the spring of this year, I became aware of a Confederate plan to initiate activities against the Union from Canadian soil. I made contact with Major Thomas Hook, Assistant Provost Marshal in Memphis, and informed him of the rebel plan. I was solicited by Major Hook to infiltrate the Canadian operation. Thereafter, I left my post with the rebel army and journeyed to Canada.
>
> "Upon my arrival in Toronto, Canada West, in July, I reported to Jacob Thompson, one of the Confederate Commissioners to Canada. Mr. Thompson and his staff shared with me the general scope of a plan they had developed to free the Confederate prisoners now being held on Johnson's

245

Island and to capture the U.S.S. Michigan for future Confederate military operations on the Great Lakes.

"I was personally ordered by Mr. Thompson to obtain as much information as possible about the operation of the Union prison camp at Johnson's Island. I was further ordered to attempt to bribe one or more of the officers or crew of the Michigan to deliver the warship to Confederate operatives in connection with the raid on Johnson's Island. Mr. Thompson provided me with the names of Confederate sympathizers in Sandusky who, he said, would assist me.

"Early last month, I arrived in Sandusky. Since my arrival, I have gathered general information concerning the operation of the Johnson's Island prison. I did so to avoid arousing suspicion among my Confederate contacts. From time to time, I would send reports of a very general nature to Mr. Thompson by special courier.

"Also, several weeks ago, I was visited by Captain John Yates Beall of the rebel army. Captain Beall had been given responsibility for recruiting and training soldiers in Canada who would take over a lake steamer by force. The steamer was to be used initially to approach the Michigan and thereafter to transport the sick and wounded Confederate officers from Johnson's Island to Canada.

During his visit to Sandusky, Captain Beall informed me of possible dates for the plan to be implemented. I knew only generally that the plan was scheduled to be implemented some time during the last half of the month of September. Captain Beall stated he would send me a coded telegram in the morning of the day he and his men would be leaving from Canada. It was to be my responsibility to have the local sympathizers ready to assist in the transport of freed rebel prisoners back to the mainland.

"I received the coded telegram from Captain Beall this morning. I was en route to the Provost Marshal to deliver the telegram and other information known to me about the Confederate plan at the time of my detention by officers of the U.S.S.

Michigan. I have since provided the telegram to Captain Carter."

Captain Carter looked up from the paper and removed his reading glasses from his nose. "Well, Mr. Cole, does that sound accurate to you?"

Cole nodded silently.

"Sir," Carter said, looking directly at his prisoner, "I must ask you just a few more questions."

Cole sat stony-faced and said nothing. He refused to make eye contact, and let his gaze turn toward a knot in the pine floor beneath his feet.

Carter continued his voice calm and measured. "Are you or are you not a rebel agent?"

Cole's head jerked upright. His back arched like that of a cat backed into a corner by a hostile dog. "Most emphatically not!" he bellowed, his voice cracking.

Hunter and Murray had been standing silently in a corner of the captain's quarters after being rebuked by their commander. But they quickly moved closer to Cole so that they could subdue him if he got violent.

Carter motioned to his two ensigns to keep away from Cole.

"Then tell me why it is that you did not report to the Sandusky Provost Marshal upon you arrival in Sandusky? Why didn't you tell him – or anybody else in authority, for that matter – when Captain Beall was here, so that he might be detained and interrogated? And why," Carter asked, his voice rising in volume and pitch, "didn't you report to the Provost Marshal immediately this morning after receipt of the telegram from Captain Beall? It was not until you were detained and questioned that you even mentioned that you had this telegram. Or, more precisely, it was not until we discovered it on your person that you felt compelled to explain it to us."

Cole's quick-booming show of defiance melted as quickly as lard on a hot stove. He knew with startling clarity that his attempt to convince Carter he was a Union double agent had failed miserably. And he knew now that prospects had increased dramatically that his life would end suddenly and quickly at the end of a Union rope.

Carter turned in his chair to his two ensigns. "Mr. Hunter," he said firmly, "take this scum-sucking dog down to the brig."

* * * * * * *

8:00 p.m.

Captain Carter had quickly left the claustrophobic confines of his quarters and moved to the bridge, where he paced nervously up and down. He was so preoccupied with his own thoughts that he didn't notice the breathtaking beauty of the sun sinking in a burst of soft red light over the horizon.

For the first time since assuming command of the *Michigan*, Captain Jack Carter had a war prize. No, he knew he hadn't captured an enemy battle flotilla single-handedly. And he hadn't chased down a rebel blockade runner, like so many of his colleagues had done. The only war prize he had was a pathetic turncoat from Pennsylvania, who was whimpering like a baby in his cell. All he had was Charles Cole.

But Charles Cole was a major prize nonetheless. He was living, breathing proof that, with diligence and bravery by his officers, a threat could be first controlled, and then eradicated.

Although Carter had no reason to doubt that Cole was a pathological liar, he also knew that at least a portion of what he had said may very well be true. The coded telegram from John Yates Beall, which Cole had carelessly kept on his person, established beyond a doubt that Johnson's Island and the *Michigan* itself were still in grave danger. Rebel forces planned to attack tonight.

Carter had done everything he could to prepare for the impending conflagration. Ensign Eddy had been dispatched to warn the Union forces on Johnson's Island. He had called his men to battle stations. Two squads of marines were primed and ready for battle, steam was up in the boiler room, and the warship's cannon had already been zeroed in on the entrance to the bay to blow away any hostile intruder, if necessary. All that could be done now was to watch. And wait.

The captain's meditation was shattered as one of the marines, positioned in the crow's nest, shouted, "Ship approaching on the port side!" The marines on the deck below all moved to the port side of the *Michigan* to take a gander at what could be the first wave of rebel invaders.

Carter strained his eyes in the direction of a tiny, bobbing dot of a boat heading out from Sandusky in the direction of the open waters of Lake Erie.

The watch in the crow's nest shouted to the captain below, "It's just a small sailboat, sir. Appears to be only a woman aboard her."

It sounded innocent enough. Just a tiny skiff. And a single woman, not a well-armored coterie of soldiers. Sailing from Sandusky, not toward it. A far cry from a rebel invading force. But something

248

didn't fit, in Carter's mind. Why would a woman, by herself, be sailing out onto the lake as the gloom of night approached? He wasn't going to take any chances.

"Mr. Murray," Carter ordered, "take four men and the barge to intercept that skiff. And then bring the woman aboard."

Jack Carter had little reason to know that he was about to sever the last, and only, warning to John Yates Beall who was waiting aboard the *Philo Parsons* just a matter of a few miles beyond the bay, set to steam directly into the waiting arms and 16 guns of the U.S.S. *Michigan*. And Annie Davis, the lone woman aboard the tiny craft, had as yet no reason to know that her desperate attempt to warn the rebel raiders would be dashed because of the confessions of her sometimes lover, Charles Cole.

20

John Yates Beall peered from the pilothouse window at the small but growing crowd of islanders gathering at Dodge's Landing. They seemed to be drawn by the curious sight of the *Philo Parsons* approaching the dock. The arrival of the *Parsons* itself was not so unusual; it stopped at Middle Bass Island on a daily basis as it made its run between Detroit and Sandusky. Its captain, Sylvester Atwood, was an island resident, and often embarked and disembarked here, trusting custody of the ship to his first mate, DeWitt Nichols, for the trip to and from Sandusky.

No, arrival of the *Parsons* was not at all an unusual occurrence. What was unusual was the fact that it had steamed back to Dodge's Landing mere hours after it had headed out toward Sandusky.

This was just the kind of potential problem John had hoped to avoid. He would've much rather stayed put off Marblehead as daylight faded into darkness and the hour of truth approached. But this little detour was unavoidable. Wood was needed to fuel the boilers for the long trip back to Canada, laden with Confederate officers from Johnson's Island who were too sick or injured to make the long march south after being liberated or to join as crew on the *Michigan* after capture. And Dodge's Landing, according to Nichols, was the only place that stocked sufficient wood to supply a lake steamer's needs.

The tiny pilothouse was crowded. Nichols, the first mate, and Michael Campbell, the pilot, were standing impassively by the big wheel. These two were closely guarded by several of Beall's men. The rebels insisted on periodically brandishing pistols and axes to intimidate their captives, much to the displeasure of their captain. And, of course, John Yates Beall himself was there. His best friend and assistant, the Scotsman Bennett Burley, stood in the doorway, since there was no more room inside the cramped confines of the pilothouse.

"Mr. Byland," John said to his long-bearded crewman, "please select three of our men from the guard detail and see to the docking of the boat."

Byland, who had become bored with the impenetrable sounds of silence emanating from the pilothouse, was glad to be given something to do again, even a matter so simple as tying up the boat to the dock. They had been cruising for nearly two hours since taking over the *Parsons*, and Byland was anxious for something – anything, really – to happen. "Yes, sir," he responded.

Bennett Burley stepped aside just in the nick of time, as the black-eyed Byland pushed his way out of the pilothouse and into the open air.

"Mr. Burley," John said, "I'm turning over control of the boat to you now, while I go down to the docks to negotiate for the wood. There should be nothing further to do, except to watch these two to make sure they don't do anything foolish. And," he said pausing and looking directly into the eyes of Nichols and Campbell, "if they do, you know what to do with them."

John tucked his Colt revolver back into his trousers, pushing the handle of the weapon down as far as he could safely do, and as close to his hip as possible. He pulled his frock coat over the weapon. A slight bulge appeared, but it was not too noticeable, especially in the fading daylight. He wanted the weapon to be as inconspicuous as possible so as not to start a panic on the docks that would get out of hand and lead to violence and, more important, which could lead to him losing control over his mission. It was bad enough in the first place that they even had to make this trip ten miles up the lake to this little outpost of Yankeedom. It would be much, much worse if everything fell apart here, of all places.

John followed Byland out of the pilothouse and proceeded down the stairs to the main deck, where his men had already lowered the gangplank. He scampered briskly down the plank and, once on the creaky, slatted dock, turned toward the island, scanning for signs of the wood yard.

He quickly spotted the place, directly at the foot of the dock. It was obvious from the cordwood stacked in little hillocks surrounding a primitive log cabin that apparently operated as the office. A large "Dodge and Sons" sign, crudely hand-painted in large black capital letters, nearly obscured the entire front of the building.

The rebel captain moved down the dock, ignoring the impassive stares and occasional questions from the dozen or so onlookers. "Is there something wrong on board the *Parsons*?" one asked. "Someone must be deathly ill," commented another.

Before John reached the foot of the dock, a man with massive shoulders came out of the Dodge and Sons office. It was obvious that this man was a lumberman. His shoulders were so broad he had to turn sideways to squeeze through the door. His plain, broadcloth shirt was open at the chest, and a river of thick black hair flowed from beneath his shirt. Gentle green eyes graced a cherubic round face which, except for a fringe of a moustache, was clean-shaven.

John put on his most civil, Virginia gentlemen face. "I'm looking for Michael Dodge," he said simply.

"And who are you?" the man inquired.

"My name is John Beall; I'm a passenger on board the *Parsons*," John responded. "Mr. Ashley, the ship's clerk, asked me to see Mr. Dodge to make arrangements to take on some wood."

"I'm Michael Dodge," the man said, putting out his hand to be shaken. "Glad to meet ya."

John noticed the woodman's grip was as firm as his shoulders were broad. "I'll be glad to assist, of course. But tell me," Dodge said glancing at some of the shaggy strangers, John's men, moving aboard the *Parsons*, "where is Mr. Ashley? What on earth is the *Parsons* doing here? Shouldn't you be in Sandusky by now?"

"I'm afraid Mr. Ashley is ill in his office," John lied. "And he didn't tell me why we didn't proceed in to Sandusky. All I know is that, about halfway down the lake, the boat stopped and then turned back here. Must have been some kind of trouble with the engine, I imagine."

"Well, what about the mate, Mr. Nichols?" queried Dodge. "Surely he would have told you why he had the *Parsons* double back here. And why didn't he come down here, instead of Ashley sending you?" Dodge shook his head. "This is all very unusual, Mr. Beall, very unusual indeed."

John had hoped that this transaction would be easier than this. Just give the man the money and load the wood, as simple as that. He had neither the time, nor the inclination, to concoct a story that this island woodsman would accept. The integrity of the mission was at stake. It was time to act.

Reaching with his right hand, John drew his Colt revolver from his trousers and, in one smooth fluid action, shoved the smooth steel barrel directly into Dodge's chest.

"Mr. Dodge, I am afraid I really don't have the time to deal with all of these inane questions," John said, his voice suddenly as cold as the end of his revolver. "The *Parsons* needs at least ten cords of wood, and it will be loaded on board. Do I make myself clear?"

John had underestimated the fury locked up inside the massive, yet seemingly gentle frame of Michael Dodge. Nobody ever threatened Michael Dodge. Never. With the roar of a caged lion, Dodge pushed John's right hand away from his chest.

The Colt discharged close, very close, to the Virginian's right ear, which immediately began to ring from the concussion of the weapon. Red flame erupted from the barrel followed instantaneously by white smoke, which wafted gently into the dusky evening sky. One of the island onlookers screamed, another fainted. A small little voice in the crowd cried out simply "Daddy!" But Dodge had not been hit. The shot had gone harmlessly into the evening sky.

"Steven!" Dodge cried out to his 11-year old son, as he struggled with John over the gun, which had clattered onto the dock. "Quickly, son," he yelled breathlessly. "Run like the wind . . . Get help! Get Captain Atwood!"

The boy stood frozen for a minute, seemingly helpless, then dashed off the dock and down the gravel road that circled the island, as a dozen rebels swarmed like bees off the *Parsons*, lighting on the back of the massive hulk of Michael Dodge.

* * * * * * *

The little lamps had been lit all around the *Parsons*, highlighting the steamer's frame against a deepening violet sky. It was the start of a clear, crisp fall night. A fat harvest moon hung low on the horizon as it prepared to begin its nightly trek across the skies. Figures moved furtively in the murky light, carrying wood from Michael Dodge's yard on board the *Parsons*.

At this rate, John reckoned it would only be another 15 minutes or so before he and his men would steam off the island and toward the culmination of their mission – capture the *Michigan* swiftly followed by the freeing of the Confederate officers held on Johnson's Island.

John Yates Beall stood alone on the bridge, surveying the scene below. The excitement in the air was palpable; he could feel it. He could even taste it; a bitter, metallic taste permeated his senses. It was just this kind of feeling that Martha – his beloved Martha – had warned him about. "Sugar," she had said breathlessly once between deep, wet, passionate kisses, "I pray you won't find the thrill of your mission to be a more compelling mistress than I." John had assured that nothing, absolutely nothing – not even his love of the South – could ever so overcome him that he would forget his pledge to her: that he would take all precautions to make sure he returned to her after the mission was completed.

Martha. In the heat of the activity over the last few days John had nearly forgotten about her. And he was ashamed. This wonderful creature that God had given to him as his helpmate deserved better. He would not forget her anymore; he would keep her foremost in his thoughts this night, subject of course to the exigencies of the Plan. Then, mystically, it seemed like some ethereal, shimmering vision of her rose, Lorelei-like, from the lake. She was smiling that oh-so-sweet smile which had first attracted John in what seemed like an eternity ago at the Runnymede Plantation in Mississippi.

John's dreamy thoughts came abruptly to an end as a sharp, piercing whistle cut through the night air like a knife. The ringing in his ear, caused initially by the discharge of his revolver, had started again. John leaned over the rail and peered into the thickening gloom, pretending to ignore the throbbing pain inside his head. He could hardly believe his eyes. It was just too incredible. Approaching the island and closing fast was another steamer, slightly smaller than the *Parsons.*

John spotted Bennett Burley on the dock below, supervising the loading of the wood. Burley and the other dozen or so men with him had also heard the whistle, and they too had stopped to stare at the belching steamer bearing down upon them.

"Mr. Burley," John cried out as loudly as his delicate, tortured lungs would dare. "Stop your loading and proceed back onto the boat at once. See to it that all of the men are alerted to the fact that we are getting some company. As many as can be spared from guard duty in the cabin should join us on the decks."

"Yes, sir," Burley replied.

"You men," the Scotsman ordered sharply, "back onto the boat with you, and leave the rest of that wood where it lies." Burley and the other rebels scampered back aboard, while John pondered this new, and potentially dangerous, development. Had they been found out? he wondered. Was there to be a battle here and now, with no hope of making it unnoticed to Johnson's Island? And, for the moment, the dreamy thoughts of Martha were replaced with the immediate reality of the steamer that was now moving ominously closer.

* * * * * * *

Captain George Orr was, by all accounts, a very controlled man. Everything about him – from the way he slicked down his thinning gray hair with pomade to his insistence that his crew address him only by use of the words "sir" or "captain" – reinforced that image. He demanded precision. And so none of his crew were surprised by his reaction to the interloper hogging the Middle Bass Island berth reserved for the *Island Queen.*

"What in the blazes is that boat doing in our dockage?" he bellowed. "Every steamer on this lake knows damned good and well that space is bought and paid for by the *Island Queen.*" Orr harrumphed some more. "What boat is that anyway?" he inquired of his mate, who was already peering through the hazy sunset skies with his binoculars.

"It appears to be the *Philo Parsons*, sir," the mate responded.

That was all Orr needed to hear. Even though their routes did not precisely overlap, the *Philo Parsons* was in competition with the *Island Queen* for the lucrative inter-island summer traffic between Kelley's Island, the Bass Islands and Sandusky. The *Queen*, built on Kelley's Island ten years previous, had no competition until the arrival in 1862 of the *Parsons.* The rivalry at this point between the two captains had become as much personal as it was business.

"Damn that Atwood!" Orr bellowed. "That scoundrel knows better than to try a cheap trick like this! If he thinks this is some kind of joke, wait until he sees what kind of surprise I have in store for him!"

A wan smile crossed Orr's face.

"So what'll we do, sir?" the mate asked.

"Quite simple, Mr. Wright," said Orr. "We really don't have a choice, since the dock is not big enough to accommodate both boats simultaneously. We're going to dock in our usual space, whether the *Parsons* is there or not. Just pull the *Queen* up beside her, and we'll tie up to Atwood's boat. We'll see how funny he thinks this is when the *Queen*'s passengers go traipsing through his ship to get ashore."

Orr chuckled out loud at the prospect. This could be seriously entertaining. In addition to his usual complement of local traffic this time of year, he was carrying twenty-five very inebriated enlisted men from the 130th Ohio Volunteer Infantry, en route to Toledo for mustering out. Those fellows should make quite a scene, which was exactly what he wanted to happen.

As the *Queen* drew ever closer to shore, Orr went down to the main deck, so he could supervise the maneuver. He could see only a few men on the starboard side of the *Parsons*; otherwise, the boat appeared to be nearly abandoned.

Once the *Queen* was within hailing range, Orr shouted through cupped palms to the hands about the *Parsons*: "You're in our space; we'll be tying up to you, *Philo Parsons.*" But instead of protestations, which is what he fully expected to receive in kind, one of the *Parsons* hands simply responded, "That will be fine. Proceed to tie up."

Orr did not expect it would be this simple. But, what the devil, why not go ahead and tie up to the *Parsons* as he had planned? It seemed as though the *Parsons* had been all but abandoned; must be some sort of mechanical problem he reckoned. If nobody's there to protest, Orr knew it would take some of the sport out of this whole exercise, but at least it will send a message to his crew that the *Island Queen* was not to be trifled with. And, more important, that he, George Orr, was not to be taken for granted.

As the *Queen* puttered alongside the *Parsons,* Orr had his men throw the docking lines to the waiting men aboard the adjoining boat. Once the lines were secured stern and aft, ladders and a single gangplank was set to bridge the space between the two boats. About thirty passengers stood behind Orr, awaiting the go-ahead to disembark. Included in their number were all of the boisterous men of the 130th Ohio Volunteer Infantry, who had become at least marginally subdued in the presence of the stern Captain Orr.

As Orr was preparing to explain to the passengers the necessity of having to go ashore by way of the *Philo Parsons*, the shrill sound of war whoops filled the air. Suddenly, the gangplank virtually exploded with pushing, shoving, shouting bodies from the *Parsons*. The men all brandished either pistols or hatchets and were headed toward the *Queen*.

Orr crossed his arms in defiance and stood erect at the *Queen*'s end of the gangplank. If this was an attempt by Atwood to up the ante on his little joke, this had gone too far! These men could hurt somebody through their reckless behavior!

"What is the meaning of this?" he demanded, to no one in particular. "See here, you cannot just barge aboard my boat like this!"

A longhaired man with a scruffy beard grabbed Orr by the arm, wheeled him around, and threw him to the deck, as others behind him clambered aboard. Orr attempted to get back up, but was pushed down again by yet another of the invaders.

As Orr finally scrambled to his feet, he heard the sound of gunfire, then screams. "Oh my God, I've been hit!" cried an agonized voice. The golden glint of the lamps aboard the *Parsons* reflected off the hatchets being wielded by some of the attackers, who were attempting to herd all of the passengers back into the main cabin.

Before he could say or do anything more, Orr caught the glint of the revolver, now squarely pointed between his eyes. He froze where he stood, uncertain as to what if anything he should do. As his eyes focused in the dim light on the features of the man holding the weapon, he was shocked that he was face to face with a man who had the look of neither a pirate nor an outlaw. Instead, he was staring at the visage of a serious-looking ordinary man, dressed conservatively in a black frock coat and trousers, with a black silk cravat and crisp white shirt.

"Captain," the man said, "let me introduce myself. My name is Beall, John Yates Beall. I am an officer of the Confederate Navy, and this ship is my prize. For your own safety, and the safety of your crew and passengers, I strongly urge you to resist no further."

Orr, mindful of the screams of the frightened and apparently wounded among his charges, felt icy fingers of fear move down his spine. For the first time in his life, he found himself in a situation he could neither have planned for nor controlled. "The ship is yours," he said meekly.

* * * * * * *

Sylvester Atwood normally would have been inclined to discount the tale of horror spilling from the mouth of the pint-sized Steven Dodge. The boy was small for his age, and looked more like he was seven years old instead of 11. He left more of an impression with people as an elf, a wraith, than as a youngster approaching the budding onset of manhood. And Sylvester Atwood knew the boy's predisposition toward taking a story and expanding it to the point it was unrecognizable.

But this time was different. The boy's deep-set eyes were filled with palpable fear, which had replaced the normal twinkle. And he was barely able to get his story out about his father being shot and wrestled to the ground by strange men from the *Parsons*. It was at this point that Steven's story took on greater interest and gained credibility with Atwood. The *Philo Parsons* was supposed to be in Sandusky by now. For the Dodge boy to insist that his boat was tied up to the dock at the Dodge's Landing, well, that was just too unbelievable for a child to concoct. Any lingering doubts Atwood had about the veracity of the boy's tale were instantly dispelled when he heard the distant but distinct popping echoes of gunfire.

He really liked little Steven; he had no children or family of his own, and the Dodge boy had become about as close as Atwood would allow any person to get to him. "Come on, boy," Atwood said softly, "let's go see what's going on." He took the child's hand into his own and headed out the front door of his comfortable clapboard cottage on the west side of the island, a good mile from Dodge's Landing. The boy was in such a hurry that Atwood felt himself compelled to half-run, half skip down the road, although that was certainly not the bearing that he, a ship's captain, normally sought to maintain.

The sun had just set, but even in the dusky twilight, the rising moon cast enough light so that, except for a few shadows, most shapes and forms were clearly distinguishable. As they drew within eyesight of the pier, Atwood could see that indeed something extraordinary was going on at Dodge's Landing this evening. From this distance, he could see that *two* boats, not one, were tied up at the dockage reserved for the *Island Queen*. And of course, he instantly recognized his own *Philo Parsons* as one of them.

Seized with a fear that nearly choked him, Atwood dashed down the road as fast as his arthritic sea legs would let him, and as quickly as little Steven's legs would allow. Whatever it was that was going on down there, it was his duty to his crew and his passengers to be there with them.

As they entered the confines of the wood yard, men were bustling everywhere carrying wood out of the yard, an armload at a time, down toward the dock. Faces faded in and out of the light of the lamps around the compound. Atwood recognized a number of the men as passengers from the day's trip out of Detroit and wondered to himself: Why weren't they in Sandusky?

Steven's hand, still clasped tightly inside Atwood's, was sweaty and strangely cold. The boy was very much afraid, and he clutched the hem of Atwood's trousers in silent desperation with his other hand. "Now, now boy," Atwood said soothingly, "there's no need to be frightened." He looked down at his silent companion, whose eyes were brimming with tears. "Let's see if we can find your pa."

As they reached the foot of the dock, Atwood spotted the unmistakable form of Michael Dodge, who stood sullenly under a lamp surrounded by three men that appeared to Atwood to be strangely familiar. More passengers, he figured.

"Pa!" Steve shouted as he spotted his father. He tore loose from Atwood's grip and ran down the dock. He muscled his way through the legs of the three men with his father. His father scooped him and hugged him tightly. No words were spoken by either father or son. None were necessary.

Atwood approached the men with Dodge. Two of them stared at him sullenly. A third, dressed in black conservative attire, smiled politely. Atwood recognized all three passengers who had boarded the *Philo Parsons* earlier in the day at Amherstburg, on the Canadian side downriver from Detroit.

"What in God's name is going on around here?" Atwood asked. "The boy here says there's been some kind of trouble. That's my boat there," he said, pointing in the direction of the *Parsons*, "and I want to know why she's not in Sandusky where she's supposed to be."

"Damn it, Sylvester," Dodge blurted out. "Get the hell out of here! These men are rebel pirates, and they've taken over your boat!"

Before Atwood could decipher the incomprehensible message Dodge had just relayed to him, a long-barreled revolver was instantaneously drawn and pointed in his direction.

"Captain Atwood, I believe it is," said the polite man.

Atwood merely nodded his acknowledgement apprehensively, uncertain as to what to say with cold steel pointed in his direction.

"I'm afraid that what Mr. Dodge has just told you is incorrect. My name is Captain John Yates Beall of the Confederate Navy. We are not pirates, but you are my prisoner nonetheless."

Atwood's jaw dropped in disbelief. Confederate Navy? Here on Middle Bass Island smack dab in the center of Lake Erie? Is this fellow crazy? The war was five hundred miles away from here!

"Mr. Byland, if you please," John said, "relieve the captain of any weapons he may be carrying and then escort him aboard the *Parsons* where he may join the rest of his crew."

* * * * * * *

"Things went pretty smoothly, don't ya think, captain?" Bennett Burley was leaning on the doorframe of the pilothouse, peering into the deepening darkness on the horizon. He took another puff from his pipe, and the embers in the bowl of the pipe glowed red, then turned gray again as Burley quit drawing. The pleasantly sweet aroma of the burning Scotch-soaked tobacco would normally have been taboo in John's presence, what with his lung condition and all. But John had decided he would tolerate whatever he had to this night as his men took their own individual measures to reduce the growing tension in the air.

John nodded, but said nothing. The heavy velvet veil of night now had fallen over the boat, and none of the usual lamps were lit, which would permit a more stealthy approach to their target. The only sound he could hear was the steady swish-swish-swish of the paddlewheel pushing the *Philo Parsons* through the placid waters of Lake Erie ever closer to Johnson's Island.

"Yep, captain, I think we're in pretty good shape," Burley continued. "Got the passengers and most of the crew to take that oath to keep silent for 24 hours. None of our men hurt neither, thank God. And we'll be in position, as planned to see Captain Cole's signal when it's time to board the *Michigan*."

John had to admit that, despite a few unexpected difficulties, things had indeed gone pretty well. He hadn't anticipated the lack of wood requiring them to take Middle Bass Island by storm. He hadn't anticipated the *Island Queen* tying up to the *Parsons*, just minutes before he was ready to steam away from Dodge's Landing. And he certainly hadn't planned on the injuries. He regretted the fact that one of Captain Orr's crew had been shot, although it appeared not to be too serious. And he especially regretted the hatchet blow sustained by one of the passengers aboard the *Island Queen*; the man had a nasty gash on the side of his head, but fortunately, it didn't appear to be life-threatening. John always hated it when innocent civilians became subject to the same depredations and difficulties that warriors could grudgingly accept. But, he had to admit, by and large Burley was right. Things had gone well so far.

Burley was in a talkative mood tonight. "Captain," he said, "we're about a mile away from Middle Bass Island now. Should we cut the *Island Queen* free?"

John had not really decided what he was going to do with his prize, now in tow behind the *Philo Parsons*. If he were back on the Chesapeake Bay, it would be obvious what he would do with the captured side-wheeler. There, he could haul her to a friendly cove on the Virginia shore, where essential hardware, lumber and supplies for the Confederate cause could be salvaged.

But this was different. Salvage was impossible so far from the Confederate homeland. And really, all he really wanted to do was to deprive Captain Orr and his crew from reneging on their sworn oaths to stay put. But he could hardly just set her adrift either. No telling who might stumble upon her.

"Mr. Burley, I believe it will be necessary to scuttle the *Island Queen*. See if you can find a sledgehammer or two, and send two of the strongest men back aboard her. Have them knock out the pony valve and then come back aboard before you cut her loose."

John knew that busting the pony valve would send the *Island Queen* to the bottom in short order. The pony valve controlled the flow of water in from the lake to the steamer's boilers. Removed, a veritable river of lake water would flow unchecked into the hold and pull the boat beneath the shimmering surface. It was the easiest and quickest was to send the steamer to the bottom, and it would be done relatively quietly.

The moon had now raised itself a third of the way into the evening sky, and it cast a soft, warm golden patina over the lake and everything on it. The beacon of the Marblehead Lighthouse pulsated in the distance on the starboard side of the boat. The lake surface was nearly glassy, with an occasional breeze kicking up a few stubby little waves. The night was deceptively calm. John might have been ensnared by the peacefulness of the evening, except for the steady clank, clank of sledges hitting the steel pony valve on the *Island Queen*. The tintinnabulation of steel against steel gave John a chill, as though it was a precursor of what was coming.

21

John Yates Beall had been exhilarated an hour previous as the *Philo Parsons* let down her anchor just a mile or so offshore from Sand Point. He was alone on the catwalk around the pilothouse. The steamer's pilot, Michael Campbell, sat on a rickety stool inside the wheelhouse, his face shoved dejectedly in his hands. John had detailed Bill Byland to keep guard over the pilot, who John learned knew more about the entrance to Sandusky Bay and the approach to Johnson's Island than anyone else.

Byland's massive frame could have blocked the one small door, the only point of entrance or egress into the wheelhouse. But Campbell wasn't running.

John's gazed fixated longingly on the western horizon, as though drawn to some Midwestern Mecca. His mind carried him as though on the wings of an eagle (to quote from the prophet Isaiah, for whom he had the greatest affection) to the other side of Sand Point, that narrow spit of silica jutting southward into the Sandusky Bay. In his mind's eye, he pictured the U.S.S. *Michigan* lying at rest, its officers and crew completely unaware that their ship would soon be in rebel hands. He could see as vividly as though he were already there the burnished bonze of the warship's cannon. Just beyond that lone Union warship, Confederate brethren languished behind the wooden stockade of the prison camp on Johnson's Island, waiting for their day of liberation.

But John's initial exhilaration of an hour ago was beginning to wane as time passed with no signal from Cole. It was replaced with growing anxiety. The progressive nervousness triggered once again those wrenching spasms in his chest. The rebel captain reached into the inside breast pocket of his silk-lined frock coat. It took him no time at all to pull out the little brown bottle. He extracted the cork with his teeth and spit it into his left hand while he pulled on the flask, harder than normal this time. The soothing elixir trickled down his gullet, its warmth and nerve-soothing power quickly spreading until the spasm had passed.

John popped the cork into the bottle with the palm of his hand, and slid it back into his pocket. He pulled the gold-plated monogrammed pocket watch, a gift from his grandfather Yates, from his vest pocket. Nine o'clock. Where was Cole's signal? He tried to suppress it, but John was growing ever more fearful that something had gone wrong, dreadfully wrong. It had been dark for some time. He couldn't just sit at anchor all night long. Someone was probably already thinking it was mighty suspicious that a lake steamer would just sit out here for so long, neither moving nor dispatching crew in a barge to the shore for help in a time of obvious distress. Fortunately, he thought, with all the lights on the ship out, it would be harder to spot. But he still was worried.

His arms locked statesmanlike behind his back, John strolled as casually as he could back to the door of the tiny pilothouse. The little room was the only one on the ship that was illuminated, and that was only because they needed light to read the charts. A single lamp flickered over the chart table. The lamp shot its amber glow about the room, and shadows danced wildly like uncontrolled marionettes off the ceiling.

Byland stepped aside as John entered. Campbell's head was still buried deeply in his hands, as it had been for the last hour.

"Mr. Campbell," John said politely.

Campbell lifted his head, crossed his arms across his chest in a show of defiance, but said nothing.

"Look," John said leaning on the ship's wheel, "I know you're unhappy about the circumstances you find yourself in. But I need your help."

Campbell sneered. "You can just go to hell, you rebel bastard!" He spat the words from his mouth like a mouthful of spoiled food. "I'd sooner pee on my grandmother's grave than help you. All you're gonna do is get some innocent people hurt. I don't want no part of that," he said defiantly.

John tried to ignore Campbell's vitriol, attributing it to the immaturity of youth. "I have given you my word as a soldier, a gentleman, and a Christian that my men and I have neither the intention nor orders to bring any harm whatsoever to civilians. We are strictly a military operation."

"Military?" Campbell smirked. "Why, there ain't nothin' military around these parts, except. . ." And then it dawned on the headstrong youth. These rebels were planning on tangling with the *Michigan*. Or mounting a raid on the Johnson's Island Confederate prison camp. Or both.

"That's right, Mr. Campbell. Except the *Michigan* and Johnson's Island. Which by my reckoning lie just around on the other side of this little spit, a few miles distant," said John, gesturing toward the shores of Sand Point rising on the horizon. He pushed the other hand through his thinning brownish hair and continued.

"I fully understand your feelings about not helping us," John said, with all the sincerity he could muster. "I'm not asking you to aid us in any of the military operation. That is not in keeping with the rules of war, and certainly not in any way what I intended. No. . ." John's voice faded momentarily as he fought back another spasm. "All I am asking you to do is to steer us through the channel into the bay."

Campbell rose from his stool and walked over to John. Byland made a move to suppress the lad, but John gestured that it was all right.

"You see that other spit of the land off the port side?" Campbell inquired, pointing to another peninsula rising just above the hazy gray waters into the moonlight sky. John nodded.

"That's Cedar Point," Campbell continued. "The entrance to Sandusky Bay is through the channel between Sand Point on the west and Cedar Point on the east. Probably all of two miles between the two points. But," he said, his one gold tooth radiating the reflected light of the oil lamp in the pilothouse, "outside the channel, the water there is six feet deep, at best. In fact, most of it is much less. The actual channel into the Bay – and it's not more than 12 feet deep – is only a couple of hundred feet wide. The channel's not well marked, either. Yep," he said, nodding his head in agreement with himself, "it would be right dangerous to try to make our way through the channel at night like this. Right dangerous."

John admired the young man's efforts to dissuade him from pursuing his appointed mission. "Mr. Campbell, I must let you know that I am not a novice at these things," John said. "I have commanded Confederate naval vessels in the Chesapeake Bay and along the Atlantic Coast. I know all about channel markers, and I know that the channel into the bay has to be marked."

"Well, you're half right, captain," said Campbell. A smirk, more than a smile, crossed the pilot's smooth face. "There used to be channel markers into the bay, sure enough. But just last month, a crew came out from the *Michigan* and pulled 'em all. Maybe they heard you fellas might be payin' a visit, and the United States Navy didn't want to make it too easy for ya." Campbell returned to his stool in the corner of the pilothouse and sat down again, this time erect and alert.

"Certainly you can find your way into the bay without the markers, can't you, after having made all of the trips on the *Parsons*?" John asked.

Campbell shook his head firmly, negatively. A longish brown lock of hair fell over his eyes, and he put it back in place by throwing back his head. "Look, captain, I ain't never come into the Bay at night, even with marker buoys. But if you insist on trying it, good luck. But you won't get any help from me."

A noiseless, painless, yet very real shock wave rolled through John's body. He did not want to believe that his mission, the Plan to save the South by taking the war to the Great Lakes, had been compromised even before it had begun. He was not concerned for his own life, but he had a responsibility to the twenty men he had with him, and to their families. And he had a responsibility to Charles Cole, who at this very moment John believed had exposed himself and the Sandusky Knights of the Golden Circle to danger by assisting in this irregular military operation, an act of war against the United States with serious potential consequences.

John knew he needed to ponder this news. Men's lives were at stake, and he was responsible. The decision-making would have been a whole lot simpler if John had known that Campbell's story about the marker buoys was a complete fabrication. The channel into Sandusky Bay was indeed well marked.

But John was not the only one affected by Campbell's lie. William Byland, the rowdy, uncontrollable oysterman from Maryland, had heard all he needed to hear. He had had doubts about this mission almost from the beginning. If it hadn't been for the bonus for capturing the *Michigan*, he would have preferred to sit in a dank, smoky tavern in Toronto and swill down beer after beer while waiting for the war to end.

Throughout all this, Byland had stood in the door, saying nothing, but absorbing the impact of the news of the imminent danger with increased concern. He could not believe that his captain could be so indifferent to the danger. He knew what he had to do. "Excuse me, captain," Byland said to John, who was leaning, silently, against the wheel for support, lost in thought. Even in the dim light of the pilothouse, the deep furrows on John's brow were obvious. "I've got to use the toilet."

John waved him on, and said simply, "I'll watch Mr. Campbell for now. Just send another man up if you're going to be awhile."

266

Byland retreated from the door and took the stairs down to the main deck two at a time. His mates needed to hear that John may not only be prepared to let them be blown out of the water, but now was giving consideration to letting them run aground, so they could be captured and hanged like pirates. But not if he had anything to say about it, that's for sure.

* * * * * * *

9:30 p.m.

John did not need to look at his watch to know what time it was. It was time for trouble. Big trouble. He knew because he could hear that loudmouth Byland ranting and raving in the main cabin below. He could hear the men's roaring approval. Damn! He should have listened to his instinct and left Byland behind in Canada. And from the sound of it, maybe some of the others, too.

And then suddenly, it grew quiet. Too quiet. Just minutes later, he heard the plates on the bottom of Byland's boots clump-clumping their way up the stairs. And then, finally, Byland was there. John stood outside the pilothouse, still mesmerized and tantalized by what lay on the other side of the narrow spit of land off their bow. He nodded to Byland.

Byland spoke first. "Captain Beall, may I speak with you for a minute?"

John stepped out of the pilothouse, closing the squeaky door behind him. Campbell was left alone inside. "What is it?" John inquired. He tugged at the lapel of his frock coat.

"The men are down in the main cabin, sir. I told 'em about what this Yankee here was sayin'." Byland shook his mangy head of hair in the direction of the captive pilot, who glared back through the window in the pilothouse door at Byland. The rebel sailor ignored him. He continued, "about them unmarked channels, and how the Yankees have known we was acomin'. They'd kind of like to hear from you, sir. They're terribly worried." Byland was more civil than John could remember. Good God, he was almost even polite.

"Who chose you to speak for your comrades, Mr. Byland? I don't recall giving you authority to act or speak on behalf of anyone else." John's voice had an icy edge to it, he knew. He put it there on purpose, just to reestablish who the captain was, and who was therefore in charge. And it sure wasn't Byland.

"Now, captain, don't get your dander up. We was just talkin'. But you're askin' us to take some risk here, and we just want to. . ."

John sighed. He didn't need his kind of problem. Not now. He had more that he could handle just worrying about whether Cole would ever signal. And if he did, what he would do. The last thing he needed was a mutiny. Although it hadn't reached that point yet, it could if he ignored this problem.

"Very well, then, Mr. Byland. I'll speak with the men. Just stay here, if you will, and watch our friend Mr. Campbell. I'd hate to see him get an idea like taking a little late night swim or something."

Byland wanted to be with the rest of the men. After all, he was the one who got them riled up in the first place. But he wasn't ready to ignore his captain's order. Not yet, anyway. That would be a hanging offense.

* * * * * * *

10:00 p.m.

This was the moment, and John knew it. Every ounce of persuasive skill he possessed would be required to quell the revolt brewing among his own men.

Most of the twenty or so under his command hung back fifteen feet or more away from their captain. They hadn't moved from the spot where they were when he had entered the grand parlor of the *Philo Parsons*.

The parlor was anything but grand at this point. The once elegant felt-covered card tables were pock marked with black holes of varying sizes, caused by innumerable smoldering tobacco products being left unattended by nervous smokers. Mounds of peanut shells mixed with the sticky ooze of stale and spilled beer on the polished hardwood floorboards. The accumulated hours of exposure to so many men had taken a toll on the décor.

Standing just to his right and a foot or so behind John was Bennett Burley. Burley projected a firm, yet warm, smile to his colleague. The presence of his right hand man and friend was a tremendous comfort to John.

As he stepped forward to the center of the main parlor, John raised his hands towards the ceiling. The nervous little whispers among the men came to a sudden complete halt.

John reached into his inside breast pocket and pulled out a slightly tattered envelope. The unbroken red waxen seal was plain for all to see as John held it in front of him.

"Gentlemen," John said simply, "I have a special message I would like to read to you. It is from the President himself, Jefferson Davis." The men cast furtive glances toward each other, their eyes revealing the shock that the President even knew they existed, much less had something to say to them.

"I received this letter just yesterday, sent to me by messenger and via Commissioner Thompson. He instructed me to share the President's message with you just before we commence the final phase of our mission. We have reached that point."

John broke the seal on the envelope, then removed and carefully unfolded the document. The linen paper crinkled like crusty snow underfoot on a frosty mid-winter's day. The parlor itself seemed to be filled with anticipation. Most of these men barely knew a colonel, and had seldom seen any general. But the President! A message from Old Jeff was unfathomable.

A heavy hush hung over the parlor as John began to read:

Sons of the South!

> *The successful completion of the mission upon which you have embarked will liberate thousands of our brothers floundering in filth and squalor on Johnson's Island and return them to their loved ones. On behalf of the mothers and daughters, sons and fathers of those suffering souls, I salute you!*
>
> *Your capture of the Union warship U.S.S. Michigan, will bring the war to the heart of the enemy, and save thousands of lives of our valiant fighting men now struggling against great adversity in our homeland. Let those Yankees drink from the same bitter cup that we Southerners have had to endure for the last three years.*
>
> *But most important, successful completion of your mission will lead to the inevitable collapse of the administration of that criminal, Mr. Lincoln. His own people will rise up against the folly he has brought on his countrymen when they see that the war can come home to them, too. With Lincoln out of the White House, I believe we will be able to achieve the sovereignty to which we are entitled.*
>
> *My thoughts and prayers, and those of our entire nation, are with you as you embark on this glorious mission. May God grant you success and shield and protect you.*
>
> *Jefferson Davis*

John carefully folded the letter, placed it in the envelope, and tucked it back in his breast pocket.

"Gentlemen," he said slowly, deliberately. "The fate of the South rests in large measure on what we do here tonight. The President knows that. I know that." He paused. "And you know it, too."

"You have certainly heard the rumors by now. That the Yankees are waiting to ambush us. Or that the channel into the Bay is not marked and impossible to negotiate in the dark. But should we so quickly abandon our bothers on Johnson's Island? Or the boys fighting back in Virginia, and Georgia and Texas? The Confederacy is counting on us, men. We can't let them down now, can we?"

John had challenged their manhood as well as their patriotism. He felt the men under his command could not just run away like dogs with their tails between their legs, no sir! He knew what he must do. He was hopeful they would stick with their captain.

But John had seriously overestimated the will of his men to fight, to take risks, to spit in death's eye. Soon, he would know just how much.

* * * * * * *

11:30 p.m.

John had removed himself to the catwalk again, hoping against hope that a signal flare would rise above the tree line on Sand Point. The little grains of sand in the hourglass of opportunity were fast slipping away. John sensed that Charles Cole had not fulfilled his part of the mission. Even he had to admit that, at this late hour, prospects for success were bleak. Cole was captured, dead, or, more likely in John's mind, vanished into the vast expanse of Middle America, where nobody would be looking for him, or even care who he was.

John heard familiar footsteps coming up the stairs from the main cabin. Bennett Burley walked silently and respectfully along the catwalk until he was right next to his captain. A funereal atmosphere hung like lead over both men. The silence was oppressive.

Burley finally spoke. He spoke in soft, measured tones. "Have you seen anything, John? Any sign of Cole? A signal of any sort?"

John shook his head, but continued staring straight ahead, his hands thrust into the pockets of his trousers.

Burley already knew what the answer must be before John had given it. He had long since abandoned any hope of hearing from Cole.

"Nothing, eh?" Burley said. "So what do we do now, John? It's nearly midnight. I don't think we're going to hear from Cole tonight."

270

"I don't know, Bennett," John said, "I just don't know." He was trying to hide his despair, to keep control, but it was difficult. John believed in his heart that the mission could be successfully accomplished. And he knew that if they were successful, the outcome of the war for the South would be forever altered. The South would have its freedom.

"John, you know I'll stand by you. Whatever you decide, why, you're the captain, and I'll follow you wherever God leads us. But," Burley said, pausing hesitantly, "the men are getting restless again, and I can't say as I totally disagree with the concerns I'm hearing down there."

A brisk breeze made its way from the northwest across the previously gentle waters of Lake Erie. The lines on the mast atop the pilothouse beat out a primitive beat as they were whipped about by the increasingly sullen wind. But John wasn't sure if the chill he experienced was due to the harbinger of wintertime or the chill of seeing the mission come to an unsuccessful conclusion.

"John," Burley continued, "the men have drafted this petition that they have asked me to present to you. I want you to know that I had absolutely nothing, nothing at all, to do with this. I have tried to prevent the situation from coming to this, but here I stand nonetheless."

John sighed deeply. "Read it." His voice was frosty, but filled more with bitter disappointment than anger.

Burley unrolled the little scroll on which John's men had staked their views. He moved a step or two away from John and under one of the lamps where there would be enough light to read.

> *We, the undersigned, crew of the boat aforesaid, take pleasure in expressing our admiration of the gentlemanly bearing, skill and courage of Capt. John Y. Beall as a commanding officer and as a gentleman, but believing and being well convinced that the enemy is already apprised of our approach, and is so well prepared that we cannot possibly make it a success, and having already captured two boats, we respectfully decline to prosecute any further.*

Burley handed the scroll to John, and saluted sharply.

"John, the petition is signed by seventeen of the men. That leaves just you, me and Bill Baker."

"I guess it's over then, isn't it, Bennett? We've failed, haven't we?"

271

"No sir, we have not!" Burley shouted. "Pull yourself out of this, man! Would you rather have us all die in a Yankee ambush? Is that what you would have us do? Is that what your Martha would want you to do?"

Martha!

The mere mention of her name filled John with the same warm tingling he experienced when they first kissed on the plantation back in Mississippi what seemed like an eternity ago.

"John!" an ethereal voice called though the sharp breeze skating across the lake. "John!" it repeated louder this time.

There was something to this voice that was intensely familiar. As he peered into the whitecaps beginning to rise on the lake, made frothy by the brisk little wind that had picked up, a visage seemed to rise from the vapor.

It was Martha. She was smiling at him, sweetly, the way that only lovers can do. The vision spoke directly to his heart.

"Come home, John," the Martha-face said. "You have done your duty. And I need you."

"John, are you alright?" Bennett Burley shook his captain gently by the shoulders.

John's vision of Martha dissipated as quickly as it had come. But it had been heaven-sent. He now knew what he must do. He tugged at the lapels of his frock coat and pulled himself erect. It seemed to Burley that John had miraculously replaced the gloom and despair of just a few moments past with pride and confidence. He was a changed man, no question about it.

"Bennett, have two of the men bring our chest up here. Quickly."

Now Burley was confused. What on earth could he want with that old chest? Shouldn't they be getting up a head of steam and turning this boat around back toward the safety of neutral Canada? They needed to get out of American waters by dawn at the latest. But he was not one to question his captain, especially not now in his hour of crisis.

Burley hustled down the stairs to the main cabin, and ordered two men to bring the old trunk up to the catwalk.

Two men lugged the chest up the narrow stairs and set it down beside John. "Here you are, sir," Burley said, his curiosity barely contained. "Is there anything else we can do?"

"Not for the moment, Bennett, but please stay here with me for a while longer." He said to the other, "You men can go back down the stairs and tell the others we're headed back to Canada. Tell them I said to weigh anchor and get underway at once."

John and his first lieutenant stood alone for a moment in near-silence. But then the breeze picked up again and the flagpole lines were beating out a new and frantic rhythm. John bent down and pried open the creaking lid of the trunk. The box was empty except for one small flat package wrapped in burlap and tied with twine. John removed the parcel gently from the trunk and unwrapped it.

Tenderly, John cradled the package in his arms. "Here, hold this just a minute, would you Bennett?" he asked, as he transferred temporary custody of the precious cargo to Burley. He had intended to do this when he took command of the captured *Michigan*, but this would have to do.

John hoisted himself up onto the roof of the pilothouse and pulled down the Stars and Stripes, unhooking it from the grommets and letting it fly away into the night. The breeze had grown, at least for the moment, into a brisk wind, which whipped the tails of his coat about and displaced his thinning brown hair from one side of his head to the other.

"All right, Bennett, hand her up!" he shouted above the gale.

Bennett Burley handed the parcel to his captain, who unwrapped the twine and lifted the contents high above his head, where it snapped to life in the wind. Even in the dim light emanating from the *Philo Parsons*' lamps, the familiar contours of the Stars and Bars were clear.

John hooked the rebel flag to the grommets then hoisted it back up the flagpole mast. The rebel standard flapped wildly in increasing northerly gusts. John hopped off the pilothouse roof, saluted the flag crisply, fighting to hold back the tears welling up in his eyes. Just at that moment, the mighty sidewheel of the great lake steamer started to churn up the emerald-black water of Lake Erie beneath them. The twinkling lights of Sandusky faded into nothingness on the horizon as the *Parsons* picked up steam and headed north to Canada and safety.

EPILOGUE

This novel is a work of fiction, but a number of the characters in the book were real people. Here's more information on what happened to some of them after the Johnson's Island expedition concluded.

Although the September 1864 Confederate raid on Johnson's Island was unsuccessful, *John Yates Beall* and his crew returned safely to Canada to fight another day. Beall was dispatched on a new mission a few months later, this time to Buffalo, New York to derail a train carrying senior Confederate officers who were to be transferred to another prison camp. He was captured at the Niagara Falls border and tried by a military tribunal as a spy in connection with the Johnson's Island affair. The tribunal swiftly found Beall guilty and sentenced him to death. Despite numerous pleas to President Abraham Lincoln for clemency, including a petition signed by six U.S. Senators and ninety-one Congressmen, Beall was hanged on February 24, 1865 at Fort Columbus, located on Governor's Island in the New York City harbor. After the war, his body was returned to Charles Town, West Virginia and reinterred at the Zion Episcopal Church cemetery there.

Charles H. Cole is a murky historical figure, both before and after the Johnson's Island expedition. "Charles Cole" is a common name and there are a number of Union soldiers listed in the records with that name, including at least five from Pennsylvania, from which Cole claimed to be at various points in time. From the Confederate side, Major Richard Pearson, a Confederate officer imprisoned on Johnson's Island, indicated that Cole had been an officer in his Tennessee unit, and Cole himself in a story after the war claimed to have been a member of a Confederate regiment from Tennessee. No Confederate service records could be found to verify this claim.

Cole was apprehended in Sandusky on the day the plan was intended to be carried out. Ironically, he initially was confined on Johnson's Island before being transferred to Fort Lafayette in New York. Other than his own often-contradictory statements, little credible evidence existed to convict Cole of anything, and he was never tried. The war ended, and Cole still languished in prison. Finally, in February 1866, nearly one full year after John Yates Beall's execution, Cole was released after a *habeas corpus* petition was filed on his behalf. After his release, he dropped from sight. Almost nothing is known about how Cole spent the rest of his years, although an 1882 story in a Philadelphia newspaper contains Cole's self-serving, post-war reminisces about his escapades in Sandusky.

After the raiders returned to Canada, *Bennett G. Burley* was arrested by authorities there who had mistaken him for Beall. When his true identify was ascertained, Union officials nonetheless demanded his extradition back to the U.S. After prolonged legal wrangling, Burley ultimately was sent to Sandusky on July 10, 1865 for trial on theft charges, ironically arriving in the city on the *Philo Parsons*, the very same boat that he and the rest of Beall's Confederate crew had taken over in September of the preceding year. The trial began the next day in Port Clinton, Ohio, the Ottawa County seat. The Bass Islands, where the theft was alleged to have taken place, is part of Ottawa County. A mistrial occurred, and Burley's confinement in the county jail continued as he awaited a new trial. Burley escaped on Sunday, September 17, and made his way back to Canada. From there, he took passage on a steamer back to his native Scotland. He then changed the spelling of his last name to "Burleigh" and in 1882 became a world-famous correspondent for the London *Daily Telegraph.* He was the newspaper's principal war correspondent and covered major military actions in Africa, Europe and Asia for the next several decades. Burleigh was also the author of well-received books about the wars he covered as a correspondent. He died in London in 1914.

Martha O'Bryan did not see John again after their final days together before the Johnson's Island expedition began. After his death, she is reported to have worn mourning clothes for the rest of her life. John was her only true love, and she never married. She returned to her native Nashville after the war and opened a school for young ladies. Martha was very active in Nashville charity circles, focusing special attention on the most needy of society. She died in 1910. The Martha O'Bryan Center, founded in Nashville in 1894, carries on today with her legacy of service to the less fortunate based on "a tradition of Christian faith."